Tor Loken
and
The Death of Chief Namakagon

James A. Brakken

Book II of the Chief Namakagon Trilogy
Tor Loken
and
The Death of Chief Namakagon

©2013 James A. Brakken

ISBN-13: 978-1492286691   ISBN-10: 1492286699

The author wishes to thank the Cable - Namakagon History Museum, the Ashland Historical Society, the Sawyer County Historical Society, Forest Lodge Library, the Wisconsin Historical Society, the Lac Courte Oreilles Community College, & the University of Wisconsin for research aid. Priceless support and assistance from my wife, Sybil Brakken, and skillful guidance from the Yarnspinners Chapter of the Wisconsin Writers Association, helped bring this story to life.

May this book inspire every professional and amateur archeologist, anthropologist, historian, detective, and treasure hunter to shed more light on the life and death of Mikwam-migwan or Old Ice Feathers, who, during the great, 19th century timber harvest, became widely known as Chief Namakagon.

Badger Valley Publishing
c/o James Brakken
45255 East Cable Lake Road
Cable, Wisconsin 54821

BadgerValley.com
Email: TreasureofNamakagon@Gmail.com
On Facebook® at Jim.Brakken

James A. Brakken's
Tor Loken
and
The Death of Chief Namakagon
An 1886 murder mystery based on fact.

Published & Distributed by
Badger Valley Publishing

BVP c/o James Brakken
45255 East Cable Lake Road
Cable, Wisconsin 54821

**Your story. Your way.
Your book. Today!**

*Top quality publishing
At bargain basement prices!*
Inquiries welcome.

**BadgerValley.com
715-798-3163**

To Sybil, my wife and light of my life ...

*... for your belief in my dreams, your enduring support,
and your tolerance in letting all my pinery
characters—from the lumberjacks and other heroes to
the ne'er-do-wells and charlatans—share our
otherwise tranquil home
for – months – on – end.*

Tor Loken and The Death of Chief Namakagon
The Chapters

Tor Loken
and
The Death of Chief Namakagon

James A. Brakken

Tor Loken
and
The Death of Chief Namakagon

James A. Brakken

Prologue

May 18, 1966
11:45 p.m.

I could not sleep. Though dead-tired, I—just—could—not—sleep.

I can't blame my restlessness on the loons calling from the bay. No, their wails had always lulled me to sleep. What had me pitching and rolling like a storm-swept schooner was a map I'd found hidden among my Grandpa's effects—a map to Chief Namakagon's lost silver mine in northern Wisconsin—a map now missing.

I put several logs on the glowing coals in the fireplace, then flopped into Grandpa's overstuffed chair, resting my feet on the hearth. Smoke from the fireplace blended with the mellow aroma of the eighty-year-old log cabin. I muttered as I struggled to re-draw the map from memory.

"Let's see ... the lake, over there, yes, and Chief's Island with an X on it. And Grandpa's lumber camp here. I remember a dotted line running north past Marengo Lake. Yes, the old Marengo Trail. Got it. Then a second X right about there. No, here!" Holding my improvised, incomplete map to the firelight, I realized it was useless—useless and worthless. And I felt hopeless.

"Grandpa Tor, I sure wish you were here to fill me in, to speak to me." I stared into the flames in the fireplace. "Oh, if only you could."

Bleary-eyed, I studied my makeshift map, suddenly seeing the teamsters, the sawyers, the skidders—all the lumberjacks working at Grandpa's lumber camp in 1886. I saw Chief Namakagon on his dogsled, speeding across the frozen lake. I imagined a young couple in a sleigh racing down a snowy trail. The boy clutched his chest, badly hurt. Eyes straining, I perceived two men fleeing danger in a heavy snowfall, descending a whitewater rapids by canoe. One's been shot! Bright red blood soaking through pure white snow.

Shaken yet spellbound by my makeshift map, I saw a dark figure wielding a bloody knife, a raging forest fire, vicious timber wolves tearing at their prey. And, there! Caked with ice, three bodies face down in blizzard-driven waves!

"What is this?" I gasped. "What happened back then?"

I stared and stared and, warmed by the fire, grew drowsy. Eyes fixed on my mysterious map, I drifted into a deep sleep—a sleep that took me back in time—back to a pleasant morning stroll along a Lake Superior waterfront and a schooner destined to set sail into dark waters.

<>O<>O<>O<>

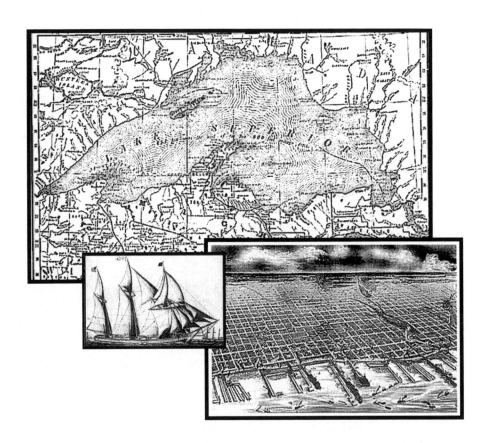

Chapter 1
The *Lucerne*

November 16, 1886

The dismal cawing of distant crows cursing the end of the harvest could not spoil this perfect Indian summer day. Strolling along Ashland's waterfront, nineteen-year-old Tor Loken opened his mackinaw coat to soak in the southwest Lake Superior breeze. He passed steamship after steamship, some laden with ore from nearby iron mines, others waiting for cargos of virgin Wisconsin white pine.

High above the steamers stretched the three tall masts of the *Lucerne*, a well-trimmed schooner stowing aboard the last of her iron ore cargo. Tor admired the handsome vessel with her scroll head and clean lines. Two men stood near the wheelhouse. One, a younger man, sported a fashionable tan suit and bowler hat. The other fellow's hat had the mark of a ship's captain. It matched his blue overcoat, adorned with gold braid and bright brass buttons. A thick, black beard hung below the cigar he chewed with the arrogance of a seasoned seafarer.

From high in the mizzenmast rigging came a sharp call. "Ay, land lubber! You come to sail the seven seas with us?"

Tor looked up. "Why, if it isn't Junior Kavanaugh, lumberjack turned sailor! You look like a gol-dang horsefly caught in a spider's web way up there in those ropes. Say, you did not have to come all the way to Lake Superior just to climb a tree. Still plenty of 'em left near Pa's lumber camp."

"Ya, Tor, but from these here poles I'll soon cross ol' Gitchee Gumi and see the world, not just some wilderness lumber outfit." Descending, Junior cried, "Billy! Say, Billy, look who come to see us off."

Billy Kavanaugh and the ship's captain stepped to the rail.

"Well, Tor Loken," yelled Billy. "Welcome to the shipping trade where the real money sits a-waitin'. Come aboard. Meet George Lloyd, Captain of the *Lucerne*. I hired the captain for a run to Cleveland before me and Junior set out for the tropics."

"What brings you to Ashland?" asked Junior, jumping the last few feet from the rigging. "Your lumberjack pay burnin' holes in your pockets? If so, there are taverns, poker rooms, and sportin' gals a-plenty here to relieve you of your money. Take my word!"

"Junior, your pa sent me. He wants you back in camp—back on the job with him and the fellas at the Namakagon Timber Company. He's worried about you workin' on the ore boats."

"Worried?" snapped Billy. "Now, ain't that Pa for you? Why, I have sailed from Boston to Brazil and Nassau to New Orleans time and time again. Not once did Pa ever show the slightest margin of concern for me, his eldest son. Junior, take my advice and just you never mind Pa. Lumberjackin' is a far sight more perilous than the shipping trade as many a shanty boy's lonesome mother and weeping widow will confirm. Many!"

He turned to Tor. "Listen here, Tor Loken. Junior is goin' off on a high adventure with his big brother. Our Pa and all you bark eatin' lumber-grubbers can freeze your gol-dang arses off by day out in them woods, then shiver in your revoltin' bunkhouse stench by night. Neither me nor Junior gives a tinker's dam. Each of us will make three times a lumberjack's winter wage on this Cleveland run alone. We are haulin' near to thirteen-hundred ton of iron ore and will soon be trading other goods in the Caribbean. Tor, you tell Pa that come summer we will call on him back on the farm in Mazomanie—each wearin' a diamond stick pin when we do."

Tor turned to Junior. "Is Billy speakin' for you, Junior? Is this what *you* want?"

"It is, Tor. Much as I like lumber camp life and the good times we had on them cold Saturday nights in town, I must do this. You give Pa a fond farewell for me. I am off to see the world, my friend. See the world and make my fortune."

"All right, Junior. I will explain it as best I can."

"Loken," said Captain Lloyd, "tell Mister Kavanaugh his boys are sailin' on the finest vessel on these Great Lakes. She's a far sight safer than them smoke-belchin' steamers. Only thing they're good for is to give a real vessel a tow when her sails go slack—which, by the by, ain't often. Tell him the schooner *Lucerne* and this here

- 4 -

captain will keep his boys safe, sound, and secure."

"I will, Captain. He'll appreciate your words."

"We have us a so'west wind and intend to ship out within the hour, a full day ahead of schedule. Will you join us for a quick bite 'fore we cast off?"

"I would like to, Captain, but I'm meetin' my girl at the depot. I know better than to keep her waitin'."

"Rosie?" said Junior, "Rosie's in town? You and your sweetheart gonna kick up your heels some?"

"No, no heels gettin' kicked up. Ashland is growin' leaps and bounds, what with all the ships, trains, mines, and lumber camps. There's talk of startin' a college here. Rosie wants to study English."

"Fancy that. Rosie Ringstadt—a highbrow college girl!"

Billy snickered. "What in the blazes for? Gol-dang waste of time, I'd say. It is shameful to fritter life away, nose stuck in a book. Tell her to take to the road. Travel's your best schoolin' by far. I plan to see the whole dang world and get rich along the way."

"Captain," said Tor, "it has been a pleasure. I hope the wind stays at your back, sir."

"Young man, our paths will again cross. I feel it in my bones. Till then, farewell, Tor Loken."

<>O<>

An hour later, Tor and Rosie walked arm in arm from the railroad yard to the waterfront. The *Lucerne,* bound for Lake Erie, left Chequamegon Bay in full sail. After watching the schooner round the point, the couple turned toward Ashland's busy downtown for a meeting with the school headmaster. As they walked, they felt the warm southwest breeze turn southeast. Stepping onto the street after the meeting, they noticed another change.

"Smells like rain," said Rosie as they boarded the southbound train.

"With fifty men in camp and a hundred more a-comin', what I long for is a gol-dang good snowstorm."

"Wishing is folly, Tor. Winter shall come when winter comes— no sooner, no later. Patience reveals change and change offers opportunities to grow."

"Sakes alive, Rosie, you are startin' to sound like ol' Chief Namakagon." They settled into a seat in the first passenger car.

"Frankly, Tor, I prefer this warm weather. I so envy Junior, off on a sailing adventure that will take him to the sunny tropics. What I would give if we could be on the *Lucerne*, too. They are so, so fortunate."

"Fortunate? Fortune is yours to find, wherever you make your camp. Chief Namakagon told me that." He put his arm around her. "Rosie, this passenger car isn't much like a camp and I know we are not sailing off on an adventure, but right now I would say there's nobody more fortunate than this north woods shanty boy."

"Why, Tor Loken! You are such a sweet talker. I hope your other flames do not hear the same."

"Other flames? Pa keeps me tied so close to camp I never meet other girls. 'Sides, Rosie, why would I want to? You are the only one for me. You know that, right?"

Rosie smiled. Two whistle blasts pierced the air.

"Well, Rosie? Rosie?"

The Omaha rolled south toward the Namakagon River Valley in hazy, Indian summer sunshine, a murder of crows soaring high above.

As the *Lucerne* sailed up the west shore of the Keweenaw Peninsula, the wind died. Captain Lloyd stepped from the wheelhouse, the chewed stub of a cigar between his teeth. He studied the slackened sails, then stared eastward.

"I'm not favorin' this weather, Mister Jeffreys. Such a sudden calm on a warm November midday has the Devil's mark. Tell the men to rig for a blow."

"Naw, Captain," replied the first mate, "she's a fine afternoon.

The wind will pick up. We'll be puttin' in at Sault Ste. Marie in no time."

"Mark my words, Robert. Something's a-brewin' in them skies. See to it we are battened down and tell Mister Kavanaugh I need to see him post haste."

"William Kavanaugh?"

"He signed the contract, Mister Jeffreys."

By the time they returned, a southeasterly wind again filled the sails.

"See, Captain?" said Jeffreys, "we again got us a good breeze. She'll be clear sailin' once beyond Copper Harbor."

"Aye, but this wind is bound to turn. I can feel it in my bones, Robert, and I don't take to it none. No siree. Lake Superior is notorious for her November gales. Mister Kavanaugh, I am droppin' anchor at Ontonagon till we see what's in store with this weather."

"Drop anchor?" said Billy. "See here, Captain. I engaged your services to deliver ore to Cleveland, not to bask in the sunshine. Winter is comin'. I say we push on."

"And I, Mister Kavanaugh, am Captain of the *Lucerne*. I am responsible for her well-being and the safety of her crew. I'll be damned if your desire for profit shall dictate otherwise!"

"One hour. If the weather then favors it, we sail. Will you accept that, Captain?"

"All right, Kavanaugh. An hour it is."

Sails struck, the *Lucerne* lay moored in waters off Ontonagon, Michigan. Again the wind turned, now southwest.

"Captain," said Jeffreys, "I still think she's a fine day for a sail. Once 'round the point, we'll make good time crossin' the lake."

The captain bristled. "Sixty minutes was my agreement, Mister Jeffreys. That's how long we wait. Now, fetch me a bottle from that case of brandy in my cabin, Robert."

One hour later the *Lucerne* weighed anchor and set out in full, billowed sail. Thirty miles beyond Copper Harbor, the eastern horizon grew black with clouds. The wind suddenly shifted, coming straight out of the northeast.

"All hands, Mister Jeffreys," shouted the captain. "Five degrees starboard. We're in for a squall." He took a pull from his bottle, jammed the cork in tightly, and stuffed it into his coat pocket. "Should've trusted my gol-dang bones."

Within minutes, snow-laden, gale-force winds drove twelve-foot waves over the decks. Ice began to build, clutching to the rigging and sails, coating every surface.

"No use, men," yelled Captain Lloyd. "There's no makin' headway against this tempest." He tipped up the half-empty bottle. "Mister Jeffreys, I am puttin' about to find us some lee waters."

"Aye, Captain."

As the *Lucerne* came about, a large wave crashed over the bow. A half-dozen ropes snapped as the mainsail collapsed, tearing as it fell onto the deck.

"Jeffreys," screamed the captain, "we've no choice now. We must run ahead of her."

"Aye, Captain," came a faint reply as Robert Jeffreys made his way through wind, snow, and ice-cold waves blasting over the stern.

"Set what remains of that mainsail, Robert. Satan will have us if we cannot keep up. I am makin' for the Apostles. We're bound to find lee water there."

"The Apostles? Sir? It'll be dark before we ..."

"Do not question me, Mister Jeffreys."

"Aye, Sir. Apostles it is."

<>O<>

As evening set in, the schooner *Lucerne*, ropes and sails heavy with ice, sped westward across Chequamegon Bay. Captain Lloyd strained to see the La Pointe light off the starboard bow. With darkness falling, the wild snow squall turned into a full-blown, fearsome nor'easter. George Lloyd realized if he saw the beacon at all, it would be too late to save his ship and crew from wrecking on the rocky, frozen mainland. Around midnight, a nearly empty brandy bottle in his coat pocket and both hands locked on the ship's wheel, he gave the order.

"Mister Jeffreys, call the crew topside, the Kavanaugh brothers, as well."

Seconds later, the sailors heard his command. "Men, I'll not further risk the *Lucerne*. We're puttin' about, bow into the wind so we can weather this here typhoon. Mister Jeffreys, on my call you drop the bow anchor, then strike the foresails quick as a whip-snap. It's the mainsails next, Robert. Then sharply drop the aft anchor and be quick about it. I mean for every soul aboard to again feel earth under his feet. I'll be damned if ol' Gitchee Gumi will take my *Lucerne* without a fight."

"Aye, Sir," came the mate's reply. Eight men soon braced themselves against the driving wind, snow, and spray, awaiting George Lloyd' orders.

Grinning defiantly, the captain spun the ship's wheel. The *Lucerne* turned windward, leaning far to port, groaning from the strain of wind versus rudder. Completing the turn, she briskly straightened up, proudly facing into the nor'easter and bucking waves now twenty feet between valley and crest.

"Now, Mister Jeffreys! Now!"

Water crashing over the bow masked the loud rattle of the chain. The anchor struck bottom, skidding across sand, barely slowing the *Lucerne* and her 1,256 tons of iron ore cargo. As ordered, the crew struck the foresails. The mainsails came next.

With words muted by howling wind, the Captain bellowed, "Drop the aft anchor, Mister Jeffreys."

"Aye, Sir," replied the mate over the roar of the storm.

The second anchor splashed into the dark water. With foresails and mainsails furled, the crew, holding tight to the icy rail, worked their way down the slick deck toward the mizzenmast. As they neared this third mast, the bow anchor wedged between rocks thirty feet below, lowering the foredeck. The mizzenmast, sails straining against wind, could not withstand the force. It snapped between crosstrees and crashed down, smashing the port rail before splashing into the lake off the stern, taking with it two men. Only Junior and the first mate heard their cries above the roar of the storm.

"Man overboard!" screamed Jeffreys. "Man overboard, Captain!"

"Nothin' to be done for 'em, Mister Jeffreys. Satan has us in his grip. Pray they do not drown or freeze 'fore washin' ashore."

"Billy! Billy!" screamed Junior. "Captain, one of those men is my brother! You must do somethin'!"

"Ain't riskin' it," Lloyd shouted. "No way to find them in the black of night—not in this devilish typhoon. You get below,

Kavanaugh."

"Damn you to Hades if you do not find them, George Lloyd!" screamed Junior. "Give me your oath you will find them—your word, Captain!"

"I'll do all I can, Kavanaugh. I will search till I find 'em if it takes an eternity! My soul will not rest until I again have my full crew. Now get below 'fore I have to fish for you, too."

The *Lucerne* pitched and rolled wildly in the dark. Making his way below, Junior heard a growling groan and deep thud as the bow anchor chain broke. Now freed, the schooner pitched, tilting and turning in the wind. Junior raced back to the wheelhouse. Captain Lloyd lay on the deck, thrown there by the fierce spin of the ship's wheel.

The vessel leaned far to port, nearly capsizing as she twisted in the storm. A gigantic wave broke on her deck, blasting the ice-laden hatch covers up and over the side and taking most of the port rail. Water rushed into the hatches. The aft anchor dragged over more rocks and, with a deep, heart-stopping snap, broke free.

Now a wind-driven leaf in the storm, the *Lucerne* rolled far to port, then to starboard in the icy, storm-driven waves. Still turning in the wind, ice fell from the masts, spars, and rigging, crashing onto the deck and crew below. They held to the rail, some throwing lines around their waists, lashing themselves to the boat.

"We have but one chance," screamed Captain Lloyd, clutching the wheel. "Pray to God she runs onto some spit of sand and don't break up on the Bayfield rocks."

George Lloyd strained to regain control of the wheel and rudder. When he did, he reached into his pocket for his final sip of brandy. Pulling the cork with his teeth, he spit it away and finished the bottle.

"Captain, a light!" shouted Junior. "There! Look! A light!"

"God in Heaven!" screamed Jeffreys. "Kavanaugh's right, Captain. It's the La Pointe light! Long Island's off the port bow. We can make the lee shore off Madeline. Take her to starboard, Captain! Hard to starboard, now! Hard to starboard!"

But the first mate's words came too late. The *Lucerne* bottomed out on the shoal off Long Island. Plowing through sand and rock twenty feet below, her hull tore open wide, spilling her iron ore cargo onto the lakebed. Lighter now, the bow thrust out of the black lake, then crashed down, taking on more water. The lower deck flooded. Next, the upper deck and wheelhouse.

"She's going down," screamed the captain. "Every man for himself. Take your chances in the lake or take to the rigging, your choice. I will find you, fellas. From here or afar, I'll find you."

Captain George Lloyd held fast to the wheel of his beloved *Lucerne* as four sailors climbed high into the rigging to avoid drowning in the icy, black waters. Two others gambled on the lake, hoping to reach shore. The schooner's hull lodged in the lakebed with a stiff jolt. The *Lucerne*'s bare mainmast and foremast protruded well above the waves while the wind in her rigging howled and howled—a thousand hungry wolves at the heels of their prey.

The snow stopped before dawn, but not the frigid wind. A bright sun and stark, blue sky hung over the shipwreck. One mile north, the keeper of the La Pointe light scanned the horizon with his glass, spotting two masts stretching skyward near Long Island.

Risking his life, he rowed out to find three ice-encrusted bodies hanging from the rigging but no sign of the other sailors. In a mere breath of time, the schooner *Lucerne* lay wrecked, her crew of nine lost to Gitchee Gumi, ill-famed for her Devil-sent, November gales.

Unaware that, along the Marengo Trail, a tenth victim, Chief Namakagon, suffered a violent death during the same storm, the lightkeeper rowed back to Madeline Island. Stroke by stroke, he heard only the rhythmic slapping of waves against his hull and the distant, dismal cawing of crows.

<>O<>O<>O<>

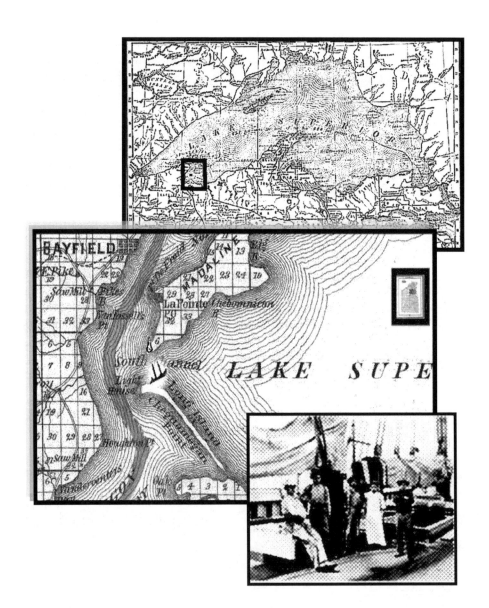

Chapter 2
The News

November 19, 1886

Word of the *Lucerne* disaster quickly reached every telegraph operator in every depot across the nation. Fifty miles south of the wreck, the stationmaster at Cable, a bustling lumber town, chose to personally deliver the news to his friends at the Namakagon Timber Company. Oscar Felsman's horse and cutter fought through twelve miles of deep snowdrifts blanketing the rutted tote road. He reached the lumber camp late that afternoon.

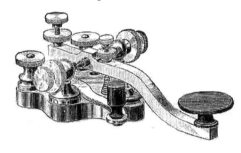

"Olaf," he shouted, throwing open the big lodge door.

"Olaf is in the barn," replied Sourdough, setting a pot of coffee on the table. "Ingman and Tor, too. What brings a stationmaster this far from civilization? You didn't come all this way to pinch me for a few nickels over a pinochle deck, did you?"

"I'm here with most dreadful news, Sourdough. News about that ore boat, the *Lucerne*. The one John Kavanaugh's boys were on."

"What of it?"

"It went down in yesterday's storm."

"Down? Down where? What in blazes you drivin' at?"

"It sunk. Got caught up in yesterday's blizzard. Wrecked off Bayfield."

"My God!"

"Sourdough, somebody must tell John Kavanaugh. Both his boys were on the *Lucerne*. Both boys lost in one night. Can you fathom that? Oh, the poor, poor man."

"Both boys drowned, Oscar? Both?"

"Three crewmen froze after tryin' to escape drownin' by climbing up into the ship's rigging. Another, the first mate, washed onto shore. Five others ain't turned up. I suppose they're at the bottom of Lake Superior."

"Then the Kavanaugh boys could be alive?"

"In that storm? In the wind we had last night? What chance would they have, Sourdough?"

"Oh, dear, dear Junior. My dear Junior Kavanaugh. May God save your sweet, young soul." Sourdough turned away, eyes wet. "Oscar, pour yourself a cup. I'll get the boss. It's Olaf's job to tell John Kavanaugh about his boys. Oh, that poor, poor man. First his wife, now both boys. Poor John. Have a chair, Oscar. I'll fetch the Lokens. Oh, my God, my dear God."

The camp cook left the lodge for the barn, suppressing a desire to scream out in rage and grief. Junior Kavanaugh, his good-hearted, adventurous, young friend was gone. He'd left to seek his fortune. Now it seemed he would never return.

Sourdough stepped into the barn. "Olaf, Ingman, Tor, someone needs to speak with you—in the lodge."

"In a while, Sourdough," said Ingman.

"You don't understand," replied the cook. "This cannot wait. You must come now."

Sourdough left the barn before the Loken family could witness the depth of his grief. They followed, crossing the camp yard to the lodge and office.

Olaf entered, his son, Tor, and Tor's uncle behind.

"Oscar, it is good to see you," said Olaf. "What brings you?"

"Sad news. The ship Junior and his brother were on was wrecked in the storm last night. Sunk off Bayfield. Both boys missing. Nine crew, every last soul, thought drowned or froze. I am so sorry to bring you this horrible news."

Tor laughed. "You are victim of a cruel joke, my friend. Or a frightful blunder. Rosie and I watched the *Lucerne* sail northeast out of port yesterday noon. Last seen, she was well east of the Apostles. By now Junior and Billy are probably kicking up their heels in Ohio, spending their newfound wealth. Somehow, Oscar, you've been duped."

"No, Tor, the wreck they found is the *Lucerne,* all right. I suffer so to tell you this, knowing you and Junior were such close pals. The storm must have blown her back across Lake Superior. The keeper of the La Pointe lighthouse spotted her at first light today. He rowed out, hoping to rescue the crew. Found no survivors. Tor, from what came across the wire, well, we will ne'er see Junior nor Billy Kavanaugh again. I am so, so sorry." He turned to Tor's father. "Olaf, their pa—he must be told."

"Yes," said Olaf. "I will tell John right away. He'll want to look for his boys, I'm sure. Ingman, you and I will go with him."

"I am going, too, Pa," said Tor. "Junior's my best friend. I have to find him and Billy, too. Surely they are all right."

"Son, this is bound to be an unpleasant journey. Your uncle and I will go with John and a few of the men."

"Pa, I have to help find Junior. I know He's out there somewhere. If I know Junior, he's wanderin' in some woods, a-whistlin' and a-waitin' for someone to shout him a hello."

"No, Tor. Better you stay. Mind the camp till we return."

"Pa, for Pete's sake! This is Junior, my best friend! I have to ..."

"Tor!" snapped Olaf. "You are stayin' here. That's the end of it!"

Without a word, Tor turned to leave. Crossing the room, he stopped when, through the windows overlooking the yard, he saw a woman approaching. Two dogs pulled her sled, plowing through the deep snow. "Look. It's Diindiisi," he said. "Alone."

"Chief Namakagon's woman?" asked Ingman. "Louise Renshaw?"

Tor rushed outside. Seconds later he helped the exhausted woman into the room.

"Louise! Welcome. What brings you?" said Olaf.

"Mikwam-migwan," she struggled to say, collapsing in a chair. "He is lost."

"Chief Namakagon lost?" said Ingman, "I hardly think so. Old Ice Feathers has lived decades in these woods. 'Tain't likely he'd lose his way. An eagle might find itself lost before old Chief Namakagon."

"No. You do not understand, Ingman Loken. Lost from the living. Lost from this place—this world."

"Lost in the storm?" asked Tor.

"No, Tor. Lost to this world. Dead."

"What?"

"That is what he told me."

"Who told you?"

"The Marengo stationmaster. I stayed there during the storm. I waited for Mikwam-migwan. He never came. I worried for him. I sang for him. He never came. Then the stationmaster told me. Namakagon is dead. He is no more."

"No," said Tor. "You're wrong. Namakagon cannot be dead."

"I am not wrong. They took him. Took my old man far away.

Away from his home. Took him to rest in the Ashland cemetery. Mikwam-migwan's spirit will not sleep so far from his home. It is wrong. His spirit is too strong. He will wander. I know this."

"You saw his body?" asked Olaf.

"I watched them put Mikwam-migwan on the train. They would not let me come close. They know not what trouble they cause. His spirit will never sleep. He will wander forever."

Tor couldn't speak. He turned to his father and uncle for consolation, for escape from all this news. Their faces confessed bewilderment as they struggled to absorb Diindiisi's grave words.

"Who found him?" asked Ingman.

"Derkson," she replied. "A lawman. Said he found Mikwam-migwan on the trail near camp. I warned my old man. "Do not go in the storm." He would not listen. Too stubborn. Now he is dead and too far from home."

"Must be Frank Derkson," said Tor. "One of the men Chief said had been followin' him, tryin' to locate his silver mine. Captain Morgan told me Derkson is crooked as they come."

"Yes. Derkson," said Diindiisi, "First to say my old man is gone."

Tor took her hand. "Diindiisi, does Sheriff Rothwell know? He needs to investigate."

"Derkson said the sheriff has too much work because of the storm. Others died, too. Some sailors. Derkson said the sheriff had no time for old Indians. Old, *dead* Indians."

"How did Namakagon die?" asked Ingman.

"Derkson said he found him on the trail dead. No more."

"He didn't say what caused it?"

"No. Maybe Mikwam-migwan was tired. He was old. Maybe he laid down for his last sleep."

"Not Chief Namakagon," said Tor. "Not old Ice Feathers. Something is wrong." He turned to Olaf. "Pa, I have to go. I must learn what happened—how he died."

Olaf looked at Ingman, then Tor. "All right, but Blackie Jackson is going along. Hitch a pair of Clydesdales to the big cutter. Son, you watch yourself. Let Blackie do the talkin'. Don't let your hot head overcome your sense of reason. If you find anything out of the ordinary, go straight to the sheriff. Good luck, Son."

"Thanks, Pa. Same to you. Find Junior. I know He's out there someplace, probably wonderin' what's takin' us so gol-dang long to fetch him back to camp. I just plain know it, Pa."

Blackie Jackson and Tor Loken stepped off the train well after dark. They crossed Ashland's business district to Front Street, checking in at the grand Chequamegon Hotel.

"Where might we find the sheriff, friend?" Blackie asked the clerk.

"Sheriff Rothwell? Oh, he is likely making his rounds 'bout now. Friday night, you know. He keeps an eye on things uptown. Between the sailors, the miners, and the lumberjacks, he has his hands plumb full. He is still tryin' to deal with the storm, too. Yep, his hands are full, all right."

"Where might we find the graveyard?" asked Tor, feeling a jab from Blackie's elbow.

"Cemetery? First you want the sheriff, now the cemetery. You got some news for our local paper? I write for the Weekly Press, now and again. You got some news for me?"

"No, no news," said Blackie, "just need to see the sheriff."

"The graveyard is south and east a ways. Other side of the Wisconsin Central roundhouse. Who you lookin' for, anyway?"

"A friend who they say died in the storm yesterday," said Tor.

"One of the sailors?"

"A man found down near the Marengo Trail."

"Oh, the old Indian? The one with the silver mine? Chief Namakagon?"

"There ain't no silver mine," said Blackie, "only rumors spread by that newspaper you work for."

"Sounds like you know all about him." said Tor.

"All I know is what Frank Derkson told the bartender at the Royale Hotel Saloon." said the clerk, rubbing his chin. "Said he found the old boy out in the woods southeast of the Marengo Station. Froze stiff. Frank said the old boy most likely drank too much fire water, fell asleep and froze."

"You mind your tongue," snapped Tor. "Chief Namakagon would not die that way, no, sir. Who, besides Derkson, might know about this?"

"Whoa, now," said the clerk. "Take it easy, there. All I know is what I heard across the Royale Hotel bar. You best be asking them questions of yours to the sheriff or to Frank Derkson in person. You will likely find the two of them together. Frank is both a deputy and a brother-in-law to Sheriff Rothwell."

"I thought Derkson was a miner," said Blackie.

"Frank? Naw. He filed a couple of claims that never panned out, but Frank Derkson is no miner. More like a mine speculator. Not many folks around these parts that ain't mine speculators nowadays, I s'pose. Few of them ever do much with their claims, though, besides letting them go back to the government."

"You said Sheriff Rothwell might be makin' his rounds right now. Is there a place where we might find him?" asked Tor.

"Were it me, I would try to find a spot near the door at the Royale. Frank and the Sheriff both have interests in some of the women who work there, if y'know what I mean. They stop in from time to time to make sure their girls are keepin' busy. Seein' as how it's Friday, you can be sure them girls will be busy tonight."

"Interests?" said Tor.

"I will explain it to you, Tor," said Blackie. "Time we get ourselves down to the Royale."

"Thanks for your help, friend," Tor said, laying two coins on the counter. "Here is ten cents for a bucket of beer and another dime to keep all this under your hat."

"Yes sir! You bet I will. Thank you, sir!"

A quarter hour later, Tor and Blackie leaned against the bar at the Hotel Royale Saloon. Outside, wagons, sleighs, and cutters lined the hitching rails up and down the street. The stores all glowed from oil lamps within. Larger lamps illuminated each intersection. The Second Street boardwalks were crowded with a mix of lumberjacks looking for winter work, sailors hoping for a last run before the shipping season ended, and miners celebrating payday. The noise from those at the bar and poker tables was masked by loud piano music. It filled the room as three women danced on the small stage.

"Barkeeper," shouted Blackie, "two beers."

"Blackie, what in blazes are we going to say to the sheriff?"

"I suppose we better let him do the talkin' till we find where he stands on all this. Let me handle it."

Two beers later, Sheriff Wendell Rothwell entered the hotel barroom, stomped snow from his boots, hung his bearskin hat and wool coat on a hall tree, and walked straight to Tor and Blackie.

"You boys lookin' for me?"

"So much for the hotel clerk keepin' somethin' under his hat," said Tor.

"News travels fast in small towns," replied Rothwell. "Now, what is it you fellas want?"

"We are close friends of the Indian found along the Marengo Trail," said Tor. "We came to claim his remains for burial near his home. You understand, right, Sheriff?"

"He has already been buried, boy. Seen to by yours truly."

Tor stood. "You already … Why? I mean, why so soon, Sheriff? What about his wife? His friends? His people?"

"Well, we thought it best to do this right now—before he putrefied on us, you know."

"In this weather?" said Blackie. "Well, no matter. We are here to take him to his final home. The ol' boy will have to get dug up."

"Boys, you don't want to go wakin' up the dead. Let him rest."

"My boss, Olaf Loken, sent us here," said Blackie. "Chief Namakagon's wife is waitin' for us at the camp. We mean to take the ol' boy back with us, Sheriff, and we would appreciate your cooperation."

"I will need an order for exhumation before we even consider it. It will take a judge to sign it and the courthouse ain't open till Monday. Boys, my best advice is to just leave the poor old soul lay where he is. The city will provide a nice marker—stone, not wood— name carved in as well. I will see to it myself."

"You will see to it?" said Tor. "Sheriff, there is a small island on a lake south of here where he lived for many decades. That land already bears his name. All we want is to take him there so his wife and friends can return him to his home according to Ojibwe ways. Surely, you can understand. Please, Sheriff, help us put our good friend, Chief Namakagon, to rest at his rightful home. It's only right."

"Not possible, boy."

"Sheriff," said Blackie, "where can we see the death certificate."

"Ain't none."

"Doctor's report?" said Tor. "Someone must have looked him over, right?"

"Listen, boys, there ain't no certificates, reports, or nothin' else to look at. He was just another old, Indian found dead back in the woods. If not for my deputy, why he would've just laid out there in the snow till the wolves ate him. Then what would you have? Not one gol-dang thing. Boys, I done him and the county a favor by plantin' his body in our graveyard. I will see to it he gets a marker, like I said. He's better off. You will be, too, when you stop troublin' me about this. You hear?"

Blackie stared down on the sheriff. "Where can we find Frank Derkson?"

"Frank? What you want him for?"

"Heard he found the body. We'd like to ask him a question or two."

"Frank is out of town. 'Sides, you have any questions for Frank, you ask 'em to me. Now, take my advice and let this whole thing be. Leave the poor old Indian rest in peace and avoid yourselves any trouble. I will tell you what, boys. I got a couple of ladies workin' for me here. How 'bout I call 'em over here along with a couple buckets 'a beer to boot and we call it all fair and square. Whaddaya say?"

"Sheriff," shouted Tor over the piano, "did Deputy Frank Derkson kill Chief Namakagon in an attempt to find the hidden silver mine? Are you coverin' up for your brother-in-law—your sister's husband? Is that what you are doing?"

The piano player stopped, turning their way. The room fell silent.

"Sonny, you will hush your damn voice or I will have you in my jailhouse for disturbin' the peace. Now you listen here and listen good. That old redskin is dead. Dead, buried, and soon to be forgotten like every other old Indian that I planted up there. Natural causes, each and every one of 'em. Namakagon froze, sonny. Got drunk and froze, see? Froze stiff in the blizzard. In weather like this, it could happen to anyone."

Rothwell stepped closer to Tor and spoke quietly. "Sonny, I'm going to do you and your oversized friend, here, a big favor. If you two are on the next train south, my deputy will not have to cart your carcasses up to our Potter's Field to plant two more dead drunks found froze along some backwoods trail. You get me, boy? Get out of my city. Get out of my city right now, the both of youse!"

The sheriff strolled back to the door, pulled on his hat and coat, and left the hotel.

"Blackie, what in blazes did I just hear? Why, he as much as confessed his part in the death of Chief Namakagon, didn't he?"

"Tor, we best skedaddle 'fore he changes his mind. Elsewise, we might find ourselves caught in a real bear trap. Drink up your beer. We need to get ourselves down to the rail yard so we can catch that southbound."

"Maybe he was lying, Blackie. Maybe, with all the problems caused by the storm, they have not yet buried the chief. Maybe he just said he did so we would let this all go. We cannot give up. We have to go look, Blackie. We owe it to the chief. To his wife. To his people."

"Much as I want to, Tor, I cannot help you. Not this time. I don't expect you to understand. I just plain cannot. I had some trouble with the law in years long passed. They would put me away for good if I run up against them now. You will have to take my word on this."

"Blackie, with or without you, I am going to the cemetery. You catch the next southbound, take the sleigh up to the Marengo Station. Wait for me there. I will be along soon."

"Your pa would hand me my walkin' papers if he knew I was leavin' this to you alone."

"This is my choice. I owe it to the chief. Go, Blackie. Meet me in Marengo."

"Much as I would like to, I know I cannot stop you, Tor. God help you if you run into Rothwell or that deputy of his. I hope you find what you are lookin' for."

Chapter 3
Potter's Field

November 19, 1886

A cemetery is no place to be on a dark November night—especially this night. Still, Tor Loken had to know two things about his friend, Chief Namakagon. Had the chief been buried as Sheriff Rothwell said? And, was the cause of death merely a case of an old man freezing out in the woods? In spite of the sheriff's threat, his warning to leave the city, Tor felt bound to investigate and now stood in the dark at the entrance to Ashland's potter's field, the final resting place for paupers, unknown deceased, indigents, criminals, but rarely Indians.

The streetlights along Front Street, though a mile away, gave a soft glow to the outskirts of town. In that dim light, Tor followed tracks in the snow. They entered the cemetery gate. One track led to three freshly dug, but empty graves. Tor followed the other to a far corner of the graveyard. There, next to a half-dug grave, sat a single, pine coffin. Tor looked back toward the gate to confirm he was alone. He struck a match. The coffin was unmarked. He pulled his knife from its sheath and, one by one, pried up each nail until he could lift the cover.

Tor struck another match. There, in this icy coffin, lay his friend, his mentor, Ogimaa Mikwam-migwan. Tor reeled from the sight and overwhelming grief. Just as it had happened on that frigid winter day many decades before, the chief's beard was covered with thick hoar frost. Tor whispered, "Mikwam-migwan, I see you remain true to your name with your face covered with feathers of ice. Tell me, how did you die, my friend? Was it the storm? The cold? Or did you fall victim to some cold-hearted treasure hunter. You must tell me."

Tor struck a third match, looking for any sign of injury. Finding none, he grasped the old man's shoulder and pulled him onto his side. On the back of Chief Namakagon's head and neck, Tor found blood-matted hair. He held the match closer, discovering more blood and a large, gaping cut. His fingers met crushed bone. He jerked away in sheer shock. "I knew it! I knew this was not your doing, Mikwam-migwan."

Gently, Tor laid his friend down, noticing the diamond-shaped medallion Namakagon always wore on his shirt was missing.

Suspicions confirmed, Tor replaced the cover, using the handle of his knife to tap the nails in place. "Sleep well, my friend. May Gitchee Manitou light your way. And may Wenebojo help me find peace for you—along with your killer."

Tor soon waited at the Wisconsin Central Railway roundhouse for the last southbound of the day. He breathed easier, relieved to be on his way home, truth in hand. The train pulled in, bell ringing, steam rushing from its airbrakes, and wheels squealing against the cold, steel rails. One short whistle from the engineer gave the all clear and steam rushed as the brakes were set.

Tor patiently looked on as eighteen travelers stepped from two passenger cars. As the nineteenth person left the car, Tor approached to board, then pulled his hat down and turned away, seeing a badge on the man's coat.

"Hold up, there, sonny," came a deep voice. "Just what makes you so shy of a man wearin' a badge?"

"Me?"

"I don't see no one else shyin' away. Who are you? Where you headin'?"

The roundtable rumbled as the locomotive and tender car rotated from northbound to south.

"Name is Tor Loken. I'm headin' home to my pa's lumber camp south of here. Lake … uh …"

"What lake?"

The locomotive rolled off the turntable and out of the roundhouse.

"One of the lakes to the south … You ever heard of Long Lake, sir?"

"What is your business in Ashland?"

Switchmen coupled the waiting cars, couplings banging.

"No business. Just stopped between trains for supper."

"Awful late, isn't it?"

The locomotive pulled past.

"You a railroad constable? I have my ticket. Want to see it?"

The brakeman waved a lantern when the passenger cars aligned with the platform. The conductor shouted, "All aboard."

"I ain't no constable, sonny boy. I am deputy sheriff here."

"All aboard," shouted the conductor again.

"You best get on board, 'fore you find yourself walking home in the dark, sonny."

"Yes, sir, Mister …uh …"

- 24 -

"Derkson. Deputy Derkson, sonny."

Tor found a seat near the coal burner, watching the door, relieved to be away from the deputy. Two whistle blasts later, the train began to inch away. As it slowly gathered speed, a rap came on the window. Deputy Frank Derkson. Tor slid the window open.

"Sonny, did you say Long Lake? I thought sure the Loken outfit was on Lake Namakagon."

The train picked up speed. Derkson followed down the platform Tor stumbled for words. "Long? Oh, you must've heard wrong. Maybe you thought you heard me say it's a long way to the lake, sir." The train rolled on. "You take care, Deputy," Tor shouted. "I am certain we will meet again."

Thirty minutes later, Tor met Blackie on the platform of the Marengo Station.

"No question in my mind," said Tor. "Someone struck the chief on the back of the head, then left him to freeze in the storm."

"That's a helluva thing to say, Tor. You absolutely sure?"

"I saw it myself. Blood all over the back of his neck and his skull bashed in. Foul play, plain and simple. I am sure of it."

"You believe Chief Namakagon was murdered? Do you know what you are sayin'?"

"I am saying someone hit him with a stout stick or rock or club of some kind. Maybe the butt of a gun. I cannot say for sure who did this, but you and I both know Frank Derkson has tried to find the chief's silver mine ever since the Ashland Press printed that story— the one about Chief trading silver for medicine and supplies in Ashland."

"Tor, there must be a dozen men tryin' to find that mine. What makes you think it was not someone else—some other claim jumper who done this? Maybe Derkson only found Namakagon, like he said."

"Then why the quick burial, Blackie? Why no death record? Why no medical examination? And why run us out of town just for wanting to bring the chief back to his home? Why lie to us? Why? I will tell you why. Deputy Frank Derkson had a hand in this. I would bet a winter's pay on it."

"All right, let us say he did. What can be done about it? The deputy and the sheriff are holding the reins."

"For now, Blackie, but not for long. Pa and Uncle Ingman will see to that."

Olaf and Ingman Loken boarded the tugboat Cyclone at the port of Bayfield. With them were John Kavanaugh and three Namakagon Timber Company lumberjacks. All were bound for Long Island to look for John Junior and Billy, John's sons, lost in the wreck of the schooner *Lucerne*.

Reaching the site of the wreck, they saw two of her masts protruding from the cold waves, stretching skyward, caked with thick ice. Fifteen feet below the waterline they made out the top deck. John then understood neither his sons nor the other sailors aboard would be rescued there. If somewhere below deck, they could no longer be alive. And if their bodies lay within, these men had no way to reach them in such frigid waters. As the tug searched for any sign of life, John Kavanaugh's tears fell into the lake that had claimed his boys. Everyone soon realized the search was in vain.

After a brief stop at La Pointe, on Madeline Island, to speak with the lightkeeper, they returned to Bayfield.

A search of the shoreline south of Bayfield yielded no trace of the captain, crew or passengers of the *Lucerne*. The men elected to return to camp. Only John Kavanaugh remained in Bayfield to continue the sad quest to find his boys. A gloomy train ride and a silent journey through the snowy woods brought the search party back to camp where Tor waited for news of his best friend.

<>O<>

"Son," explained Olaf, "we found no sign, no trace of either Billy or Junior. The lightkeeper said the waves last night were higher than he had ever seen or heard tell of. He figured no man could have survived such a shipwreck. John still has hope of findin' them, of course. And, truth be told, if anyone will find 'em, John Kavanaugh will."

Tor took this news as hard now as he'd taken it a day before. How could his closest friend, Junior Kavanaugh, be gone? And Junior's older brother, Billy? And Chief Namakagon, his mentor and trusted companion? How was it they could all be lost during the same storm? What mysterious force, unseen power ...?

Olaf interrupted his thoughts. "What of Chief Namakagon, Son? What did you learn?"

"Plenty, Pa. There's no question in my mind that old Ice Feathers died at the hands of another. I saw the evidence first-hand. On top of that, when Blackie and I asked the sheriff about the nature of Chief Namakagon's death, we were run out of town. Rothwell said if we did not let this lie, we might end up in the same cemetery. I know he was killed by another, Pa. And I am bound to prove it."

"Now, Son, you ought not go flyin' off the handle. I know this is all hard to accept, but …"

"Pa, listen. The sheriff told us Namakagon was already buried. It was an outright lie. Ask Blackie. He will tell you the same. Sheriff Rothwell knows dang well the chief was murdered. And, Pa, I think I know who did the murderin'—his deputy, Frank Derkson."

"Derkson."

"No question about it, Pa. Frank Derkson. I know it."

"Son, I learned a while ago not to doubt you. But, whether you know this to be true or not, you keep your hunches under your hat for now. Both Rothwell and Derkson are lawmen. They have power and influence that could be used against any accuser. And, Tor, both men carry guns. I know you would like to charge right in and make them stand tall for this. But, if you want justice done and done right, you best be patient. Meanwhile, it might be good to take a look 'round the chief's Marengo camp. Likely that's the last place he spent time. I will take care of things here. You and Ingman can head up there first thing tomorrow. Keep an eye peeled. The old chief had plenty of men looking for his silver mine. Hopefully you can get there before any of them do. Better take your snowshoes along. You will need them."

Still reeling from news of the violent deaths of both his mentor and his best friend, Tor Loken stepped outside. He stood on the porch, listening to the wind whispering through the tall pines. He imagined he could hear his friend and mentor, Chief Namakagon, the Ogimaa, Mikwam-migwan, chanting his songs. He heard the same chant Ice Feathers offered before a hunt—a chant of anticipation, a song of satisfaction, a mantra of deep sorrow. Feeling the rhythm of the Anishinabe song, Tor chanted along with his mentor and the whispering pines swaying above.

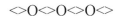

Chapter 4
Seventeen Months Earlier

June 5, 1885

Like most mornings, the restaurant in the Hayward depot was crowded with travelers. In the far corner of the waiting room, Rosie Ringstadt, a red handcart displaying her flowers, stood surrounded by passengers. Bouquets of white and lavender lilacs trimmed with yellow ribbon and petite arbutus corsages she made earlier that morning were quickly selling. The aroma of her flowers filled the air, almost masking the persistent odor of smoke from cigars, pipes, and locomotives.

"Ten cents, sir," she said to a tall, clean-shaven gentleman. "Three for a quarter-dollar, should you prefer."

By the time passengers stepped from the noon train, the last of her flowers had sold. She wheeled her empty cart past the loud locomotive, its bell ringing, steam hissing, and thought she may have heard someone call her name. Turning, she saw only the crowd of travelers.

"Rosie!" came a call from the depot platform. "Rosie Ringstadt!"

She turned again. "Tor?" she said, still wondering if her imagination was playing tricks.

Tor Loken jumped from the platform, sprinting across the gravel and cinders of the railroad yard, shouting, "Rosie!"

"Tor! Sakes alive, what are you doing in town?"

"Came to see you, Rosie. What else?"

"I know your pa better than you think, Tor Loken. He keeps you hidden away out there in that lumber camp of his. Now, confess. Why are you in town on a Friday in June?"

"Ya, you are right. Pa sent me. Wanted me to check on some rail he ordered." Tor hugged her as he continued, "S'posed to be coming in this week—all the way from Cleveland—for our railroad line. You know, the track we are running through the eastern sections of our cuttings. Remember?"

"Remember? Oh my, yes, Tor, I remember. Your pa and your uncle are the talk of the town. Or maybe I should say the laughing stock of the town. Everyone wonders if you Lokens have not gone plum crazy, building a railroad that goes nowhere but back in the woods."

"Nowhere? You think it goes nowhere? Why, it's gonna wander all over the dang pinery, haulin' men and equipment out to the cuttin's and then haulin' timber to the mills. The rail due here this week is for a grade we plan to cut that will connect our camp with Pratt. Think of it, Rosie. No more river drives. No risk to our men. And no pine wasted."

"That log drive is the only time half of your lumberjacks ever bathe. You may be depriving the public of a valuable service."

"Very funny, Rosie. Why, I bet in five, ten years there will not be another log drive on the Namekagon River. Can you imagine that? Every log we cut hauled out by rail? And we Lokens right there, standin' first in line?"

"Pratt, you said? You are building a line to Pratt?"

"Uncle Ingman's got a crew up there right now layin' out the way, preparin' the grade."

"Tor, will I be able to take the train from Hayward to Pratt and, from there, catch another up to your lumber camp?"

"You betcha. Well … more or less. You might have to wait at the Pratt depot for a time, but only until another trainload of Loken pine is delivered from the camp. See, we don't run on a schedule like the Omaha line or the Wisconsin Central."

"Then, likewise, will my beau be able to take the train to Hayward? I mean, more often than now?"

"You betcha, Rosie. If Pa says it is all right. Isn't this great? If the connections are right, I can make the trip in two hours instead of half-a-day. Imagine! Chief Namakagon, Uncle Ingman, Pa, and me. Why, we could be here every Sunday for your ma's fried chicken dinner!"

"I should have known."

"Hmm? Say, Rosie, speaking 'bout food, how 'bout I treat you and your ma and your sisters to supper at the hotel?"

"Why, that would be nice—very nice. But … well, Mama's got boarders to feed and my sisters need to help her. No, I fear they will not be able to come."

"Oh, oh. I suppose we can eat at your ma's, then."

"No, no, Tor. We simply mustn't burden Mama with another place setting. You sound like you have your heart so set on supper at the hotel. I would not dream of letting you down merely because Mama and my sisters cannot come. I will dine with you … well, if that's what you want. Is it what you want, Tor?"

"You mean just the two of us? You and me? Alone?"

"If that's what you want."

"You gol-dang betcha it is what I want. I … I mean … that would be wonderful!"

"All right, just the two of us. Supper for two at the restaurant in Johnny Pion's Hotel. I will have to ask Mama, but I know she will approve. Mama will do anything for you. You have charmed her, Tor Loken."

"I have? Me?"

"You certainly have. And you have charmed me, too." She hugged him, then turned her cart toward the hill and her mother's boarding house. "You may call on me at four o'clock today, Mister Charming," she said with a wink.

<>O<>

Shortly after four, the couple sat at a corner table near the front windows of the busy hotel restaurant. Rosie noticed two young men, one short and stocky, the other tall and slender, strolling down the boardwalk. They passed Pete Foster's Saloon and the land office. Turning, they crossed the rutted, muddy street, entering the Pion Hotel through the lobby doorway. They turned into the restaurant and stood in the doorway, looking over the tables as if searching for someone.

The shorter man wore a well-pressed, wool business suit and a matching bowler. The other wore the attire of a lumberjack, yet looked uncomfortable in these clothes. His bright green wool shirt and matching wool britches appeared too new to have had the starch washed from them. New too were his slouch hat, suspenders, shiny, calked boots, and the yellow and black plaid wool mackinaw carried over his arm. Upon seeing Tor and Rosie, they approached. The young man with the bowler bowed to Rosie before turning to Tor.

"Are you Tor Loken? Namakagon Timber Company?"

"I am. But if you fellas are lookin' for work, my uncle is the man to see. Ingman Loken. He will be hirin' gandy dancers soon. If it is pinery work you seek, well, you best come back in October."

"I'm not looking for work. No sir, I am looking for you."

"Me?"

"My pa and my little brother told me to look you up if ever I came near Hayward. My name is William Kavanaugh. Them that are my friends call me Billy." He stretched out his hand. "This here is my friend, Reginald."

Tor leaned back in his chair. "Billy Kavanaugh? Well, I'll be a gol-danged, mud-suckin' snappin' turtle! Billy Kavanaugh! Junior has told me so many tall tales about you that I was startin' to think you were cousin to Paul Bunyan."

"Who?"

"Paul Bunyan. Paul ... well, you will hear about him if you stay in these parts long."

"Tor," whispered Rosie, "Tor ..."

"Oh. Oh, yes. Rosie, this here is Billy. You know, Junior's brother. And his friend, um ... Reg ...."

"Reginald. Yes, I heard."

"Reginald, Billy, this is my girl, Rosie. She's a flower peddler."

"I am a florist."

"Hmm?"

"I am not a flower peddler, Tor. I am a florist."

"Oh, yes, yes. That's what I meant, fellas. Rosie is a flur..."

"Florist, Tor. Flor - ist."

"When she's not peddlin' flowers, Rosie helps her ma who runs the best boarding house in town—up by the new courthouse."

Rosie rolled her eyes in amazement.

"Her ma serves up the best gol-dang food you will ev...."

The taller of the two young men took Rosie's hand and, bowing gracefully, gently kissed it. "The pleasure of making your acquaintance, Miss Rosie, is completely mine. I must say, your beauty and poise are far beyond words. And, please, call me Reggie."

Rosie blushed. Tor was speechless. Billy shook his head in disbelief, saying, "Reggie already went and booked us here in the hotel. Otherwise, we would room at your ma's boarding house, Rosie, right Reggie?"

"I say we cancel our hotel stay and patronize Rosie's mother, William."

"Oh, no, no," said Tor, "you needn't do that. You are far better off downtown. Why, you will find it much more interesting than a stuffy old boarding house."

"Stuffy old boarding house?" snapped Rosie. "Stuffy? Tor Loken, you never once before said anything about Mama's boarding house being stuffy. And how in blazes could it be old? You know very well there was not one house built in this town until the railroad came three years ago."

"Now, Rosie ..."

"Stuffy and old indeed! I suppose you say the same about Mama, too. Maybe even me. Perhaps, Tor Loken, you should just stay here in the hotel, too. Far more interesting than a stuffy, old boarding house."

"Oh no, Rosie. I did not mean it was stuffy for *me*. I like it stuffy. I mean ... well, Billy and Reggie will be fine here at Johnny Pion's Hotel. I will take my regular room at your ma's." He put his arm around Rosie who continued to scowl. "Fellas, maybe you should excuse us now. Rosie and I were about to order supper."

Fuming, Rosie interrupted. "Why, Tor, how dreadfully impolite of you to not ask our new friends to dine with us."

Reggie was quick to accept. "William and I would love to join you, Rosie. How very gracious. But you must allow me to pay the fare."

"Then it is done," said Billy. "Waiter, two more chairs and a bottle of champagne—no, two bottles. And four glasses ... clean ones."

"And here is a dollar in advance for your good service," said Reggie, "and another dollar for the piano player. Have him play some waltzes to put us in the mood for dining."

Tor, his quiet evening alone with his flame now shattered, looked at Rosie, forcing a smile.

She turned from him to Reggie. "What kind of work are you in? Are you a sawyer perhaps?"

"Sawyer? Oh, dear me, no."

"Not a dentist, are you?"

"Dentist?"

"A sharpener. Saws and axes and such."

"Rosie," he said, laughing, "I am not accustomed to such labors as your stalwart men of the woods."

"But, your ... attire ..."

"Oh, yes. I see. You wonder about my apparel. You see, in my wanderings, I choose to don the garb of the commoners in those localities wherein I visit. It helps me fit in, somewhat. No, Rosie, I am not here to work. Rather, I am here to negotiate the liquidation of my financial holdings—my timberlands. You see, I recently inherited my grandfather's properties. And me, a person having absolutely no interest in the timber trade, well, I intend to turn them."

"Turn them? Turn them into what?" asked Tor.

"You know, turn them—offer them up for sale. Whether for profit or loss, I intend to rid myself of their burden. Several St. Paul and Chicago corporations have expressed some interest, although I wonder if one of the firms already invested in this region might make a better offer. If I play my cards correctly, I stand to leave the pinery with a tidy sum, I dare say. Billy, here, claims he will be able to advise me in this sale."

"Your grandfather," said Tor. "Who was he again?"

"Oh, I thought I mentioned it. I am so sorry. Grandfather's name is the same as mine—Muldoon. I am Reginald Muldoon. My grandfather was Phineas, although you folks probably knew him as King. King Muldoon."

Rosie looked toward Tor, then asked, "You are Phineas Muldoon's grandson?"

"The one and only. And, his only heir. You knew grandfather?"

Tor tried to change the subject. "So, Billy, what are your plans?"

Rosie interrupted. "Reggie, surely you must know what most people here thought of your grandfather, right? He was not held in high regard. In fact ..."

"Grandfather was not well-regarded in any of his circles, including his own family. Phineas was a miserly old curmudgeon, a penny-pinching, mean old rapscallion. Now, after all these years, the greedy old scalawag will finally share his wealth. His demise was a blessing to all—a godsend. I have come to make certain of it. I intend to liquidate the old miser's assets and share a good portion with the public. Perhaps an opera house would befit this community. Or a library, perchance?"

"Goodness gracious," said Rosie, "In Hayward? A Library? An opera house? Really?"

"Only a start, Miss Ringstadt. Only a start."

Tor turned to Billy again. "Billy, what did you say you were planning to do here?"

"Insurance, Tor, an up and coming industry. I'm planning to sell hospital scrips to the lumberjacks. With so many good men bein' injured and in need of doctorin', it only makes sense for them to purchase their hospital stay *before* they need it. I have arranged to sell, for a paltry five dollars, a certificate bound to get you a week stay in the Ashland hospital—doctor's care, included, mind you. What is more, I have, at my own personal expense, printed up five thousand copies. I expect to sell every last one between the first snowfall and Christmas."

"My word!" Rosie said. "May I ask, Billy, how much you earn from this?"

"Me? Well, let me just say the hospital gets the lion's share."

Reggie laughed. "Do not let my clever friend, here, pull the wool over your eyes, Rosie. After the hospital takes their 'lion's share,' William pockets two dollars and sixty-two cents. Perhaps more, if he can arrange a better deal."

"My word, Billy. That comes to thirteen thousand, one-hundred dollars. Are you planning to earn more than thirteen thousand dollars in only three months time?"

"Well, less my expenses. In spite of what Reggie says, I don't really make out so well in the final tally. Still, it is enough to live on. But, say, Rosie, you are quite swift with your numbers. If you are lookin' for work, I could use me a bookkeeper. I can offer you ... "

"Don't let William fool you," said Reggie. "He will bank all of that thirteen thousand along with much more from the sale of his stock in the Deer Creek Silver Mining Company."

Tor turned toward Billy. "You own a mine? A silver mine?"

"Yes. No. I mean, well, ... what I own is the deed to some land north of Deer Creek, and ten thousand certificates of stock I had printed up in Milwaukee. I plan to sell the shares so cheap that a person would be a fool not to buy one or two. A mere dollar apiece. If and when the mine pans out, each shareholder gets a percentage. The more you buy, the bigger cut you get. Now, does that not sound like a great investment opportunity?"

Reggie laughed again. "Mind you, the cut William mentions is reduced by fees he deducts for managing the business and for his commission, mining equipment, laborers, tools, and the like."

"So, where is this Deer Creek?" said Tor.

Billy smiled. "Gol-danged if I know. Someplace nearby a train stop called Marigold. No, ... no, Maringold ... Maran ..."

"Marengo?" asked Tor.

"Marengo! Yes. I bought the land from a fella who homesteaded up that way. Preemption grant. The old fellow put in three hard years but could not stand the cold of one more winter up here. Suffered frostbite somethin' awful, he did. Fingers, toes, ears. Had one cut clean off by some sawbones up here. He wanted nothin' more to do with the place. I got his land for a paltry three double sawbucks. The forty even came with a lean-to big enough for a man and a couple of workhorses. Not a bad deal once I sell the shares."

"What made you settle on a dollar apiece for each share?" asked Tor. "Why not two or three?"

"Oh, I have gained some business sense in my travels. I learned you can shear a sheep every now and then but you can only skin him once. I make the price so low, folks tend to spend all they can muster."

"What happens if you don't find any gold or silver?" asked Rosie.

Billy smiled. "Well, that's mining for you. Life comes with risks, you know."

"Reggie, how much land you plannin' on sellin'?" asked Tor. "We Lokens might take the whole works off your hands."

"Grandfather's lawyers tell me there are about four hundred square miles, several dams, some sawmills, and a boom company on the St. Croix River."

Stunned, Tor replied, "Oh, oh, I see. Well. I will let my pa and uncle know. I doubt they will show much interest in a boom company or river dams. We haul our pine out by rail starting this winter. Modern days call for modern ways, you know. We Lokens are going into the railroad business. Railroads and timber—that's where the future lays a-waitin' up here in the pinery."

"Lies, Tor," said Rosie.

"What?"

"Lies."

"What the heck do you mean, 'lies.'"

"Lies-a-waiting. Not lays-a-waiting."

"Hmm. Oh. Yes, lies, yes."

Reggie filled four glasses with champagne. "Miss Rosie, if you were not tethered to this railroad magnate, I swear I would be inspired to bring you bouquets of roses and write poems for you every day. Your beauty, your poise, your grace have simply, well, simply lifted my heart."

"Oh, my. Reginald, how very sweet. Poems and roses. Tor has never once written a poem for me."

"What? He has never felt the quill dance across the papyrus as words of love appear from the heart?"

"Not once, Reggie."

Tor drank down his wine. "Rosie, you know I am kept very busy up at the camp—cutting timber, laying track, and all. But I can get you roses. Why, anyone tall enough to reach the window in the telegraph office can get roses delivered on the Omaha. I could write poems, too, if I had the time."

"Poems? You?"

"Why, sure I could."

"All right, Mister. Show me."

"Hmm?"

"Show me."

"You mean … here? Right here? Right now?"

"Yes, Tor, right here, right now, a poem. A poem for your sweetheart."

"Well, all right, but you have to give me a minute. Us poem writers cannot be rushed, you know." Tor poured more wine in his glass, then gulped it down.

"Let me see … Hmm. Rosie is the one for me. Sweet as … apples on a tree. Pretty as a flower petal. Heart as warm as … um … as a hot teakettle. There, see Rosie? Nothin' to it. Say, I'm hungry. Where is that waiter? Waiter? Say, waiter!"

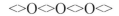

Chapter 5
A Piece of Pie

June 6, 1885

Tor was dressed and shaved before breakfast, his hair neatly combed. He seated himself between other boarding house guests at the table. Rosie's sisters soon brought fresh baked cinnamon rolls, a platter of sausage, another of fried potatoes, and serving bowls heaped with scrambled eggs.

"Milk, Tor?" asked Daisy.

"Milk? Me? Oh, no. Never touch the stuff, nowadays. Up at the camp we jacks prefer coffee. Black and hot, by gum. Yessir, Daisy, we have to have our coffee."

"Sure wish Mama would take us up to your camp again someday. It must look a lot different in the summer than it did when we were there last Christmas."

"Pretty hard to get to the camp these days. You have to take the long way around the lake and the tote road is not much more than a muddy cow path right now. A fella who comes by way of that trail after a storm passes through had better plan on spending time cutting out windfalls, too. Now, if I knew when you were coming, I could meet you at the dam with the Empress Karina and you could ride in high style across the lake. You would like that, Daisy. Say, where is your big sister this morning? Still countin' sheep, is she?"

"Rosie? Oh, she's already down at the Omaha depot with her flowers. She says the seven-fifteen northbound carries some of her best customers, especially for the bouquets. The lilacs and arbutus will be done soon so she works hard to sell them while she can."

"So, young man, you are a lumberjack, are you?" asked the man seated next to Tor.

"Yessir. That I am. Day in, day out durin' the wintertime. Cuttin' and haulin' pine, that's my trade. My family owns the Namakagon Timber Company. 'Bout half-a-day east of the Cable station. And you?"

"I'm here for some trout fishing. Have any secret trout holes I can try?"

"Trout. Hmm. Well, my Uncle Ingman would be the one to ask. He is an expert when it comes to angling. He would say if you really want to catch trout, big trout and plenty of 'em, here is what you do. Find yourself any cold creek that flows into a river used for driving timber. See, when the log drives come down in the spring, the water gets so stirred up and muddy that the trout hightail it up into the small, cold creeks. It has been two months since the spring drive so some of the trout have returned to the river, but my uncle would say your best bet is still up in the creeks. Mind you, stay away from any country that has been clear-cut. Soon as those trees are gone, the water warms up, the rains wash the dregs into the streams, and most of the fish die. Not a pleasant sight to see, hundreds of big trout floatin' belly up in a pool.

"'Twas me, I'd take the train to the Long Lake Station. A sternwheeler there will cart you up the lake to the northeast bay. From there, hike due east, oh, about two, maybe three miles, to Eighteen Mile Creek. I've heard of anglers taking fifty big brook trout out of one pool, then moving upstream and taking fifty more."

"So that woods has not yet been cut? Water is in good health?"

"Eighteen Mile? No. Not cut yet, though I heard Ezra Cornell bought up much of it. For a fella who never comes 'round, he sure buys a lot of timberland. You might run into some jacks building dams, bridges, or slushin' out railroad grades with oxen, but there will not be any cutting goin' on. Lumber outfits cannot cut and haul in summertime. Nope, a fella needs snow cover, ice. Lumberin' is winter work. Yep, always will be."

Adeline Ringstadt came from the kitchen. "Good morning, everyone," she said in a sing-song voice. "How are we all doing? Can I bring more rolls?"

"Mrs. Ringstadt," said Tor, "your breakfasts are delicious. Why, you should have Rosie write down every recipe you know and make one of those cookbooks they sell down at the mercantile."

"Well, Tor, how very nice of you. However, I cannot imagine anyone taking interest in my cooking. More coffee, anyone?"

"Now how would a young lumberjack know about such things as cookbooks?" asked the fisherman.

"Hmm? Oh, Sourdough keeps stacks of cookbooks at the camp."

"Sourdough?"

"Our camp cook. Got it that name because he claims he can make everything taste better by adding his own sourdough concoction. He says it dates back to the Pilgrims, though he's been known to exaggerate some. He keeps a tall stack of cookbooks. The one most worn out is an army cookbook from the Civil War. If you get near our camp, stop for supper. Let me tell ya, you will not regret it."

Tor finished his breakfast and paid for his stay.

"Mrs. Ringstadt, I meant what I said. You should have Rosie write up your recipes. You're a fine cook. Why, I bet you could get together with Sourdough and have the finest cookbook around."

"You certainly are a flatterer, Tor Loken. But I think you would be better off saving your flattery for Rose. She is the one you should be shining up to. She has a soft spot in her heart for you. Maybe you two should think about spending more time together. I mean, she *is* seventeen. Not getting any younger. Most of her friends—other girls her age—well, they've been married for some time now."

"Pa's plans to expand the company don't favor me spending much time here. 'Sides, we have plenty of time. I mean, why rush?"

"Why rush? Tor, there are hundreds of young bachelors here in the pinery and very few eligible young ladies. Why, one of them could just come along and scoop Rosie up. What a pickle that would be. Many a young lady has found herself swept away by the wrong man. It would pain me to see that happen to my daughter."

"Swept away? My gosh, what should I do?"

"You could start by visiting more often. Maybe you and Rosie could take the Omaha to Clear Lake for the day. Or you two could go on a picnic. Oh, there are plenty of things a young couple could do together. Whatever you do decide, dear, you dassn't dawdle."

"I'm afraid I don't know much about courtin'."

"Please don't get me wrong, now. I know it is not my place to give you such advice. But, I know you lost your mother years back and, well, if you will pardon my sticking my nose in, you can feel free to ask my advice on any questions you might have asked your own mother. Seems it is the least I can do, considering she's gone."

"That's kind of you, Mrs. Ringstadt."

"Oh, Tor, why not just call me Mama, like Rose and the girls?"

"I best be off. Pa gave me some business to tend to. But first, I am going to buy Rosie a piece of pie at the depot restaurant and make some plans for that picnic."

"Good for you, Son. Good for you."

His rucksack on his shoulder, Tor crossed the tracks and entered the depot waiting room. In the far corner stood Rosie's red flower cart but no Rosie. He crossed the room to find the cart empty—every bouquet and corsage gone. He approached the ticket window.

"I'm looking for Rosie Ringstadt. Any idea where she could be?"

"Who?"

"Rosie. Rosie Ringstadt. That's her red cart over there."

"The flower peddler?"

"Um, florist."

"Huh?"

"Ya, the flower peddler. Have you seen her?"

"She was here a while ago. I seen her talkin' to some jack. Tall fellow."

"Tall fella? Was he wearin' a yellow mackinaw?"

"Yep. That's him."

"You see which way she headed, by chance?"

"Nope. You try lookin' in the depot restaurant?"

"Ya. She's not there. How many trains have come in today?"

"Only the seven-thirty northbound. But there's another due at …"

"Thank you, friend. Say, if you see her show up for her cart, let her know Tor Loken is lookin' for her."

"Tor Loken? Is that you? You the Tor Loken who stopped them train robbers last year?"

"Hmm? Oh, yeah. That's me, I s'pose. Say, let Rosie know if you see her, all right?"

"And weren't you in that fight at the dam—where King Muldoon got killed?"

"Ya. You will watch for Rosie, then?"

"Yessir, Mister Loken. I'll keep an eye peeled. Surely is a pleasure meetin' you."

Tor walked through the depot restaurant, leaving by the south door. He crossed the tracks again, headed for Hayward's downtown. As he passed the large windows of the Hotel Pion, he caught a glimpse of yellow—a yellow mackinaw, hanging over a chair in the restaurant. Cupping his hands around his eyes, he pressed up against the glass. There, staring back at him was Reggie Muldoon seated at a table. Across from Reggie sat a young woman with dark, flowing hair. Tor entered the hotel and turned toward the restaurant.

"Rosie?"

Reggie pulled out a chair. "Tor! Come join us for breakfast. Say, what a beautiful June day, eh? Sunny and bright, blue sky. Makes me wonder if I should keep a few square miles of land up here in the wilderness. Maybe a section or two on some river or lake."

"Rosie, I thought you would be at the depot."

"I was. Then a wonderful thing happened. Reggie bought every one of my bouquets and corsages. How grand! He bought them all and gave them away to every person who stepped off the train. I never saw so many happy travelers."

Tor sat down. "Why … why that's great, Rosie."

"Loken, you should have seen all the smiles gracing the faces of those common folks. I swear we made forty new friends by the time Rosie's flowers were gone. How fun!"

"And I needed not spend my morning selling flowers. Reggie, that was such a thoughtful deed."

"The pleasure was mine and mine alone. But I must say, there was an underlying reason."

Tor stared at Muldoon. "What reason?"

"I am unaccustomed to taking breakfast alone. When I observed Rosie strolling down Iowa Avenue with her delightful, dainty red cart, right then and there I knew she was the one."

"The one?"

"Yes. She was the one who must share my breakfast table this morning—at any expense." He turned to Rosie. "Think of it! That's the effect you have had on me in only one day. Imagine how my heart might spin in a week or two."

"Reggie, you are so very sweet."

"A week or two?" said Tor.

Reggie took her hand. "Rosie, what say you and I set off on a picnic today? After all, your daily chore is done. Perhaps you can delight me with a tour of some local sites?"

"Oh, Reggie, what a wonderful plan! I will have Mama pack a nice dinner. I know a farmer on Round Lake who will let us use his rowboat. It is such a fine day for it."

"Reggie, do you know how to swim?" asked Tor.

"Swim?"

"Just in case the boat sinks or a black bear capsizes you."

"Black Bear?"

"Tor, you stop that right now," said Rosie. "Reggie, Tor is teasing. Pay no attention to him."

Reggie squirmed. "Black bear?"

"Been known to tear the face off a man. Seen it once myself. Not a favorable sight—a man with his face torn clear off."

"Tor, that's quite enough. You said you were looking for me in the depot. Was there something you wanted to tell me?"

"No. Well … yes. I mean … I was wondering if you might like to, well, go on a picnic or something."

"A picnic? You were going to ask me to go on a picnic? Hmm, where have I heard that before?"

"No, Rosie. It's true. Ask your ma."

"Mama? What does Mama have to do with this?"

"Oh, nothing really. I was telling her over breakfast how it would be a nice break from work at the camp if we went on a picnic or maybe take a train ride somewhere."

"You? You thought we should do that?"

"Well, your ma and me, we talked it over some."

"Just what I thought. Mama is putting ideas in your head. Are you unable to come up with your own? Do you need Mama to do your thinking, Tor Loken?"

Reggie leaned back in his chair with a smirk.

"Rosie, Pa told me to take care of the company business first thing today and then get back to camp. Instead, I looked for you. I hoped you would let me buy you a piece of rhubarb pie. That's all I wanted to do. Honest, Rosie. Buy you a piece of pie and ask if we could spend some time together some day—maybe at the camp, or a picnic, or we could even take the Omaha up to Bayfield or down to Clear Lake for the day. But I see now that you are … well, too busy. So I will be on my way. I s'pose I'm not in the mood for pie anyway. You have a good time with Reggie. Maybe next time I come to town I will look you up, Rose."

He turned to Reggie. "You enjoy your boat ride, Muldoon. Keep one eye peeled for those bears, now, 'specially those she-bears. No tellin' when one might turn on you."

Rucksack in hand, Tor left the hotel, for the Omaha freight office. When he bought his ticket an hour later, Rosie's red handcart was still in the waiting room. He took a seat in the passenger car, far from other travelers.

<>O<>O<>O<>

Chapter 6
Diindiisi

June 7, 1885

Noisy loons woke Tor early the next morning, pleading with him to gaze across the mirror-like surface of the lake. Three-quarters of a mile away, a thin column of smoke rose from Chief Namakagon's early morning campfire. With no breeze to disturb its ascent, the wispy-white shaft climbed high above the island before vanishing into the blue. Tor threw on his work clothes and laced his boots. In minutes he was in his canoe. To the east, the sun peeked through the trees as he pulled onto shore, greeted by Chief Namakagon's dogs, Makade and Waabishki. Tails wagging, they bounced in and out of the birch canoe and led him up to the lodge.

"Mikwam-migwan," he called, climbing the bank. "Smoke from your morning fire invited me to share your coffee."

"Hello, young woodsman," came a muffled reply from the chief's lodge. "It is high time you arrived. The loons have been complaining how they must begin their workday hunting for fish while you sleep the morning sun away. Come. Breakfast will soon be ready."

Chief Namakagon's dogs circled the fire, flopping down near the warm stones. They waited for the old man to turn the sturgeon slabs soaking in the smoke. Tor sat between the dogs, scratching their ears. He glanced at the lodge entrance where an unfamiliar walking stick leaned. The brightly decorated, feathered staff seemed too short for the tall Namakagon who now stepped into the morning air.

"Woodsman, I would like you to meet someone," he said. A woman followed him from the lodge. "This is Diindiisi, who for many years I have known."

An Ojibwe woman in a dark blue deerskin dress with white beading stepped into the sunlight. Her long, black hair, braided neatly and tied with a white, braided leather cord, lay across her shoulder. She approached, eyes smiling.

Tor stood. "I am honored, Diindiisi. Chief, here, calls me Woodsman, but Pa and my uncle call me Tor. Tor Loken. I am from the Loken lumber camp across the lake. Namakagon Timber Company."

"I know of your father's camp, Tor Woodsman. This old grouse told me many tales about you. I imagine a few may have been true."

"Grouse? Diindiisi, you call me a grouse?"

"It has more than one meaning, old man. One seems to fit you well from time to time."

"Grouse. Yes, I suppose, as you say, time to time I do grouse."

She stepped closer to the fire ring, stretching her palms toward the heat. "Long ago, this old man gave me the name, Diindiisi, the Blue Jay."

"Long, long, long ago," said the chief, grinning.

"He enjoys giving others their names. I think he liked the blue of my dress. I am also called Louise Renshaw. That's my city name. I have come to help the old man with his chores."

The chief winked at Tor. "Help me? You came to bother me. Maybe I call you Blue Jay because you squawk, squawk, squawk, morning till night."

"There are times when this old man grouses about my squawking. Other times he grouses that I do not squawk enough. He is not easy to please. The song of a blue jay, like the grousing of an old man, can sound different to different ears. I will tell you, though, Mikwam-migwan praises my songs more than he complains."

Namakagon poured coffee into tin cups before turning the slabs of sturgeon. "It frightens me how often she is right. Perhaps we should change our discussion from birds to fish. This will be ready to eat in another minute."

"Diindiisi," said Tor, "where did you find blue hide to make your dress? Not from Paul Bunyan's blue ox, I hope."

"The color comes from dogwood bark, blackberries, and sumac leaves. My grandmother showed me how to make this along with others. She could turn animal hides many colors. Visiting her village was like walking through a rainbow."

Namakagon offered slabs of smoked sturgeon and steaming coffee to his guests. "I met your uncle along the Marengo Trail two days ago. He said you will soon lay the steel for your railroad."

Tor sipped his coffee. "According to the freight office in Hayward, it will be delivered to Pratt today. We will start layin' track there and work our way up the grade to Atkins Lake and beyond. Uncle Ingman has seventy gandy dancers hired for the job. If the weather cooperates and my uncle can keep them away from the whiskey, we should have the first leg done in two weeks."

"I have seen the grade. Many curves. Steep hills. Maybe too steep. Much work."

"Pa already has contracts to haul for seven other camps besides ours. Uncle Ingman says our railroad will pay for itself in no time."

"No time?" said the chief. "Time is an odd notion. Time does not exist until it suddenly appears. We do not know it arrived until it has passed. By then, it is lost forever. Lost time is no time."

Diindiisi laughed. "Again the old grouse tries to mimic the wise owl. No time, lost time, past time? Mikwam-migwan, your notion that you are some wilderness sage may come from smoking too many pipes or eating your own cooking."

"Too many pipes? Bah. I only speak my heart." Namakagon sat. "Oh, how delighted Wenebojo must be when he sees the effect of a woman's tongue on a man's brain." A wide grin spread across his face as he turned to Diindiisi for her reply.

"And where, old wise one, might Wenebojo ever hope to find a man's brain? Surely not in your lodge!" Blue Jay's retort brought silence—then laughter from all three.

"Uncle Ingman bought our first engine, the old ninety-nine from the Omaha line," said Tor. "Came with nine flatcars, a tender, and a caboose. Says he is buyin' three old passenger cars, too. Louie Thorp, our carpenter, will outfit two of 'em with straw bunks for the men. The third will become a rolling cook shanty. Sourdough has been bellowing like a mule caught in a thorn apple thicket ever since he found out he will be cooking out in the cuttings and not at the cook shanty by the lake."

"Who will run this locomotive?" asked Namakagon.

"My uncle and Gust Finstadt, our blacksmith, are lookin' for someone. It's not like being an engineer on the mainline, though. We will not have folks buying tickets and expecting us to meet a time schedule. No need to go more than five or ten miles an hour, either. Our train will do nothing but haul timber out of the cuttings, then bring feed for the animals and food for the men back in. The sawmills will provide slab wood for her fuel in trade for some switching of cars now and then. Uncle Ingman says he has it all figured out."

"What of the work horses and oxen?" asked Diindiisi. "What will happen to them?"

"Well, we will not butcher them, if that's what you are wonderin' about. No, we still need them to get the pine out to the rail line. I doubt there will ever be a day without horses or oxen pulling sleigh loads of timber out of the Wisconsin pinery. Right now we are using our oxen to slush out the grades back into the cuttings."

"Slush out?" said Diindiisi.

"Ya, each ox team pulls a big metal scoop they call a slush bucket. It's designed to scrape up dirt. Then the teamster drops the dirt in the low spots. He does this over and over until the grade is even. A team of horses then runs a drag up and down the grade to smooth the whole she-bang out. Y'know, it's downright amazing how much work two oxen can do in a day just by draggin' a slush bucket. All for a forkful of hay now and then.

"Say, Chief, I finally met Junior's brother, Billy Kavanaugh. I was in Hayward eatin' supper at Johnny Pion's Hotel with Rosie when he just showed up out of nowhere."

"I sometimes wondered if Junior actually had a brother or if his stories were just more lumber camp tales."

"Oh, he has a brother all right. And Junior was not exaggerating when he said Billy was a high roller and a wheeler-dealer. Quite the character, he is. He has plans to sell thirteen thousand dollars worth of hospital insurance scrip before the snow flies. Can you imagine? That's more than a year's payroll for a hundred-man lumber camp."

Diindiisi nodded. "In Michigan they stopped a man from selling insurance scrip that was no good."

"Oh, Billy's scrip is on the up-and-up. Least, I think it is. I suppose we will not know till some poor jack gets his foot stepped on by a hay burner or waylaid by a widowmaker."

"Or run over by your train," said Namakagon. "Diindiisi, what happened to the man in Michigan? Was he sent off to cheat other people? Sent to work at the capital city, perhaps?"

"No. He will not cheat anymore. They made sure."

"Made sure?" said Tor.

"The lumberjacks lynched him."

Tor's eyes widened. "Really? They strung him up?"

"Yes. Hung him from a tree. Left his body out in the woods to feed the timber wolves. No one cried for him. No one cared. How terrible it must be to face death knowing no one will care."

"Diindiisi, I will be sure to let Billy know when I see him. I will tell him to stay on the up and up. I 'spect he will be visiting all the camps to sell his hospital scrip and his silver mine shares."

Namakagon looked up from his plate. "Silver mine?"

"Up in Marengo country somewhere. Forty acres. Billy printed up a whole pile of stock certificates. Ten thousand. He plans to sell them, and then use the money to dig for silver."

"He is one of many who hope to get rich from Marengo River silver and gold. Only a few who scratch in the earth for riches are able to find enough for both food and whiskey. Most go home with no more than a worn out shovel, a sore back, and an angry woman waiting at the cabin door."

"What about your friend, Captain Morgan? I heard he is doin' pretty well."

"Yes, Dan Morgan. He is different than the others. Knows the earth. Respects it. One of the few miners who refuses to use dynamite."

"Then how does he ...?"

"The old way. Our ancestor's way. By searching, not blasting. I doubt Junior Kavanaugh's brother knows there is an old way."

"Billy had a friend with him, too. One of those fancy-pants fellas from out east. Chief, you will remember his grandfather."

"His grandfather?"

"King Muldoon."

"Muldoon? He is the grandson of Phineas Muldoon? He is here?"

"'Fraid so. Says he came to sell off his family holdings. Says, too, he will donate much of what he gets back to the folks who live here. I will not believe it until I see it."

"Muldoon's grandson. Not good. Not good. Tell Olaf and Ingman they must remain aware of all their surroundings until he is far away. You, too. Family ties are strong, Woodsman. This could bring trouble."

"I think not. From how he speaks, I would say he disliked the greedy old shark even more than we did. Sounded to me like he was pleased to finally be able to reach inside his grandfather's pocketbook. Says he wants to make it right for folks 'round here, too. Plans to build an opry house or something of the sort."

"Where is he now?"

"Well, that's sort of a touchy subject. You see, right about now I figure he is courting my girl."

"Rosie?"

"Only one I would call my girl, Chief. I'm afraid she is downright bedazzled by his Eastern ways, taken in by his falderal and the weight of his pocketbook. Why, when Rosie heard he might use his grandfather's money to build an opry house in Hayward, she seemed to melt right there at the supper table."

"Yes, I have noticed Rose is charmed by wealth and extravagance. She is like the butterfly in spring when every flower has nectar sweeter than the one before."

"I swear, when I had to leave Hayward for the camp yesterday, I had visions of Muldoon taking my Rosie away forever. Probably with her right this very minute, plying her with poems and roses, flattering her mother, and buying licorice whips for Rosie's sisters."

Diindiisi shook her head. "If you feel you two are truly meant to be together, then you must return to her and tell her so."

"I doubt that I could do that, Diindiisi."

"Ask yourself what is important. Far too many loves are lost because words are not spoken, feelings not expressed."

"Pa would not hear of it. Why, he would ..."

"You do not listen, Tor Loken. Ask yourself what is most important. If the answer is your love for this girl, then go. Go find your butterfly."

Chief Namakagon put his hand on Tor's shoulder and looked into his eyes. "Woodsman, though it pains me to admit, Diindiisi is right. You must go."

"But ... what do I do about Pa?"

"I will explain to Olaf."

"Boy, oh boy, I don't know about this."

"He would have gone for your mother. He will understand."

"But ..."

"Tor," said Blue jay, "My ancestors left these words for all to follow. Listen to them. There is but one thing in this life worth living for. And there is but one thing worth dying for. Both are the same. Both are love. If you love this girl, this Rose, if you feel she is worth living for and dying for, you have no choice. You must follow your heart. You must go. Go, now."

<>O<>

The Omaha twelve-fifteen southbound rumbled past the Phipps dam on schedule. As the locomotive crossed the trestle north of Hayward, one passenger, Tor Loken, realized he had neither luggage nor the slightest idea of what might happen next. It did not matter.

Chapter 7
The N<u>o.</u> Wisconsin Lumber C<u>o.</u>

June 11, 1885

The thick scent of fresh-cut pine filled the air outside the enormous Hayward sawmill on this quiet summer morning. In the holding pond, workers walked atop logs, sorting and sending the pine to the multi-bladed gang saws. Upstream, the lake lay so jam-packed with timber that workers could walk shore to shore and step onto dry land with dry boots. The whine of water-driven saws resonated up and down the Namekagon River Valley.

The thick scent of fresh-cut pine filled the air outside the enormous Hayward sawmill on this quiet summer morning. In the holding pond, workers walked atop logs, sorting and sending the pine to the multi-bladed gang saws. Upstream, the lake lay so jam-packed with timber that workers could walk shore to shore and step onto dry land with dry boots. The whine of water-driven saws resonated up and down the Namekagon River Valley.

As hundreds of logs moved up and into the mill, wagon after wagon, heavy with lumber, rolled down the ramp and into the yard. There the stacked boards dried in the summer sun before being loaded onto railroad cars and shipped to emerging Midwest cities and towns, all eager for Wisconsin pine.

The sign on the office door read, *North Wisconsin Lumber Company, A. J. Hayward, President*. Mister Hayward's secretary announced the young man.

"Come in. Come in. Have a chair, Reginald," said Hayward. "I have been expecting someone from your family to pay a visit for quite some time now. Ever since old Phineas ... well, shall we say ... left this world for a better one?"

"Then you know why I am here."

"I imagine I do. Your grandfather assembled quite a collection of assets around here. Old Phineas owned a good portion of the timberland and a number of mills. I would venture either you want advice from me about how to succeed as my competitor, or you want to know how much I will offer to buy you out. One of those choices will get you a few more minutes of my time. Which is it?"

"Mister Hayward, I prefer the competition of the rowing scull and the polo horse. I came here to liquidate the old fellow's holdings. And although I have been here only a few days, I have already grown tired of your woodtick bites and the persistent buzzing of your miserable mosquitoes, not to mention their annoying itch. The sooner I can arrange to convert Grandfather's properties into cold, hard cash, the sooner I can return to the city life I so prefer. Frankly, I cannot understand how anyone can tolerate life in this desolate wilderness."

"Small price to pay for the financial rewards of life in the pinery."

"Perhaps for A. J. Hayward, but not for Reggie Muldoon. My attorney prepared this list of Grandfather's assets. Make me an offer." Reggie slid a sheet of paper across the oak desk.

A. J. Hayward studied the list. "Reggie, as much as I would like to write you a fat check for all this right now and take it off your hands, I must decline. All my assets are tied up in this company and my own personal timberlands. I could not squeeze another thousand dollars from the bankers at this time. The best I can offer is to manage your grandfather's properties and send you an annual payment toward the principal."

"Not interested, A. J."

"I suggest, then, you speak with Mister Robert McCormick."

"McCormick?"

"One of my investors. We are partnering on some projects. I think he might be interested in helping you out. You will find him up on the hill near the new courthouse. He built a home there. Look for the largest house on the hill. Yes, Robert McCormick is the man to see, Reggie." A knock came on the door. "Yes, come in Freddy," said Hayward. "I was hoping you would stop in. There is someone here you should meet."

A thin man dressed in plain, loden green work shirt and pants stepped into the office, a stack of papers in his hand.

"Reggie," said Hayward, "I would like you to meet our business manager. This is Frederich Weyerhaeuser. Should you find need for financial advice, Frederich is your man. Knows all there is to know about the timber trade."

"Weyerhaeuser? Why, I believe I may have humiliated some of your relatives on the polo field."

"I am not one for games, Mister …"

"Muldoon. My grandfather was …"

"King Muldoon?"

"You have heard of him."

"You will not find a soul in these parts who hasn't. Not well-liked, old Phineas. In fact, most folks downright despised the cunning old rascal."

"And you? Did you despise the old troll?" Reggie said over a distant whistle of a train.

"Me?" Weyerhaeuser stuck his pencil behind his ear and placed his hand on Reggie's shoulder. "I would not have offered the time of day to Phineas Muldoon, the man. However, as a businessman, I must admit King Muldoon was quite shrewd—shrewd and very successful. I imagine you now appreciate how successful he was, no?"

"Yes. Yes I do. In fact, I was telling A. J. here that I plan to sell off my grandfather's timber holdings. You might consider cutting yourself in. It may take several partners to assume my properties. I am on my way now to see Robert McCormick."

"Young man, I appreciate this information. Before you finalize any arrangements for a sale, you let me know your plans. Perhaps we can come to terms in some fashion."

"Will do, Freddy. Will do."

<>O<>

Reggie knocked on the large front door of the McCormick home. A maid escorted him to the parlor where he explained his intentions to liquidate to Robert McCormick.

"Yes, Reginald, I believe we can come to terms on a sale," said McCormick. "I am knee-deep in some other company business right now. Headed for St. Paul tonight, as a matter of fact. Expect to return within the week. Meanwhile, like you, I know how hotel lodging can wear on a person. Reggie, there is no need for you to rub elbows with the riff-raff. You are welcome to stay here if you wish. We have an upstairs guest room waiting for you, if you so please."

"I would be delighted, Robert. Your words ring so true. These

- 53 -

small town hotels, as convenient as they may be for some, are sheer punishment for we who prefer sophisticated travel. I will check out of Pion's first thing in the morning. Meanwhile, you have a safe, speedy trip, sir. St. Paul is a delightful little city … well, delightful, save the excessive horse manure in the streets. You would think the city fathers would tend to that issue."

<>O<>

By the time the Omaha southbound rumbled across the Hayward trestle, Tor was ready to disembark. The closer the train came to the depot, the more his anxiety grew. Palms wet with perspiration, he was across the platform and into the station before Conductor Williams called the all clear. Neither Rosie nor her red flower cart were in the waiting room. He rushed through the depot restaurant, checking the counter and tables before heading downtown in search of his girl.

His apprehension growing, Tor peered through the windows of the Pion Hotel as he passed by. He turned the corner onto Iowa Avenue, noticing the boardwalks were all but deserted in the mid-afternoon sun. Two empty rigs waited in front of the general store and only a few horses stood hitched to rails near the saloons. The tall, brick-faced buildings, standing shoulder-to-shoulder, blocked any relief a cooling summer breeze might bring. Stores up and down the street all had their front doors wide open to help weather the heat and humidity.

Paying no heed to the heat, Tor trotted up the hill past the new courthouse, turned the corner, and scaled the front steps of Adeline Ringstadt's Boarding House, taking them two at a time.

"Rosie? You here? Rosie?" he called, wiping his brow.

"Tor?" came a call from the kitchen. "What in the world? Dear me! Is everything all right? Your pa is all right? Your uncle?"

"They are fine, Mrs. Ringstadt."

"What brings you back to town so soon?"

"Rosie does. She had stars in her eyes after meeting that fella Reggie. I came here to set things right. Let her know … well, let her know what is in my heart. Is she here?"

"I sent Rosie and the girls to the market. They should be back soon."

Tor breathed a sigh of relief.

"What do you mean by set things right? Is something the matter?"

"Oh, I said some foolish things, I'm afraid. I surely don't know what to do, Mrs. Ringstadt."

"Mama, Tor, please. You were going to call me 'Mama.' Remember?"

"Hmm? Oh, ya." He plopped down in an overstuffed chair in the parlor.

Adeline smiled. "Tor, we all say foolish things, time to time. You are concerned about that new boy? Reggie?"

"He sashays around, flaunting his hoity-toity ways and talking his highfalutin' talk, throwing his money around like it grows on trees in one of his estates. Seemed Rosie was acting as though she might follow him over the rainbow if he should ask."

"I wonder if you are not imagining things."

"That slicked-up, tin horn, popinjay with his shiny new boots and gold ring bought up every last bouquet she had just to purloin her away from her flower cart!"

"Hmm. Rosie did mention he bought some flowers."

"Some? For Pete's sake, he bought the lot of them! Every last blossom, leaf, and stem. Then he gave them away willy-nilly. Now, how am I supposed to match up to that? 'Specially when I have to tend to my work at the camp."

"The way you match up, Tor, is simply by being yourself. Rosie is a bright young woman. She might dream of castles in the air now and then. And, why not? Lord knows I did. Still do! Nevertheless, you mark my words and mark them well—Rosie may have her head in the clouds now and again, but she knows to keep her feet steadfast on the ground as well."

They heard the back door to the kitchen open and close. Tor stood.

"Mama," cried Daisy, "tell Violet to stop mocking me."

"Mama," came the echo, "tell Violet to stop mockin' me."

"Please, Mama, make her stop."

"Please, Mama, make …"

"Violet," snapped her mother, "Show your manners, young lady. We have guests here." Adeline stepped toward the kitchen.

"I swear, Mama," said Rosie, carrying packages into the kitchen, "These two disobedient urchins are an embarrassment to us all." She placed a wrapped and tied bundle in the icebox, slamming the door. "You should have heard them bickering in the candy store. They are impolite brats. Never again, Mama. Never again will I take them …"

"Tor is here, Rose."

"What?"

"Waiting for you in the parlor."

She peeked around the doorway. "Tor?"

"Hello, Rosie."

"What in the world ..."

"I came to see you, Rosie. To try to ... to let you know that ... to see if ... well ..."

"Stop beating about the bush, Tor."

"Well ... Rosie ... would you like to go on a picnic?"

<>O<>

Adeline Ringstadt had the basket packed in minutes. Tor hitched the mare to the buggy and, within the hour, Tor and Rosie sat beneath a towering birch tree overlooking the river. Cooled by a southwest breeze and clouds, now blocking the sun, they soon shared a dinner of cold fried chicken, deviled eggs, biscuits, rhubarb pie, and iced tea.

Tor searched for words. "Rosie, I have to know. Do you have designs on Reggie Muldoon?"

"Designs? On Reggie? Wherever did you come up with such an idea?"

"At the hotel. You know, when we had supper the other day. You seemed so ...well, it just looked like you ... well ..."

"For crying out loud, say what you mean to say."

"I just got the feeling you might think a fella like Reggie Muldoon, with all his money, could be your ticket to the world. Seemed like every time he said something about traveling here or there or doing this or that, you sort of wanted to do the same. It just seemed ..."

"Tor, Tor, Tor. You poor boy." She put her hand on his. "I see now what Mama meant when she said men have trouble seeing the forest for the trees. No, Tor, I have no designs on Reggie Muldoon or, for that matter, anyone."

"You sure?"

"Anyone but you, you big knucklehead." She leaned in, kissing him on the cheek. "Look at those clouds over there. I think it is going to rain."

"You sure?"

"About the rain?"

"Rain? No. About you havin' designs on me and not Muldoon."

"Am I sure? Well, of course I am sure. Look, Tor Loken, there is not a girl in Wisconsin, or anywhere else, for that matter, who does not fancy thoughts of traveling to the world's finest hotels, dancing in glorious gowns on the floors of the grandest ballrooms with a charming, handsome, polite young man. But these are a girl's dreams. Pipe dreams, Mama calls them. And we know pipe dreams rarely come true. So we reach for those fantasies and hope for the best. I doubt I will ever travel to the world's finest hotels, dance in the grandest of ballrooms, and wear glorious gowns, although I have not given up hope quite yet. But some of my dreams have come true. I have the most charming, handsome, polite, young man of my dreams, although I must admit he utters some very peculiar words now and again."

Tor grinned. "Namakagon said the same. Says it is far better to speak little and let people think you are wise than to jabber away and convince them you are not."

"You and your wit and wisdom of Chief Namakagon."

"So, you say Reggie Muldoon is not …"

"No, Tor, No designs, no interest, no nothing. I showed Reggie and Billy around town, introduced them to Mama and to Reverend Spooner, but they were more interested in the businesses on Iowa Avenue—especially the sporting houses. That Billy Kavanaugh, I swear! Acted like he never saw the inside of a brothel. And he, a sea-going salesman. I left them both downtown and spent my evening at Mama's piano. Tor, you can discard any foolish ideas you may have about me and anyone but you. Here, have a cookie."

"Hmm?"

"Would you like one of Mama's cookies?"

"Mama packed cookies?"

"Mama? You called her 'Mama'?"

"Well, that's all right, isn't it? I mean, me calling her 'Mama'?"

"Well …yes. Yes, I think I would like that. I would like that a lot. You call Mama 'Mama', and I will call your father 'Papa.' You think it might rain?"

"You want to call my father 'Papa'? Oh my. The whole camp would give me the berries for it. Can you imagine the razzin' I would get? They would never let up. Say, just look at those clouds. You think it will rain?"

"Tor, I've been asking you the same question since we arrived."

"You have? Oh, oh, ya. We'd best go or we will get caught for sure."

Rosie began repacking the picnic basket. "All right, then. When I see your father, I will stick with Mister Loken—for now. But someday ...when I finish my schooling ..."

"Someday, Rosie. My, just look at those clouds. We better get goin'."

"Meanwhile, Tor Knucklehead Loken, I have no interest in anyone but you, rain or shine." Rosie kissed him on the cheek as the first raindrops fell.

Chapter 8
No Winks, No Nods, No Whiskey

August 1885

The clock in the lobby of the Chequamegon Hotel rang half-past ten in the evening. A tall man in a dark green, oilcloth rain slicker stepped onto Ashland's Second Street in the drizzling mist. The heavy odor of coal smoke hung in the air as he made his way, searching tavern to tavern for someone to hire. His search ended at the Crows Nest bar.

"Then you will take the job?" he asked in a hushed tone to the man near the end of the bar. "You will do it?"

"You got the got the money?"

"You get half tomorrow. The rest when the job is done."

"I ain't no fool, now. You best not try to stiff me, mister."

"Shh, keep your voice down. I will not stiff you, friend. Why would I? Money means little to me. Not only will you get your pay, but, if you follow my instructions to the letter, I will have three more jobs for you. Why, by the time we have things all squared up, you will be sitting on a fine purse—a regular bankroll."

"These 'jobs' of yours, exactly how do you want them …"

"Accidents. A string of everyday, pinery accidents. Nothing unusual. Your job is to make each look like an ordinary, out-of-the-blue accident. Do that and nobody will be the wiser."

"And if an accident cannot be arranged?"

"Then, my friend, you are on your own. That's your decision alone. I will pay you either way."

"All right. You got your man. But, if this is gonna be so damn easy, why not do it yourself?"

"Oh, I would that I could. People know me—know who I am, what my business is—what my ties are. Besides, I am not cut out for this kind of work. I don't have the stomach for it."

"Stomach? I say it is backbone you lack, friend."

"Look. I can find someone else. Do you or do you not want the job? Plenty of others around—men out of work who would jump at the chance."

"All right. All right. Like I said, you got your man."

"Good. Take the Omaha to Hayward tomorrow. Meet me in the alley behind the Pion Hotel. Ten-thirty sharp. You'll get half your pay then, along with the rest of the details. Meanwhile, I don't know you. You don't know me. This is the first and last time we are to be seen together in public. Should you chance upon me on the street, offer nary a nod nor a wink. We will both be the better for it."

"No winks, no nods. Ten-thirty, tomorrow night behind Johnny Pion's. I will be there."

"And you dassn't come with your brain muddled with spirits."

"No winks, nods, no whiskey. Humph."

"Here is a sawbuck to show I am serious. Tomorrow night then?"

"You dang sure better have two hundred in hand."

"Oh, yes, I will have it for you. And soon after, you will have twice as much in your pocketbook."

The man in the dark green slicker stepped onto the dreary street, leaving his new acquaintance sitting at the far end of the bar at the Crows Nest examining the ten-dollar bill. He slapped it on the bar. "Barkeeper! Set me up again. No more of your watered down rot gut, neither. Pour me your best bourbon. I got me something to celebrate."

"Ya? And what might that be?"

"I believe my ship has finally come in, friend. Pour the whiskey."

<>O<>

Shortly after the morning train pulled up to the Cable station, Conductor Clyde Williams carried a stack of newspapers into the waiting room. He plopped the bundle onto the ticket counter with a thud and picked at the knot, then, impatient, cut the string with his pocketknife. Williams sat down on the nearest bench and studied each page while waiting for the engine to take on water. Suddenly, he sat up straight, shouting into the back office.

"Holy old jumpin' up Jehoshaphat, Oscar! You will not believe what is in the morning paper. Page two. Listen to this! *The old Indian hermit, Chief Namakagon, known also by the name Mikwam-mi-migwan, or Ice Feathers, has been seen trading raw silver for medicine and other goods in Ashland. Those who have inspected said silver profess it to be of highest grade, indeed not in need of shipping off to the refineries.*'

"Hear that, Oscar? Sounds like ol' Chief Namakagon struck it rich! *'It is not known where the Chippeway hermit is procuring such valuable a mineral or how much he may have already set aside.'* Are you listenin' to this, Oscar? *'This newspaper suspects the silver came from the vicinity of the Marengo Station, as the old hermit frequents the Marengo Trail between Ashland and Lake Namakagon and recently built a lodge near there.'"*

The engineer sounded the train whistle, bringing Clyde to his feet. "Did you hear that, Oscar? Oscar?"

The depot door opened and the telegraph operator stepped into the waiting room followed by the stationmaster. "Morning, Clyde," said Oscar. "Anything new in the morning paper?"

The engineer gave another whistle, somewhat louder than before.

"News? I should say so! News that's bound to have folks 'round here jumpin' like a long-tailed cat in a room full of rockin' chairs!" Another whistle sounded. Clyde handed the paper to the stationmaster. "Here, I got myself a schedule to keep. Read it for yourself. Page two. You will not believe it, Oscar. No siree."

Clyde rushed out. A second later he poked his head in the door, saying, "Oscar, you owe three cents for that paper," and quickly vanished again as the train pulled away.

Oscar turned to page two, reading the short report. "Well, imagine that! Why, that sly old devil must have himself quite a diggin's. By golly, when folks get wind of this, life is gonna change and change fast for ol' Ice Feathers. Every last man jack with a pick and a shovel will be hounding him like a bunch of crows on a dead moose. My, my, my. Poor ol' Chief Namakagon."

Oscar took the paper into the office, poured himself a cup of coffee, and sat back in his oak chair. He studied each page in order, then finally reached the last page where he found more.

"'King Muldoon Holdings All Sold. Those estate and business interests in Bayfield, Ashland, and Sawyer Counties previously owned by Phineas 'King' Muldoon have been conveyed to the North Wisconsin Lumber Company, effective immediately. Workers are now being hired to fill the former Muldoon camps this coming winter. Manlookers have been dispatched by the North Wisconsin office to St. Paul, Hudson, La Crosse, Menomonie, and Chippewa Falls in search of experienced lumberjacks.'"

"So ends the sordid tale of King Muldoon," Oscar mumbled.

"What is that, Oscar?" came a voice from the doorway.

"Oh, hello, Bill. Say, take a gander at today's paper. Page two. I think you might be interested."

The railway constable opened the paper. "Well, I'll be danged. The old chief found himself a silver mine. I wonder where it is."

"Wish I knew, Bill. He has been spending a lot of time up near

Marengo lately. Built a cabin."

"I heard he has some timber rights up there."

"Maybe he is taking timber from above and silver from below. Ever think of that?"

"No, not the Chief Namakagon I know. He has little use for money. His wealth comes from his love of life and land and such."

"Just once I would like to find myself a silver mine, Bill."

"Naw. Up in this country most miners go bust in no time. You plan on joinin' that bunch?"

"Me? Well, if I had the …"

"Oscar, you are no miner. Besides, you have been blessed with inside work, good pay, and on top of that, your family rides free. I do not think you would want to trade all this for anything risky as a silver mine."

"Trade? Mercy no. I did not mean to imply I would trade jobs. No sir. Folks count on me. I perform a valuable service to the public. I would not want to disappoint the good folks around here by neglecting my duties. But, I sure would like a silver mine on the side."

"Wishing will not make it so. Say, Oscar, how about you go in with me on a mine? I will provide the pick and shovel and point the way, then you go do the digging. We will split fifty-fifty."

"Very amusing, Constable. I suppose for the time being, I will content myself tending to my tasks here. How 'bout you, Bill? You cannot tell me you would not like to own your own private silver mine."

"I have one."

"You? You have a …"

"The corner table in the Cable House bar."

"Hmm?"

"Poker, Mister Felsman. A game of chance for many, game of skill for me."

"Pshaw. You cannot make money playin' poker. Not you, Bill."

"No? From November to April, I mine the shanty boys' pockets. I dare say I have become rather good at it. It is a rare night when I share the table with someone who really knows the game. Oh, I'm not saying I win all the time. No. But I usually leave with more jingle in my pocket than when I came. And I need not step on a single shovel nor swing a solitary pickaxe to do it."

"Poker is for the rude and the crude, Constable. Pinochle! Now there is a game! Yessir, show me a man who can prevail with cards cast from a pinochle deck, and I will show you a *real* card player."

"Child's play, Oscar. Penny ante. Not worth my time. No sir."

The waiting room clock struck nine.

"Dear me," said Oscar, "I best be sorting the last of the freight. Ed Williams will soon be here for his dry goods. Hell hath no fury like Ed when he has to linger whilst I sort his goods!"

"Say, before I make my rounds, I noticed there is no paper in the depot privy. Might you have a catalog to spare?"

"Here, Bill, take this newspaper. You need to see what is in it, anyway."

"Why, thank you, Mister Stationmaster. And, by golly, you are right."

"Hmm?"

"You do provide a valuable public service, after all."

Eight miles east, Chief Namakagon knelt by the lake scrubbing a cast-iron frying pan with sand. Waabishki and Makade sat behind him. Makade growled.

Namakagon looked up to see a canoe rounding his small island home. It nosed onto shore. Two strangers climbed out, each carrying a shovel.

"Boozhoo! What brings you to my camp?"

"You know what we are here for, Chief," said the taller man.

"No, I am certain I do not, friend. Perhaps you will tell me."

"The silver mine."

"Silver mine?"

"Don't play the fool, Chief. I ain't one to be bamboozled by no Indian. We know it is here somewhere."

"Here? Silver? You are mistaken."

"Said so in the Ashland paper, Chief. No point in you denyin' it. Now where is it?"

"There is no silver here. It is newspaper that has bamboozled you, friend. Look south of Pratt. You will find a mine or two up there. Perhaps there you will quench your thirst for easy wealth. Now, leave my home."

"Bud," he said to his friend, "You look 'round here. I will scratch around up by his camp. That silver mine must be somewhere hereabouts."

Both dogs were growling now. "Animosh, go!" ordered the chief, throwing a hand signal.

Waabishki and Makade, teeth bared, growling, charged. The men dropped their shovels and raced for the canoe. They awkwardly jumped in and pushed off, the canoe rocking and tipping, then capsizing ten feet from shore. Both dogs, snarling and snapping, splashed into the lake, threatening the floundering prospectors.

"Animosh, come!"

Makade and Waabishki bounded from the water and back down the shore. They shook, spraying the chief with lake water and interrupting his laughter. The floundering men pushed their canoe into knee-deep water near shore and climbed in, fumbling for paddles.

"Say, Chief! Throw us our gol-dang shovels, would ya?"

"Only if you pledge to never return, Mud puppy."

"Huh? Well, I cannot say we …"

"Do you or do you not want your shovels?"

"All right, all right, we ain't comin' back. That don't mean others ain't comin'."

As Namakagon tossed the shovels to the men, he made out two more canoes far across the lake heading his way.

"Makade, Waabishki, you may have your work cut out for you for a while. Seems our silver is both a blessing and a curse. I hope this old man is up to the challenge."

As the canoes approached the island, shovels appeared. "Animosh, speak!" he ordered. Waabishki and Makade tore down the shore, barking and snarling their warning. The canoes changed course and both dogs returned, tails wagging. "Yes, my friends, you may have work to do."

Chapter 9
The Hayward Yard

September 1885

Olaf Loken left A. J. Hayward's second-floor office in the big mill, descending the outside steps. He folded a document, stuffing it into his coat pocket. The signatures at the bottom were his and that of Anthony Judson Hayward, the company's president. The contract would allow the Lokens to expand the Namakagon Timber Company, adding another fifty men, a dozen more flatcars, and more rail. Olaf paused on the stairway landing to look across the expansive yard, admiring row after row of towering stacks of rough-sawn pine boards drying in the September sun. The next northbound train would arrive soon. Olaf noticed a shortcut to the depot, straight through the yard, a perfect route that would allow him to explore the canyon-like alleys between the mountainous stacks of drying lumber.

Neat, towering piles of pungent, white pine boards shaded him from the hot midday sun as he strolled through the yard. Between the rows to his left he saw a horse team and wagon half-loaded with pine. Hoping to meet the men loading the pine, Olaf turned between the next two stacks and turned again to the rig. He found no one there. "Dinnertime?" he wondered aloud, pulling his pocket watch. "At one-thirty?"

As Olaf slipped the watch back into his pocket, it happened—an avalanche of pine planks fell from above. He dove, rolling under the wagon, barely avoiding a thousand pounds of falling boards. The horses, struck by the pine, bolted, screaming. Olaf reached up for the axel and held on, letting the frightened animals pull him to safety as the top half of the twenty-foot lumber pile thundered to the ground.

The rig came to a stop near the holding pond. Seeing the injured horses and nearly demolished wagon, two men sorting logs out in the pond jumped from log to log, running across the pine to shore. They reached the rig in seconds to find Olaf climbing out from under. He felt his pockets. The contract was there, as was his pocketbook and watch. Turning back toward the fallen pine he saw no one in the cloud of dust now encompassing the mass of tangled planks.

"You hurt, mister?" yelled one of the workers.

"Hurt? No, seems I'm all right. You boys have any idea who was loading that pine?"

They looked at each other before one man said, "We keep our eyes on the pine under our feet, not that what is stacked in the yard. You best talk to the yard boss."

Wondering if others were injured, the three men searched the nearby alleyways of lumber. Up and down rows they turned and turned again before coming back to the wrecked wagon. There, they found the yard boss tending to the horses. He glared at Olaf, pulled a nickel-plated revolver, cocked it, turned, and shot one of the injured horses behind the ear. It collapsed, dead before the pistol's loud crack could echo off the surrounding buildings.

Then, pointing the muzzle at Olaf, the yard boss yelled, "What drove you to knock down my pine and spoil my mare, mister? And, what the devil are you doin' out here in my yard in the first place?"

A. J. Hayward opened his second-floor office window. "Forsythe, what in creation is going on down there? Who fired that damn shot?" Seeing the revolver pointed at Olaf, he shouted again. "For God's sake, Forsythe, put away that pistol before someone gets hurt!"

"I fired that shot, Mister Hayward." He pocketed the revolver. "I had to put a horse down. Poor thing got its dang leg broke on account this fella here tipped a load of pine onto her."

"He is wrong, A. J." shouted Olaf. "'Twas not me who knocked down that stack of pine. I was merely walking down the row. I neither caused this nor do I think it was an accident. I would like to talk to the man who left that wagon there."

"Dammit, Forsythe, I want you and the men responsible in my office in ten minutes. Get to it or I will have a new yard boss by morning. And get some men over here to straighten up that lumber. Makes the whole yard look a mess."

"Yessir, Mister Hayward. Right away sir."

The discussion in A. J. Hayward's office led nowhere. The wagon was not supposed to be where Olaf found it, yet no one knew how it got there. Nor did anyone know what caused the lumber pile to fall. The men all returned to work. Olaf headed straight for the sheriff's office.

"Mister Loken," said the sheriff, "I understand your concerns, but, frankly, I think you are way off the mark. You came awful near to getting hurt—hurt bad—maybe even killed. It is common to jump to conclusions when such a thing happens. I agree it's mighty queer that lumber pile fell just when it did and all, but that does not mean it fell by design. Now, you tell me, Loken, who in his right mind would attempt such a thing? Only a fool, right? Why, it would be · plumb folly for some ne'er-do-well to think he could get away with such a crime."

"You would not have thought it folly had you been under that wagon, Sheriff. Someone pushed that gol-dang pile over, then made himself scarce as hen's teeth. Otherwise, Sheriff, what was that rig doin' there? You tell me! Who left it right there—right on the spot where the pine just happened to fall at the very moment I stood below? And tell me this, why would the man who left the wagon there not show his face? Unless, of course, there was some dirty work afoot? No Sheriff, something is amiss here, and dreadfully so. I know full-well that lumber pile did not fall on its own. Someone tried to kill me."

"Look at this from my side of the fence, Loken. Old A. J. Hayward is the backbone behind this whole town. How do you suppose it would look if I started an investigation about something like this? Why, win or lose, it would besmirch his reputation and likely cause his buyers to look elsewhere. First thing y'know, we have men laid off—bills not paid—people unable to patronize our businesses—and the gol-dang county board askin' why I went ahead and caused all this commotion. No, Mister Loken, this was an accident, plain and simple."

"And you can say that with a clear conscience, Sheriff? You can stand tall and say that?

"My conscience has little to do with it. It's the reputation of the mill, the integrity of the whole town what is at stake."

"Sheriff, someone tried to kill me today. You're the only law I can turn to. Can you ask around, find out who might be behind this?"

"Loken, why, in Heaven's name, would anyone try to kill you? You tell me. You are a respected businessman in these parts. Known as a good boss. Your men like you. Respect you. No, Mister Loken, you are imagining all this. You just happened to be in the wrong place at the wrong time. Bad luck, that's all this is. Just plain bad luck."

"Luck is one thing, Sheriff. This had nothin' to do with luck."

"Mister Loken, I will speak with A. J. Hayward's yard boss. And I will keep an ear to the rail. If I learn anything, anything at all, I will get word to you. Elsewise, I suggest you forget about all this. It was bad luck. Put it behind you 'fore it draws more bad luck."

"Might be easier to say than to do, Sheriff. I spent too many years in a wheelchair from my last lumber wagon accident. No, I will not soon forget this."

Twenty minutes later, Olaf knocked on the boarding house door. Adeline Ringstadt was both delighted to learn he had missed the afternoon train and disturbed to hear of the incident. In honor of the surprise visit, she made a special dessert for supper—peach cobbler topped with homemade vanilla ice cream, Olaf's favorite. That night he slept in his old room, a room where he spent over two years convalescing from his earlier accident. Olaf slept an uneasy sleep.

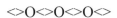

Chapter 10
Billy Kavanaugh's Miracle

November 10, 1885

The scent of fresh-cut white pine from the northern Wisconsin sawmills filled the early morning air. Billy Kavanaugh climbed the steps of the church parsonage. After pulling a diamond stickpin from his tie and dropping it into a vest pocket, he knocked on the door. The curtain  moved, a latch tripped, and the door swung wide. The smell of fresh-baked bread greeted the young man.

"Good day, ma'am," said Billy with a tip of his hat. "My, my, such a delightful aroma—the baking bread, I mean. It is as delicate as that handsome lace borderin' your apron."

"Why, thank you, William. How nice of …"

"Ma'am, I was wonderin' if I might speak with the parson. I have a most troublin' matter and know not where to turn but to the patience and wisdom of you and the reverend, the good shepherds of this fine community."

"Why, certainly. Come in. The Reverend Spooner is in his study perfecting his sermon for Sunday's service. Please, William, have a chair in the parlor."

Billy stepped in, plopping down on a gold velvet chair near a window overlooking the street. He watched wagon after wagon pass by, each piled high with pine boards. Two Hamm's beer wagons and a farmer with a load of hay followed, then more lumber wagons.

Lumberjacks looking for work crowded both boardwalks along the muddy, rutted street. Down the way, a locomotive's whistle announced the departure of another trainload of lumber. The sights, sounds, and smells declared Hayward, a town that did not exist three years earlier, the lumber capital of northern Wisconsin.

"Good morning, William," said the preacher from the hallway. "I apologize for keeping you. These sermons I write do not favor interruptions. Once I get my steam up, I dassn't let up on the old throttle till I have crossed the trestle, rounded the last bend, and pulled into the station."

"Hmm? Uh, what?"

"Oh, don't mind me. In this week's sermon, I strive to compare the Church with the railroad industry, Andrew Carnegie and all. You know … how the railroads now reach every nook and cranny in the wilderness, bringing sinners to the stations one day and saints to save them the next. And how the immense weight of the heaviest trainload of sin can be borne by the rails below, provided those rails are crafted with steel as pure as the love of Jesus. Do you see where I am going with this, my boy? Do you see the beauty in it? Seems Heaven sent, don't you agree? I mean … trainloads of sin? Lifted by steel rails as pure as Jesus' love? Well, what do you think?"

"Reverend, I fear you may have a difficult time tryin' to convince the gandy dancers who line the bar down at the Rail Inn that they are spreadin' the word of the Lord. Although I can attest they do call out his name now and again. Undoubtedly more often than you would prefer, sir."

"I believe you may have missed my point. What I meant …"

"Excuse my interruption, sir, but … well, I fear I have a pressing matter to share—a most troubling issue. I do so need your advice, sir. I know not where else to turn."

"Please, do go on."

"Reverend, I seem to have got myself stuck neck-deep in a pickle barrel. And after hour upon hour of searchin' my soul, I realized the church, your church, sir, should be the first place I turn to for salvation."

"I am listening, my son."

"Reverend Spooner, I fear I have failed my fellow man. In the interest of providing a service to the thousands upon thousands of poor, vulnerable lumberjacks risking life and limb out in the pinery, I entered into a … well … what some would call an embarrassing financial blunder of sorts."

"Oh, dear."

"With so many men facin' peril out there in the woods, I somehow found a way to provide each man injured on the job, each poor, helpless soul, with a guarantee of good health. For the afflicted, it would mean a free stay in a hospital and good doctorin' until their injuries are tended and their bodies are mended."

"Why, William Kavanaugh! What a selfless gift and fine service you offer these young men."

"A sacrifice I felt I must make, sir. But now ... well, it seems I have overextended. You see, my interest in the well-being of my fellow man apparently clouded my good business sense. I now find myself, well, holdin' the bag, sir."

"How so?"

"I fear I overdid it. I am now unable to see my way clear to continue my quest—my struggle to care for the injured and infirmed—all due to, one might say, a budget shortfall."

"A budget shortfall?"

"Pastor, I'm dead broke. Sittin' on five thousand hospital certificates and not a gol-dang penny to spare for your Sunday collection basket."

"Oh, dear, dear. I find it heart wrenching to see you struggle so. But our small church is hardly in a position to rescue you from your business predicament. I can, however, offer you a meal, suggest a place where you could reside, perhaps find work until you are back on your feet. Come to think of it, I believe Buster Jewel, across from the Sawmill Saloon, needs a stable boy. Knowing Buster as I do, I can assure you he will not pay well. But, with winter coming on, it might be a fine opportunity. You could sleep in his loft. Plenty of hay in the mow to keep you warm on the coldest of January nights."

Billy stifled a cringe. "Oh, thank you, Reverend. I so appreciate your effort to assist me in my time of trouble. You are so, so kind. Yes. I will consider paying Buster a visit. But, in the meantime, whatever shall I do with these hospital certificates?"

"Please tell me about them, son. Perhaps I will be able to offer an idea or two about ..."

"Oh, no. You've already done enough. You needn't trouble ..."

"No trouble, young man. All part of my service to my flock."

"But ..."

"Please. For me, William?"

"Well, sir, it works like this. For a fistful of pocket change, a lumberjack can purchase a certificate—a document assuring him of a weeklong stay at the Ashland hospital if said lumberjack meets with a broken arm or leg or other injury requiring doctorin'. Many a man has found himself out in the cold, you might say, after gettin' busted up on the job. The certificates give the fellas comfort in knowin' they will get tended to by a boney-fide sawbones who knows what he is doin' and not just the usual horse doctor or camp cook. Reverend, it gives the fellas faith. Faith and trust and belief. And you know the value of faith, trust, and belief, right?"

"Oh, yes."

"And all for a paltry donation of one five-dollar bill. Chickenfeed! A pittance for a certificate that will guarantee a lumberjack's good health. And here I sadly sit with five thousand certificates—five thousand and no way to deliver them to the poor, hard-workin' men who so depend on them. Reverend Spooner, I need a miracle. That's why I came to you, sir—you, the shepherd of this fine church. I know you visit the camps now and again. You could deliver these miraculous certificates. What a wonderful, generous service you could provide the lumberjacks—these poor lost souls of the woods. And at a mere five dollars apiece, you could have the lot of 'em sold before Christmas. A Christmas miracle, sir. And a tidy profit, I might add. Fair compensation for the good shepherd of this here fine church."

"You say you have five thousand of these certificates William? Five thousand?"

"Five thousand, Reverend."

"They go for five dollars each?"

"Half-a sawbuck."

"Good for a full week at the Ashland hospital?"

"Complete with a saw-bone's care and comfort of a nurse."

"Good for how long?"

"One year from date of purchase. Keep in mind, though, the lumber camps are all shut down by May. Reverend, do you see where I'm going with this? Do you see the beauty in it? Heaven sent, do you not agree?"

"Five thousand certificates of good health?"

"Multiply that by five dollars and you see the value of this opportunity, this … miracle."

"And my cost would be …?"

"Normally, twenty-two-thousand-five-hundred. But, well, you can see I'm in a real fix. I suppose, for you and the Missus, and the church and all, I can let the whole lot go for, say, twenty-one thousand? You would stand to profit four thousand. I am certain you could have them five thousand scrips gone in no time flat. Four thousand dollars in your purse by Christmas Morning. Not a bad poke, I would say."

Reverend Spooner stared into Billy Kavanaugh's eyes considering the young man's words.

Motionless, masking his anxiety Billy waited and waited until …

"Fifteen thousand, William. That's all the church can muster."

"Nineteen and we can shake on it, Parson," he said, finally exhaling.

"Seventeen. Best I can do."

"I will take eighteen-five, knowin' your flock will benefit, sir."

"I will go seventeen-five, William. Please do not ask my parishioners for more."

"Done! Seventeen thousand, five hundred dollars. I will have the certificates ready for you in twenty minutes."

"The Lumberman's Bank opens at ten. Bring the notes."

"Reverend," said Billy, returning the stickpin to his tie, "thank you on behalf of those poor lumberjacks who risk their lives out in the pinery. This is a fine and generous service you offer them, sir. I will see you down at the bank."

Billy Kavanaugh took the ten-thirty northbound. He stepped onto the Ashland Depot platform and asked for directions to the city hospital. Minutes later, the hospital door closed behind him.

"Can I help you, sir?" asked the clerk.

"Yes. I wish to speak to the man in charge of billing."

"That would be me, sir. Patrick P. La Pointe, at your service. Do you wish to pay your bill?"

"Oh, I don't have a bill, Patrick. Well, that's to say, I do not have a bill as yet. I would like to make a down payment on a future bill."

"Future bill, sir?"

"I want to give you some money in case one of my … um … *clients* is injured."

"I am sorry, sir. We bill only after service is performed."

"Look, Patrick. I have money—right now—right here—in my pocket. I will not have money later. I wish to give you some money now just in case one of my clients should suffer injury on the job. It's called insurance. Sort of a new concept 'round here. I'm willin' to deposit one-thousand five hundred dollars against future care."

"But …"

"Let me finish. If any of my injured clients show you a hospital certificate bearing both their name and my signature, you can deduct

- 73 -

from my deposit the cost of up to a week's stay. You can also use up to ten dollars for any doctorin' needed. Now, Patrick, I wish to pay you today. Do you or do you not want my money?"

"How much did …"

"Fifteen hundred."

"Let me fetch my receipt book, sir."

Billy Kavanaugh spread fifteen one-hundred-dollar bills on the desk. "Now, Patrick, understand two things. First, if one year from today, there is any money left over, that amount is to be refunded to me. Second, if my fifteen-hundred gets used up, do not expect any more. If anyone comes in with one of my certificates after the money is spent, you either take care of him on your own or tell him there have been so many accidents this year that the fund plum got used up. Understand?"

"Yes, but …"

"Patrick P. La Pointe," said Billy, stuffing a bill in the clerk's shirt pocket, "this is for you. I imagine this amounts to a months' pay. My friend, there is more where that came from. If you need to reach me, I reside at the Pion Hotel in Hayward."

As Billy walked to the door, the clerk pulled the bill from his pocket and held it to the window light. "Gol-dang! A double sawbuck! Thank you. Thank you very much, Mister Kavanaugh!"

Billy turned back. "Say, Patrick, one more thing."

"Sir?"

"Just where might I find the nearest printer's shop?"

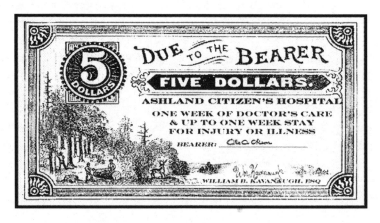

<>O<>O<>O<>

Chapter 11
The Blizzard

March 1886

Junior Kavanaugh rose early, chased from the bunkhouse by the roar of a hundred snoring lumberjacks. In the dim, predawn glow, he put four lids on the charred, cast iron bean pots and set the pots on the hot coals in the bean hole. He covered the pots with more coals and ashes. There, outside the cook shanty door, they would bake until the lumberjacks returned for supper. Junior stared at the faint reddish blush beyond the treetops before stepping back inside.

"Feels like a snowstorm a-brewin', Sourdough," he said to the camp cook. "I would say we are in for a good one. 'Bout time, too. Them ice roads are gettin' bare in spots. Mighty tough on the horses to skid timber on bare trails. Half-a-foot of snow would keep us a-haulin' pine a few weeks more."

"Snow? Pshaw! We will not see a snitch of snow today, Junior. Nary a flake." He licked his finger and touched the oven door to feel the sizzle. "Say, fetch me a sack of corn meal from the pantry, will ya?"

"Just how might an ornery old pole cat like you know that?" Junior dropped the fifty-pound sack on the butcher block with a thud.

"I can tell from how the water boils in the coffeepots. And you watch your sassy tongue, whippersnapper."

"Coffeepots? Hogwash. You will not hoodwink me with your Paul Bunyan claptrap."

"Listen, Kavanaugh, I been out in this here pinery for six years now. I know when a gol-dang snowstorm is comin' and when it ain't, see? My coffeepots do not lie."

"Oh, it is bound to snow, all right. I can tell from the horses."

"Horses?"

"Yep, they eat more 'fore a storm. Just ask my pa. He'll tell ya."

"Bah! Here, make yourself of some use," the cook said as he slid a tub of lard to the boy. "Grease up them pans for my johnnycake. And this time don't miss no spots, hear?"

Junior scooped up a handful of lard and slapped it into a pan with a splat. Using an old dishrag, he smeared around the grease. "What? You don't trust the wisdom of a horse, old man? You?"

"No sir, I do not. And I ain't your old man."

"And, here I thought you had some horse sense."

"Hmm? What? Why, you watch yourself, sonny boy, lest you find a handful of red pepper in your coffee cup some mornin'. You hear me?" he said, waving a large wooden spoon dripping with batter. "I mean it, Junior. Sometime when you are looking the other way I could slip it right in, stir it up and, in the wink of an eye, the deed would be done. You would be in a real fix, you would."

"Oh, it's gonna snow all right. I can smell it. There's a light breeze blowin' straight out of the east. It's the last Saturday of March and somethin's in the air, I tell ya."

"Bah. Nothin' but blue sky and sunshine, once ol' Sol makes it up over the pines."

Junior grinned. "I'll put a sawbuck on it, Sourdough. You game?"

"No, I am not game, gol-dang it. Nor am I bound to put no sawbuck on it. You have pinched me for enough of my winter's pay. Find some other poor dumb sap to swindle."

He opened the firebox door on the huge, Monarch kitchen range and tossed in three split maple logs. "I swear, Junior, you are the luckiest dang weasel in the woodpile when it comes to such wagers."

"Luck? No, 'tain't luck at all." Junior slid the greased pans across the butcher block and tossed the greasy rag back into the lard tub. "Every wager I make is based on good ol' common sense and nothing but. Certainly not lame-brained notions that fellas like you pull out of the south end of a northbound horse, old man."

"I'm warnin' you, whippersnapper, from here on in, you best be tastin' your coffee 'fore you swallow it." He poured the thick cornbread batter into the pans.

"Hah! I double-dang dare ya."

"Don't be so cocksure of yourself, boy."

"And, why not? By not takin' me up on my bet, you are admittin' to the world that you ain't sure about it not snowin'. Is that not what I heard between all that red pepper falderal, old man?"

"All right, wiseacre, I will take your gol-dang money. You cannot match wits with me, sonny boy. Ten dollars says it will not snow by suppertime. Not a dang flake, Kavanaugh."

Within minutes, Zeke and Zach Rigsby, the cook shanty cookees, began hauling pots of steaming coffee to the tables along with flapjacks, hot molasses, fried pork, blackjack, and Johnnycake. Yesterday's leftover beans rounded out the fare. The men filed into the cook shanty slower than usual.

"My bones ached somethin' awful last night," groused Tex Ketchum, the oldest man in camp. "I got me an inkling snow is a-comin'."

"Hear that, Sourdough?" shouted Junior. "Ol' Tex feels it in his bones. You might as well fork over my sawbuck right now." He poured two cups of coffee and sat down next to Tex.

Sourdough bristled. "Old bones or no bones, I do not figure I will be donatin' to your purse, Junior. You will be squeezin' no greenbacks out of me today."

"We will see what we will see, Mister Cook. It's a matter of Tex and his old bones up against you and the hind end of a horse." Junior ducked as a wet washrag flew past his head.

Tex jumped up, spitting his coffee onto the pine floorboards. "Consarn it! Who in tarnation made this here gol-dang Mexican coffee? I thought I was rid of such poison when I tied up with all you Swedes and Norskies!"

Junior laughed as the camp cook slipped into the pantry. "Tex, I think ol' Sourdough was just tryin' to warm up your old bones some. We dassn't hold it against him. He is about to donate ten bucks so you and me can quench our thirst next time we get into town."

"Ya? Ten dollars? In that case, young fella, go on and pour me another cup. 'Tain't so bad after all."

<>O<>

The men left camp in the early morning glow, arriving in the cuttings at first light. Saws sang out and trees soon fell, were swamped, bucked, skidded, and chain-loaded onto the sleighs. By nine o'clock, snowflakes started falling. The easterly breeze turned into a wind as the snowfall increased. Men, horses, and sleighs were soon white with the wind-driven snow. The sky darkened, the wind grew stronger. Within minutes, the blowing snow turned into a white-out blizzard.

A mile east, beyond Superstition Creek, Ingman Loken, woods boss and top-loader for a chain-haul crew, made the call. There was no point in continuing. They would finish the load then wait out the storm. The crew of five and their two horses hunkered on the lee side of the loaded sleigh, letting the logs shelter them from the wind.

"Boss, how long you gonna keep us out in this here wind-driven tempest?" shouted Leroy Phipps. "You can hardly see the hand in front of your face. I would say it's time to make for camp."

"Show some gol-dang lumberyack gumption, Leroy. This cannot keep up. We will be back on the yob in a wink or two. We only got us a month in the cuttings till we button up for the year. Every day lost is yust money up in smoke."

A shout came from somewhere in the woods. "Hello to the chain-haul crew. Are you there?"

Ingman peered around the end of the sleigh as a teamster emerged from the sheer-white curtain of blowing snow.

"Swede? For cryin' out loud, is that you?"

"Ya, Boss. Me and me saw crew."

"Come on down. Might yust as well hunker down here as anywheres."

As Swede approached, the saw crew appeared, walking in the track of the single pine log dragged behind their snow-blanketed Clydesdale.

Now, huddled near the loaded sleigh, ten men and three horses endured the blizzard. Strong gusts whipped and drove the snow into every crack and crevice, down every neck and into every cuff. The men soon shivered in the wind, soaked to the skin.

"That's it, fellas," yelled Ingman. "No tellin' how long this will last. We are pullin' up stakes—headin' for camp 'fore we get stranded here for good. I will not have my name or yours in the *Ashland Press* come spring as being another lumberyack found froze somewhere out in the pinery. Leroy, I want you to make your way over to Blackie Yackson's crew. You tell Blackie I called her off for the day. And, Phipps, you make gol-dang sure every man and horse comes out of the woods with ya. I don't want nobody lost to this tempest. You get word to Blackie. I will let the other crews know."

Nine men and three horses trudged toward the lake, a mile away. Meanwhile, Leroy stuck to the ice road, head down, feeling his way with his shoe pacs, leaning into the wind. By eleven that morning, the men were back in camp, shaking snow from their coats and hanging wet wool socks above the stoves.

Sourdough and his cookees laid out dinner as the men crowded in, a tide of red flooding the cook shanty. Most wore only their damp longjohns and shoe pacs.

"Kerwetter," yelled Blackie, "when the blazes are you gonna sew them missin' buttons back onto your butt-flap? They been gone least a month."

"Ya, Blackie? Here I thought it was the winter wind."

"Confound it, Klaus, where is your gol-dang self-respect?"

"I s'pose you are right. I will tend to it today."

"Well, I should say so. We have seen more than enough."

"Say, Blackie," yelled Rusty from the end of the far table, "is it just me or are you the only bloke in camp who has taken such notice of Klaus's hind end? Maybe you need a trip into town one of these nights." Quiet laughter rolled down the rows. "Say, fellas, anyone else notice Kerwetter's flap a-flyin' like a flag in the breeze?" The men stared at each other, then looked toward Blackie. "See, Blackie? High time you get to town, all right."

Max Wiley walked up and down the rows of tables. "Say now, where do you suppose ol' Leroy Phipps might be a-hidin'?"

Ingman stood on his bench to scan the hundred-man crew. "Anybody here seen Leroy? Anybody?"

There was no answer.

Ingman removed his hat, scratching his head. "Blackie, might you know which way Leroy went after reachin' your crew?"

"Ya, Boss. He said he was gonna go get Junior and help him button up the donkey engine."

"Yunior? You see him?"

"Not hide nor hair, Boss."

"Then how'd you know you were s'posed to come in?"

"Elmer told me when he brung up the last sleigh from the northeast forty. Said we been called off the job. I shut down the donkey engine myself. Drained her down, too."

"Fellas," shouted Ingman, "looks like we have got one of our own out there in that storm. You know well as me that in such a blizzard a man can get turned 'round in a hurry. Much as I do not want to spoil your noon dinner, we are headin' out right now to find Leroy Phipps while he still has a chance, slim as it might be. We will divide into six teams usin' the tables you are settin' at to divide you up. Now, listen, men, we do not want anyone else wanderin' off. I want each one of you to keep an eyeball on the others in your group. Stay on the skid trails and don't wander off from your pals."

Sourdough stepped from the kitchen pantry. "What about my dinner fixin's? Me and me crew worked dang hard to put ..."

"It will yust have to keep," snapped Ingman. "All right, everybody, up and at 'em. Daylight's a-wastin'."

Grumbling and grousing, the lumberjacks slowly pushed away from the tables. Ingman stepped back onto the bench. "For cripessake, stop your gol-dang complainin'," he shouted. "Could be any one of you bums lost out there. Every man who knows Leroy Phipps likewise knows he would not gripe over searchin' for you, so yust wise up and shut your gol-dang yaps. Now get a-goin'!'"

Steam rose from plates of roast pork and venison, baked beans, sweet potatoes and warm yellowjack as the men left the tables. The room fell silent as the lumberjacks donned wet britches and mackinaws, then filed out into the blowing snow.

Before the search party reached the center of the lumber camp yard, a ghost-like image appeared down the trail. The faint shape slowly approached and Leroy Phipps gradually emerged, caked with snow, slogging toward camp.

"Look, fellas," shouted Blackie, "danged if it ain't Leroy himself!"

A loud round of cheers filled the lumber camp yard. Blackie, Ingman, and Tor rushed to the straggler while the rest of the camp piled back into the cook shanty.

"You see that, Tor?" said Leroy. "I ain't never once had such a fine welcome." He slapped snow from his coat with his hat. "Warms a fella right up to know he has so many good friends." They followed the others inside.

"Ingman," said Blackie, "should we tell Phipps why the men were cheerin'—I mean their dinner not gettin' any colder?"

"Naw, Blackie. Let him have his fancy. I would venture ol' Leroy has been through enough for one day."

<>O<>

Olaf stood face to face with his brother before the lodge fireplace.

"You shouldn't oughta done it, Ingman. Not without my say-so."

"You were not out in that storm today. You would've done the same dang thing—made the same call."

"Not with spring right around the corner, I wouldn't. We need to put up as much timber as possible 'fore the season is all petered out. You should've know that. You could've sat it out for a while longer. I am payin' a dollar a day, you know. A dollar a day, damn it! A hundred fifty dollars went up in smoke when you called it off this mornin'—all thanks to you."

"Listen here, Olaf, I am the woods boss, not you. I am out in the cuttings with my men day after gol-dang day. You best be stickin' to your pencil pushin' and let me run the camp as before."

"I lost a hundred and fifty dollars ..."

"And no men! You lost no men, today, Olaf. Ever take that into consideration? It is not always about money. At sixty dollars a tree, you will make thousands upon thousands and still keep your reputation of being a good lumber company boss with nary a man dead in what, seven, eight years? Tell me, what is that worth to you? What is your reputation worth? Your name? Our family name? Tor's name? And what is a man's life worth to his family?"

"Don't you go and twist this around, Ingman. Say what you might, I still own this camp, lock, stock, and barrel. My name is on the deed. I make the decisions, dammit. If you cannot abide by that, then go start your own gol-dang timber company. I will not stand in your way."

"Olaf, this is my camp yust as much as yours. You and I built it up from little or nothin'. You know dang well this outfit is what it is today because of the both of us. Your name might be on the deed, but my signature is all over this outfit. Every tree we ever send downriver had my stamp on it. NTC. You might own the land, but *I* am the NTC, the Namakagon Timber Company."

Olaf was silent.

"And, tell me, Olaf, who the heck ran this camp after you laid wreck to that wagonload of pine and busted yourself all up? Who did both my work and yours while you were laid up and sittin' on your arse in that boardin' house for nigh onto three years? Who, Olaf? You tell me!"

"You know how much I appreciated what you did."

"Well, ain't it about time you showed it? I took charge and the camp prospered like never before. I doubled our acreage and added man after man, the best men in the pinery, at that. I hired the best camp cook anywhere to be found. I built the barn, bought the livestock, constructed most the tote roads. Me! While you were layin' back on a sofa bed, I built this into a fine lumbering outfit. I did it, Olaf. I did it dang-near alone and you dassn't deny it! What do you say to that?"

"Ingman, before you make any decision affecting this company— our company, you will first speak with me. When it comes to this outfit, I make the decisions."

Ingman turned toward the door. "Ya. You make the decisions, all right. Yust keep in mind, Olaf, decisions have consequences—some good, some bad." He pulled his collar up and hat down before tramping through the snowdrifts to the cook shanty. Although dinner was through, most of the men remained at the tables.

A shout came from the back of the room. "Boss, are we headin' out this afternoon if the storm lets up?"

"Men, I don't give a dang if the sun shines, the snow melts and the birds all whistle *Oh, Susannah*. I'm the woods boss for this here outfit and, gol-dang it, what I say goes. Light your pipes, fellas. We are done for the week. That's my decision."

Chapter 12
The Poet Winslow Winters

March 1886

Coffee steaming, Ingman reached for a piece of blackjack. "Where is Whistlin' Yim Engelbretson?"

"Over here, Boss."

"Yim, get your squeeze box out. Play a few ditties, will ya?"

Whistlin' Jim put two fingers to his lips and blew a shrill shriek. "Say, Kelly," he called to the back of the room, "bring your banjo up here. Time we put some life into this here grayback palace."

Kelly Thompson tuned his banjo to Whistlin' Jim's concertina. Soon they had the men stomping their feet to one lively tune after another. In spite of the howling wind outside, the music carried across the yard to the barn, bringing a dozen more men.

"Ya, ya, ya," sang Sourdough as he beat a wooden spoon on a copper pot in time with the beat. "Fetch the checkerboards and cards. Long as we're snowed in, might as well make the best of it."

Throughout the afternoon, the men sang and danced, played checkers, and spun yarns. As the daylight dimmed, the oilcloth-covered tables were set with platters of roast moose, fried onions, squash pie, baked beans, blackjack, and hot coffee. Oatmeal cookies came next, along with more coffee. The men ate their fill, the tables were cleared, pipes were lit, and the songs and stories resumed.

"For Pete's sake, Tex," yelled Rusty, "you have told that same Pecos Bill yarn three times now. Have you no others?"

"Oh, I got others all. But none that your mother would allow me to tell, O'Hara. You're too dang wet behind the ears for my tales."

Ingman turned to Winslow Winters. "Say, Windy, how 'bout you dig out that book of poems you keep hid in your bunk? The ones you been writin' all winter now. Will ya read us a few?"

"Naw, Boss, nobody wants to hear my rhymes and ramblin's."

"C'mon, Windy," begged Tor. "You and I both know you have some good poems there. Whaddaya say, Windy? One little poem?"

"All right, all right. But first time I see a fella yawn or hear him laugh, I am settin' my book aside."

Winslow Winters opened his journal midway, thumbed through a few pages, and stopped. "All right, fellas. Here is one you will all appreciate. I call it 'The Ballad of Ole Johnson.' It goes like this."

"Far up the old Wisconsin
Lie the bones of Ole Johnson.
His ghost it swims the river night and day.
Ole's looking for a tool
That he dropped in a deep pool.
When the log jam he was fightin' did give way.

The dynamite they used
Was not correctly fused
And blew the pine high above the bay.
As for Ole Johnson's crew,
Across the logs they flew!
But Ole lost his footing on the way.

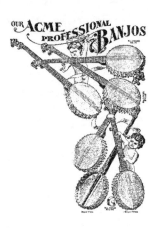

His men their god did thank
When they made the river bank.
But Ole dropped his Peavey in the drink.
So he dove into the pool,
This timber-drivin' fool,
Before he even took the time to think.

Up Ole came for air
But only logs were there,
A-turnin' in the churning icy foam.
And, way beyond the shore,
He cursed the logs and swore
That he'd bring that Peavey back or ne'er come home.

Pine floatin' overhead,
Ole swam the river bed,
He hoped to bring his precious Peavey back
And, above the river's noise,
Shout, "Found it!" to his boys,
The mark of any worthy lumberjack.

His men all stood and stared,
Their concern for Ole shared,
Watching all the thrashing, bashing pine.
While below, Ole did swim,
The chance now growing slim
That they'd see poor Ole Johnson down the line.

Far up the old Wisconsin,
Lie the bones of Ole Johnson.
His ghost it swims the river night and day.
Ole's looking for a tool,
He lost in a deep pool,
When the log jam he was fightin' did give way.

A thousand pounds each log did weigh,
Or even more, I would say,
Half-a-million floatin' to the mill.
Ole Johnson down below,
A-countin' as they go,
And the ghost of Ole Johnson counts them still.

Now, if you take a float
In a canoe or a rowboat,
On a Wisconsin crick or creek or river, too,
And you feel a sudden bump
Or you hear a muffled thump,
Know that the ghost of Ole Johnson counted you.

And if a Peavey you should see
Below a river flowing free,
Know that Ole left it on the river bed.
Leave it there for Heaven's sake,
Or Ole's place you'll surely take,
Just a-countin' logs a-floatin' overhead.

Far up the old Wisconsin,
Lie the bones of Ole Johnson,
A-countin' all the logs as they go through.
If you feel a sudden bump
Or hear a muffled thump,
Know the ghost of Ole Johnson counted you.
Now my tale of Ole Johnson is all through."

"Say, Windy, that was a fine one," said Ingman. "Got any more?"
"Well, I s'pose one more would be all right." He thumbed through his book again. "Here's one I wrote about the lot of you. It's called 'The Ne'er-do-well Boys.'"

Cheers and laughter rolled through the crowded cook shanty as Kelly tuned his banjo, before they broke into song.

"Way up in the pin'ry they tell of a night
When ten hearty lumberjacks got in a fight.
Now, gather 'round people. My story I'll tell
Of the boys from the lumber camp called Ne'er-Do-Well.

In the back room of the Sawmill Saloon
Sat Rusty O'Hara a-whistlin' a tune,
Sharin' a whiskey and raisin' some hell
With the boys from the lumber camp called Ne'er-Do-Well.

Now the Ne'er-Do-Well boys were a rough-tumble bunch
Who drank, cussed, and gambled and, I've got a hunch
Would stand close beside, if you needed them there,
But show you no mercy if your dealin' weren't square.

Now a fella named John Bob, he pulled up a stool
And tossed in his ante, this Norwegian fool.
The Ne'er-Do-Well boys, their eyes couldn't believe
When he dealt from the bottom with cards up his sleeve.

Rusty O'Hara, he was first to speak.
He said, "Johnny Bob, now, we weren't born last week.
We see that you're fixin' to swindle away
From Ne'er-Do-Well lumberjacks their hard-earned pay."

"Them's fightin' words mister!" ol' John Bob did shout.
That's when our boy Rusty punched him in the snout.
Out onto the street these big brawlers did go,
A-punchin' and a-fightin' in two feet of snow.

By a boot John got waffled, right square on the chin.
He spit out two teeth, then stood with a grin.
"You'll have to do better, you Ne'er-Do-Well men.
I'm bound to not let you knock me down again."

They fought and they floundered with snow underneath.
John Bob lost an ear lobe to Ole's old teeth.

Swede, Pete, and Elmer next got in their licks.
Them Ne'er-Do-Well boys they don't put up with tricks.

They wrestled and battled up and down the street.
But John Bob he managed to stay on his feet.
They fought all that night long and into the day,
When Rusty said, "Boys, I got something to say."

"Any man willin' to fight through the night
'Gainst ten other men, right through to daylight,
Is certainly worthy of friendship with me
And the Ne'er-Do-Well boys in the big pinery.

"John, if you quit swindlin' and cheatin' at cards,
We'll share us a whiskey and all become pards.
O John Bob, you're all right so come sit a spell
With your newly found friends from the camp Ne'er-Do-Well."

Now, in the back room of the Sawmill Saloon,
Sits Ol' Johnny Bob tryin' to whistle a tune,
Sharin' a whiskey, raisin' some hell
With the boys from the lumber camp called Ne'er-Do-Well."

A round of cheers filled the room.
"One more, Windy! Ya?"
"All right, Swede. But that's it, then." He held his journal to the kerosene lamp. "This here one is meant to be recited by a young woman, but, considerin' the boss don't allow women in camp, well, you fellas will just have to close your eyes and use your imagination. Here she goes."

"Johnny Boy, oh, Johnny Boy,
How I love you so.
Johnny Boy, my Johnny Boy,
How was I to know
That you'd take a job a-drivin' pine
Down the old Saint Croix?
Now I yearn, both day and night,
For my Johnny Boy.

A lumberjack came to me
With news so dark and grim.
He said while rastlin' with the logs,
They sent you for a swim.
'Tis then they chose to close on you,
Far too far from shore.
Now the only sound you hear
Is the river's roar.

Johnny Boy, oh, Johnny Boy,
How I love you so.
Johnny Boy, my Johnny Boy,
How was I to know
You'd take a job a-drivin' pine
Down the old Saint Croix?
Now I yearn, both day and night,
For my Johnny Boy.

Johnny Boy, oh, Johnny Boy
A blackbird you became,
A-drivin' logs down to the mill
In April's pourin' rain.
Now you lay below the ground,
Oh, my lumberjack,
In icy water you did drown,
Never to come back.

The other drivers stood and watched
As Johnny Boy did drown.
'Twas revenge the spirits sought
For cutting timber down.
So many boys the river claims,
Each and ev'ry drive.
We know not many of their names,
Nor who's left to survive.

So many wives and sons remain,
Darling daughters, too.
So many teardrops fall upon
Wisconsin waters, cruel.

I'll say a prayer to honor you,
And sadly bow my head.
And send the news on down the line,
Our Johnny Boy lies dead.

Johnny Boy, oh, Johnny Boy,
How I love you so.
Johnny Boy, my Johnny Boy,
How was I to know?
My sweet darling, Johnny Boy,
You meant so much to me.
I'll come tonight to river's edge,
For with you I must be.
Yes, I'll come tonight to river's edge,
For—with—you—I—must—be."

The room was silent except for a man sobbing far back in the room. Winslow closed his book. "Gosh, fellas, I meant not to spoil the merriment. After all, they're only poems, you know."

"Whistlin' Jim," shouted Tor, "You better play us a lively tune. Cheer things up a bit. Can you do that for us?"

Jim whispered something to Kelly who stomped out a beat and Steven Foster's "Camptown Races" brought the room to life with everyone singing along, some in tune, others not, and all shouting out "Do-dah, do-dah," every time it came around.

Returning from the camp latrine, Tex Ketchum danced into the room. As the song ended, he stood on a table. "Fellas," he yelled, "the storm is spent. Right now there's more gol-dang stars out than a man can count in a fortnight and the northern lights are just a-shimmerin'. Them who don't believe me, go see for yourselfs."

The cook shanty emptied, the full compliment of lumberjacks trudging and tramping through snowdrifts to view the spectacular sight. The storm was over. One more month of cutting lay ahead for the men of the Namakagon Timber Company. Across the pinery, logs would soon roar down wild rivers. On nearby Gitchee Gumi, ships laden with clear white pine lumber and iron ore would again set sail—ships that included a handsome, three-masted schooner known as the *Lucerne*.

<>O<>O<>O<>

Chapter 13
Windigo Creek Gold

April 1886

Junior slammed the cook shanty door behind him, slung his rucksack over one shoulder, and set out across the yard. "C'mon, Tor. Day's a-wastin! We have work to do if want to make it to Windigo Creek and back, and fill our pockets on top of it all."

"Dang it, slow down, Junior. I've nary a notion why I let you talk me into this. We are lumbermen, not gold prospectors."

"Oh, I think you know very well why. Here it is, the second Sunday in April. Snow is dang-near gone and we are done cuttin' for the season. We could do like the rest of the men in camp and spend the day sitting on the dock watching the ice melt or we could embark upon a true adventure. Think about what Billy told us last week. Reports of gold being found up in Windigo Creek. The newspapers are full of notices of claims filed, Tor. Silver, copper, and gold to boot. Why, we could stumble upon a fortune, pal. A fortune!"

"Tell me, Junior, if your brother is so all-fired sure there's gold to be found, then why is he not out there looking for it?"

"Billy? Now, you know that's not his way of doing things. He works mostly with his head, not his back. You are more likely to find him buying the gold from some prospector and selling it at a profit than rummaging for it himself."

"That does seem to be his way, all right. I have yet to see any dirt under his fingernails."

Two miles down the trail, Junior stopped. "Look! Up there! That must be the shortcut Billy told us about. Three ax cuts on that oak. Billy said it will take a half-hour or more off our tramp."

They stood in front of the oak, staring at three weathered hatchet cuts and the trail it marked.

"This doesn't look like much of a trail to me, Junior. Must not get used much. Maybe it's the wrong tree. Heck, most deer trails are better than this."

"You sayin' Billy is wrong?"

"No, Junior, I'm not sayin' that. It could be the right trail. It's just that, well, it's just not what I expect a trail to look like."

"Well, I got faith in Billy," said Junior. "This here's the trail. I just plum know it. C'mon, Loken. Our fortune beckons."

Following the neglected path proved difficult. Patches of lingering snow often masked the way. They climbed over windfalls, skirted blowdowns, and, after losing their way several times, found themselves backtracking. As the trail neared Windigo Creek country, it diminished to a mere deer trail. An hour passed before they crested a hill and finally reached their goal.

"Eureka!" yelled Junior, running down the steep bank. "C'mon! We found our river of dreams come true!"

"You sure this is the right stream, Junior?"

"There you go again, doubtin' my brother. No question in my mind that this is the right stream. Flows right to left, just like Billy said."

"Unless you happen to be standing on the other bank."

"Hmm? Oh, ya, I s'pose. But we are not, are we? No sir. This is the Windigo. Time to strike it rich!"

The small stream bubbled wildly from the spring runoff. Junior splashed in, then pulled his rucksack from his shoulder, removing two gold pans. He tossed one to Tor.

"Where in tarnation did you find these?"

"Billy gave 'em to me last time he was in camp. Won them in a card game. Most likely filled with gold, if I know my brother."

"You know how to use these things?"

"Why, sure. Billy said all you need to do is dip it in the water, scoop up some sand and gravel, swish it around a bit, and dump the gold in your pocket."

"Seems too easy. Might be there's more to it than he knows."

"More than Billy knows? Billy Kavanaugh? 'Tain't likely, Tor."

Standing mid-stream, Junior dug into the creek bottom, scooping stones, mud, and sand from the streambed. Ice-cold water flowed over his hands as he swished the pan around and around, water spilling onto his britches. "See? Nothing to it! Just splash it around and watch all the worthless stuff wash out. Wishy washy wishy washy and voila! Next thing you know, you are sittin' on top of the rainbow, lightin' your pipe with a five dollar bill."

Junior finished washing his first scoop and silently stared into the bottom of the pan.

"See anything, Junior?"

"Naw, nothing but black sand," groused Junior, rinsing the pan. "Maybe upstream a piece. Billy said to try our luck under any big rock in the creek. Told me sometimes gold likes to hide out there.

C'mon!" he shouted, splashing as he ran.

Junior rolled a large rock to the side and dug into the ice-cold streambed. He washed and washed, then discarded the sand in disgust. "Say, we should try 'round the bend a ways," he yelled back to Tor as he half-waded, half-ran upstream. Water splashed onto his coat and hat. Stopping, he thrust the pan into the icy water, bringing a full scoop of sand and gravel to the surface.

"Just think of it, Loken, there could be a week's worth of lumberjack's pay in this pan right now. What in blazes are you waitin' for? Dig in, for Pete's sake! Don't you hanker to be rich?"

"Something tells me I should stick with white pine and leave the gold nuggets to you, Junior."

"Look! Up there! I thought I seen something sparkle. I could swear it! C'mon," he yelled as he ran upstream.

Pan after pan yielded only muddy water, numb fingers, and wet britches. Two hours later, they sat on a large boulder near the stream. Clouds now hid the sun as they ate the smoked venison and biscuits Sourdough had stuffed into the pockets of their coats back at camp.

"Junior, I am getting a bit weary of this prospecting business. Neither of us has seen a glimpse of gold. My hands are about to fall off from this freezin' crick water. I sure would like to be sittin' with my feet to the woodstove in the cook shanty sippin' on a hot cup of tea. Whaddaya say we button up and head back to the camp?"

"Head back? Why, we barely got here! I'm pondering the thought of going upstream a bit more. You never know what could lurk 'round the next bend."

Tor pulled his watch from his pocket. "It's goin' on two o'clock. We're leaving at three. No later. If we leave by then, we should reach camp before dark. That gives us 'bout another hour to pan."

"Three o'clock it is, my friend. Y'know, if we stumble upon the right hole, you and me could both be rich by then. Say, Sourdough's biscuits are better right out of the oven than soaked in creek water, huh?" Junior wrung water from a biscuit and tossed it into the stream. A trout snapped it from the surface with a splash.

Tor shook his head. "Wish I had Pa's fly rod instead of this gol-dang pan right now. Maybe we'd have something for our troubles."

"Why, that ain't the Tor Loken I know. You need a positive attitude. You never know when Lady Luck is gonna come a-knockin'. Billy told me that. Always be positive, no matter what."

"Positive? I don't see your brother out here soakin' wet, cold from head to hind end, up to his knees and elbows in ice water and mud. Of that, Junior, I am positive."

The two novice prospectors worked their way upstream. Pan after pan yielded only sand, gravel, mud, and frozen fingers. Tor looked at his watch.

"Five of three, Junior. Time we head out."

"Tor! Look. A nugget! A gold nugget! I'm sure of it! Look!" Junior held a pea-sized piece of yellow metal in the air. "This is it, the spot we have been searchin' for!"

Excited, both boys scooped, swished, and dumped pan after pan of creek bottom, but found no more yellow metal. They worked their way up to a fork in the stream when Tor said, "Junior, it is goin' on four o'clock, an hour past our agreed-upon time to make tracks for camp. You and I have been at this all day. If we don't leave now, we will be in the woods after dark. Not on the tote road, mind you, in the woods. As it is, if we leave this minute, the owls will be hootin' long before we make the cook shanty."

Junior scooped one last pan from the creek, washed it, then dumped it into the icy water. "Dang it! I just know the mother lode is somewhere nearby. I wish we had more time."

"Well, we don't, Junior, and that's the truth of it! Unless we head out now, we will end up spendin' the night in the woods. Now, c'mon. We have to go."

The two boys waded downstream until they found the trail. Hoisting rucksacks onto shoulders again, they climbed the bank.

"Is this the right trail, Tor?"

"I'm not certain. Looks to be rather well worn. Seems the other path was hardly beat down."

"I think our route is farther downstream. Follow me."

"With this cloudy sky, we better dang sure have the right trail."

"Trust me, Tor. I can find the way. C'mon."

The two prospectors dodged briars and low-hanging branches, looking for the trail. A half-hour later, they came upon a stream.

"I can't recall crossing this creek on the way here," said Tor. "You suppose this is Superstition Creek?"

"You are askin' me?"

"Well, if not the Superstition, what in tarnation could it be?"

In the fading light, they slid down the bank, crossing the stream.

"Junior! Look at that rock upstream. Is that not where we ate our gol-dang dinner?"

The boys waded upstream.

"Dang it all!" shouted Tor. "We are back at Windigo Creek!"

"Windigo?" said Junior. "Naw, it cannot be. We left Windigo an hour ago!"

"We've been walking around in circles, my friend. I s'pose we followed our eyes instead of using our wits. Seems, we have come right back to where we started—right back to gol-dang Windigo Creek!"

"What do we do now, Tor? It'll be dark soon."

"Dark? With no moon and a cloudy sky overhead, it will be black as the inside of a moose."

"And to think I could've stayed right here, panning for my fortune instead of wandering through the woods with you this past hour."

"Dang it all, Kavanaugh! Here you are thinkin' again about gold instead of getting back to the safety of our camp." Tor pulled his watch from his pocket. "We best make camp. No point in traipsin' through the woods once darkness falls."

"Make camp? You mean stay out in the woods all night?"

"What choice do we have? No stars above to help us out. No compass between us."

"Go ahead and make your camp if you want, Tor. I will have no part of it. I intend to find my way back to the tote road and to camp."

"Junior, do not play the fool. Why, you will get yourself so confounded that you'll never find your way out."

"You go ahead, Loken. Make your camp. As for me, I am off for the warmth of the bunkhouse and a good, hot meal, with you or without."

"Do what you must, Junior. If you are not back at camp when I get there tomorrow, I will send a search party out to find you—or whatever is left of you. Who knows, maybe you will stumble across the trail to the lumber camp tonight. Most likely you will just stumble, fall, and end up food for the timber wolves."

"Timber wolves?"

"I'll be seeing you, Junior."

"Golly, I never thought about the gol-dang timber wolves. You think that …? Well, maybe I should stay the night. Get a fresh start in the morning."

Chapter 14
Lost

April 1886

 Tor and Junior found a nearby balsam windfall. They snapped off branches, piling them to make an insulating cushion between their bodies and the frozen ground. More balsam limbs layered above would help hold in their body heat through the chilly night.

"Junior, looks like I'm clean out of matches. You have some?"

Junior searched his pockets. "Soaked through and through. Cannot even light my pipe. No matter. Tobacco is soggy too to burn."

"Well, this is a gol-dang fine how-do-you-do! Here we are, wet, cold, bound to spend the night in the woods, and not a gol-dang match between us. I don't suppose you have a flint and steel, either."

"Nope. You?"

"Ya. Sitting back at camp next to my compass."

"You will likely remember it next time."

"Next time, Junior? You really think there will be a next time?"

Lanternshine glowed from the windows of the Loken lodge. Ingman, Olaf, John Kavanaugh, and Chief Namakagon sat before the fireplace.

"Olaf, for cryin' out loud, stop your gol-dang worryin,'" said Ingman. "Any minute now those boys will come a-stumblin' up the steps. Who knows? Maybe they will cart back a pocketful of gold. Why, chances are they don't even know we are concerned. You and I were the same when we were young bucks. I remember Pa tannin' our backsides more than once for comin' back after nightfall."

"Say what you will. Tor and Junior are out there in the gol-dang dark of night. You know how the woods can turn on you after dark sets in. I hope Tor has the good sense to make camp and wait things out."

Namakagon stepped closer to the glowing fireplace. "Tor will camp, make a fire. We will see him come morning. Junior will be alongside or close behind. Nothing out there will harm them. Only their pride will suffer."

"Dang it," said John. "I don't see why we are standin' around jawin' about this. Olaf, I think we should round up a search party to look for them. Poor boys must be scared stiff."

Olaf glanced toward Ingman, then said, "John, Blackie, if you want to take a few of the men with you down the east trail, you are sure welcome to. Take the gabreel with. Let the men know I have an extra week's pay for the fella who finds them first."

"Olaf," said Chief Namakagon, "I feel your concern. But know they are strong, capable young men. We will see them tomorrow, if not tonight. And if not tomorrow, then the next day or the next. Rest easy. Nothing bad can come to a lost woodsman who does not panic. Like the deer, the bear, all the animals in the woods, they will simply survive."

"Like the wolf?"

"Yes. Like my brother, the wolf."

Ingman struck a match, lighting his pipe. "Chief is right. I know Tor. He will keep his head about him. They will both wander into camp shiverin' with cold and worn to a frazzle. Rest easy. No point in us a-frettin' and a-fussin'."

"Rest easy?" snapped John Kavanaugh. "I will rest easy after my boy is back, safe and sound. Not till then. No sir."

Olaf paced with worry till morning. At first light he was on the trail north and east. He was not alone. John Kavanaugh, Ingman, Blackie, and Chief Namakagon were with him, along with one hundred thirty-one Namakagon Timber Company lumberjacks, all intent on returning by day's end with two more men and a pocketful of reward money.

<>O<>

Junior and Tor lay shivering between balsam branches at daybreak. Early morning light in the east gave them the sense of direction needed to search for the trail to camp. Hungry, wet, and cold, they stumbled through the forest, trying to maintain a westward bearing.

Within an hour, a heavy gray sky masked the sun and any hope of using it as a beacon. Hoping to see anything other than trees, Junior climbed a tall white pine, then descended, dismayed. On they trudged, desperately seeking yesterday's trail, using only lichens and moss on tree trunks as their guide. A murder of crows burst from branches overhead, their sharp caws voicing displeasure with this interruption by the forest floor vagabonds. All flew off in various directions. A single raven, much larger than its crow cousins, circled. It called as it did, then landed in a tall pine and stared down at the two boys.

Tor watched it light on a bare, dead limb that bobbed and bounced from the bird's weight. "Junior, maybe we should just stay put. Somebody will find us. Chief told me that rescue comes soonest to those who stay put. He said …"

"Dang it! There you go with your words of wisdom from that old Indian! It could be a week before anyone finds us out here. Least we can do is to get closer to the tote road where they might have a ghost of a chance. 'Sides, who says they are even lookin'? You can stay put if you want. Not me."

Three more calls from the raven pierced the air.

"Whatever we do, we have to stay together, Junior."

"That's fine by me," he replied. "My gut tells me west is this way. Time to be off."

Tor looked up at the raven, flung his rucksack onto his shoulder, and followed Junior who, within minutes, led them into a thick cedar swamp. Their travel slowed to a crawl. Branches pulled at coats and britches and swiped their hats from their heads again and again.

A tangle of windfalls soon blocked their way. Junior plopped down on the trunk of a fallen birch in disgust. "We are making no headway. I say we double back and try to skirt these cedars."

"I know it is slow going, but I agree with what you said before—about your gut feeling. If my hunch is right, we will soon stumble onto the east tote road somewhere north of the lumber camp. It cannot be more than two miles." The raven flew beyond them. Tor watched it perch in a distant pine.

"Two miles? Two miles through this swamp?"

"Probably less. Probably not all swamp."

"I'm goin' around, Tor, not through. I know I can make better time. 'Sides, it might be better to split up. Whoever gets back to camp first can get help to look for the other. Make sense?"

"No. Makes not a lick of sense. Not a smidgeon. We have to stick together. It will save the search party from half their work. 'Sides, what if one of us should twist an ankle? Who will be there to help? No, best we keep together. C'mon. We are wasting daylight."

"Well, listen to you—Tor Loken, boss of the woods. I have had it with you telling me what I can and cannot do. Go ahead. Just you try to make it through this swamp. I will let your pa know where I left you when I reach the camp."

"Don't play the fool, Junior."

The raven repeated its call.

"I'm finished with it, Tor. We're splittin' up. Meet you in camp."

Junior threw his rucksack on the ground and disappeared behind the thick cover of cedars.

"Junior," Tor yelled. "Junior, stop this folly. You hear me, Kavanaugh?" Silence. "Junior!"

Tor continued his plod. Rain fell, turning to snow, then rain again. He soon found himself under a canopy of white pine. More windfalls interrupted his course and left him wondering if he had changed direction. He and Junior had circled the day before. Had these thick, gray clouds stolen his sense of direction? Could he be circling now? On he trudged, at times confident in his hunches, other times not.

From somewhere ahead, another call from the raven prompted Tor to stop. He listened for the next, though knew not why. Silent now, desperate to find his way home, his imagination almost conjured the faintest sound of a gabreel far in the distance. The raven flew to another tree and called again. Once more, the barely audible tone filtered through the trees. Tor began stalking this vague, occasional resonance. Again he tramped through the pines before seeing the coal-black raptor fly high into another tall pine. Pursuing, he now believed it flew the same direction that might lead him to safety.

The raven moved once more. Stopping to track its direction, Tor again heard the faint sound of the camp cook's trumpet, this time a bit louder. Motionless, now, he strained to listen, finally catching the faintest sound of the horn.

He turned toward the sound and clearly heard the faraway yet distinctive tone of Sourdough's tin gabreel. His heart lifted, the lost lumberjack picked up his pace, following more calls from the raven and the clear song of the cook's signal horn. Stopping to listen again, he heard something else—the distant shouts from the men in the rescue party. Chasing these voices, raven in the lead, he suddenly stepped onto the tote road east of the camp. Knowing he was safe, he took a deep breath and knelt down in the middle of the lane, exhausted and relieved. The raven flew past again, alighting on a dead limb not ten feet above. The bird turned its head, looking down on the rescued rover who whispered a word of thanks to it and any spirit willing to listen.

As the raven disappeared into the forest, Tor checked his pocket watch. "Three thirty-five, Junior. I am a good seven or eight miles from camp. I wonder where the heck you are."

<>O<>

Mile after mile, Junior slogged through the woods, trying to keep the cedar swamp on his right. He prayed he was headed south or west or somewhere between. The thick April clouds lent the forest a gloomy, menacing manner. Rain fell, turning to snow, then rain again.

Dusk approaching, Junior stumbled on a creek. Knowing if he crossed, he would likely be going farther from the camp, he followed the riverbank upstream. A ruffed grouse flushed from near his feet, its erupting, exploding wing-beats startling him. Junior lost his footing and slid down the steep bank into the water. He jumped to his feet and waded to a large rock where he rested. His surroundings slowly became familiar.

"Devil be damned, Windigo Creek again!" he screamed down the stream. "Danged if I ain't back where we ate our gol-dang, muck-sucking, dirty dog of a dinner yesterday! Son of a biscuit! Son of a gol-dang, dirty dog, waterlogged biscuit!" He lowered his head, holding it in his hands, staring at the water running between his feet. "Dear Lord up above, please, please help me. Help me get out of this dang bear trap, will ya? I swear I will quit my cussin' and even go to Reverend Spooner's sermons should I ever get to Hayward on a Sunday mornin'. I ain't such a bad fella, you know, unless you count the gamblin' and cheatin' at solitaire. Oh, and that night with Mabel Durst at the Cable House. But you prob'ly remember more about that night than do I, seein' as how I was pretty drunk and all. Anyway, help me, dear Lord. I'll pay you back two to one odds if you do. Heck, I'll even make it three to one."

As Junior stared, head in his hands, down into the flowing water, he noticed a glint of light in the stream. Reaching elbow-deep, he picked up a small gold nugget. "Lord, I'm not sure you heard me right. I mean, I sure appreciate this and all, but what I need right about now is to find my way back to the camp—back to my Pa and a good meal and dry britches. But, thank you, anyway, Lord. Least it is somethin'."

Dropping the nugget into his pocket, the lost boy climbed the stream bank. Junior found the balsam windfall where he and Tor slept the night before. There he lay, cold and wet, shivering in the dark under the same balsam boughs as the night before.

Rain fell through the night, stopping shortly before sunrise. In the dim, morning light, Junior lay half-asleep on balsam boughs, wet, weak, and hungry. He wanted to not move, but knew he must. The howl of a nearby wolf woke the lost boy with a start. He jumped up shouting, "You will not feast on me, wolf. Leastwise, not yet!" He pulled his collar up around his neck, straightened his hat, and, soaked to the skin, Junior Kavanaugh tramped on.

Chapter 15
The Third Day

April 1886

The early morning light in the eastern sky again offered Junior a sense of direction. He headed west, rain dripping from overhead branches. Reaching the cedar swamp, he turned south now, hoping this would take him to the original trail and out to the tote road. Shivering and weak from two days without food, he trudged forward, coming to a deep, narrow ravine. He stood at the edge, gazing down as the wind picked up.

"Well, now," he mumbled, "ain't this a fine how do you do! I can go leftwise back toward where I come from, rightwise into that gol-dang tangle of cedars, down into this gorge and up the other side, or stand here pondering. Of all the gol-dang luck! I swear, if it ain't one thing, then it's sure to be another. Looks like I am bound for a climb."

Junior broke two dead limbs from a nearby pine, looked them over, then chose the strongest to use as a walking stick. Dropping the other, lighter limb where he stood, he began the treacherous descent, the rain resuming. Nearing the midpoint, he slipped in the mud, his feet flying from underneath. Down he slid to the bottom of the ravine, flipping and turning and tearing his britches, losing his hat. He lay in muddy water wondering what injuries he sustained. Temporary pains from the fall slowly ebbed as he stretched and flexed. He fumbled for his walking stick and stood upright. Sore from the fall, he looked up at the high wall before him. Water dripped from rocks and roots above. Shivering, alone, frightened, he began his slow, silent ascent.

Above, thirty-six Loken men combed the woods on either side of the ravine. The men shouted his name as they searched, but their calls, muted by rain and wind, failed to reach Junior, far below. Other men clawed their way through the cedar swamp. Their shouts were difficult for each other to hear, much less anyone in the bottom of a deep ravine. The lumberjack nearest the precipice looked down now and then, though never expected anyone might venture into such a perilous gorge.

Junior climbed toward the daylight above. After slipping and falling several times, he managed to crawl out, rolling away from the edge. No one near now, he lay in the rain, waiting to catch his breath.

"I'm not givin' up. No I am not! Not me, dang it. Not Junior Kavanaugh. Not Billy Kavanaugh's brother, no sir. Not givin' up."

He stood, peeking over the edge into the deep ravine, then turned to press on, stepping on the lighter of the two walking sticks—the one he left behind before descending into the gorge. Junior picked up the stick, staring at it in disbelief. He looked over the edge of the ravine again then at the stick. Tears filled his eyes as he began his second descent, vowing to reach the other side this time.

A half-hour later, covered in mud, the lost boy pulled himself to the surface and rolled away from the ravine's edge. He lay on the forest floor to rest before continuing his trek, then struggled to his feet and trod on, unaware he was crossing the footsteps of his fellow lumberjacks, men who had passed through only an hour earlier.

The rain stopped, but not the cold, April wind. Chilled, Junior ran when he could to regain some warmth. Between his running and walking, his wool clothes began to dry. But, two days without food, the lost boy soon tired. Sitting on a log to rest, he stretched his legs, retying his boots. He looked up, beyond the tangle of tree limbs and branches above. "Lord, I hope you ain't forgotten about all my chin-waggin' last night. I am still in a pickle—still need your help if you think I am worth the trouble. Sure would be kindly of you."

A single loon flew over, calling to others. Junior watched it, wondering. "Are you headed toward the lake, loony bird? Should I follow? Or, maybe you are heading away? Naw, with so many gol-dang lakes around here, you could be headed anywhere."

Junior started to rise, then, weak and wobbly, plopped down again. "Say, Mister Loon, maybe you are a sign from above. If my pal Tor was here, he'd be sure to say you are ol' Wenebojo or some other Indian spirit that he's always jawin' about. I swear that Tor Loken is pretty well sold on ol' Wenebojo bein' real. Well, who is to say he ain't? I will tell you this much, if ol' Wenebojo were to set down right beside me on this log and tell me he was gonna lead me out of this bear trap, I would give him a pat on the back and say 'lead on, Wenny!'"

Exhausted from his ordeal, Junior walked again, too drained to pay attention to direction. As he trudged, he mumbled. "Wenebojo, Gitchee Manitou, Lord in Heaven— to me it don't matter no more who sends help. I'll take it gladly from any one of 'em. Who knows?

Maybe they's all the same fella anyhow. Who is to say? Who is to say? Who is to say, who is to say, who is to … Tor Loken, that's who. He is the boss. My best friend. Tor Loken. 'Twas that gol-dang Tor Loken that got me into this mess in the first place. Tor Loken. He got me caught in this bear trap. By God, he should've come with me, the son-of-a-biscuit. The two of us would've made it out long ago. Got plenty a nerve tellin' me what to do. Gol-dang Tor Loken. Probably lost in them cedars back there. Probably dead and gone. I s'pose that's what they figure they are gonna say about me—lost and dead and gone. And who in blazes would give a gol-dang. Well, I'm gonna show 'em. I ain't gonna let gol-dang Tor Loken be the end of me, no sir. Nerve. That's what Tor Loken had, gettin' me into this here mess. A whole lotta gol-dang nerve. I'll show him. I'll show him. I'll show him. I'll show him. My Pa is gonna find me. I know he will. And Billy. Billy and Pa are probably comin' right now."

He looked behind. "Billy? Pa?" he yelled, "is that you? Is that you come to my rescue?"

There was no answer. Junior stood, staring into the woods, then turned, resuming his plod, mumbling, "Billy and Pa, Billy and Pa, Billy and Pa, Billy and Pa, Billy and Pa, Billy … Say now, my brother Billy—there's a big shot for ya. When I get out of this here gol-dang, no good tangle, I am taking off with my brother Billy. We'll be livin' high on the hog, we will. No more of Sourdough's soggy biscuits, soggy biscuits, soggy, soggy …"

Junior tripped on a log, collapsing face first on the forest floor. Within seconds he was unconscious, dreaming disjointed dreams of ships sailing port to port in warm Caribbean seas. The boat rocked gently as, in his delirium, he and Billy counted stacks of bananas and baskets and money. Beautiful, dark-skinned women brought them mugs of beer and bowls of fried pork skins from the Cable House bar. In the distance, the whistle of another ship broke the silence. Junior and Billy rushed to the rail, peering across miles and miles of blue, sun-bathed water and searching the horizon for the ship. The whistle sounded again. Billy pointed. Junior squinted, straining to see the ship. The whistle blew louder. In the hot sunlight, Junior squinted. It blew again. Billy pointed, laughing silently. Junior then saw it—the ship, no, a train. A train coming to them—the Omaha—no—the Wisconsin Central—there! Right there atop the ocean! A locomotive! A locomotive in the ocean? There! Billy laughed and danced and laughed. The locomotive rolled across the ocean, the engineer waving. A smoky old locomotive! A locomotive carrying pine logs—pine logs and bananas and baskets and money—and beautiful dark-skinned women—and Mabel Durst from the Cable House with mugs of beer! Mabel Durst. And Rusty O'Hara. And Junior's Pa, Sourdough, and Gust Finstead. And Tor Loken. Tor Loken high atop a sleigh full of pine, calling to his team of Clydesdales. The whistle sounded again.

Junior, face-down on the wet forest floor, rolled on his side, his eyelids fluttering. He felt warm. Warm and comfortable. His breathing slowed. "So warm and sunny," he tried to say. No words came from his lips. He lay there, warm and comfortable on the deck of a ship with his brother, drinking beer, eating bananas and ...

The whistle sounded again. His eyes opened wide. "A train?" he tried to shout, surprised to hear only a whisper come from within. "A train! Which way?" He listened, hearing only wind in treetops. "Must be dreaming. Still dreaming ...still ...drea..."

The locomotive's whistle sounded again. Junior tried to push himself up and to the left, staring at the trees before him, waiting. Again the distinct resonance of an engineer's whistle cut though the wind and woods, this time straight ahead. Junior slowly stood, then trudged forward. Step after step, he moved in the direction of the welcome sound, a sound of others—of warmth and food and shelter. Suddenly revitalized, he determined, once again, to not give up.

On and on he tramped toward the train's whistle, soon hearing the chugging of the steam engine. The whistle blasts were regular—one long blast every half-minute. The signals led him back through the woods to the same stream where he and Tor had panned for gold. He sighed, shaking his head as he stood on the bank above, then sat, sliding down the bank into the stream. He crossed the creek, stepping onto the bank to begin his climb, but weak and wet, he fell back, hitting his head on a rock in the streambed. The icy water washed over him, bubbling and gurgling, washing the mud from his boots, britches, and coat. He lay there immobilized, helpless. The stream bathed him in clear, ice-cold water as he again fell into unconsciousness.

<>O<>

The engineer was first to see the movement in the shadows of the woods. Pointing out the locomotive's side window, he shouted to the conductor. "Otis! Say, Otis! Look! Over there, beyond those willows. See? See them?"

"Huh? See who? Don't see nothin' but woods, Paul. You gone daft?"

"No, I ain't gone daft, ya pot-licker. Over there." He turned to his fireman, standing on top of the tender. "Say, you see 'em, Farley?"

"Sure do, Paul. Looks like two 'Jibwas to me. You?"

"Ya, maybe so. I was hopin' it would be that lost fella."

"Don't look like no lost man. Better keep blowin' that whistle."

The engineer pulled the chain. Another whistle blast cut through the woods.

"Now I see 'em, Paul," yelled the conductor. "Looks to me like two Indians draggin' out a deer. Maybe they want to sell it to us. I am plum out of venison."

"We will know soon, Otis. They's comin' straight this way."

The railroad men watched as the two Ojibwes approached.

"Say, Paul," said Farley from atop the tender, "if my eyes ain't deceivin' me, that deer they're draggin' is wearin' a red mackinaw."

"Well, I'll be danged, Farley. That must be the fella what got himself lost. Glory be! Ain't that sumpin'! We found him, fellas. Here I thought we were sittin here a-spinnin' our wheels on a gol-dang greased rail. Wait till the Milwaukee office hears 'bout this! We are gonna be heroes, Farley. Heroes! They will have my picture in the paper! Yours, too, maybe. Let's pray that poor lost fella ain't dead yet."

"He ain't lookin' too good from up here. They are draggin' him on a travois."

"Ya? Then I'd bet my wife's horse he's still alive."

"How do you figure?"

"Were he stone-cold dead, Farley, there would be no use for a travois. They would just drag him out with a rope. You know, like you would a dead deer."

The conductor and brakeman met the two Ojibwes.

"Found him in Windigo Creek—near drowned. Acted confused, stupid," said the taller Indian. "The spirits were looking out for him today. If the suckers were not running, we would not have been there to find him."

"Now, don't that beat all," muttered Otis. "Saved by a gol-dang school of suckers. The Lord must've been watchin' out for him."

"Now, tell me, Otis, if the Lord was lookin' out for him, how'd he get himself in such a fix in the first place? No, I'd say the boy fell on bad luck then good, that's all. Let's hope he has enough good luck left that he pulls through."

The train rolled in to the Mellen railroad yard ten minutes later. Two men carried the unconscious boy from the depot to the doctor's office while the telegrapher sent a message to Oscar Felsman, the Cable stationmaster. Soon a messenger was running to the Namakagon Timber Company camp with news of Junior Kavanaugh's rescue.

Ingman, Olaf, and Blackie called in the search teams. All the men were in camp that night, drying their coats, shirts, socks, and britches. John Kavanaugh, Blackie, and Sourdough joined Olaf, Tor, Ingman, and Chief Namakagon in the lodge to toast the successful recovery of the two lost prospectors.

"Olaf," said John, "I would like to go see my boy tomorrow—bring him back to camp when he's up to it. Slim Waterson says he can tend to the barn chores till we return. All right by you?"

"Ya, you bet, John. You and your boy take all the time you need. Give him a pat on the back for us."

"John," said Tor, "you tell your boy we need him back here to pilot the Empress Karina when the log drive starts. That's sure to raise his spirits."

"Sourdough," said Olaf, "looks to me like the ice will last a day or two more. We have little work for the men to do tomorrow. High time we bent the rules a bit. There's two cases of brandy under my desk. Have your bull cook and the cookees send a few rounds to the men. They served well today. Let 'em whoop it up a bit—on the Lokens."

Ingman piped in. "You tell 'em I said no brawlin'. I do not want our gol-dang cook shanty broke up."

"Or the men," added Tor. "Least not till after the drive."

"Young woodsman," said Namakagon, "you have not yet told us what you found on your gold hunting expedition."

"What I found? Well, I s'pose what comes first to mind is a song Rosie plays."

"What song is that?" asked Ingman.

"'Be it ever so humble, there's no place like home.'"

Chapter 16
Murphy's Pocket

May 1886

Billy Kavanaugh had a late breakfast at the Cable House, choosing to eat at the bar. At the far end, sitting on top of three wooden whiskey crates, sat the only other customer. His head lay on the bar. Timothy Murphy stopped snoring and looked up only long enough to order another beer, then lowered his head into his folded arms again. The bartender filled the glass, taking a dime from the change next to Murphy's morning paper.

"Now, don't you be forgettin' to bring me the nickel you owes me, Walter," mumbled Timothy.

The bartender slapped the nickel down next to him. "Wake up, Murphy. It's goin' on half-past nine. Have you no place to go?"

"Mercy Mother Magee! Walter, you have no call to wake the dead." Murphy said into the polished mahogany bar. Raising his bleary, bloodshot eyes, he muttered, "Why in the world would I want to go anywhere? Everything I need is right here—your delightful cookin', your stale beer, your friendly pleasantries … I ask you, who could want for a better life than all this?"

"Don't get me wrong, Timothy, we value your business, but …"

"Oh, no! Mercy me! Walter, did I miss church again?" He sat up straight. "Walter, please tell me I did not miss the Sunday service again."

"Church? For Pete's sake, Murphy, it's Tuesday mornin'! Why, you been camped out here in the barroom for most of a week. Now, you are askin' me if you missed church? Yes, Murphy, you missed church."

"Oh, my, my. Me sweet mother, bless her heart, would not approve. No sir. Better pour me another brew, Walter. Would you do that for me, now?"

"Timothy Murphy, for cryin' out loud! You must have something better to do than drink your gol-dang life away. You are a young man. Go get yourself a job. There's plenty of work in the pinery for a strong fella like you. Why, you could …"

"Get meself a job? I have a job. Why in blazes would I want another job? I squirrel away more than enough greenbacks during the spring drive to keep me in navy beans and beer for the whole year, Walter. And enough to pay me bills at the bawdy houses, to boot. I am livin' the good life, me friend. No siree, no other job for me. I will be as rich as the bloomin' bishop of Chicago a month from now."

Billy Kavanaugh moved to Timothy's end of the bar. "Say, I couldn't help overhearing, friend. I am curious how a man can work for only a week or two in April and make enough to carry him through the year. I am always on the lookout for a fast dollar. What kind of work do you do?"

"Why? Who are you? You with the law? I ain't doin' nothin' them timber companies ain't doin' to everyone else."

"Me? The law?" said Billy. "Why, that's a knee-slapper, friend. I specialize in stayin' far clear of the law. No, I am in the tradin' game."

"I got nothin' to trade. Me, I trade with the mills once a year. That's plenty."

"Name is Kavanaugh. Billy Kavanaugh. And you are …"

"Thirsty."

"Walter, give us a beer on me, would you?"

"Hear that, Walter?" shouted Murphy. "And see if you can find a clean glass this time." He turned to Billy. "Walter rarely wipes them off unless reminded. So, who did you say you are?"

Billy laid a half-dollar on the bar. "Take out for my breakfast, too. And a nickel tip for your patience, Walt." Billy turned. "I'm Billy Kavanaugh."

Murphy looked up before laying his head on his folded arms again.

"It's a pleasure, Billy Kavanaugh. Much obliged for the beer."

"So, you are a river pig? That's how you make your money each spring? You drive logs?"

"Me? Not a chance. Far, far too risky. No, you will not see old Timothy Murphy ridin' out down the river on those man-killers. No siree, Billy."

"Then, …"

"I have me a gold mine."

"You are a miner? But, I thought you said …"

"Green gold."

"Green gold? What?"

"Pine, Billy Kavanaugh, white pine. Ask any lumber baron. White pine is green gold."

"Oh, I see. So … you cut and haul timber?"

He put a finger to his lips. "Shhhh." He grinned. "Cut, yes, but don't haul."

"What? Who …, I mean, how …"

"You see, Billy Kavanaugh, I let them loggin' companies cut and haul for me. They are so much better at it than old Murphy could ever hope to be. Professionals, is what they are."

"But, then …"

"Why, I could never be a lumberjack. No, no, no. Not Timothy Murphy. No siree."

"Then how …"

"Oh, I tried it once. Spent a whole winter in Ole Olson's camp 'fore the spring drive came along and I seen me the road to riches."

"The road …? What road did you see?"

"More like a river of wealth, I s'pose."

"Tim, I'm not followin' you."

"Timothy."

"Hmm?"

"Me sweet mother, bless her heart, called me Timothy. You can, too."

"So, Timothy, just what is it you do for work?"

"You see, Billy, I only help meself to a few here, a few there. The lumber camps have plenty—more than plenty—certainly more than they need."

"Plenty of what?"

"They never miss a-one."

"What?"

"Hmm?"

"What is it they don't miss?"

"Logs. Pine logs."

"Logs? But, …"

"You say you might be lookin' to make some money?"

"If the right opportunity knocks. I've never yet turned down a chance to snag the brass ring. But, Timothy, you still ain't said …"

"Brass ring? Oh, yes, this is the brass ring, all right. Shiny and bright as the morning sun on the deep, briny sea."

"What kind of work are you …?"

"Shh, I'll tell you, but only if you give your word to not spread it around, Billy Kavanaugh."

"You have my word, Timothy."

"It's as simple as me mother's apple pie, my friend. All winter long," he straightened up and stretched his neck, staring down the bar to make sure the bartender could not overhear. Then, in a hushed tone, said, "All winter long the timber outfits cut, cut, cut. They haul hundreds of thousands, maybe millions of logs to the lakes and rivers, right?"

"So ...?"

"So, in April, when all them logs come a-floatin' down the river, there stands ol' Timothy Murphy, pike pole in hand, waitin' for 'em, eager to help out. Why, every river pig what passes me by waves a fond hello and smiles when they see me givin' them a hand, see?"

"And that's how you make your money? Helping camps drive logs?"

"Well, while I'm helpin' them, Billy, I am also helpin' meself."

"Yourself."

"Yep. Helpin' meself."

"Oh, I see, Murphy. You help drive their logs while you drive your own."

"You could say that. Yes."

"So, you have a one-man lumber camp."

"Nope. Just a stamp."

"A stamp?"

"That's all a fella like me needs, Mister Billy Kavanaugh, a stamp and a big ol' log to smack it on."

"Timothy Murphy, you are makin' no sense whatsoever."

"Look," Murphy said in muted tone, "I will spell it out for ya."

"That would be good, Murphy. So far you're speakin' nay but gibberish."

"All right. Pay attention, Billy. Come springtime, when the drive commences and all them logs come a-floatin' down the river, there stands ol' Timothy Murphy, pike pole in hand, waitin', eager to help out. Why, every river pig who passes by waves a hello and smiles when they see me givin' them a hand."

"I got that. But, how ...?"

"I'm gettin' to it. I'm gettin' to it. See, as soon as they disappear 'round the bend, ol' Murphy sinks the point of a picaroon into a fine, fat pine log and drags it up the creek into me own private pond just a bit off the river." Murphy drank his beer, slamming the empty glass on the bar. "Billy, in no time at all, I have sawed off both ends and marked the log with me own stamp hammer, see? I have givin' it me very own sign, me mark of distinction, me brand, you might say. About then I check to see there is nobody comin' downstream. If the coast is clear, I push the bloomin' log back among the others. It goes floatin' down the merry old stream while I grab me the next. Them other fellas, the river pigs, they labor hard to get each and every last stick of pine to the mill—including old Timothy Murphy's. They keep the logs from jammin' on the bends, keep 'em floatin' all the way to the mill pond. When the mill workers sort 'em out and tally 'em up, the mill pays each and every timber outfit what is due them. Whether a camp is big or small, a hundred men or one man, the mill pays the same rate per log."

"So, what timber outfit do you work for? I mean … who pays you?"

"I told ya, Billy Kavanaugh, I work for meself. As you said, I am a lumber company of one. I am the One-eyed Moose. Now you sees me, and now you don't."

"But, how in blazes …?"

"Beautiful, ain't it?"

"Murphy, you continue confusin' the daylights out of me. Who is it you said pays you? Some one-eyed moose?"

"No, no, no. Now pay attention. Like I told ya, all them logs from all them backwoods camps make their way downriver. But, before they make it to the mill, I pinches one here, one there, cuts off the end, stamps me own mark on it, then sends it on its merry way. Later on, the logs get sorted out by the mill hands, see? After they tally up each outfit's total number of logs, the mill pays out. And, just like the other camps, logs bearin' me stamp are tallied under me own name."

"You mean …"

"Yes, Billy. I get paid for each and every last one of them logs marked by me stamp. Ain't nobody knows the difference. Nobody. I get me pay same as every other timber outfit boss. Of course, the other camps have to pay their workers. Me? I only pay meself—and me partner, when I have one."

"Well, fathom that! Timothy Murphy, you are no more than a gol-dang river pirate."

"It's a title I accept with honor."

"A gol-dang sneak thief."

"Sneak-thief? Rather harsh. And it lacks the same spirit of adventure of a river pirate. But, I s'pose so.

"You, sir, are a ..."

Businessman, Billy. And I'd say I got me a rather a nice little business, ay?"

"More akin to a nice little swindle, I'd say. You are a red fox stealin' chickens from the henhouse, Timothy Murphy."

"I like to think of myself more akin to ... oh ... a raccoon snatchin' up a few surplus beans from what boiled out of the bean pot."

"Amazing!"

"Or a blackbird snitchin' a kernel of corn from your sweet grandmother's garden when she ain't lookin'."

"My granny only grew flowers. But had she grown corn, she'd have shot any blackbird that ..."

"Or, Billy, think of me as a weasel in the woodpile, takin' a mouse now and then."

"Weasel in the woodpile? In the eyes of the lumbermen, you are more like a skunk under the woodshed, Murphy."

"I've been called worse. So ... you want to go in with me?"

"Murphy, have you thought about what would happen if you got caught. I mean ..."

"Oh, they'll never be catchin' me. That's the beauty of it. Won't be catchin' you, either if you're game. Are you game for it, Kavanaugh?"

"Why bring in a partner?"

"Well, me one-man saw is not nearly as efficient as a two-man crosscut. Two men workin' a crosscut can do three times the work. Why, you and me could be sittin' on easy street in just a few days' work. No bills to pay. No overhead. Pure profit, 'cept for the whiskey."

"How much profit?"

"Oh, say, two hundred."

"Two hundred?" Billy rubbed his chin. "Damn good wage, two hundred a month."

"A day."

"What?"

"A day, Billy."

"A day? Two hundred a day? Why, that's more than a man's wages for the entire winter. Murphy, are you tellin' me you can make a lumberjack's winter wage in only one day?"

"Multiply that by six days a week."

"What? That's six years' wages! You sayin' a man can make that kind of money, six years of pay in less than a week?"

"At least. Two of us would do better."

"So, why six days and not seven?"

"Seven? May the good Lord forgive you and the angels in Heaven forget you even asked the question! Mercy me, Billy, the seventh day is the Lord's day! Why, I would not dream of goin' agin' the word of our maker. Oh, my! What would me sweet mother think?"

"Six years' worth of lumberjack pay in only six days. The very sound of it takes my breath away."

"Do I have me a partner?"

"Why shouldn't I just go off on my own?"

Murphy leaned in closer, "Because, friend, I have me the perfect spot," he whispered. "Me cabin is on a wee little creek that opens onto a pond along the river. Indeed, I call it 'Murphy's Pocket.' Many a pine log has disappeared into Murphy's Pocket, Billy Kavanaugh."

"Where might I find this cabin of yours?"

"East of here. Not too far. Near to a small oxbow, it is. That oxbow hides me shenanigans from the drivers. You game, then?" Murphy extended his hand.

"When do we start?" replied Billy, shaking Murphy's hand.

"Breakup comes in two, maybe three weeks, Billy. That's when you and me go to work. Me cabin is, oh, half-an-hour east of here, a wee bit south of the east trail and just off the Namekagon River. Meet me there tomorrow and I will show you me setup."

"Put on your coffeepot, Timothy. I'll be there."

"Billy, you and me are bound to be rich by the end of the month. Mark me words."

"Long as I'm not in the calaboose, Murphy. A fella cannot spend his fortune sittin' in the calaboose, no matter how rich he is."

<>O<>

The next day, Billy knocked on Timothy Murphy's cabin door. "Murphy, you up? Murphy?"

"Down here, William," came a shout from the pond. "Come have a look at me outfit."

Billy followed the path to the pond, already free of ice. There stood Timothy Murphy, hammer in hand, knee-deep in ice-cold water.

"I am building us a ramp to help roll the logs up. That way we can cut 'em on the sawbucks instead of standin' up to our arses in freezin' pond water like last year."

"So you had a partner last year?"

"Last two years. Pinky. Pinky Collins. Least that's what he went by when he did not call himself Johnny. Not the first fella I met up here whose true name I never knew."

"So, Murph, what jail is Pinky sittin' in?"

"Now, there you go again, thinkin' 'bout gettin' caught. I hate to disappoint, Billy, but ol' Pinky did not get arrested. Nor will you."

"So, if this is such a fool-proof operation, why is he not here? Where is he?"

"The other side of the rainbow, I'm afraid."

"Rainbow?"

"Pinky is dead, I'm afraid."

"Dead?"

"Stone cold dead, bless his wayward soul."

"But, …"

"Now you dassn't go quiverin' in your boots, Billy. Pinky was not done in for pinchin' pine logs."

"What, then?"

"Jealous husband."

"No! Really?"

"Yep. Happened right after we split our earnin's last spring. Pinky hopped a southbound train, took all his pay straight to the gambling parlor of the biggest hotel in Chippeway Falls. Roulette wheel, I heard. Poor Pinky. Lost all but a few greenbacks. From there he went to the hotel bar. Got good and drunk.

"Sometime in the middle of the night, four gunshots woke up the whole dang hotel. Seems some fella come back to his room from a night on the town to find his wife under the blankets with ol' Pinky. Shot the both of 'em dead as dead can be. Such a shame. Judge let the fellow go. Called it justified. Like I say, I s'pect ol' Pinky's somewhere on the other side of the rainbow, drinkin', chasin' the skirts, carryin' on like always."

"Poor Pinky."

"Poor Pinky? Why, that's precisely how I want to go out, Billy"

"How's that?"

"Jealous husband."

"What?"

"I want me tombstone to read 'Here lies Timothy Thomas

Murphy, age one hundred and one. Killed by a jealous husband.'"

"I marvel at your ambition, Mister Murphy."

"Come on, William. Let me show you me little money factory."

Billy made his way to the shore.

"We saw off the ends of the logs here, then toss the log ends straight into the fire pit. Pay heed, now. Not one log end can float downstream or we risk bein' found out. We'd surely be in the pickle barrel if that happened. Besides, the log ends make for a nice fire to boil up our tea and keep us from the shivers.

"Now, with both ends trimmed off, we stamp each log twice on one end and likewise on the other. Then, it's back into the pond with her. We float the little darlin' down the creek and out to the river. Like I told you before, we give a look upstream, then down. If nobody is around, we send our little sweetheart on her journey to the mill and she's soon in the company of a thousand other logs and nobody's the wiser. Next, we grab us another darlin', float her back up here and dance another dance. Billy, in honor of our new partnership, I have even built walkways along the creek to keep our feet dry, unlike them poor blokes who drive our logs for us. Most are wet from head to toe, daylight till dark."

"We work all day, then?"

"All day and all night, too, if the moonlight and our achin' backs allow. Oh, I never said it ain't hard work, but it surely don't come near what the river pigs must bear. You know, I sort of feel sorry for them, soakin' wet, shiverin' and shakin' dawn to dusk like a willow leaf in the wind. And takin' all the risk on top of it all. Poor fellows."

"How do we know when the drive will start, Timothy?"

"By keepin' one ear to the rail, William. When you see beer wagon after beer wagon lining Iowa Avenue, you'll know the drive is forthcomin'."

"Murphy, those wagons have been rollin' into town all week."

"Then it shan't be long. The minute Lake Namakagon breaks up, all the drive bosses will let go the logs and the drivers with 'em. I 'spect the bankers and businessmen are already countin' their profits."

"Timothy, as soon as I hear the rumble of the logs comin' downriver, I'll be a-knockin' on your door. You and me are going to make us some money, we are. Yessiree, my friend, *real* money."

Chapter 17
The One-eyed Moose

May 1886

"Ffisssssss."

The sound of another barrel of beer being tapped filled the room, followed by cheers from the crowd. Outside, in full uniform, the City of Hayward's four-piece marching band played "The Battle Hymn of the Republic" as they marched up and down the three-block-long business district. As they did, they dodged horses, cattle, horse apples, and cow pies.

Billy Kavanaugh raced across the railroad yard as the train pulled out. He tossed his rucksack onto the steps of the second passenger car and vaulted onto the steps as it gained speed. Conductor Clyde Williams met him there, glaring at him over his glasses as Billy pulled a silver dollar from a pocket.

"Young man, you have no ticket?"

"No, sir. Here is a dollar. I only need to go as far as the Cable station."

"Unless you have never before ridden a train, you surely know you must purchase your fare *prior* to boarding, not after."

"Yes sir. A dollar more than covers it. You keep the extra."

"I could let you off, you know."

"Is a quarter gratuity not enough, Conductor?"

"This is not about the money. It is about railroad company policy."

"Policy be damned. You keep the quarter and, here, have another. That, sir, is a fifty cent prize. Will that do? Or should we stop at Phipps where I can purchase my fare, get back on the same train and save myself the half-dollar? Now, you tell me."

"Well, …"

"Good. No need to stop then. Now may I take a seat? Or do I have to ride out here in this draft?"

"Yes, well, find yourself a seat, young man. I will make the necessary arrangements regarding your fare."

"I am certain you will, Conductor."

Clyde Williams dropped the two coins in his vest pocket as the train rumbled north, crossing the river twice. At each of the two trestles, Billy witnessed the first few of what would soon be over a million logs floating downstream, helped along by a thousand river pigs. More logs and log drivers soon came into view on the creeks feeding into the Namekagon River. The locomotive labored, climbing the final grade to Cable. It pulled into the station, bell ringing, steam rushing, and smoke rising skyward. Billy Kavanaugh jumped from the still-moving train before the engineer gave the all clear, eliciting a final glare from Clyde Williams, Omaha Conductor.

Billy rushed through the waiting room and out the east door of the depot, through the park and down the street before following the east trail out of town on foot. Thirty minutes later, he was at Murphy's Pocket, the pond named by his new friend.

"Down here, William," yelled Murphy. "You are just in time. We can pull a few logs in before the river is crowded with drivers. C'mon."

They stepped out onto the narrow, wooden walkway Murphy built weeks earlier. A pike pole hidden in the brush was all Murphy needed to guide one of the huge logs up the creek. Billy slammed the sharp point of his picaroon into the log and coaxed it up the narrow stream and into Murphy's Pocket. By the time he returned, Timothy had a second log on the way.

"No time to lose, Billy. There will be river pigs comin' along any time now."

Twenty minutes later, they had nine logs in Murphy's Pocket, ready to saw. The sharp crosscut sped through the pine with ease. Four solid smacks with Murphy's stamp hammer marked the log as their own. Billy tossed the first two log ends into the fire pit and the next log soon lay waiting in the sawbucks.

"Time to send 'em on their way," Murphy said when all nine were ready. "Now we better keep us an eye peeled so we don't raise any suspicion. If someone should happen by, you let me do the talkin'."

The logs floated down the creek with ease. Then, caught in the rushing current, they raced downriver, mixing with thousands of others. Billy again fished his pike pole from the brush.

"Hide that picaroon!" whispered Murphy. "Drivers a-comin'!"

"Hello there on the oxbow," came a shout. "What camp you boys hail from?"

"The One-eyed Moose, yelled Murphy. How 'bout you boys?"

"Castle Creek Company. Say, I ain't never heard of the One-eyed Moose. Who is the head push? Is that Ole Swenson's outfit?" The men stepped log to log, crossing the river, then jumped onto Murphy's narrow walkway.

"Ole Swenson?" said Murphy. That's a knee-slapper, friend. No, it is old man Murphy who runs it, the cantankerous old crank. Slave driver, he is. Murphy's cook ain't no good, neither. The old grouch makes you listen to him readin' the Bible, docks your pay for every cussword, and makes you sleep two to the bunk, besides. I am tellin' you, friend, you do not want to work for mean old man Murphy."

"Dang! Thanks for the tip-off. A fella don't always know what he has stepped in till he finds himself stuck knee-deep in the muck. But, how is it you work for him? Must be some reason you boys stay with him. How is the pay?"

"Fair. At least it's fair when he forks over. He is one of those who takes what he wants and divvies up the leftovers. One year he told us he run out of money and we would need to wait till fall for our pay. When one of our teamsters told him that his barn and office would soon be set afire, he suddenly found more money and paid up on the spot."

"Dang! I'm sure glad we bumped into you, friend. We will stay clear of the One-eyed-Moose. Well, Swede, you and me best be movin' on. Say, friend, you never did tell us just why it is that you work for this Murphy character."

"We got here late last December after most all the hirin' was over with. Rest of the outfits were pretty near full up. Say, how far downstream you headed today?"

"Us? Oh, we are s'posed to hang near the bend above the Cable trestle. The logs tend to bunch up on the first bend downstream."

"Okay, then. You fellas watch yourselves now. When you see the train cross that trestle, wave to the ladies in the passenger cars for me, will ya?"

"Ya, ya!" shouted Swede. "Ve vave plenty."

Billy found his picaroon. "That, Timothy Murphy, was quite the yarn you spun."

"William, as long as they see us here, movin' logs downstream, they have no reason to suspect anything. We are merely two more river pigs, pushin' logs and tryin' to make a livin'. The only time we need be concerned about getting caught is when we are seen pullin' one of the logs up to the pond."

"So, why did I have to hide my picaroon?"

"A picaroon has no use to a log driver. Pike poles and Peaveys are the tools of the trade out here. Any fella that uses a picaroon is bound to be up to no good. Now, what say we stab ourselves another twenty-dollar-bill?"

<>O<>

By sundown their arms and backs ached from the work. Billy's muscles, in particular, complained, unaccustomed to such strenuous, all-day labor. He sat near the fire on a stump, tossing the last of the log ends into the flames one-by-one. Murphy fetched a bottle of whiskey and a slab of smoked venison from his cabin. They ate, drank, drank more, and tallied the day's work. Old Man Murphy's One-eyed Moose lumber camp floated eight hundred dollars' worth of pine downstream on the first day.

"This is one gol-dang quick way to reap the benefits of the timber harvest, Murphy. Why is it there ain't a lotta other fellas doin' the same?"

"There are some out there. No one knows just how many. Most are so careful that nobody ever knows about 'em."

"What about those who get found out?"

"Well now, I have heard a tale or two, about others gettin' pinched. Not often, though. You see, Billy, the lumber companies don't like word gettin' out that someone figured a way to cut in on their profits so they try to keep it on the hush when they catch someone. I s'pose there's no tellin' how many get caught."

"The men who do get caught—what happens to them?"

"If a fella's lucky enough to be turned over to the law, he'll get by with a small fine. You see, the judge has no way to be sure how much of the fine should go to this camp or that, so the county just keeps the money. Works out good for them, so they don't mind lettin' the thief off with no time in the hoosegow."

"What about those caught by the drive bosses?"

"Well now, that's a bit more serious. I keep a wad of cash hidden in a stump that I can trade for me life if it comes to that. Never had to use it yet. If I did get nabbed, I figure I could offer a drive boss a winter's pay and he would take it with a grin and a tip of his hat. Those log pinchers that have no way to buy their way out, no poke to trade, well, they usually disappear."

"Disappear?"

"Drowned, usually. Beat to a pulp then drowned. By the time a man makes it downstream a mile or two, he has been pounded so much by these pines that he cannot be recognized. Billy, half the men who lie buried along this river are neither identified nor does anyone have a notion how they died, or why, for that matter."

"I'm not sure I should be part of this, Timothy. I don't mind sneakin' something past the law now and then, but I am not one to stick my neck out too far."

Murphy grinned and passed the bottle. "Naw, you worry too much, Kavanaugh. We shan't be found out. Look. In two days there will be a full moon. Nobody works the river at night. Them drivers that ain't sittin' in camps, dryin' their dungarees, are sittin' in taverns. I wager we can do twice what we sent downstream today."

"All right, Murphy. All right. The money is too dang good to pass up. But you keep that wad of bills handy, just in case."

"Oh, you bet I will. And, by this time next week, I will walk into A. J. Hayward's office and lay claim to the timber receipts of old man Murphy's One-eyed Moose lumber outfit. And you, Billy Kavanaugh, will earn half of what goes in and comes out of Murphy's pocket."

<>O<>

Timothy Murphy stood with a grin before the broad, brightly polished desk of the North Wisconsin Lumber Company business manager. A line of lumber camp owners stood behind him.

"Mister Weyerhaeuser, according to me tally, I figure you have near to three-hundred-sixty logs bearin' the stamp of the One-eyed Moose."

Frederich Weyerhaeuser thumbed through his ledger. "One-eyed Moose. One-eyed Moose. Yes. Here it is, Mister Timothy Murphy. By our count you have three-hundred-and four logs in the bay. That's quite a rise over two years ago. You've expended?"

"Well, sir, you might say I doubled my crew," replied Murphy. "But I feel certain we sent more than that downstream. Where, now, would you be supposin' the rest of my logs are a-hidin'?"

"Oh, they could be 'most anywhere. Lost in the brush, sitting in some backwater, or, who knows? Maybe they fell victim to log thieves. I will tell you, Mister Murphy, unlike you and me, there are plenty of scoundrels out there not willing to put in a day's work for their wages. Pirates can lurk around any bend in the stream, you know. They get far too many logs from us honest men." Weyerhaeuser counted a stack of bills, counted it again, then slid it across the desk with a receipt. "Sign here, Mister Murphy."

"Timber pirates? In these parts? Say, now, they must be a courageous lot." Murphy stuffed the stack of bills into his pocket.

"Mister Murphy, are you not going to count that money?"

"Come now, Mister Weyerhaeuser, I know it is right. Were it your intention to swindle me, you would have simply made a slight mistake in your log count. After all, how could I dispute it? No, Frederich, there would be no point in you shavin' down this pile of bills. It is the log count you would reduce, sir. And, I agree. Pirates can lurk around any bend in the stream. Good day to you, Mister Weyerhaeuser."

Billy was waiting when Murphy stepped outside. "You got paid all right?"

"Paid? Oh, yes, they paid, although not quite as much as I expected. Still, here is your half, fair and square."

"My, my, look at that. Six days work and nearly three thousand dollars." Billy slid the bills into the inside band of his hat and plopped it onto his head. "I am off to the bank, Timothy. You too?"

"Lumberman's Bank? Oh my goodness no. Can't trust 'em. They will not see my earnin's. I have more faith in me hollow stump."

"Well, then, Timothy Murphy, you keep the wind at your back and your feet on the ground. If you are up for it and I find my way here next spring, we will do this again. Meanwhile, my friend, do us both a favor and stay clear of jealous husbands … at least till you reach the age of a hundred and one."

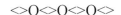

Chapter 18
Captain Dan Morgan

July 1886

Peering through brass field glasses, Deputy Frank Derkson watched the Marengo Station from his perch in a tall pine, high on the ridge. The Wisconsin Central locomotive rolled up to the depot right on schedule. Chief Namakagon, carrying a walking stick, stepped from the passenger car onto the platform, his two dogs—one black, one white—at heel. The old man took the path behind the water tower to the west tote road, disappearing around the bend.

"Ain't no way you are sneakin' off on me this time, old man. I will know where your silver is hid by suppertime." Frank stuffed his binoculars into his rucksack and climbed down.

The road wound down along the river to a shallow crossing, then ascended, cresting the next ridge. Each time the trail straightened, he caught fleeting glimpses of the Indian and his dogs. Footprints left by the soft moccasins were almost imperceptible and the trail would have been nearly impossible to follow if not for the distinct sign left by Chief Namakagon's staff. The stick's unique, round mark punctuated every other step.

About three miles west of Marengo Station, the road forked. Moccasin tracks, walking stick marks, and dog tracks, led down both trails. Confused, Derkson studied these, then flipped a coin, following the southern route. It wound down into a thick tangle of spruce and took him across a small stream, through knee-deep muck, and up another steep, rock-strewn trail to a ridge-top. The tracks vanished among those left by deer, bear, and moose. He found no sign of old Ice Feathers, his dogs, or the walking stick. Disgusted, hoping to locate his quarry again, Derkson climbed high into another pine. He scanned and scanned the hills and valleys with his binoculars, seeing no trace of the Indian or his dogs.

"Jaybird," came a shout from below the tree, "you must be lost. I have observed you following me since Marengo. Did I violate one of your many laws, Deputy?"

Slowly descending, Derkson yelled, "You know very well why I'm following you, Chief. Same reason as half-a-dozen others who want to know where your dang silver is hid."

"You will not find silver high in a pine tree, Jaybird. You might consider looking elsewhere—perhaps, say, on the ground?"

"You dassn't mock me, old man. I will find it, sooner or later. Say, how about I pay you to take me to it right now?"

"The location of the silver, if there is silver, is not mine to sell, Jaybird. It would belong to my people and to the Earth Mother. You and the others like you should seek out your own silver. Trust my words, Jaybird, if I have silver, you shall never find it."

Derkson continued his descent to the thick bed of white pine needles blanketing the forest floor, saying, "A hundred dollars if you take me there right now, old man."

Chief Namakagon and his dogs had vanished. "Dang it all!" he bellowed into the woods. "This is the third time you left me standing empty-handed, Ice Feathers. I will find it. You know I will. Mark my gol-dang words old man!"

<>O<>

Two hours later, Chief Namakagon followed the Marengo River upstream, his dogs exploring every stone, twig, and track along the way. The river brought him to a narrow gorge and the mineral claim of Captain Dan Morgan.

"Boozhoo," he shouted as he neared the mine entrance. "Captain Morgan, it is Mikwam-migwan come to visit."

"Mikwam-migwan," came a shout from within a shallow cavern. Dan Morgan, slapping his hat on his dust-covered coat, stepped out, squinting in the daylight. "Welcome to my humble camp. I plum run out 'a coffee, but I will boil up some tea if you have time to sit a spell."

"Time?" said the chief, "Time I have, Captain. I may move

slower than in years past, but time is a gift I still enjoy. And sharing it by the fire with a friend is, in my mind, a fine way to spend it."

"I swear I must look like a leftover Johnny Reb 'neath all this here dirt." A cloud of dust surrounded him as he slapped, snorted, and spit. "The men I led against General Lee would laugh if they found me wearing gray instead of blue." He placed a pot of water on the hot coals of the campfire. "You headin' off to your diggin's, Chief?"

"My diggings? Ah, then you know, too."

"'Fraid so."

"Seems there is no rest for these old bones. Ever since that newspaperman, George Thomas, announced that I paid for some medicine with silver, I have been … haunted. They follow me everywhere I go—everywhere. Even to the latrine. No, I cannot travel to my silver by day. And my old eyes are no longer reliable in the forest at night. But, tell me, Captain, how is the Earth Mother treating you? Is she offering up any bits and pieces of wealth?"

"Yeah, well, you will not see any claim jumpers after my riches, if that's what you mean. Oh, I've been able to get by. But, the gold vein I was followin' last month played out. Stopped cold, it did. Vanished. I was hopin' it would branch out into a lode. No such luck."

"This is a story often told by miners here, Dan Morgan. Old Wenebojo has a hand in this trickery, you know."

"Wenebojo? The spirit? Bah!"

"He tempts miners with a fleeting glitter of gold or silver, knowing their thirst for wealth will pull them away from home and family. The miner's life is one of contradiction. Searching for the easy life, a miner soon finds himself working harder than ever, often earning far less."

"And you think your Wenebojo has a hand in this?"

"Oh yes, Wenebojo is a mischief-maker all right, especially when he senses greed. Miners, those who dig down into the Earth Mother's womb, are of particular interest to him, being the son of the same Earth Mother. He has little patience for those who violate her. Very little."

"But, you take silver from your mine, do you not?"

"Never without reverence. Those who understand the way of my people know the Earth Mother provides many treasures—the air and waters, the trees, the sun, stars, and moon—all that surrounds us. It is there for us to enjoy—to share. Like nectar for the bees, she offers us her abundance. She allows us to pluck what she offers so we may sustain ourselves, nourish our bodies, gain strength that we may serve her. But she will not suffer having her wealth destroyed by those who want more than their share."

"Nonsense, my friend, the abundance of ore under these hills is here for anyone to take, provided the taker is willin' to work for it."

"To take, yes. But not forsake. Would you cut down the tree in order to get the brightest apple? Would you drain a river to harvest the fish?"

"Dang it all, Chief, if one man doesn't take the easy pickin's, another man will. Early bird gets the worm, ol' friend. Ever hear of that?"

"The Anishinabe have long lived by such words. They rose early to harvest the bounty of the land, then shared that bounty with others. Look at what your ancestors have done. Great forests once standing across Europe are all but gone. The rivers and lakes are spoiled—all to make a very few very wealthy. No wonder so many Whites come here to live. How long before this land suffers the same consequence?"

"No, Namakagon, you are wrong. This land is so rich, so thick with fish and game, so fertile, why, the time will never come when these treasures fade. Take your white pine. They say it will take a thousand years to cut down the Wisconsin pinery. A thousand years! By then, other trees will grow. It will never end."

"I have heard these words. But, Captain, have you noticed how fast the pine vanishes from our hills and valleys? Have you seen how wasteful most lumber companies are—eager to gain the greatest wealth in the shortest time? A thousand years? More like fifty."

"What about us who come here, then fall in love with this land? Why, I would never do anything to harm our woods and waters."

"Yes. You respect the woodlands and waters. However, many come only for profit, leave only waste. They care neither about the future of these lands nor those who depend on them to survive."

"Your Wenebojo does nothing to those who plunder."

"His ways are not easily explained. Wenebojo knows no restraints of time and place. Some who squander Earth's gifts soon feel his reprisal. Others? In time. But know, Captain, all who suffer insult on the Earth Mother shall, one day, themselves suffer."

"Hogwash!"

"You have seen this, Captain Morgan. You have stepped from your mine to hear the cold wind whip across the valleys and hills clear-cut by the lumber companies. With the trees gone, the rain and snow and sleet sting your face more than before. The soil runs into the streams and lakes, killing the fish. Songbirds that once made their nests here are no longer. These are minor problems and discomforts we see now. Over time the changes will be more severe. All are the result of pain suffered by the Earth Mother. Wenebojo delivers nothing man has not earned by his actions, his treatment of the earth and each other."

"My claim does little harm to the earth."

"You are right. You and the others with small mines have little impact on the land and waters. I doubt you risk the wrath of Wenebojo by taking metals from your mine. You are collecting only what is there—what comes of your hard work. But when the miners use blasting powder and dynamite deep in the womb of the Earth Mother, when their actions fill our streams with mud, flood our lands, kill our fish, and cause the deer and bear to take flight, that's when skies darken for all people. No, Dan Morgan, take what you find. Harvest what the Earth Mother offers, but take it gently—not in greed. Take it because it is there to sustain you. Then, like late summer blackberries in your pail, share your bounty that others might also benefit. One day, all will abide by these words and the dark skies shall be lifted."

"Dang it if your words don't ring true. It ain't what we were taught growin' up, but, you are right. It only makes sense to care for the land. I just hope ol' Wenebojo ain't watchin' if I slip up now and then."

"We all slip up now and then, Captain. Wenebojo knows the difference." Chief Namakagon stood, motioning to his dogs. "I must go now. I expect the deputy will soon stumble up the river. When he arrives, mention I was here and point in the direction I now go. Will you do that for me?"

"I surely will, if that's your pleasure."

"Oh, it will please me, my friend. Animosh, come!"

Captain Dan Morgan watched old Ice Feathers cross the river, walking stick in hand and dogs running ahead. They soon vanished among towering white pines high on the hill.

Carrying his walking stick now, Chief Namakagon circled, again crossing the Marengo River. Knowing Derkson would not find his track, he headed for the Loken camp, a half-day south.

Within a quarter hour, a glance behind showed another man following. Namakagon sighed. "Makade, Waabishki, this tires me so. If these men worked as hard looking for their own silver as they do seeking mine, we would all be far better off." He laid his staff on the trail. "Enough of this," he said to his dogs. "Animosh, hide!" Waabishki and Makade disappeared into the woods. Chief Namakagon hid.

As the man reached for the walking stick, a shadow fell over him. He looked up into the eyes of a great, black makwaa with a diamond-shaped, white blaze on its chest. The bear stood on its hind legs, its huge, sharp-clawed paws well within reach of the treasure hunter. Frozen with fear, the man trembled, turned white, and fainted.

As dusk fell, the man stirred. Recalling the sight of the bear, he sprang to his feet and ran down the trail shouting at nothing there.

Miles to the south, Waabishki, Makade, and Ogimaa Mikwam-migwan, walking stick in hand, entered the Namakagon Timber Company yard. Hearing loons calling from the lake, the old Indian smiled, imagining them laughing at the events of his day. He called back softly, yearning for a life as simple as theirs.

Chapter 19
Billy Kavanaugh, Flimflam Man

July 1886

When the front door of the Uptown Saloon crashed open, the mare tethered to the rail tore free and raced down the dusty street. Glass shattering, Billy Kavanaugh flew across the pine-plank sidewalk into the dirt. His derby hat soon followed, along with rolling laughter from the men in the tavern.

"Take your worthless mining shares somewhere else, Kavanaugh," shouted someone from inside. "We know there ain't no silver on your forty and we ain't about to line your pockets for shares in a mine that ain't dug!"

"And never gonna be dug, neither, ya two-bit pole cat!" yelled another man.

Billy gathered his certificates from the rutted street, stuffing them into his coat pockets. Brushing off dust, he plopped his crumpled hat on his head and mustered his remaining dignity before moving on to the next tavern. Summer was here and he had yet to sell any of the ten thousand shares of his speculative mining company—shares he had printed two years earlier. "High time I fine me a new fiddle for unloading this dang mining stock," he muttered.

He peeked through the front window of Pete Foster's Saloon, then entered, confident in appearance, apprehensive within.

"Say, ain't you John Kavanaugh's boy," said a huge man with a thick, black beard.

Billy back-stepped to the door, ready to run. "Who's askin'?"

"Name is Blackie Jackson. Me, your pa and your little brother all work at the same lumber camp—Namakagon Timber Company—Olaf Loken's outfit.

The bartender poured Blackie another beer and turned to Billy. "What'll you have, sonny?"

"Glass of port, if you have it."

"Make it a mug, Pete," said Blackie. "Go ahead and drop a couple hens' eggs in it, too. This young fella looks like he needs a meal."

"I am most obliged for your concern, Blackie, but …"

"Pete, you got any pickled pigs' feet in the crock?"

"Some."

"Bring 'em over here—the whole crock. Looks to me like the boy needs somethin' solid in his belly."

"Pigs' feet?" said Billy. "Why, funny you should mention 'em. That's what we ate up in Marengo when my diggings came in. Pickled pigs' feet and Hamm's beer. 'Fore the night was out, I had nine new investors."

Blackie squinted. "Investors? Investors in what?"

"Like I said. My diggings, my mining claim."

"Your what?"

"You know, gold, silver, copper. I got me a mining operation up near Marengo"

"Gold, you say?" All eyes in the tavern turned to Billy.

"Gold, silver, copper ..."

"Bullfeathers."

"Oh, it's real all right, Blackie."

"Why you sellin' it off then? Seems like you been dealt a pat hand and you are throwin' aside the best cards."

"I ain't cut out for it, Blackie. Too much work for one man to handle so I'm sellin' it off cheap, sharing the wealth."

Blackie squinted at him, raising one eyebrow. "So you say."

"Yep. A fella could get rich up in my diggin's. Rich as a king."

"Sounds too good to ..."

"Look, Blackie. Look here." Billy reached in his pocket and laid a wrinkled stock certificate on the bar. "Boney-fide shares. E Pluribus Unum. Anno Domini. Legal and binding, free and clear and marked right there with the words, "In God We Trust.' You do believe in God, do you not?"

"Say," said a grime-covered railroad worker far down the bar, "I could not help overhearin'. Where did you say your diggin's are?"

"Marengo River country. Not far from the Northern Belle Mine."

"Northern Belle?" said Pete. "Why, ain't that the gold mine everybody is jawin' about?"

"There ain't no gold 'round here," mumbled a teamster into his beer.

"Bullfeathers!" replied the rail. "That Northern Belle operation has been shippin' high grade gold ore down to Chicago for three years now. Somebody's gettin' rich, I'd say. Gol-dang rich, at that."

"Yep," said Billy. "I would wager you can find four, five, maybe six hundred men up there in the Marengo River Valley, all lining their pockets with silver and gold. Yessir."

Pete Foster placed the mug of port wine before Billy and cracked two raw eggs into it.

"To the Northern Belle," said Billy. "May she continue to make men rich overnight." He slugged the drink down, wiping his chin with his sleeve.

"Boy, oh boy," said the teamster, "what I would not give to get in on somethin' like that. Pete, give this fella another drink, will ya?"

"Why, much obliged, friend." Suppressing the urge to make his sales pitch, Billy pulled the pickled foot of a pig from the Redwing crock.

Pete poured Blackie another beer, saying, "I see a few of those miners here in my tavern now and again. Out on a bender, usually. I must say, they always got money to burn when they come to town. I been thinkin' 'bout filin' a claim myself."

Billy bit into the pork. "What is holdin' you back, Pete?" He spit a bone onto the floor.

"Well, problem is I would not have a ghost of an idea where to go. A man cannot just start diggin' hither and thither, you know. Takes a fella with experience to point the way. So, how'd you find your claim, anyway?"

"Me? Oh, I ran into a miner who said he got tired of life in the wilderness. Wanted to spend his riches elsewhere—Chicago, St. Paul, Milwaukee. Said there was nothin' here to spend his money on. So, I offered to buy him out—lock, stock, and barrel. I spent a pretty penny on it, I did."

"Wish I could be so gol-dang fortunate as to lay my hands on a mining claim," said the teamster. "What I would not give for …"

"Fellas," Billy piped in, pulling a stack of crumpled mining shares from his coat pocket. "I got just the thing for you. Like I said, my claim up there in the gold country is far and away more than I need for myself. And, look at me. Do I look like a man fit to swing a pick? You seem like good, honest men. Let me give you a chance to get in on it while the gettin' is good. I'm offerin' you each a stake in my operation."

"Free and clear?" asked the teamster.

"Dang near, fellas."

"Up in Marengo River country?"

"Best mineral country around."

"How much, then?"

"Dollar a share. Take as many as you see fit."

"Dollar a share? That's all you are asking?"

"Like I say, boys, I have enough and figure it's time to spread the wealth."

"I s'pose other fellas are already workin' the claim, no?"

"No, not as yet. Soon, though. Course, first men in the diggin's will get pick of the litter, cream of the crop. That's how it works in the ol' silver and gold mine game."

"What did you say your name was?" asked the rail.

"Hmm? Billy. Billy Kavanaugh."

"Kavanaugh," said Pete, "just how many shares you plan on ...?"

The teamster set his empty beer mug on the bar. "Kavanaugh," he muttered. He turned to Billy. "Kavanaugh. Kavanaugh. Where have I heard that name?"

"We got some Kavanaughs in our camp," said Blackie. "Fact is, this fella is related. I can vouch for his pa, John."

"No," said the teamster, "that ain't it. I seen that name someplace else." He pulled a wad of papers from his pocket. "Here! Here it is, William Kavanaugh, Esquire. Signed right here on this gol-dang worthless hospital scrip! Is that you? Is this your sign, Mister?"

"Me? No, well, yes, but the hospital is responsible for those scripts, not ..."

"I bought this from some gol-dang preacher last fall. Cost me five bucks. Then, when I busted my gol-dang arm not a month later, the Ashland Hospital told me the funds were all used up. Gone. Spent. They sent me on my way, busted arm and all. The way I see it, Kavanaugh, you owes me four dollars for the doctorin' and twelve dollars for the hospital stay. Better add another five for this useless hospital scrip, too, gol-dang it."

Billy gulped down his wine. "Well, that's betwixt you and the hospital, friend. I am a mere salesman. I cannot be expected to ..."

"Twenty-one dollars, Kavanaugh. That's what you owe and that's what you are gonna pay.'"

"I would like to help you out, my friend, but I am a little short of cash at the moment. Tell you what, though, I can pay you right now in mining shares." He started counting them out on the bar. "Lady Luck is smilin' on you, my friend. Why, with this much stock, you will be sittin' on easy street in no time—no time at all. Fifteen, sixteen, seventeen ..."

"Wait a while, sonny. How do I know your gol-dang shares are not as worthless as your gol-dang hospital scrip?"

"Sir, are you suggesting ..."

"I ain't suggesting nothin', sonny. I am sayin' outright that you and that paper you are peddlin' is downright worthless. Admit it, sonny. Worthless. No good, just like you."

"What about it, Kavanaugh," said Pete, "you tryin' to sell us worthless mining shares?"

"Worthless? No, no, they are not worthless. I mean ... well ... it is Marengo River country. There is gold and silver a-plenty 'round there." He edged toward the door.

The railroad man grabbed Billy by the collar. "Hold on there, William Kavanaugh, Esquire." He turned to the others. "Fellas, looks to me like this fella is tryin' his best to swindle us honest folks any way he can. I say it's high time we made an example of one of these here charlatans. I work for my pay and I am gol-dang tired of scoundrels like this tryin' to swindle me every time I turn 'round. I say it's time for a tar and featherin'."

With a jerk, Billy tore free from the railroad worker's grip, kicking the rail in the shin. A shove sent the man into the crock on the bar. The crock slid, tipped, and spewed vinegar, onions, and pickled pigs' feet down the bar, splashing onto the rail's grease-stained coat and britches, and running into his boots.

Billy dashed down the length of the bar with the railroad man close behind, dripping juice, scattering pork and onions across the floor. The teamster grabbed the crock and flung it toward Billy just as Pete rushed around the end of the bar closest to the door. The crock hit Pete square in the chest, throwing him and more pigs' feet to the floor. Billy jumped over him, crashed through the door, ran onto the street, and raced toward the depot.

In the bar, the rail let go a long string of cusswords as he came to his feet, then slipped on pickle juice and fell again.

Blackie Jackson burst out laughing.

"Who you think you're laughin' at, bark eater?" yelled the railroad man.

Blackie couldn't catch his breath to reply.

"Nobody laughs at me, by gum!" The rail's fist flashed through the air.

As Blackie raised his right arm to block the blow, the beer mug he held slipped from his fingers and flew into the air toward the teamster, also struggling to his feet. It caught the teamster in the head, sending him to the slippery floor again.

The incensed rail took a second swing at Blackie.

Still laughing, Blackie ducked, causing the railroad man to slip again, falling back into Blackie who lifted him by the armpits like a rag doll and plopped him on the bar.

"Gol-dang you, bark eater!" shouted the rail, winding back for another poke. "I will learn you to tangle with an Omaha Railway man!"

Now roaring with laughter, Blackie reached down, grabbed him by the boots and tipped him back, dropping the rail head-first onto the floor behind the bar.

Near the door, Pete stood up and, looking into the mirror over the back bar, straightened his collar. He plucked a piece of pickled pork from his sleeve, took a bite, then tossed the rest back in the crock. Grinning at Blackie, still doubled over with laughter, Pete let go a belly-laugh of his own. The other two men looked at Pete, then Blackie, then each other, and they, too, burst into laughter.

As Pete Foster stepped behind the bar to pour another round, Blackie caught his breath long enough to say, "I'll tell ya, Peter, I ain't had such a gol-dang good time since ... well ... since I just cannot remember when." He turned to the others. "Say, if either of you fellas ever run into that silver-tongued charlatan again, you be sure to thank him for me, will ya? Well ... thank him right before you ring his gol-dang, mud-suckin' neck!"

Chapter 20
Doctor Henry White

July 1886

The heavy glass door of Doctor White's Second Street Apothecary swung closed behind Billy Kavanaugh. The large front windows shook when it slammed.

Before him, Billy saw a narrow aisle flanked floor to ceiling by jam-packed wooden shelves. Both right and left, the shelves sagged under the weight of hundreds of tin canisters, identical if not for hand-written paper labels. Among these tins stood almost as many bottles, some brown, some green, some clear, each capped with cork or glass stoppers. The room had a peculiar odor of pungent herbs combined with noxious chemicals, concoctions created by the good chemist, Henry White.

"Doc?" Billy called.

No reply.

"Doctor Henry White? Are you there?"

Billy stepped to the counter, finding a small, brass bell. He shook it vigorously. "Doctor White!" he called again.

The faint sound of footsteps ascending a wooden stairway came from far in the back. Down the dimly lit aisle, Doctor Henry White emerged from the darkness.

"Doctor White, is that you?"

"Well, of course it is! Who in tarnation did you think would show up when you called my name?"

A short, fat man wearing a white apron and collarless shirt waddled to the front of the store. Standing in sunlight streaming through the large store windows, he slapped his apron. A cloud of powdery dust rose to envelop him.

"What is it you need, young fellow? Be quick, now, I must return to my mixing table. I feel I may be on to a cure for gout. Or perhaps baldness. I do not yet know."

"Doc, I have been sent here by a Mister Vaughn. He said you would ..."

"Vaughn? Samuel Vaughn?"

"Yes. Sam told me ..."

"Then you are not here for medicine, I take it?"

"No sir. No, I am here for ..."

"Vaughn! Why, if that old snapping turtle sent you here to try to get me to sell my share of his mine, let me tell you, young man, it's a fool's errand you are on. Furthermore, both you and he are wasting your breath ... and my time. Good day." He turned.

"No, sir. Not that. You see ..."

"Then what is it? Speak up. Can you not see I am engaged in important work here?"

"Yes, well, I apologize for interrupting ..."

"Interrupting? Of course you are interrupting. And I greatly resent those who interrupt. Now, for Pete's sake, what is it you want?"

"Mister Vaughn said you might ..."

"It is a significant social ill, you know."

"Sir?"

"Interrupting."

"Oh. Um ... yes. I suppose it ..."

"A sign of very poor upbringing."

"Yes."

"We see a lot of it nowadays. Interrupting, I mean."

"I suppose we do, sir. But back to my reason for coming ..."

"Never used to be that way when I was young. People showed more respect for each other. Why, back then I would not dream of ..."

"Interrupting. Yes, I know, Doctor White."

"Hmm? Well, as I was about to say before ... "

"Y'know, Doc, I have been from Brazil to Boston and I can tell you the problem is spreading like bacon grease on a hot griddle."

"You have been from Brazil to ...?"

"Wherever you go nowadays, people are interrupting. America, Mexico, Cuba, Argentina, even Peru."

"Peru? Argentina? Really? You have traveled to ..."

"I have. And you can take it from me, Doc, they all interrupt. I cannot make heads nor tails of it. But, the reason I am here is not about that or your medicines and potions. No, you see, Mister Vaughn said you might have a couple of samples of high grade silver ore I could take on my travels—to show to the natives down there. I would like to purchase a sample. You have any silver for me, Doc?"

"Silver? Yes. Yes, as a matter of fact, I do. Came from the old hermit, Namakagon. Marengo country, I suspect. Or maybe near Pratt. He would not say. Tight-lipped, that Namakagon is." Henry White reached under the counter. "He traded it for medicine—not for him, mind you. For his people. Very high grade. He brought it in just last week. Shows what is out there if a fellow is willing to look for it, no?"

Billy inspected the fist-sized samples. "How much for this one, Doc?"

"I have no plan to sell ..."

"What is it worth, Doc? Six, seven dollars?"

"Well, I should say so! At least that much. Why, it ..."

"Eight? Nine dollars, Doc?"

"Nine-fifty would be a fair ..."

"Fine. Here is a sawbuck, Doc."

"I will get your change ..."

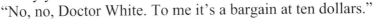

"No, Doc. You keep it."

"But, that's half-a-dollar too much. Certainly you want ..."

"No, no, Doctor White. To me it's a bargain at ten dollars."

"Well, all right, but ..."

"And, Doc, please do accept my sincere apologies.

"Accept your apologies? Apologies for ..."

"Interrupting, Doc. It's a significant social ill, you know. Good day."

The windows shook as, silver in hand, Billy Kavanaugh left through the heavy front door of Doctor Henry White's Second Street Apothecary.

<>O<>

The three-and-a-half-pound chunk of high-grade silver ore lay on the counter of the assay office.

"Mister Kavanaugh, based on this sample, I would say your mine is capable of a net yield of somewhere 'twixt ninety-five and one hundred dollars per ton. It's a rare find, sir.

"Exactly what I had hoped to hear, my good man."

"I can provide a more accurate assessment, but you will need to bring in a somewhat larger sample."

"Oh, no, that shan't be necessary at this time. If you will be kind enough to give me a written estimate of that yield you just quoted, it will do for my present needs."

"Consider it done, sir. That'll be seventy-five cents. Anything else?"

"Yes. I wonder if I could ask a small favor. I have taken a room across the street at the Royale. I see by the sign on your door that you close at six o'clock. If you would be so kind as to bring both my estimate and my ore sample to me there after work, I will sweeten that amount by two dollars and buy you a whiskey to boot."

"Two dollars, sir?"

"Not enough?"

"Oh, no sir. Two dollars will do fine."

"Very well. Six o'clock then."

<>O<>

The Hotel Royale barroom was crowded well before six. Billy found a place to lean near the end of the bar and ordered two shots of Old Crow. The assay agent walked in, spotted Billy, and placed the assay estimate face-up on the bar with the ore sample on top. The bartender and several men at the bar watched Billy as he moved the silver and read the paper.

"Holy Mother of God in Heaven!" shouted Billy, turning to the assayer. "Mister, you sure this is right?"

Everyone turned.

"Well, um, yes. Yes, that's what we ..."

"Hoorah! Hoorah! I struck it big! My silver claim has finally come in!" yelled Billy into the room. "Bartender!, Here is a double sawbuck. Drinks are on me—me and my silver claim!"

"Three cheers for this young fella," shouted a well-dressed man wearing a tall top hat. "Hip hip ..."

"Hoorah!"

"Hip hip ..."

"Hoorah!"

"Hip hip ..."

"*Hoorah!*"

<>O<>

Billy left the bar at the Hotel Royale at eight-thirty, every share of his Marengo forty in the pockets of others and their money in his. Dodging a beer wagon, he strolled toward Front Street, looking for a restaurant where he could celebrate the success of his recent venture. The restaurant he chose was off the lobby of the Chequamegon Hotel.

"Champagne," he said to the waiter. "Your best champagne, at that. What do you recommend for fish, tonight?"

"The whitefish is fresh," came a deep voice from behind. "I brought it in just this forenoon."

Billy turned. The man at the next table wore a gold-corded hat and the long, double-breasted, blue coat of a sea captain, complete with bright, brass buttons.

"Delicious, too. Had it for dinner and orderin' it for supper, I am. The cook here knows his way 'round a galley, I would venture."

"Waiter," said Billy, "I will have the whitefish." He turned again. "What port you hail from, Captain?"

"Cleveland."

"Steamer?"

The sailor bristled. "Bah! I cannot stand the smell of burnt coal, sir. No, you will not catch me on one of those smoke-belchin' barges. It is canvas for me, sir."

"A schooner, then?"

"Aye. And a fine one she is, too."

"Two-master?"

"Three. And enough sail to keep any steamer far to me wash, assumin' the wind is right."

"I hired out a three-master once." said Billy. "I was runnin' coffee and bananas from Brazil up to New Orleans. That haul was more pleasure than work, other than the spiders that stowed away in the bananas."

"Ya? Ever get bit?"

"Never bit, but there was many a night when I'd wake up with one crawlin' in my hammock. The mere thought of it gives me a chill."

"Of late, I hang tight to the Great Lakes," said the captain. "Plenty of ore to haul. Good money. Andrew Carnegie sees to that."

"May I share your table, Captain …?"

"Lloyd. Captain George Lloyd of the *Lucerne*—the finest schooner on the western Great Lakes. And, yes, please do join me, young man. Maybe we can swap a tale."

Many stories later, the waiter brought a third bottle of wine for Billy and a second pint of brandy for the captain.

"So, William, what made you shed your sea legs for work here?"

"Plenty of money in the pinery, Captain. I have dabbled in some ventures here. Done all right, too, I suppose. But, Captain, after speaking with you tonight, I realize I have been away from the sea far too long. The shipping trade is where the money is. I have had my fill of woodticks and man-eatin' mosquitoes. High time I returned to the work I enjoy best."

"Ever consider iron?"

"Captain?"

"Iron Ore. A dozen trains a day haul it down from the Bessemer mines. Most every shipload ends up in Cleveland or one of the cities 'long Lake Erie. Easy runs they are. Short enough that a man can see his wife and little ones now and then but long enough that a man can get away from them, too. I will be makin' for Cleveland in two days, matter of fact. A week in port there, and I will soon be droppin' anchor in Chequamegon Bay again. What could be better?"

"Money to be made, Captain?"

"Money? I should say so! Andrew Carnegie money, William."

"Sir, your words have a nice ring to 'em. So, when can a fellow make the most profitable of runs?"

"Mister Kavanaugh, few know this, but the big companies shy away from runs in the late season, due to the risk of gettin' froze in for the winter. That's when old Andrew Carnegie pays the most. The later in the season you haul, the more money you make. Course you would need a sizeable loan to hire a ship."

"Loan? Oh, Captain Lloyd, there would be no trouble getting a loan. I have a friend I could interest in this proposition. Well-to-do, he is. No sir. No trouble with financing. So, late in the shipping season is more profitable, you say?"

"Aye. The later, the better, long as you don't find yourself froze up for the winter. November and December runs pay the most."

"Your *Lucerne* is available for booking then, Captain?"

"She is, William. Ship, captain, and crew."

"Well, then, Captain Lloyd, I do believe this chance meeting may well be the work of fate. My brain is a bit befuddled from the wine at the moment. How about you and I meet here for breakfast? We can make a pact to thumb our noses at Old Man Winter and make us a small fortune. What say you, Captain George Lloyd?"

"I say, 'aye, aye,' Mister Kavanaugh, 'aye, aye!'"

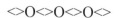

Chapter 21
The Mason Mill

September 1886

"Here you go, Clyde." Ingman Loken handed his ticket to the conductor. Clyde Williams punched the ticket four times.

"Heading for Mason, I see."

"Ya. Looking at buying a mill there."

"On the White River?"

"Right across from the landing."

"Oh, Andrew Hanover's mill. My brother works there. They sure put up a lot of pine."

"That's what I am counting on, Clyde. Olaf and me need a mill close to the Omaha line so we can ship our pine out with ease. Many-a camp drive logs down the White these days. But it's a long haul to Lake Superior. Mason sits right in the way, a perfect place for a man to snag that pine, mill it, and send it our by rail. It's a chance for a man to make his own fortune."

The train rumbled north through a large cutover, crossed a wide marsh, and climbed the grade to the Mason depot. Ingman stepped from the passenger car and followed the road to the river. A narrow iron bridge over the river and steep road took him up the hill to the mill where he met with Sven Severson, the mill foreman.

"She's a fine sawmill, she is, Mister Loken. Mister Hanover would say the same were he here. He rarely shows up 'fore dinnertime."

"That's fine, Mister Severson. I figure I can learn more from the men on the floor than the fella behind the desk. If I like what I see, I will meet with Mister Hanover later. So, tell me about your mill, then."

"The boss set it up in seventy-nine. Had it hauled piece-by-piece from Lake Superior. Came up the White River on barges pulled by horses. Took us all summer, it did. Lost two horses and one man bringin' all this upstream. Good horses, too. Percherons. Worth the trouble, I s'pose. This sawmill runs like a ten dollar watch, she does. All water powered, mind you. No need for a steam engine."

"And your yield?"

"On a good day, we mill, oh, seventy, eighty thousand board feet, though it could be more. Once, just to see what we could do, we made a hundred and ten thousand in one shift. Couldn't do that regular, though. Too hard on the men to keep up such a pace."

"That's less than half of what A. J. Hayward's mill makes."

"Oh, there is no chance we could catch up to the Hayward operation. See, Mister Hanover holds tight to a twelve-hour day, Monday through Saturday. Now, if a fella wanted, he could run twenty-four hours and double our yield. Of course, he would have to double the crew. Would not hurt none to put in them new Disston saws, neither. They cut like a hot knife through a lard."

"How many workers you employ?"

"Inside, eight sawyers, one mechanic, one sweeper, and one foreman, that would be me. Outside I have one tallyman and two pond men sortin' logs and five yard men haulin' and stackin'. That's about it. Oh, I forgot one—Mister Hanover's nephew. He helps out here when he's not down at the tavern. He gets paid half-a-dollar a day straight from Mister Hanover's pocket so we don't see the need to keep him on the company books."

"Nineteen men. My, that's quite a crew."

"Walter Wimbly, our bookkeeper, makes it twenty. He keeps to the front office. Two days a week, only."

"Twenty men. And your total cost for labor?"

"You will have to ask the boss about that. He will show you the books. The other day I heard him complainin' it cost him thirty-seven dollars per day in labor, though I have my doubts. He is tight as the bark on a dang oak tree."

"You know what's the mill's income after the lumber camps get paid for the timber?"

"Oh, I figure Mister Hanover makes four hundred to five-fifty per day, more or less. All depends on the timber market and shipping. Most of our pine ends up in St. Louis and Kansas City nowadays. Where it goes from there I wouldn't know."

"Any other expenses I should be made aware of?"

"Hmm. Mister Hanover greases a few palms of inspectors who come sniffin' around. You know, the regulars. Calls these his 'insurance' expenses. Says it protects his business. Truth is it keeps the county out of his business. Keeps his ne'er-do-well nephew out of jail, too. If you ask me, we would all be better off if his nephew was in jail and out of our way here in the mill."

"Is that it, then? No other expenses I need know about?"

"No, that about covers it, Mister Loken."

The foreman walked Ingman through the factory. Below, near the river, logs floating downstream were guided by men with pike poles to a holding pond. From there, the logs were pushed into sluices and measured for length and girth by a tally man with a log scale before being fed onto steel log carriers. A conveyor with sharp hooks gripped the logs, lugging them, end-first to a sawyer in the mill whose saw trimmed one side flat, discarding the unwanted slab and sawdust onto another conveyer.

Using a cant hook, the sawyer turned the log, trimming flat the next side and repeated this until a squared pine timber remained. The timber, caught again by hooks, was dragged toward a gang saw that sliced it lengthwise into two-inch planks. A third conveyor belt took the planks to the next saw where each plank was sliced into narrower boards before being sent out to the yard for stacking and drying. The constant drone of spinning flywheels powering the gang saws made conversation difficult.

"All right, Sven," shouted Ingman, "I have seen plenty. High time I make tracks if I hope to catch the southbound back to Pratt. You tell Mister Hanover to come up with his askin' price and get it to me. You let him know that, if it's low enough to cause the Namakagon Timber Company to be curious, he might yust see me stoppin' back for a chat. I best be on my way, Sven. My train is due in soon."

Ingman left the sawmill, headed for the station. Crossing the narrow bridge spanning the White River, he heard, behind, the rumble of an approaching rig. He turned. Racing down the hill came a horse team pulling a wagon. He ran for the far end of the iron bridge. Glancing over his shoulder, Ingman realized he could not make it across in time. He lunged over the rail, plunging into the river, narrowly missing the logs floating downstream. The river's current swept him into submerged rocks. He swam with all his might for shore. Suddenly, crushed between two logs, he felt his arm go numb. Ingman jerked his arm free and dove under the logs. Resisting urges to surface for air, he scrambled along the riverbed under the logs until he reached quiet water near shore. Ingman waded out, collapsing on the ground with the roar of the White River in his ears. Seconds later, he sprang to his feet, found his hat, and ran up the hill looking for the teamster responsible for the runaway rig. No wagon there, he stopped at the first tavern, dripping wet.

"Old Crow, double it up," he said to the bartender, whose hands and apron were covered with feathers and blood. "Bartender, you happen to notice a wagon go by? Real fast? Say, yust about five, maybe ten minutes ago?"

"Cannot say as I did," replied the bartender, wiping his hands on his apron and pouring the drink. "I been butcherin' chickens. You miss your ride, Mister?"

"More like he missed me." Ingman laid a dime on the bar.

"Say, how is it you are so wet?"

"Wet? Me? Oh, ya. I yust took a dip in the White to cool off some. You sure you didn't see nor hear a rig go by?"

"No sir. Like I say, I been butcherin' chickens. Out back on the stoop. Maybe you should check over to the depot, ya?"

"Ya. I will do that."

Ingman downed his whiskey and headed for the depot, boots sloshing at each step. Finding no wagon, no horse team, he boarded the southbound seconds before it rolled out of the Mason yard. Still soaked, he sat watching the landscape rush by, rubbing his injured arm, and wondering about that wagon.

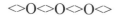

Chapter 22
Engine N$^{\underline{0}}$ 99

September 1886

A silent rain fell across the pinery through the chilly September night, soaking the lush, boreal forest. The showers stopped after dawn. Patches of blue sky strained for a stronghold as bright beams of sunlight stabbed through the hazy mist.

Tor climbed into the cab of the Namakagon Timber Company's locomotive number ninety-nine, purchased from the Omaha Railroad Company. He joined Klaus Kerwetter, a teamster turned engineer. Behind the huge, black engine, the tender car was stacked high with hardwood slabs for fuel. Seventeen cars came next, each loaded with white pine timber headed south to sawmills in Chippewa Falls, Eau Claire, and Menomonie. Farthest down the track, the last car carried the latest Namakagon Timber Company investment, a steam loader. Permanently mounted on a flatcar, it could lift the heaviest of pine logs on and off the railcars.

"Klaus, have you seen my Uncle Ingman? I swear he said he wanted me to join him here today."

"Ingman? Oh, ya, ya. He vent on ahead. He told me to tell ya 'bout the change of plans. Said he vould be a-vaitin' for ya at da Pratt depot. Prob'ly on his vay dere, as we speak."

"Pratt? Did he say why?"

"Ingman said he vould go to Mason to look at some sawmill dere. Might buy it, he thought."

"Sawmill. Yep, sounds like Uncle Ingman, all right." Tor leaned out the cab window, looking down the line of cars. "Who's the brakeman?"

"Vashburn, I tink is his name. Ya, Nick Vashburn."

"You figure this Washburn knows the ropes—knows this is a steep downhill grade?"

"Oh, ya, ya, Tor. Vashburn knows railroadin'."

"How about you, Klaus? You got the hang of this hand-me-down iron horse?"

"Tor, you know vell as me I prefer usin' my oxen. But, gol-dang it, times are surely changin'. Changin' awful fast. Gust and Ingman both give me a pretty good schoolin' on the ninety-nine. Yunior, too. Say, dat vippersnapper, Junior, sure knows dese dang machines, ya?

I swear dat little fella stands a foot taller ven runnin' a steam enyun."

"So, Klaus, you are sure you know how to handle this locomotive?"

"Oh, ya. Sure as shootin'."

"You actually made a run with her?"

"Made a run? Tor, I already I made me tree runs down ta Pratt mit no problem. Ninety-nine's boiler I got stoked up real good. Old girl's got her steam up and she's a- rarin' ta roll. You comin', den?"

"You bet. Throttle up when ready, Mister Engineer."

Klaus pulled down on the brim of his hat and gave two blasts on the engine's whistle. Far behind, the brakeman leaned out, waving a flag. "All clear, den." He tapped a gauge, checking the boiler pressure one final time, opened a valve, released the air brake and firmly pulled back the hand-throttle. "Here ve go."

With a rush of steam, the huge piston, responding to the pressure, pushed the massive connecting rod rearward, turning both enormous drive wheels. They shrieked and spun on the wet rail for a moment before gaining traction, then slowly lugged the engine forward. As they did, each successive coupling in the line of cars pounded the next with a loud slam as the massive weight went into motion. Engine straining, the train crept forward, slowly gained speed, then soon rumbled northwest toward the mainline junction some twelve miles ahead on the steep downhill grade.

Pressure in the boiler soon brought the train up to a comfortable speed. Klaus backed off on the throttle, now letting gravity take over. As they approached the bend at Trappers Lake, Klaus opened the brake valve slightly. The train slowed before entering the bend.

Now, with the bend behind and a hill ahead, two whistle blasts cut through the air. The engineer spun the brake valve, closing it. Then he opened wide the throttle to make the ridge. Smoke billowing from the stack, the locomotive grunted her way up the grade, made the curve at the hilltop and started her final, three-mile descent to the station. Approaching the steepest section of track, the engineer cut back on the throttle and reached for the brake.

"Tor, give me a hand mit dis valve, ya? Seems she's stickin' a bit. Must be gummed up, some."

They tried to turn the brake valve's brass wheel as the train slowly but steadily gained speed. Grabbing a wrench, Klaus loosened, then tightened the locknut behind the valve's wheel.

"Looks to be froze up tight, Klaus. Grab that hammer. I'll turn the wheel while you give her a whack."

Tor strained to open the brake valve as the engineer slammed it with the three-pound hammer.

"Again, Klaus!"

Klaus grunted a loud grunt as he brought the hammer down on the brass valve. The wheel snapped, yet the valve remained closed.

"Lord Mother Mary help us!" Klause screamed. "Ve lost our gol-dang airbrakes!"

"Set the hand brake before she gets up too much speed."

Klaus pulled back on the lever. They heard the locomotive's steel wheels squeal against the cold rails. Smoke billowed out from behind each wheel, but the heavily laden lumber train continued to gain speed. Klaus reached up, gave three short whistles, then three long followed by three more short. He then gave a long succession of short blasts, alerting anyone down the line to clear the track.

"Klaus, the hand brakes on each car have to be set. I'll work my way back. Hope Washburn is already workin' his way forward."

"Tor, vatch out, she might not hold da track. Be set to yump!"

"Jump? No, we have to stop this train."

Trees flashed by as Tor climbed across the top of the wood-filled tender. When he saw, far behind, smoke billowing from under the flatcar, he knew the brakeman had set the hand brake and uncoupled the car. Seeing it drift back behind the rest of the train, Tor descended the ladder and stood on the coupling behind the tender. Holding on with one hand, he turned the wheel, setting the brake.

Again, smoke billowed from behind and below as he climbed to the top of the next car. Successive blasts on the engine's whistle pierced the air, followed by another round of three short, three long, and three short whistles. Tor scrambled across the logs in the next car, seeing another end car safely falling back. Knowing Nick Washburn could handle the trailing cars, Tor stood on the next coupling. He set the safety brake, then grabbed the coupling release and, with a stout jerk, freed the cars behind. The air-hose snapped and a shriek of air told him the brakes behind were now set. He watched the cars drift back. Making his way forward toward the engine again, he knew now what must be done.

"Klaus," he shouted, climbing back into the cab. "I need you to uncouple the tender. I'll handle things here."

"I am da dang enyineer, Tor. You go set free da tender."

"No, sir, Klaus. I'm taking her in. I need you to uncouple that

tender and the car behind her. Now, Klaus."

"I ain't lettin' you do my verk!"

"All right, then. You are fired!"

"Vhat?"

"Now drop those cars and stop your gol-dang bickerin'!"

Knowing he was closing in on Pratt junction, Tor pulled and pulled on the overhead chain, throwing whistle blasts down the grade ahead. With a jerk, the tender and first car uncoupled. Looking over his shoulder, he watched them drift back, Klaus Kerwetter standing on top, waving farewell.

"Klaus," yelled Tor, "You're hired again. Due for a bonus, too!"

"You dassn't wreck my ninety-nine, ya pot-licker!" Klaus replied, drifting back.

One hand sounding the whistle, the other hammering the broken valve, Tor raced toward Pratt, the locomotive still gaining speed.

Blast after whistle blast cut through the valley, echoing off the hills and alerting every lumberjack, miner, and railroad man of a pending train wreck. Tor, leaning out the window again, spotted the station ahead. Now a ferocious, iron bull, the ninety-nine screamed her warning over and over and over as she sped on, passing houses, stores, taverns and Pratt's grand hotel. People lined the street and peered from windows and doors as the great, black, belching locomotive streaked by, whistle screaming warning after warning. Far ahead, a man threw a switch before racing from the track as the ninety-nine flew past. The engine shuddered as it blew across the switched rails, through the junction, onto the mainline, across the huge trestle spanning eighteen-mile creek, and up the next grade. Tor kept up his quick whistle blasts, then felt the locomotive slow as she climbed the hill. He took a deep breath, exhaled, and finally felt his muscles relax.

The ninety-nine slowed and slowed, stopping for a moment, then began rolling back down the hill. Still with no brakes, Tor worked the throttle only enough to keep the engine's backward descent in check. The locomotive ambled downhill, crossed the trestle again, and backed down the mainline track to the station. Moments later, the boy engineer stopped engine ninety-nine next to the platform, sharing the same sense of relief as the many onlookers. Tor looked up the grade to see Klaus Kerwetter's tender and car slowly rolling toward the engine. As they did, Klaus tightened the hand brake to slow the two cars. With a loud bang, they coupled with the locomotive, bringing a round of cheers from onlookers who then noticed the rest of the train slowly rumbling toward them with Nick Washburn in control of the hand brake on the lead car. He stopped the string of loaded cars short of the station to the sound of another round of cheers filling the air.

Tor stepped onto the platform to more cheering. After a hug from his uncle and a handshake from the stationmaster, Tor and Ingman sat in the depot restaurant for a discussion of the near-catastrophe.

"Uncle Ingman, there is something that bothers me about all this. Oscar told me he had the ninety-nine refitted with those new Westinghouse airbrakes. He said they are known to never fail."

"Ya, well, there has to be a first time for everything, don't there?"

"Ya, I s'pose. But, remember winter before last, when that fella tried to wreck one of our sleighs on the downhill run to the lake?"

"Remember? Not a man in camp will soon forget that day. Why? Do you think somebody … No, Nephew, nobody wants to see our business go under no more. Ain't no timber outfit competin' with us or tryin' to do us harm. This was yust an accident. All there is to it."

"But, what about that lumber stack that almost fell on Pa?"

"Olaf was in the wrong place at the wrong time. What goes up, must come down."

"How many close calls does it take to become more than coincidence?"

"Think about it, Nephew, we have no competitors. So, who would do such a thing?"

"Maybe it's not business, Uncle. Maybe it's personal."

"Bah. You are inchin' out onto a mighty thin limb. I can't for the life of me imagine anyone wishing ill toward us. Or willin' to run the risk of gettin' caught at such a crime. Wreckin' a train? Pshaw!"

"Ya, I s'pose you are right. Pa always tells me I make too much of things. Says I am always leapin' before lookin' for the rocks in the way. Surely this was bad luck, pure and simple." Tor drank the rest of his coffee. "So, Uncle, how in blazes did you get so wet? Get caught in the rain?"

"Yumped into the gol-dang White River. You should've seen it!"

"Really? Naw, you are pullin' my leg, right?"

"Wish I was. Got run off the road by some runaway wagon. Dang near run me down on the bridge south of the Mason depot. It was a matter of choice—get run over or take to the river."

"Really? You jumped over the rail? Into the White? I'll be gol-danged. Wish I was there to see that! Quite a sight, I imagine. I can almost see the driver of that rig fishin' you from the drink right now. You must've been fit to throttle him."

"Found neither hide nor hair of him. You would think he'd come back to help—or at least see if I made it out of the rapids. I asked around and, you know, I never did find out where he come from, or where he went. I figure he had his mind on his team and yust did not see me. Oh, well, water under the bridge, in more ways than one."

"Another coincidence? You don't think this is ..."

Before Tor could finish, a switchman approached. "Don't mean to interrupt, but I figured you fellas ought to see this," he said, placing a bent steel bolt on the table. "We found it when we went to fix the shut-off valve for the air brake. It was jammed in tight. Those brakes could not have been set if Paul Bunyan himself was turnin' that brake wheel."

Tor examined the bolt, passing it to Ingman.

"Mister Loken, much as I hate to be the one to say it, this here was no accident. No sir. Some ne'er-do-well must have it in for the boy, here. Were I you, I would call in the law."

"Uncle, you were supposed to be on that train, not me. Someone has you in his sights—wants you dead. Someone is trying awful hard to make it look like an accident, too."

Ingman stared at the bent bolt in silence.

"Uncle, looks to me like whoever is behind this will do whatever it takes, even if that means wrecking a train, maybe killing other folks. Don't tell me I am again jumpin' the gun. It was guesswork before." He took the bolt from his uncle's hands. "This is evidence."

Slowly his coffee, Ingman looked into his nephew's eyes. "Tor, send a telegram to Captain Morrison at the Chicago office of the Pinkerton Detective Agency. Tell him we'd like him to yoin us on a fishin' trip. If I know Earl Morrison, he'll be on the next northbound train. You let Earl know. We will soon get to the bottom of all this."

Chapter 23
Stranger in a Brown Tweed Suit

October 1886

A tall man in a dark brown, tweed suit and matching derby hat stepped off the northbound train and entered the Cable depot. He placed his leather satchel on a bench, snapped open both clasps, and pulled out a nickel plated pocket revolver. He flipped it open. Seeing five cartridges, he snapped it closed and slowly rotated the cylinder with a click-click-click-click before slipping the handgun into the inside pocket of his coat. Satchel in hand, he stepped up to the ticket window calling, "Boy?"

There was no reply.

"Boy!" he called again.

The man in the next office replied. "Be with you in a jiffy, Mister."

A thin fellow wearing a visor stepped to the window. The sleeves of his white collarless shirt were rolled beyond his elbows and held fast by black garters. He slid his pencil behind his ear, saying, "Sir?"

"The stationmaster. Oscar Felsman. Is he on duty today?"

"Yes sir. In the next office. Checkin' in the last of the freight."

"Fetch him for me, would you?"

"Can I tell him who is asking for him, sir?"

"Just let him know an old acquaintance is asking for him."

"Right away, sir."

Oscar Felsman entered the office from the freight room door and plopped a stack of papers on his desk. "Well, I will be gol-danged! Earl Morrison! Good to see you again, Captain. It's been a while, I'd say. Must be better than a year since you and your deputies hauled off those Chicago bandits who tried to upset the Loken outfit. No?"

"Hello, Oscar. Two years, four months, nine days. I had plenty of time to recall that case on the way up."

"My, my. That long? You know, Earl, city folks still make the journey, come all the way up here to Cable just to hear about that brawl at the dam, the train robbers who were undone by Tor Loken and Chief Namakagon, you and your Pinkerton men, and all the rest. I am happy to fill their ears, too. I must admit, though, the story I give 'em gets better and better each time I tell it. Why, I paint you and the Lokens as true, gun-totin' heroes, I do. And Chief

Namakagon as a wise old Indian leader who came to the rescue of the lumber camp and saved the day. Why, those city folks cannot get enough of my tall tales of pinery justice. I am even pondering the idea of writing one of those dime novels. You know, like those Billy the Kid and Black Bart the Poet Highwayman books. Earl, we got ourselves a real wild west story going here."

"So I have seen. You know, the Tribune will not let go of these tales about the perils of life up here in the wilderness. The newspapers have been scratching for such stories ever since, five years back, Jesse James got shot and killed down in Saint Jo. Your so-called pinery justice story might fill the bill for 'em. Why, you should see some of the gol-dang whoppin' tall tales those yarn spinners now write about northern Wisconsin!"

"Oh, yes. I know what they write. You know, Earl, we are not so remote that we don't get the Chicago papers up here. Chicago, Milwaukee, Saint Paul Pioneer Press, to boot. Often a day or two late, but we still get 'em. We see the stories all right. In fact, the Tribune sent a man up here to gather stories. Maybe you know him. A fella called Thomas, I believe. Yes, George Francis Thomas. Seems he grew to enjoy life here so much that he up and put down

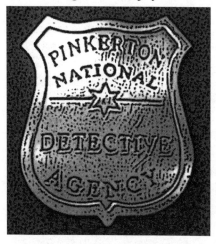

roots. Settled in Ashland. Frankly, I don't care much for his writing. Seems to mix facts with daydreams, he does. I suppose that's what writers must do. Folks will not buy papers if the stories are not fancied up enough to sound interesting."

"That's fine till what they write is less like truth and more like what is between the covers of those dime novels, though I will admit, they do tend to pin your ears back."

"That they do. And, like I say, plenty of folks come to hear the tale you were part of. I make it a point to mention the Pinkerton Detective Agency helped save the day."

"I believe Allen Pinkerton's front office would like that. Good for business."

"Good for business up here, too," replied Oscar. "Hotels,

restaurants, and taverns, I mean. And for the railroad company that employs me, to boot. Four cents a mile. That's what folks pay to come here to hear my stories, you know. Four cents a mile. You think the Omaha would give me a raise? Compensate me? Heck no, the penny pinching cheapskates."

Oscar stepped from the office and checked his watch. A second later, a distant whistle announced the approach of the next train. He pocketed his watch, mumbling, "Minute early. I'll be danged."

"Still the same old stationmaster, I see."

"I keep 'em running on time, in spite of the Chicago office. Public demands it, you know. One train arriving late can set the whole schedule on its backside. Five minutes late up here can mean a dozen trains arriving an hour late in Saint Paul, two hours late in Omaha. Folks do not see that. They cannot appreciate how one late train affects the next and the next. Regular folks don't have a grasp of the situation. Not like we railroad men do. No siree."

"Yep, still the same old stationmaster."

"So, Earl, you here for work or for play?"

"Here for both. Tor Loken hailed me. Offered to take me out in search of brook trout in trade for my help with some small matter."

"I thought as much. I only hope you have time for the trout."

"Oscar, I don't plan on leavin' without a catch. Whether it will be fish in the creel or some rapscallion in handcuffs is yet to be seen."

"Well, best of luck to you. Say, Earl, the bartender at the Cable House can get you set up with some ice out of Cable Lake. Good ice. Clear as glass. All the taverns up and down Main Street use it in their drinks. Before you leave, you throw a block of that ice and a hundred brookies in a crate, cover it with a blanket, and your wife and young ones will have fresh fish for a good while."

"No wife or young ones, not in my line of work. But I appreciate the tip, Oscar. Right now, I'm off for the Loken camp. High time I find out what concerns them so much that they are willing to let slip the whereabouts of their favorite trout hole."

"Say, Earl, you tell Olaf and Ingman to quit pinchin' their pennies and come to town for some pinochle one of these days."

"I surely will. Now you keep those trains running on time, Mister Stationmaster."

Chapter 24
Neck-deep in Deviltry

October 1886

At the lumber camp, Earl Morrison listened to the Loken's concerns over supper then turned in early. At dawn, he took the Marengo Trail north and soon found the road to the Marengo Station where he bought a ticket to Ashland. The sun was high in the sky when he stepped from the Wisconsin Central passenger car. The Pinkerton detective crossed the busy railroad yard, dodging a switch engine and a long chain of ore cars. Unpinning his badge and slipping it into his vest pocket, he headed for Front Street and the Chequamegon Hotel.

Earl signed in under the name of Charles Gunderson, not wanting to be recognized from newspaper accounts of Pinkerton Detective Agency successes such as the conflict at the Lake Namakagon Dam, the death of the lumber baron, Phineas Muldoon, and a law assuring fair access to navigable waters. The law, initiated by Governor Jeremiah Rusk also guaranteed public ownership of every dam on state waters.

Now a new case was developing. The accident at A. J. Hayward's sawmill was suspicious to say the least. Olaf could have been killed. Then there was Ingman's close call on the bridge over the White River near Mason, equally suspicious. The sabotaged break valve on

Engine Ninety-nine clinched the Loken's decision to call in professional help. The Lokens were now certain of foul play and asked their friend, Detective Earl Morrison, to investigate. As he did, one name continued to surface—Frank Derkson, Ashland's Deputy Sheriff.

Morrison hauled his grip up the hotel stairway. His third-story room overlooked a serene, sun-drenched Chequamegon Bay and beyond, her emerald-like Islands of the Apostles. Morrison packed his pipe, opened a flask of bourbon, and sat back on the veranda, contemplating the task before him.

That evening, in the Chequamegon Hotel restaurant, he dined on fresh whitefish fried with potatoes and onions, rutabaga soup, and white wine imported from France. He signed for the bill before making the rounds of the local saloons, quietly seeking out information about Frank Derkson. Tavern by tavern, he explored the city, beginning at the wharf and ending on Second Street, filling page after page of his notebook with names and places related to curious or unexplained deaths.

Morning found Morrison at the office of the Ashland Weekly Press, combing through old papers looking for news stories to reinforce his notes. By noon, the Pinkerton man's notebook listed seven suspicious deaths or disappearances in the past four years, each directly linked with Frank Derkson. As he finished each paper, he replaced it in the wooden file box. When done, he set the box on the counter.

"Find anything helpful regarding your kinfolk, Mister Gunderson?" asked the editor.

"No I'm afraid not. Seems there are Gundersons a-plenty 'round here. None seem to be relations of mine, though. I might have guessed as much. Could be they settled in Ashland, Ohio and not Ashland, Wisconsin. Pa never did specify. Merely called them our Ashland kin."

"I seen you writin' notes in your pocket book, there. Thought maybe you found somethin' out."

"Oh, that? No, just odds and ends, places to visit 'fore I return to Chicago. Say, thank you for helping me with this task, my good man." Earl slapped a quarter-dollar on the counter. "Let me buy your noon dinner, my friend. I'm much obliged."

<>O<>

Two blocks south, leaning against the far end of the Hotel Royale bar, Frank Derkson spoke in hushed tones with his brother-in-law.

"Gol-dang it, Wendell," said Frank, "sheriff or not, you sure got plenty of gall tellin' me I cannot take on a side job now and again."

"Side job? You call this a side job? Dang it, Frank, a side job is one thing. This is another. This is more than a lawman should take on. Sure, if some tavern needs you to keep the brawlin' outside or if a hotel needs you to evict a deadbeat roomer, well, that's all well and good. But, this goes too far. This is beyond what a man bearin' a badge ought be caught up in. And, Frank, I know full well you are not givin' me the whole story."

"You and me is kin, Wendell. Does that not enter in?"

Just because you wed my sister, don't think you can take advantage of me and my office. Yes, we are kin. Be that as it may, Frank, I cannot have my deputy runnin' off to Hayward doin' odd jobs, some of which you and I both know ain't in accordance with the law."

"But …."

"No, Frank. You tell that high roller who hired you that if he wants someone to help him out, he better look someplace else. There's plenty of men between jobs this time of year. He will find someone."

"But Wen, the money is good—real good. Too good to be true. Let me cut you in. 'Tween us two, we can get this all cleaned up in a few weeks, end up with a fine roll of bills in our pocket."

"I want no part of it, Frank. Whatever it is you are doin', I know it is beyond the law. I cannot stop you from goin' out on a limb here, Frank. Just keep it out of Ashland and don't get found out, hear? And Frank, whatever comes of this, you be gol-dang sure my name don't come up. Kin or no kin, I swear, if you cause me to lose my badge, I will personally see to it you are hauled in, convicted, and sent away."

"But, Wendell, I …"

"Listen, Frank, and listen good. I want nothin' to do with whatever you are involved in. Like I said, you are on your own. Keep me out of it. That's as far as I can go. You hear me, Frank?"

Derkson stared into his brother-in-law's eyes, saying nothing.

"You hear me, Frank?"

A tall man wearing a brown tweed suit and a matching derby hat entered the Royale. He spoke to the bartender who pointed to the two lawmen. Sheriff Rothwell studied the tall man now strolling toward him.

"The barkeeper says one of you is the sheriff."

"That would be me," replied Rothwell. "And who are ..."

"Then you must be Deputy Frank Derkson."

"Might be. Who are you?"

"Morrison. Captain Earl Morrison. Pinkerton Detective Agency. Chicago office." His stare remained on the deputy as Rothwell spoke.

"Pinkerton? What in tarnation are the Pinkertons doing in Ash..."

"What do you want with me?" Derkson snapped.

"What makes you think I want anything, Deputy?"

"Well, you ..."

The sheriff stood. "Let me handle this, Frank." He turned, putting his hand on Morrison's shoulder, turning him. "What is the nature of your business, Detective?"

"Captain."

"What?"

"Captain Morrison—not Detective Morrison," he replied, staring at Derkson again.

The deputy stood. "I ain't done nothin' wrong."

Morrison smiled. "I don't seem to recall saying you did, Deputy."

"Then, why are you ..."

The sheriff interrupted. "Dang it, Frank. Shut your fool mouth. I said I would handle this."

Morrison stared into Derkson's eyes, but spoke to both lawmen. "You fellas seem rather nervous. You always act like this? Or, perhaps you only get edgy when a fellow peacekeeper shows up in your town."

"What do you want, Morrison?" snapped the sheriff. "Spit it out. You're wastin' my time."

"I am looking into some complaints from friends of mine. The Lokens. You know 'em?"

"Heard of 'em. Cannot say I know 'em."

"You know 'em, right, Deputy?"

"Me? Why would you say that?"

"Seems as though all the folks in the Namekagon River Valley know about you. I hear your name come up right often down there."

Sheriff Rothwell stared at his deputy now. "And tell me, Morrison, what are these folks sayin'?"

"Captain Morrison, Sheriff."

Derkson blurted out, "Nobody down there got no right to say nothin' 'bout me. I ain't done a thing."

"Sheriff," said Morrison, "your deputy sure seems nervous. Bein' a fellow lawman and all, you and I can easily spot when some fella is sittin' on a pile of guilt. Deputy, why not just come out and tell us what the trouble is—what you have been up to. Make it easier all around."

Derkson shook with rage. "No gol-damn Chicago dandy claimin' to be a lawman has a right to come in here and accuse me …"

"I don't recollect accusing you of anything, Deputy. Sure sounds like you have some heavy burdens built up inside, though. Best thing you can do is to share 'em, you know. Get 'em off your chest."

Derkson pulled a revolver from his vest pocket, yelling, "I ain't gonna stand for no more of this!" As the words left his mouth, Morrison's hand came up, pulling the pistol from the deputy's grip and smashing it into his jaw, sending him across the barroom floor, over a chair and into the wall. He jumped to his feet and dove toward Morrison who stepped aside. Derkson landed face first on the bar. As the Pinkerton man ejected six cartridges from the deputy's pistol, the sheriff lifted his deputy by the collar.

"Enough, Frank. I need you to get over to the office right now. Sweep it out. Check on them two drunk sailors. You hear me?"

"Dammit, Wendell, you ain't gonna let this …"

"Get out, Frank! Not another word."

Derkson picked up his change from the bar and stomped from the room. "I ain't done nothin'. Nothin', you hear? Morrison, you tell Ingman and Olaf Loken and them other shanty boys down there to stop spreadin' lies or they'll suffer for it." He slammed the barroom door.

Morrison said nothing, offering the unloaded pistol to the sheriff who snatched it from his hand.

"By God, Morrison, I've a mind to throw you in jail for disturbin' the peace. If you had any evidence against my deputy you wouldn't have done all that chin-waggin'. Instead, he would be in handcuffs and you and him would be on the southbound. Am I right, Morrison?"

The detective said nothing.

"Yes. That's what I figured. You were hopin' to trip Frank up. Well, it didn't work. Now, take my advice. You get your arse out of my city—not tomorrow, not tonight, right now. Next train leaves at the top of the hour. You best be on it. Morrison, I will take no responsibility for what happens if you fail to heed my words. You hear me?"

"Oh, I will be on the southbound, all right, but not because of your warning. I don't pay much mind to empty threats from penny-ante coppers. I have some advice, Sheriff. You put some distance between yourself and that inept deputy of yours. It is clear he's involved in something crooked—involved in matters that could send the both of you off to prison. If you're not already neck-deep, you need to take steps to protect yourself. And, if you are involved, rest assured I will have you in shackles as well as that ham-headed, loose-tongued, brother-in-law of yours. Understand?"

Rothwell said nothing.

"Yes, I believe you do."

At a loss for words, Wendell Rothwell watched as the Pinkerton man strolled to the front door.

Gathering his nerve, the sheriff shouted, "Be on that train, Morrison."

The detective opened the door replying, "It's *Captain* Morrison. Good day."

Chapter 25
Bushwhacked

October 1886

Two days later before dawn, Frank Derkson saddled his horse and followed the Marengo Trail south. Reaching Lake Namakagon, he took the east tote road toward the Loken camp, his eyes scanning the tops of pines along the trail. About a half-mile from the camp, he dismounted, walking his horse into the woods, dropping the mare's reins. A long rope over one shoulder, he crossed the trail again, climbing to the top of a pine overhanging the trail. He threw a hitch around a dead limb, tossed the rope to the forest floor across the trail, and descended. Derkson rolled a boulder onto the trail. Threading the rope through the brush, he tied it to the saddle horn. He watched, hidden in the brush, one hand on the halter, not caring who came along, as long as the victim of his trap was a Loken.

A half-mile south, Olaf, Tor, and Ingman stood near the file shed. Olaf flexed a two-man crosscut saw, showing the maker's mark to Ingman. "Be sure to order Disston saws, Ingman. Their new saws are a sight better than the others. Pick up some spare handles, too."

"What about axes?" asked Ingman. "Must be we lost a dozen or more last winter with all that snow."

Tor grinned. "Snow snakes get 'em?"

"Ya. Snow snakes," said Olaf. "More likely we have a few men who pay no attention to where they dropped 'em. I will have a talk with the crew. See what can be done. No point in leavin' our tools for the porcupines to chew on come spring."

"Four Peaveys and two pike poles went by way of the river last spring," said Tor. "Not bad compared to Ole Swenson's camp, I hear. With Ole havin' fewer than half our number of men, he lost many more tools and a greenhorn log driver besides."

"Ya," said Olaf. "I s'pose we have no right to complain. The Loken camp has been very fortunate. Very few injuries and not one man killed since we started up six years back." He pulled a pencil and notebook from a pocket. "With a hundred and fifty men comin' in this fall, we better stock up some. Last thing we want is for our boys to sit idle for lack of proper tools." He scribbled a list.

Tearing it from the book, Olaf said, "Here you are, Ingman. This should do it. Tell Basil at the Ashland Mercantile to put it on my account. Mention I will be along with full payment for all we owe as soon as A. J. Hayward's mill squares up with us. As for me, I'm headed down to speak with A. J. today. Bob McCormick, too. Seems they are looking for a partner in this area for their new outfit."

"What outfit is that, Pa?"

"They're callin' it the North Wisconsin Lumber Company. Those two high rollers been buying up timberland like there's no end."

"You thinkin' about throwin' in with them, Pa?"

"I see little point to it. Our method is to cut only the prime timber and maintain the quality of the land. They tend to cut everything, then turn the land back to the government while they seek out more timberland. Be that as it may, I figure I should meet with them, if nothing more than to be a good neighbor. 'Sides, I am curious to see what kind of a deal they are hatchin' up."

"Might I tag along, Pa?"

"I need you to keep an eye on things here. I'll be back tomorrow."

Ingman stuffed the list in his pocket. "I s'pose I best be off for Ashland if I hope to get back before dark with the tools and such."

Twenty minutes later, Ingman's wagon rounded a bend in the east tote road. He pulled back on the reins when he saw a large boulder in the way. His horse grew uneasy, tossing her head back and abruptly stopping the rig.

"Easy, Lady, easy," he said, sliding from the wagon's bench seat. "Nothin' to fret. Let me get this ol' rock out of your way, girl."

As Ingman rolled the rock from the trail, a horse suddenly flashed through the brush behind him. Ingman heard a loud *crack* above. He dove away from the sound, but felt something strike him on the shoulder and back. Lying alongside the road, he turned to see a huge, dead tree limb whisk into the brush. The widowmaker disappeared.

Jumping to his feet, Ingman rushed to his wagon, grabbing his ax. Seconds later, a horse whinnied and crashed out of the brush and onto the trail far ahead. Behind it trailed the dead pine limb. It caught on a tree and snapped with a loud crack. The horse fell, then recovered, vanishing around the bend.

Ingman waited, ax in hand, watching the trail and the woods. Minutes passed before he coaxed his mare to turn the wagon around on the narrow road. "Easy, girl," he said, rubbing his arm and bleeding shoulder. "It's all right. It's all over—all over for now."

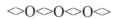

Chapter 26
In Hot Pursuit

October 1886

Ingman Loken knew his injuries would heal. And he trusted Earl Morrison would capture the man who did this. Earl would have the best guide—a skilled tracker—Ogimaa Mikwam-migwan, known by many as old Ice Feathers. Tor would be in on the search, too.

"You find this fella," Ingman told them. "I will wager he is behind all of these so-called 'misfortunes' we have seen lately. You find him and bring him to me. I will tend to him—give him a taste of his own medicine." He put his hand on Tor's shoulder. "Nephew, you stay close to Earl and to Chief Namakagon, hear?"

"Sure, Uncle. I'll keep a close eye on them for you."

"Ingman," said Morrison, "make plans for that trout fishin' trip. The three of us should have no problem catching up with this scoundrel. Soon as we have dealt with him, I plan on tangling with some of those brook trout."

"Ya, it will be good to take a few days off after this commotion, turmoil, and such."

<>O<>

Tor, Namakagon, and Earl Morrison left camp on foot. By midmorning, they were three miles north on the trail of the culprit. Derkson was also on foot, his horse gone lame from dragging the hundred pound pine limb. They found the animal dead in a ravine, shot twice behind the ear. Its brand had been sliced from the rump and the scorched remains of the saddle lay under nearby smoldering coals.

Chief Namakagon followed the sign. Tor and Captain Morrison followed the chief. The heels of the assailant's boots cut deep into the soil.

"This bandit makes no attempt to cover his tracks," said Morrison. "Must figure nobody is following him. That's good."

"City dweller," said Namakagon.

"Now, how in blazes can you tell that from a few boot prints?" asked Earl.

"His footsteps are those of a man who does most of his walking on pavement—city streets—not the forest floor. Look how his tracks spread apart at the toe of the boot. Now, look at Tor's. The young woodsman has steps that point straight ahead. Mine show the toes pointing in. And yours, Captain? Yes. Those who walk on concrete and stone have toes pointing apart."

"Well, I will be gol-danged," said the Pinkerton. "City dweller."

A half-hour later, the trail left by their quarry abruptly changed. Though harder to follow, Namakagon stayed with the boot prints.

"We are close," said the chief. "He now knows we follow him. Look, he steps carefully, trying to not leave sign. He will have to do much better if he hopes to escape."

"Maybe we should split up," said Tor. "I can swing around ahead and cut him off."

"No," said Morrison, 'we will catch him soon enough. Better to work together like wolves on the heels of their prey."

"Yes," said the chief. "He flees his pursuers like a snowshoe hare—running ahead, circling, hiding in the brush until he sees us. Then he runs ahead again. He knows very little about evading hunters—leaves far too much sign even when trying to leave none. He fears we will soon have him trapped, bound for camp. This is not good."

"Not good?" said Tor. "We have him on the run, don't we?"

"Fear leads to desperation, young woodsman. It matters not what animal you trail. We do not want this rabbit to act out of desperation. We do not want him to make it difficult to predict his next move. If he feels trapped, he may strike in some way we cannot foresee."

Tor studied the sign. "However we do it, I am eager as a dog on a bone to hog-tie this bandit and drag him a-spittin' and a-kickin' to camp. Uncle Ingman has something in mind for this outlaw, yessir. Probably skin him alive and throw him in Sourdough's biggest stewpot."

Morrison laughed. "Your pa will not allow any such thing, Tor. This rabbit, as Chief calls him, will be in the state prison for a long while. It could be the only time he ever leaves will be in the undertaker's wagon."

"Can't say I am a bit sorry," mumbled Tor.

The three trackers pressed on. Soon the would-be assassin's trail ascended a ridge straight into the stiff, midday wind, a ridge so steep that Chief Namakagon had to stop twice to rest before reaching the top.

"I am not the young man of times past. I can no longer keep up with you young bucks."

Earl laughed. "Keep up? Why, I have had trouble staying abreast of you all morning. We will soon crest this ridge. I imagine I will again be breathing hard in order to meet your pace."

Nearing the top, Namakagon studied the trail. "Odd," he muttered. "His tracks no longer circle. He seems to have a place to go. Or a purpose." He studied the sign. "Look. See how the distance between footfalls has increased? He is taking longer strides. He runs straight into the wind. Our rabbit has something in mind. Something has changed. He has a plan."

"Must be he is scared that we are closing in," said Tor.

"No," said Namakagon, "I think not. Look at his tracks. They are now the tracks of a running man—far apart—heels digging in—toe pushing off. He runs, yes. But why? It will only wear him out. This makes no sense—no sense at all."

Studying the tracks, again, Tor said, "I s'pose I would run, too, if I had tried to kill someone and knew ol' Ice Feathers was on my trail."

"Namakagon stared at the sign. "No, Tor. This is different. He does not run to escape. He has no need to run. He knows we must travel slowly to read the sign, to follow. No. Something else is afoot."

"Could it be this here fella is in a blind panic?" suggested Morrison. "Many a man has gone berserk when pursued."

The three trackers followed the fugitive's trail into a wide valley of cutover pine. They climbed over dry limbs and dead treetops scattered across the landscape by earlier lumberjacks. Tor, Earl, and Namakagon fought their way through tall grass and dry brush, over and around pine stumps. The runner's footprints continued into the wind.

"Strange," said Namakagon. "A wise rabbit would keep circling until we lose his track. This is very odd. Why does he run? And, why into this wind? Why?" The chief pulled some pemmican from the pouch on his belt and sat on the ground. "We have followed this rabbit through this cutover for two, maybe three miles. I dislike the feeling I have in my heart. He knows something we do not."

"I know this country fairly well," said Tor chewing on the pemmican. "Nothing much ahead. Nowhere to run, least not this direction. This cutover goes mile after mile, halfway up to Lake Superior, I would say. And now our rabbit, as you call him, runs more like a scared deer."

"No," said the old Indian. "That, young woodsman, is the twist. A deer runs into the wind so he can smell danger ahead and avoid it. Why would a desperate man do this? He has no danger ahead. Couldn't smell it if he did. This confuses me."

Tor and Earl stretched out on the ground, resting their feet and chewing the pemmican. Suddenly, Chief Namakagon turned his head, sniffing the air.

"Smoke!" said Chief. "Tor. Earl. Do you smell smoke?"

Tor leaned forward, inhaling. "Faint, very faint. Must be a trapper's cabin close by—or maybe a mining camp."

"No," said Namakagon. "No camp. No cabin." He jumped to his feet. "We must leave—leave now."

"What? Why?" asked Morrison.

"Do not ask. Run!" Chief ordered, pulling Tor to his feet. "I know why the rabbit led us into the wind—why he ran ahead. Come. This way! Hurry!"

Earl followed, shouting, "Why? What in blazes is it?"

Namakagon turned, shouting as he ran. "He wanted us to be far downwind when he set the woods afire. He knows, with enough distance between us, the fire will grow large—too large for us to escape. Run!"

"What in tarnation are you talking about? What fire?" Earl shouted, trying to keep up.

"The rabbit has set fire to the woods upwind," replied Namakagon. "That is why he ran. The smoke we smell is from a fire that will soon be half-a-mile wide and upon us. This rabbit knows the strong wind, dry limbs, fallen treetops will create a fire so fierce, so wide that we will have no chance—no escape. Come this way. Hurry! We must prove him wrong."

The old woodsman and his companions ran through the cuttings, perpendicular to the wind. Tripping over limbs, brush, and branches, they stumbled, crashed, and clattered their way to a narrow creek. By the time they reached the stream, smoke filled the air.

"Water!" Tor shouted, cupping his hands and quenching his parched throat. "We can stay in the water."

"No. Keep going. This fire will be too large for such a small stream to help us. There is a lake downstream from here. It might save us. Wet your clothing and follow me. Run!"

All three men plunged into the stream before climbing the bank, charging through the brush, and scrambling ahead over dead limbs and treetops. Along the horizon, Tor noticed flames spreading across the cutover. Smoke grew thick and the wind stronger and hotter.

A doe and her fawn burst out of the brush, almost plowing Tor to the ground. For an instant, Chief Namakagon, Tor, Earl Morrison, and the two deer ran together, partners in their desperate flight, until both deer hurdled a fallen treetop, leaving the men behind.

Sparks began falling around them. Looking back at the fire, Tor tripped on a dead limb, flying face-first to the ground.

"Get up, Woodsman! Run! Run!" ordered the chief, pulling Tor up by the arm. "We are almost there!"

They crashed through the brush, Tor's long legs a blur and his boots barely touching the ground. Bellows from a bear calling her cubs came from behind Tor. He did not look back. Ash and sparks dropped from the black sky. Flames flared as dry grass and pine ignited around them. Lungs ached from hot, thick smoke. Overhead, fire roared in the wind. Ahead, beyond flaming debris, Tor caught sight of the lake.

"Do not stop!" gasped Chief from behind. "You will make it! Run, Woodsman! Run!"

Shielding his face with his arm, Tor vaulted up, over, and through the fierce flames, now nearing the shore. Never slowing, he blindly dove head first into the water, colliding with a terrified moose calf swimming for safety. Behind came the cow, much bigger and faster. Tor dove, hoping the cow's hooves would miss him as she sped by. Surfacing, he turned to locate his friend. From the mix of thick smoke and flames came more animals fleeing the violence of the forest fire. On shore, standing dead pines, left behind during the cut, burst into flame from the scorching wind and sparks. Other dead trees fell to the hellish furnace of the forest floor.

"Namakagon!" screamed Tor, treading water. "Namakagon!" he shouted over the fire's roar.

"Here! I am here."

Looking across the lake, Tor could only see animals swimming for safety and a large, scorched log floating a few yards away. "Namakagon," he called again.

"Here, woodsman," said Namakagon. "take hold of this log before you sink to the bottom." Tor reached for the floating log as Namakagon peered around the end, coughing and gasping, "Tor, get the log between you and the fire and hold on tight. It will support you. We can drift to the other shore."

"Chief, we must find Earl!"

"He is not with you?"

"No. He must have fallen behind." Tor turned to the shore, now engulfed. "Earl!" There was no answer. "Earl Morrison!" screamed Tor into the roar of the inferno. "Morrison!" There was no reply. "Morrison, can you hear me? Morrison! Morrison!"

"Woodsman," shouted Namakagon, "we must flee this fire. We have not a minute to spare."

"What about Earl?"

"Perhaps he already made the other shore. If he is alive, we will find him."

"What if that shore burns, too?"

"The fire will circle the lake, but with this wind, the woods near the lake will be spared."

Tor wrapped an arm around the floating log as a red squirrel struggled up and onto the log, then chattered its displeasure.

"Mikwam-migwan, you gave me quite a scare. I thought I had lost you to the flames."

"No, Woodsman. Not yet. Like this noisy squirrel, you and I will survive this. I wonder if the rabbit will be so fortunate."

"And, Earl Morrison?"

"We will look for him."

"Chief, when we find him, we must take up our chase, get on this rabbit's trail again."

"No need. Sooner or later he will come to us. He will come to see if we escaped his trap. He is determined. For whatever reason, he will seek us out. When he comes, he will find us all right—find us waiting."

By nightfall the flames had died. Smoldering wood, plants, and peat threw a thick blanket of smoke into the air. The smoke hung low, hugging the blackened forest floor, making each breath a challenge. Still, there was less risk in staying the night than in trying to hike out. Tor and Namakagon did their best to sleep near the shore of the small lake, taking turns calling for the Pinkerton man while watching the landscape glow with flare-ups through the night.

The following morning, a change in wind cleared the air. The two survivors, coughing and spitting from hours of breathing soot and smoke, began their search for one more. Determined to find any sign of Earl Morrison, they moved slowly, picking their way around the lake. Soot wafted into the air from each step. Then, backtracking as best they could, they crisscrossed the black hillsides.

Scouring the charred terrain for any sign of their friend, they plodded across the hot forest floor from beyond the creek where they'd last seen him, all the way to the lake. Next, Tor and Namakagon circled the shoreline twice, hoping not to find Morrison in the water, certain he would be dead if found there. Sky growing dark and feet burning from hours of walking on smoldering embers, Tor Loken and Chief Namakagon climbed a scorched hill and called Morrison's name again and again. Their cries brought eerie echoes from the bare, blackened hillsides, but no reply from their friend, the Pinkerton Detective, Captain Earl Morrison.

Interlude
May 19, 1966

2 a.m.

The flames in the fireplace now licked high. My hot boots woke me with a start, my feet still resting on the hearth before the fire. I struggled to untie the laces—laces bent on remaining secured. Finally able to remove one boot, I thrashed at the other, opened my pocketknife, cut the laces, and rubbed my hot feet to ease the pain.

I walked into the kitchen for a glass of water. Returning, I pulled Grandpa's chair away from the heat, sliding it across the eighty-year-old pine plank floor. As I did, my crude map fell to the floor. I held it to the firelight. Stare as I might, nothing moved, nothing changed. No images of the old camp, no lumberjacks, no Chief Namakagon behind his dogsled. Tor and Rosie were nowhere to be found. I saw nothing but my preposterous pencil marks and—my useless, hopeless map. I crushed it into a ball and pitched it into the fireplace. Distracted by the call of a loon, I didn't notice the ball of crushed paper bounce off the andiron and fall back onto the hearth.

I stepped to the window to see the shape of a single loon outlined by the reflection of the moon descending toward the treetops across the lake. The loon called again. Another swam across the white path of moonlight dancing on the still water. Then, another appeared, and another, until eight loons again graced the bay.

"Foolish loons, why are you so intent on staying here in this bay? Is there something I can do for you? Something I should know?"

Another loon called. I laughed at my absurd fantasy that these loons could somehow communicate with me.

"Crazy as a loon," I mumbled, sitting back in Grandpa's chair again. That's when I noticed the crumpled map on the hearth. I picked it up and flattened it between the palm of my hand and my knee. Staring at it again, I tried once more to recall the other map, the one I found the morning before, the treasure map now destroyed. I strained to recall, to imagine, to conjure those faint pencil lines, those scratchings that appeared drawn in such haste onto the back of an 1884 grocer's bill. I stared at my map, my pitiful drawing. As I stared, the moon descended the sky, the woods fell black and I again drifted off.

<>O<>O<>O<>

Chapter 27
Four Days before Chief Namakagon's Death

November 1886

Earl Morrison was missing. It had been weeks since he was last seen fleeing the raging forest fire, running for his life. Ingman and Olaf coordinated the search effort, asking neighboring camps to help. Chief Namakagon brought many friends to scour the burned-over hills north of the camp. In spite of days, then weeks of searching, no trace of the Pinkerton detective surfaced. The man-hunt continued, though no one now expected to find Captain Morrison alive.

Bill Burns, the constable for the Omaha line, also searched, though not in the burned over forest and not for Captain Morrison's remains. Burns saw to it every railroad depot, post office, and tavern from Chippewa Falls to Lake Superior had a poster offering a two-hundred dollar reward for information leading to the capture of the man who set the deadly forest fire. Despite the constable's efforts, the name of the arsonist remained a mystery. Determined, Burns met with every lumber camp owner, stationmaster, tavern keeper, and lawman in the area. His interviews included one with Frank Derkson. The deputy seemed astonished that anyone would attempt such crimes. He scoffed at Burn's claim that the fire was intentional, blaming it on a homesteader burning off a tract of land or a hunter losing control of his campfire.

"Tell me, Burns," Derkson said with a grin, "this fella Loken, the bark eater who claims someone dropped a widowmaker on him—did you see any liquor bottles layin' in the back of his wagon? I heard he's a hard drinker. You bother to check his breath?"

"Ingman Loken wasn't drunk."

"Sounds to me like he was oiled-up. Pickled. Three sheets to the wind, Burns. You ask him how much he had to drink before all this happened? Did you, Constable?"

"No, but …"

"That's what I thought. You railroad constables don't know what in blazes you're doin'. Overpaid night watchmen, that's all you are. You have no business tryin' to act the role of a lawman. You constables are always too quick to blame a fella for what is really a natural cause. You'll not be satisfied till you send someone to prison even though your so-called crime might be an act of God. You do believe in God, Constable, do you not?"

"Don't try to twist this …"

"Then you don't believe in God?"

"Listen, Frank, there's no doubt in my mind that the murder attempt on Ingman Loken was intentional. We found the trail blocked, like Ingman said. We tracked the horse through the woods, found the tree limb that dang-near killed him and we found the poor horse shot dead because of a lame leg due to all this. I do not know how good you are at solvin' crimes, Frank Derkson, but it is clear to everyone else that …"

"Everyone else? Listen, Burns. Everyone who thinks a crime took place here is guilty—guilty of jumpin' the gun. And you, Constable, are the reason why. You come 'round with your tall tales and reward posters, gettin' everybody all riled up. First thing you know, the whole dang pinery is out looking for a murderer that ain't there. That's how innocent men get lynched, Burns. Is that what you want? Is that what you're after? You want some innocent fella to hang for this? Is that what it will take to satisfy you? Bill Burns, get out of my town before I jail you for disturbin' the peace. That's what you are doin', you know—disturbin' the dang peace."

Of all the people interviewed by Constable Bill Burns, only Frank Derkson criticized his investigations. And, though the constable's other interviews resulted in no leads, he continued his effort, widening his search, determined to get some answers to the series of suspected murder attempts. There had been too many close calls. Morrison was missing. Burns wanted answers before the next murder attempt was made—before the next attempt succeeded.

Meanwhile, in spite of many search teams scouring the site of the forest fire, no sign of Earl Morrison, Pinkerton Detective surfaced.

<>O<>

On the evening of the thirteenth of November, 1886, returning from another day of searching the blackened landscape, Tor led his mare to the barn for the night. He handed the reins to the camp barn boss, John Kavanaugh.

"Say, Tor," John said, "I was wonderin' if I could ask a favor."

"Sure, John. You want me to rub down my mare? Bed her down?"

"No. No, I will tend to her. That's my job. It's something else."

"Anything, John. You name it."

"I am worried about Johnny."

"Johnny? Oh, Junior. You worried about Junior?"

"Tor, my youngest has taken up with his brother to sail the seas and I don't care for it none. You see, William, my oldest, well, he's an independent one, he is. That boy can find his way, yessir. Always has been able to take good care of himself. My Johnny? Well, Johnny is not so savvy, though he wants everyone to think he is. You have seen that, Tor, the way he struts like a rooster tryin' to stare down a coon. Johnny's not a man for the seas, neither. No sir, not by a long shot. 'Sides that, it simply ain't safe out there. They mean to sail the Great Lakes, then head for the Caribbean. God knows what kind of ships they will be workin' on or where they might end up. My Johnny ain't no man of the world like his brother, William."

"Junior has been letting on about this ever since I first met him, John. He looks up to Billy. First thing I ever heard Junior say was that someday he was gonna go off with Billy and learn how to be a big shot sellin' bananas and baskets and such."

"Tor, my Johnny already left for Ashland with William. They plan to ship out in three or four days on a boat called the *Lucerne.*"

"What? Why, I spoke with Junior only a few days ago. He made no mention they planned to leave this soon. Sure wish I could have talked to him 'fore he left. Might have changed his mind, though I don't know if I would have tried. Sometimes a fella has to take a gamble in life. The chief taught me that more than once. My pa, too. Pa would not be where he is today if he never took a chance in life."

"Well, be that as it may, I am still worried about my Johnny. It is no secret that William and me do not see eye-to-eye, Tor. I am sure his intention was to purloin Johnny away, tempting him with women, wine, and wealth."

"From the little I know of your son, Billy, I cannot disagree. So, John, what is it you would have me do?"

"Tor, if you are willin' I would like you to go up to Ashland, find the *Lucerne* and have a talk with my boy. My Johnny and me already had some harsh words over this. I want you to let him know … well, let him know he is welcome to come back to the camp and, come spring, join me on the farm again. Will you do that for me, Tor?"

"You know I will, John. Your son, already knows he is welcome here. I'll do my best to convince him to stay, at least for the winter. Maybe then, as you say, he'll return with you to the farm come spring, if that's his wish. I'm off to Hayward tomorrow but I will be in Ashland before that boat departs. You can depend on me, John."

<>O<>

Opened wide, the parlor windows of Adeline Ringstadt's Boarding House allowed music from her mother's upright piano to flow down the street—music cool and sweet, like water flowing downriver on this Indian Summer day. Tor strolled up Iowa Avenue, the heart of Hayward's business district, hearing Rosie's music from far down the street. He climbed the boarding house steps, stepped into the foyer, and peeked into the parlor. There, nine guests sat enjoying her performance. He looked on as Rosie spoke.

"This next song was written by Winslow Winters and Whistlin' Jim Engebretson, two of the men at my beau's lumber camp. Jim put Winslow's words to the tune of an old Irish ballad called *Danny Boy*. I think you will like it. She turned to the piano.

"Oh, Lumberjack,
You don't know how I fear for thee.
Out in the cold
And snowy pinery.
From dawn to dark,
You risk your very life for me.
I pledge to you,
Your love I'll ever be.

Beyond farm fields
Wisconsin pines they call to you.
All winter long,
You slave your life away
To keep our farm
From banker's hands. That's what you do.
Dollar-a-day is what the bosses pay.

Majestic pines,
They stretch almost to heaven's door.
When they descend, run far beyond the crown.
For, should you fall,
Your handsome face I'll see no more.
They seek revenge on those who cut them down.

- 176 -

Oh, Lumberjack,
You don't know how I fear for thee.
Out in the cold
And snowy pinery.
From dawn to dark,
You risk your very life for me.
Oh, Lumberjack, I pledge your love I'll ever be.

Now what's this news?
You ne'er returned to shanty door
A falling pine
Seems was the death of thee.
And now I learn
The comp'ny boss had pushed for more.
And a widowmaker stole my man from me.

So here we are,
Your son and wife now wearing black.
Awaiting you
But no more to embrace.
The lumber train
Will bring you down the railroad track
Just one more man the comp'ny must replace.

Oh, Lumberjack,
I weep for thee, I weep for thee.
Out in the cold
And snowy pinery.
It breaks my heart,
You gave the pine your life for me.
Oh, Lumberjack, I pledge your love I'll ever be.

The boss man says
You failed to work the winter through.
And now I learn, we shall not get your pay.
The bank's foreclosed.
Now leave this farm is what we'll do.
No coin in hand and nowhere else to stay.

And so we, too,
Must venture to the pinery.
A sporting house
Is where I'll earn my keep.
And your sweet son
Will soon become a lumberjack.
While in the dreary graveyard you do sleep.

Oh, Lumberjack,
I weep for thee, I weep for thee.
Out in the cold
And snowy pinery.
It breaks my heart,
You gave the pine your life for me.
I pledge to you,
Your love I'll ever be.
Oh, Lumberjack, know that your love I'll ever be."

With tears rising in the eyes of those listening, a tall, thin man stood, stepping behind Rosie. As the small audience applauded, the young man placed his hands on Rosie's shoulders, massaging them.

She brushed them off, scolding, "Reggie Muldoon, I have told you before, I do not favor you touching me."

"Now, Rosie, you know I mean no harm by it. Mercy sake, can I not show my appreciation?"

"You can take your appreciation downtown to one of the many bawdy houses you frequent."

"Now, now, Rosie …" He reached for her again.

As he did, another young man dashed across the room. Almost instantly, Muldoon was on the floor looking up at Tor, standing with fists clenched. A woman shrieked. Two men moved between them.

"Muldoon, I swear, you lay one more finger on …"

"What is going on here?" said Adeline from the kitchen doorway.

"It's all right, Mama. Reggie was just leaving. He will not be staying for supper. Tor will."

"You will regret this, Loken," said Muldoon. "I will see to it."

"Muldoon, you think your money allows you to do whatever you want. You are no different than your grandfather—both cut from the same cloth, I'd venture. Cheap muslin, at that. Nobody 'round here cares for you anymore than they did for Phineas. Fetch your fancy hat and take your leave. Go someplace where you're less likely to get hurt."

Muldoon slowly stood. "I will leave when I so choose."

Tor stepped forward, grabbing Muldoon squarely by the collar. With one hand he dragged him across the parlor, through the foyer and out the front door. Using his foot, Tor gave Muldoon a push, causing him to somersault down the steps and onto the dusty street.

A round of cheers came from those watching through the windows of the parlor.

Muldoon scrambled to his feet, turned and charged up the steps in a fury. As he reached the top step, Tor stretched his arm straight out and his clenched fist met Muldoon square on the nose, sending him down the steps and onto the street again. Bleeding, whimpering, he struggled to his feet and stumbled down the dusty road, both hands to his face.

"Don't come back, Muldoon. You're not welcome here."

Another round of cheers came from the parlor.

"I never did care much for that fellow," said Adeline, speaking over Tor's shoulder. "Come in and have a seat. Supper is nearly ready. Tor, I believe you just made yourself the guest of honor."

<>O<>

After supper, Rosie and Tor strolled through the town in the warm Indian summer weather. Rosie took Tor's hand.

"Tor ..." she said.

"Hmm?"

"Mama and I have been talking about this and that."

"This and that?"

"You know, the future?"

"The future. Rosie, you best say what you mean to say before our tramp is over and we find ourselves back at the boarding house."

"Well, you know how much I enjoy literature and all, and ... well, I have decided to continue my schooling."

"Why, that's wonderful, Rosie. Somehow I figured you would. You sure got the wit for it. No question about that. And the gumption, too. Is there somebody around here who can be your teacher?"

"No, I am afraid not."

"You mean ... Rosie, are you goin' away?"

"Away? Yes. But not far, Tor. I hear talk there will be a college in Ashland soon."

"Ashland? Ashland, Wisconsin?"

"I am going to speak with them about enrolling."

"And you want to study literature?"

"Oh, I would so like to study literature. I may even write my own book one day."

"I think that's a wonderful idea, Rosie."

"You do? Really?"

"'Cept … what about your flower peddlin'?"

"For Pete's sake, Tor Loken, how many times must I tell you? I am not a flower peddler. I am a florist, a florist, Tor. And I intend to continue until the school term begins, then take it up during summer again to help pay for my tuition."

"When does all this start? I mean the classes and such."

"I do not know yet. I plan to take the train to Ashland soon to speak with the new Board of Education."

They walked in silence a while. Then, "Rosie Ringstadt, I think it is outright wonderful you want to study literature and such."

"Then, I have your approval?"

"Approval? Why, sure. Perfectly all right by me, although we both know well you would do this with or without my say-so."

"Yes, I suppose I would. Still, I would much rather know you think this is a worth-while endeavor."

"Imagine, my gal Rosie in a college. Just the very thought of it is worth while, I'd say. My gal Rosie in college!"

"Say, Rosie, John Kavanaugh asked me to speak with Junior before he sails out of Ashland in a couple a days. I'm headed there this week. Why not join me? We can make a day of it. I could find Junior, and you could visit with the college folks. Will you, Rosie?"

"I would like that. I would like that very much, indeed."

"Day after tomorrow sound all right? I could leave camp early and meet you at the Ashland depot."

"Perfect. I will finish my morning chores at Mama's and be on the nine-thirty northbound day after tomorrow. Maybe I can sell a few corsages on the train."

"Good. I will look for the pretty, dark-haired, flower peddler."

"Florist, Tor. F.L.O.R.I.S.T. And, Tor …"

"Hmm?"

"I so dread depot waiting rooms. Do not be late."

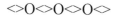

Chapter 28
Four Days after Namakagon's Death

November 21, 1886

The storm that wrecked the schooner, *Lucerne,* had passed. Junior and Billy Kavanaugh were among those presumed dead. No one knew what had become of Captain Earl Morrison, lost in a raging forest fire a month earlier, and Ogimaa Mikwam-migwan lay in his grave. The whereabouts of his silver now piqued the interest of many. Bringing Chief Namakagon's murderer to justice became the quest of his friend, Tor Loken.

The door to Chief Namakagon's Marengo cabin stood open to allow in light. Deputy Frank Derkson was inside. He knew no one would be this far out in the woods this soon after the blizzard. He knew no one would have the pluck, the backbone, the stamina needed to challenge this weather, this deep snow. He knew no one would come here so soon after the burial of the Ojibwe chief. He never suspected he might be interrupted as he rifled through the chief's belongings.

Quietly pawing through Namakagon's few possessions, Derkson looked for maps, records, any clues to the old man's hidden silver mine. "I shall have your silver, one way or another, Namakagon," he mumbled into the empty room. "Do not think for one minute that I will not. There must be something here, some clue. Make it easy on me, old man. Don't tell me that I done you in for nothin'. There's a cavern full of high-grade silver out there somewhere, I know it. Let us not waste my time, Indian. Show me a clue. A clue, dang it!"

Caught unaware, Derkson jerked with surprise when he heard the voices. He swiftly ducked out of the cabin, leaving the door ajar and loping through deep snowdrifts into the nearby woods. Thick balsams hid his escape, but not his tracks.

Seeing tracks in the snow and the door open, Tor and Ingman cautiously approached Namakagon's modest cabin. After standing their snowshoes on end in the snow, they entered to find the interior in a shambles.

"Uncle, Chief Namakagon would never leave his camp in such a mess. Someone else did this. And look here. Look at this snow on the floor. It hasn't been here long."

"Probably from the man whose tracks we found outside."

"My guess it was that egg-suckin' weasel, Frank Derkson."

Ingman held up Namakagon's hatchet. "Whoever it was, this fella was not yust rummagin' for something to steal, for this would be a prize. I'm thinkin' he hoped to find something more. A map, maybe?"

"A map? Chief would never leave a map. No sir. Kept all his maps tucked away in his head. Only map he ever showed me was one from years ago. Said it came from someone called School ... Schoolcraft."

"Henry Schoolcraft?"

"You know of him?"

"Worked for the government. Explored this area, they say. Set up some trading posts. I wonder how Chief came to have a map of Henry Schoolcraft's."

"He didn't say. Just told me I should have it. Said he memorized it and had no use for a piece of paper 'cept maybe to start a campfire."

"I don't s'pose it showed any silver mines, did it, Tor?"

"No such luck. It's a map pointing the way from Lake Superior down to the Mississippi River. I will show it to you when we get back to the lodge. I keep it in my dresser. Not much of a map. Not a road or a railway anywhere to be seen."

"Tor, look here!" Ingman held a fist-sized chunk of metal in the sunlight filtering through the floursack curtains. "Must be silver. Now, why would someone ransack a deserted cabin and leave this behind—a three-pound lump of silver?"

"Maybe Derkson overlooked it."

"Right here in plain sight? I don't think so. I think he didn't take it along because he did not have time. Tor, I think we surprised him. He most likely got here right ahead of us, then fled when he heard us comin'. Could be he is right outside waiting for us to leave."

"Or drawing a bead on us right now, Uncle."

"No, I think not. Derkson has no cause to harm us. For all he knows, we yust stopped to check on Chief Namakagon's camp. So far, he has no reason to think we are a threat to him."

"We will see about that. Uncle, need to find a way to tie him tight to the murder. Or ... maybe get him to confess. Make him admit his guilt."

"Yust how do you suppose we go about that?"

"Hand me that lead pencil you carry with you." Tor pulled a slip of paper from his shirt pocket.

"What are you up to, now?" said Ingman, handing Tor the pencil.

"This is an old invoice for some goods we fetched from Morse a while back. All that talk of Namakagon's old map gave me an idea. I believe the backside of this bill will put that weasel in the state prison."

Tor drew a crude map of the lakes and streams in the area. He added a line to represent the Marengo Trail and placed an X on Chief Namakagon's island camp, then another near the Marengo River not far from where they now stood. A few more marks and unintelligible words and his map was complete. He folded it twice and hid it under the shredded tobacco in the tin canister above the window.

"That should do it," he said. "Whether it is Derkson or some other hooligan, if somebody is out there watchin', he is bound to return lookin' for something of value. He is bound to look in the chief's tobacco can."

"And, if he does not see the map there?"

"Oh, I'll wager he will find the map, all right. With tobacco costin' what it does nowadays, he will surely fill his own pouch and his pipe."

"And what good will that be?"

"Uncle, if my hunch is right, we are going to catch Deputy Frank Derkson with my map in hand and this here raw silver in his rucksack. If that's not enough to bring him before a judge, nothing is. Derkson will know it, too. Probably dig a deep hole when he tries to talk his way out. C'mon, high time we gave him his big opportunity."

"You surely do conjure up odd ideas. Must be the Norski in ya."

Snowshoes on again, Ingman and Tor left, following their same trail out. After cresting the hill, they cut into the woods and circled, hiding under the limbs of a large, snow-covered spruce within sight of the lodge. They waited, chewing on sticks of dried venison Sourdough had stuffed in their pockets that morning.

Their wait was short. And their hunch was on the mark. Frank Derkson, a rucksack and a double-barreled shotgun over his shoulder, stepped from behind the balsams, not fifty feet from Chief Namakagon's single-room cabin. Tor and Ingman watched him enter. Sounds of breaking glass and upset furniture came from the lodge. Through the side window, Ingman and Tor saw glimpses of the deputy as he reached high, bringing down the tobacco canister. Minutes later, Derkson emerged, stuffing two chunks of silver into his rucksack. He pulled out a compass, looked at the map, and headed southwest into the woods.

"Well, I'll be danged! He took the bait, Nephew. Must be heading for the lake. Derkson must know there are canoes stored for winter under the spruce trees where the creek comes in. If we can get to the island first, we will have him cold."

"You noticed that shotgun, right, Uncle?"

"This coward will not think twice about using it on a red man, Tor, but he dassn't use it on a white. He'd get lynched for sure and knows it."

"Then, Uncle, we are off to Lake Namakagon. Looks as though we've got us a gol-dang weasel to trap!"

Chapter 29
Namakagon's Island Camp

November 21, 1886

Frank Derkson paddled across the north end of Lake Namakagon to the island, skirting ice now forming in the wind-sheltered bays. He pulled his canoe onto shore and, in seconds, stood before the chief's lodge. After brushing snow from a stump near the door, Deputy Derkson pulled Tor's hand-drawn map from his shirt pocket, then sat to study the drawing.

"Well, now, what might you have there, deputy?" came a voice from within the lodge. Ingman stepped into the sun, Tor close behind.

"What? Who are ... Wait! I seen you at the old man's cabin. How did you ..."

"We know these woods a might better than you," Ingman said. "You see, we live here."

"And we know enough to wear snowshoes when the snow calls for it," added Tor.

"Name is Loken. Ingman Loken."

Derkson's eyes widened. "Loken?"

"This here is my nephew."

"You, young fella, do I know you?" Derkson began to stand when Ingman placed his hand on the deputy's shoulder, forcing him down onto the stump again. Derkson stuffed the map in his coat pocket.

Ingman snatched the map from Derkson's hand. "Let me see that. Hmm. Why, looks like a map. Ya, it surely does look like a map. Say, this wouldn't be a map to the old Indian's silver mine, ay, Frank?"

"You have no right to that. What are you and the boy doin' here anyhow? You been followin' me, Loken? Is that it?" He tried to stand. Again, Ingman's powerful hand returned him to the stump.

"Following you? Why deputy, how is it we are here and you show up out of nowhere? Seems more like you are following us!"

"Loken, I ask you again. Why are you here?"

"Maybe we are lookin' for treasure, yust like you, Deputy."

"Give me my map."

"Where'd you get it?"

"Give it here."

"How did you come by it, Frank? The ol' chief give it to you?"

"Yes. The old chief gave it to me. So what?"

"Chief Namakagon?"

"Yes. Hand it over."

"Now you tell me, Frank, why under God's blue Heaven would our good friend, Chief Namakagon, give you a map to his silver mine? Why, Frank? Tell me!"

"Loken, you hand me my map right now or I will arrest you for thievery. You hear me?"

"First, Deputy, you tell me why he would have given you this map?"

"That's it! The both of youse are under arres…" He tried to stand again. Ingman pushed him down, harder this time.

"Why, Frank? Why would Chief Namakagon give you a map?"

"Loken, the next charge will be assault. Is that what you want?"

"Derkson, you are not arresting me, my nephew, or anyone else and you damn-well know it. Now, if you will not tell me why old Ice Feathers gave you this map, then at least tell me when."

"What?"

"When, Frank? Did you steal it from his lodge?"

"I never stole nothin' from no Indian Chief."

"So he gave it to you before he died then?"

"Yes. Before."

"On the trail to his lodge?"

"Yes. On the trail, Loken."

"Before the storm?"

"The storm? Yes… I mean … No."

"Well, I am damn sure he did not hand it to you after the storm. He was dead by then."

"He gave it to me during the storm. All right? During."

"During the storm. On the trail to his lodge?"

"Yes, Loken. Yes!"

"Before or after you hit him on the back of the head, Frank?"

"What? No. I never …"

"You and I both know he did not volunteer to give you a map to his silver mine, Frank. That can only mean one thing. You took it! You took it, Frank, and when you took it, he fought back and you smashed in his skull with that shotgun you carry—the shotgun down in your canoe. You killed him, Frank! He was yust another old Indian and you figured nobody would care if you gave him a tap on the back of the head with your double-barrel. A little harder than usual, right, Frank? A little harder than you would hit a sailor or a lumberyack or a miner or any white man. But he was yust an Indian. You hit him, right, Frank? You hit him!"

"All right, I hit him. Is that what you want to hear? I hit him and he slumped down and sat there. Just sat there in a daze. But I didn't kill him, Loken. I swear I did not kill him. He was alive when I left him there, see? I took the silver decoration he wore on his shirt and I left him. This medallion." He reached in his shirt pocket, then tossed the diamond-shaped medal to Tor.

"When I found out he did not show up at the Marengo Station where his woman was waitin', I went back. There he was. Sittin'. He never got up. He just sat there, Loken. Sat there starin' at me with those dark, frozen eyes of his. Starin' at me. I did not kill him, Loken. He died from the cold."

Tor wiped tears from his eyes. "That's why you buried him in a rush. You had to bury him right away—before anyone looked him over. You knew if a doctor got involved, there would bound to be trouble. And a death report. You knew without a doctor, there'd be no death report. You and the sheriff saw to it he was six feet under before anyone knew the better. I will wager there's no death record, no burial record, nothin'. Right, Frank? Right?"

"So what? So the old man is dead. Nobody cares. Another old Indian is dead and we have a map to a silver mine. Look, we can work it together. Even split. Right down the middle. The Derkson-Loken mine. What say you? Partners?"

"Many men have been made fools of chasing such rainbows," said Tor. "Your greed has you dreamin' dreams of riches you will never realize. What kind of fool believes in such nonsense?"

"You don't believe there's a mine? Then tell me, sonny, what do you call this?" Derkson pulled a chunk of raw silver from his pocket. "Look at it! Silver. High grade silver from the old Indian's mine."

"Why, that looks like the same piece of silver Billy Kavanaugh was showin' off," said Tor. "He must have given it to the chief."

"Given?" said Ingman. "Billy more likely traded it for something, I would venture."

"Then tell me," said Derkson, "what about the map?"

"This map?" said Ingman, holding it high. "This map? My nephew here drew this map not more than a few hours ago, Frank. You think this map will guide you to easy street? The only place this will take you is to prison. Prison, Frank Derkson, prison for murdering an old, unarmed man—crushing in his skull and leaving him out along a trail in a blizzard to freeze to death, you spineless coward. You are damn lucky Wisconsin allows no death penalty or your 'easy street' would lead right on up to the gallows."

Blood drained from Derkson's face. "No! That map is real. You are out to swindle me, Loken. You want the silver for yourself. It's real and I know it's real! I found it in the Indian's tobacco can. By rights it's mine. Nice try, Loken. Now hand it over. Give it here in the name of the law!"

Ingman held the map out of Derkson's reach. "I cannot imagine how the Ashland city fathers ever hired such a dimwitted idiot! Must've been your brother-in-law's doin'. Look." Ingman showed the side opposite the map. "See this? This is a receipt for goods bought and paid for by Olaf Loken of the Namakagon Timber Company. Olaf Loken, Frank. My brother. Tor's father, you mule-headed fool. You have been done in, Derkson. You are guilty of murder and thievery and you will be comin' with us for a visit to the sheriff, one way or the other. The Hayward sheriff, Frank. Not your brother-in-law. Now get up."

The deputy sat silently on his stump, staring at the chunk of high-grade silver ore in his hand. He stood slowly without taking his eyes from the silver. Suddenly, he swung, striking Ingman on the jaw with the piece of ore. Ingman collapsed. Tor reached to catch him. Both fell back. Derkson sprinted down the trail to the lake. He stepped into his canoe. One foot in his canoe and the other on shore, he gave a shove. The canoe glided out onto the quiet water. Frank paddled out and waited.

Ingman and Tor ran down to the shore, finding Derkson, shotgun at the ready.

"Loken, you and the boy best not follow me. Whether that map is real or not matters no more. If you forget all this happened, you can have the whole she-bang."

"That will not do," shouted Tor. "You need to account for your crimes, Derkson. You murdered Chief Namakagon and you are going to stand before a judge."

"Loken, you tell your nephew to wise up. You and I both know there ain't a judge in Wisconsin willin' to try me, a lawman, for tappin' some Indian on the head—some Indian who was disturbin' the peace, resistin' arrest. Case closed. I'm givin' you the map, the silver mine, the whole she-bang. That should be enough, Loken. I'm washin' my hands of the whole deal. I have had my fill of this country. You dassn't follow me, now. You go back to your lumberin'. Leave me alone. Hear?"

Tor and Ingman watched as Derkson paddled east, rounding the point to the south.

"Where do you suppose he's headed?" said Tor.

"Must be makin' for the river outlet. He said he had enough of this country. Easier to go downstream than up."

"He's headed for the river?"

"Goes all the way to New Orleans, Nephew, and no train fare to pay."

"You think he figures we won't follow him?"

"I am sure of it. Derkson is counting on us takin' more interest in the silver than him. He thinks we want it for ourselves."

"If he is bound for the river outlet, he will have to go all the way around Bear Point. We could cross the point, Uncle. We could cut him off above the dam."

"You're right. We could."

"We cannot let him get away, Uncle Ingman. We owe it to Mikwam-migwan, to Diindiisi, to him. Derkson must pay for his crimes."

"Then, Nephew, I say we best ready our canoe. The chase is on!"

Chapter 30
Whitewater, Buckshot, and Blood

November 21, 1886

Deep snow slowed the Lokens' portage to the river outlet. As they reached the lakeshore again, preparing to launch their birch canoe, they saw Frank Derkson come around the Bear Point. Crossing the bay as they hid on shore, the rogue lawman entered the narrows leading to the dam and river below. Having lost the element of surprise, the Lokens followed, keeping well behind their quarry.

Tor turned from his bow seat. "What do we do when we catch him, Uncle?"

"He doesn't know we're close behind. Surprise is still on our side. Once we catch up, we hang back out of sight till the time is right."

"Time is right? How will we know?"

"We will know it when we see it, Nephew."

Silently following the winding river, they soon caught sight of Derkson. They stayed back, waiting for the right opportunity. Every time they rounded another bend, they would spot him far ahead. Then, skirting a small island in the river, they saw Derkson, much closer.

"Make for the alders," whispered Ingman.

The Lokens ducked into an alder patch along shore, waiting until Derkson rounded the next bend.

Resuming their stalk, they now moved at a snail's pace, not wanting to overtake Derkson until the right moment. They crept silently downstream, waiting to see him. Bend after bend, revealed no sight of him. Frank Derkson, it seemed, had vanished.

Tor turned again. "He may have seen us, Uncle," he whispered. "The coward could be hiding anywhere along shore. Maybe in the woods or even up some creek. We won't see hide nor hair."

"That's what I am counting on, Nephew. If Derkson pulls onto shore or up some creek, we might pass by, unnoticed. Then we can get ahead of him and lay in wait. Or make our way to one of the camps downstream to get help."

"But, how will we know if we have passed him by?"

"If we pace ourselves, if we slowly float downstream, we should see sign where he pulled onto shore. We have good snow. He will leave a good track."

"And, if he slides up some creek? What then?"

"Look for snow knocked from overhanging branches and off rocks. It's not easy to hide your trail with this much snow on the ground."

"What if Derkson sees us first? Sees us passing by? Then what?"

"If that happens, there's nothing for us to do but to go for help. If we can reach town before him, get to Bill Burns, get to the telegraph office, we can stop him from escaping downstream.

"He has that shotgun, Uncle Ingman. You plum sure he will not use it? 'Specially out here where he could leave us in some swamp, neither to be seen nor heard from again."

"No, Derkson would not be so foolish as to risk using that shotgun on a white man. He knows it could mean life in prison, unlike what he's already admitted to."

"I disagree, Uncle Ingman. If he did use the shotgun, what would folks hear? A distant shot. Nothing you don't hear now and again this time of year. And who would hear him out in this country? Nobody around for miles, most likely."

"There are lumberjacks a-plenty workin' all 'round here. Ole Swenson's camp, for one. Say, I believe Arnie Peterson's outfit has a camp yust ahead. We can put in there and find out if anyone saw Derkson go downstream."

Tor and Ingman cautiously floated another half mile before reaching the Peterson lumber camp landing.

"Hello in the camp," Tor yelled from the canoe. Two men in kitchen aprons came down the riverbank. "We are lookin for ..."

"For a friend," said Ingman. "Maybe come by here, oh, 'bout a half-hour ago."

"Cannot say as we seen him, Mister. No, nobody come by here that we know 'bout."

"Ingman paddled closer to the bank. Anyone else here that might have seen him?"

"Nope. They's all out in the cuttings. Must make hay when the sun shines, you know. Why you lookin' for him? Ain't lost is he?"

"No," said Tor. "Friend of mine. I owe him some money and wanted to get it to him before he left to look for work down in Chippeway Falls."

"You could leave it here with me. I could keep a lookout for him and see to it he gets it."

"Why, that surely is kind of you to offer to do that for us," said Ingman. "I think we will keep on searching, though. We are bound to find him."

"You certain? We'd be pleased to be of help."

"Much obliged," said Ingman, pushing off.

With a single thrust of his paddle, Tor had the canoe out into the current again. It pulled them slowly downstream and around a sweeping bend. He turned to speak.

"Uncle, do you think they knew…"

"Seems they acted rather strange. I wouldn't be surprised if … Nephew, look … over there!" He pointed to a clear track made by a canoe dragged into the woods. "It must be Derkson. I got a feelin' that he pulled beyond the camp, onto shore with plans to circle back."

"Maybe he is looking for food," said Tor.

"Or, maybe he has friends here. Those two fellas could have been lying through their teeth for all we know."

As they paddled closer to shore, a shotgun blast shattered the quiet river valley. Ingman slumped to the bottom of the canoe.

"Uncle! Uncle Ingma …"

A second shot tore a dozen pea-size holes through the canoe near Tor's knee. He jammed his paddle into the river bottom and pushed out with all his might, snapping the spruce blade. The canoe, caught in the current, slowly turned broadside to the hidden assassin. Tor leaned far back, fumbled for his uncle's paddle, found it, and turned the canoe downstream. Paddling furiously, a third shot rang out and the water to his left seemed to explode as the buckshot ripped into the river's surface. A balsam windfall caught the bow, turning the craft sideways in the current again. A fourth shot came from the woods and balsam pine needles flew into the air, falling like rain on Ingman who lay motionless in the bottom of the canoe. Three quick strokes of his paddle and the tree separated killer and canoe. Tor paddled desperately, hoping the spruce blade would stand the strain. Another shotgun blast tore through the tree, then another. Finally, as Tor rounded the next river bend, dead silence.

"Uncle, Uncle!" shouted Tor.

"Paddle!" Ingman forced from his lips. "For mercy sake paddle! He's bound … to run downstream … through the woods. He could be … upon us any second. Don't fret 'bout me. Paddle … for your … life or … he'll have us … both!"

Ingman slumped further down. Blood soaked through his wool coat and soon coated the bottom of the canoe. Tor paddled and paddled, eyes wide for any movement on shore. He raced downstream, trying to avoid exposed rocks and overhanging tree limbs.

"Uncle, how bad are you hurt?"

"Yust paddle ...for your life, Tor!"

"You're bleeding. We have to stop it before you bleed to death!"

"Do as ... you're told. Man running ... through the woods ... can keep up ... with canoe. You must ... outrun him ... to Swenson camp ... 'bout six miles ...downstream ... Paddle."

Tor's muscles burned and shoulders ached from the strain of furious, deep paddle strokes. The canoe raced around bend after bend, closing the distance between the site of the vicious ambush and Ole Swenson's camp.

The silence of the river valley soon changed to the soft sound of wind in the pines. Tor paddled on, ever closer to the help he sought ahead. The sound of the wind increased prompting a skyward glance. Something was wrong. The trees did not sway. Their branches were still. Yet, the sound of wind grew louder and louder. He suddenly realized why.

"Uncle!" he yelled. "Hang on best you can. Rapids ahead!"

"You must ... keep tight ... left bank ... till past ... red granite rock ... then stay ... midstream. Don't let ... low branches ... steal your hat ... Nephew."

The canoe made the final bend above the rapids. Tor's eyes widened. The wild roar of the whitewater rapids masked his words. "Lord help us, Uncle Ingman. Hold on!"

The current pulled at the canoe, trying to turn it crosswise in the stream. Racing downriver under the force of the raging stream, Tor paddled with all the strength he could find, gradually guiding the birch canoe close to the left bank. Using his paddle to steer, he ducked as they flew under overhanging tree limbs and dodged protruding, ancient rocks. Far ahead, he spotted the huge red granite boulder. Reaching it in mere seconds, he pulled back on his paddle, trying to turn toward midstream. The canoe did not turn. With a loud "thud," the canoe hit the exposed boulder, then hit another and another. Water splashed up and over, drenching both passengers. The canoe spun sideways, then spun again as they hit another rock. More water splashed in. Sailing downriver stern-first, Tor planted his paddle on a rock and pushed. The canoe spun again, tipping, almost capsizing, then righting itself, now in midstream. The canoe straightened out. Like a hunter's arrow, they sped down the white, raging river, narrowly missing boulder after boulder and sliding over others just below the surface. Ahead, Tor made out the tail of the rapids. He guided the leaking canoe past the last rocks and into the quiet water below, then breathed a deep breath of relief.

"We made it, Uncle! We're beyond the whitewater."

Ingman made no reply. Tor turned. Three inches of red water sloshed in the canoe. Ingman Loken lay motionless, drenched with his own river-thinned blood.

"Uncle? Uncle Ingman!" shouted the boy. "Uncle!"

Ingman Loken raised his head enough to see his nephew out of one eye, then lowered it again. "S-still got ... your hat ... I see."

"Still got it, Uncle Ingman."

"Your paddle?"

"Got that, too."

"Good. Next one ... is worse."

Tor pulled onto a snow-covered spit of sand and shifted his uncle, making him as comfortable as he could for the next leg of the trek. Using his hat, he bailed some of the bloody water and took the stern seat, knowing he would have better control. In less than two minutes he was on the water again, back to his feverish pace, trying to distance his canoe from the last sight of the shotgun-wielding assailant and hoping to find help for his uncle. Stroke after stroke, the blade sliced into the frigid, foamy water. Down the river they sped, Ingman's breathing now labored, his nephew's muscles burning, and the canoe again filling with ice water. Large flakes of snow began to fall, melting on contact with Ingman's mackinaw. As the snowfall increased, it stayed, turning Ingman's red and black plaid wool coat a bright white and then red again as more blood soaked through the wet snow.

"Stay with me, Uncle. It cannot be far. We will make it. You will see, Uncle Ingman. I bet Ole's got someone in camp who is as good at doctorin' as old Sourdough. Dang it, I sure wish old Sourdough was here now. He would fix you up." Tor dodged a windfall.

"Yessiree, Uncle, Sourdough could have you mended in no time—no time at all. He would make you drink down some of that godawful lemon extract of his. Yechh. Ever taste that terrible elixir of his, that lemon extract? Might be fine for pies, but it sure is horrible for drinking. Worst tasting stuff around. I swear it tastes as bad as that kerosene Leroy Phipps hoodwinked me into drinking that time out in the cuttings. You would probably like it though—Sourdough's lemon extract, not the kerosene. Boy, I sure got Leroy back for that one—the kerosene, I mean. Remember? We dumped ol' Leroy Phipps' skinny butt right into the muddy water down by the dock. Why, the whole camp was there to bear witness. Every lumberjack in camp saw it. That was something, right, Uncle? Uncle?"

Ingman did not reply.

"Uncle Ingman, you hold on now. I will get you to Ole Swenson's camp right soon. Don't give up, Uncle. You cannot give up."

Tor paddled, wiping sweat, melting snow, and tears from his face with the sleeve of his coat. The snow continued flakes as large and soft as angels' pillows, as his mother used to tell him. In the bow, his uncle lay motionless. A thick layer of white soon conquered the red of the blood seeping below. Stroke after stroke, Tor raced ahead. The sound of wind came again, though the snow gently floated straight down. The sound grew and grew as before.

"Wenebojo!" Tor screamed into the snowy forest. "Wenebojo, for Pete's sake, show us some mercy! Remember us? We are the Lokens—the ones who try hard to take care of these woods and waters, and we could use a little help!"

The falling snow and ever-increasing roar of rapids ahead absorbed Tor's words. The river narrowed, its current carrying the canoe faster and faster downstream. Tor rounded the next bend and shouted again.

"Hang on if you are able, Uncle Ingman. This is it. No turning back!"

The river necked down to a narrow channel between steep, rocky ridges. Huge midstream boulders created white rooster tails and eddies that pushed and pulled the canoe, rocking it, jerking it violently as Tor tried to steer by dragging the blade of his paddle on one side, then the other. The bow slid up and over one submerged rock after another. Tor's view of the waters ahead was obscured by the heavy snowfall. It mattered little. The river had control. The canoe bounced over rock after rock, hanging up on some, slipping across others. Finally, Tor guided the frail, leaking craft through the tail of the rapids and into quiet water again. But he knew he could not rest, could not relax. He paddled and paddled, harder than before, knowing time was working against his uncle.

"We made it Uncle. Whaddaya think about that? We made it past both rapids. Dang. I hope to see no more rocks for a piece. We are taking on water fast enough as it is. Uncle? Uncle Ingman?"

Ingman Loken lay still, silent, the snow on his coat washed away, and more bloody water sloshing side to side as the canoe moved downstream.

"Uncle Ingman, you hang on. Ole Swenson's outfit must be close. Wenebojo will get us there. Got us past that last washboard, he did. I know we can count on him. Old Ice Feathers told me that. And the Chief knew from what he was saying, I'd say. I'm telling  you, Uncle, once we get out of this here bear trap, once we get you on the mend, I'm going to make things right. Old Namakagon should not have died like that. No sir. He lived a good life. He never meant any harm to a soul. I'm telling you right now, Uncle, Frank Derkson is gonna pay for what he has done. He murdered Chief Namakagon. He peppered you with buckshot. Who knows what other evil things he has done. By God, he is gonna pay and pay dearly. We are gonna track him no matter where he goes. We will get him, Uncle. Mark my gol-dang words, sooner or later, hell or high water, Derkson will pay and pay dearly."

Arms burning, weak, Tor kept the canoe in the midstream current, paddling when he could. He tried to keep his eyes on the river ahead, though distracted by the sight of his uncle who sprawled before him in the bottom of the bow. Down the river they descended until, through the softly falling snowflakes, came an unexpected but familiar aroma of a hardwood fire.

"Smoke! Smoke, Uncle Ingman! Smell it? We must be nearby the Swenson camp. Yaheee! We made it! Look, Uncle, look!

Downstream! The landing. Right there! Right there!"

"Hello in the camp." Tor screamed. "Help us! Help us, fellas! My uncle has been shot! Help!"

A bell rang out as the canoe nosed up onto the landing. A cook and a man wearing the leather apron of a saw filer raced down the hill with other men behind.

"My uncle has been shot. Lost a lot of blood. Who does your doctoring? We need …"

"Slow down there, sonny," said the cook. "We will take care of him now. Our barn boss will see to it your uncle is tended to proper." They pulled the canoe onto shore.

"Barn boss? You look like the camp cook. Can you patch fellas up?"

"Our barn boss does our camp doctorin', whether it is swine, horses, or people," replied the man in the white apron. "If your uncle can be saved, Clive Schmidt will do the savin'."

"I'm obliged, fellas. My uncle Ingman and I are deep in debt to you."

"Ingman, you say? Not Ingman Loken, is it?" He lifted the brim of Ingman's hat. "Why, sure enough. Boys, get him up to the cook shanty. Make haste, now. Robert, you go get Clive. Tell him not to dally. This fella owes me a dollar-thirty-five in poker table change, and, by golly, we're gonna see to it I get paid."

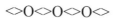

Chapter 31
Lady Luck and Horse Liniment

November 21, 1886

Ingman Loken, pale from blood loss, lay motionless on a cook shanty table in Ole Swenson's lumber camp on the Namekagon River. Clive Schmidt, barn boss and substitute doctor for the Swenson outfit, leaned over, ear to Ingman's face, hoping to hear breathing. Seven men looked on including Ingman's nephew.

"Not good," said Clive. "Robert, fetch me your shavin' mirror."

He held the glass close to Ingman's nose.

"No use," said Smiley. "He's dead."

"No. Least not yet," said Clive as the mirror fogged slightly. "There, Smiley, see that? Still breathin'."

"Just barely. He would not get the attention of any field surgeon I ever met. No sir."

Another wisp of moisture fogged the mirror. "Well this ain't the U.S. Army, Smiley. Be glad for it. Go ahead and cut off his coat and shirt. Robert, bring me a dishrag and half-a-bucket of hot water. James, you will find some rolled-up bandages in the lard can above the wood box. Fetch me a few rolls."

Tor helped pull his uncle's mackinaw and blood-soaked shirt free. "You can save him, right, Doc? My uncle won't die, will he?"

"By the looks of it, he lost a good deal of blood. Barely breathin'. Right now I believe your uncle is in Lady Luck's hands more than mine. I will do what I can." He turned toward the cookstove. "Robert? Say, Robert! Where is that gol-dang dishrag?"

"Here you go, Clive. Watch it, she's hot as a poker."

The backwoods doctor squeezed excess water from the rag. As the hot, wet cloth met his chest, Ingman gasped.

"So, Smiley, you still think he is dead? This fella is in what you call, shock. We got to get him warmed up. Get what little blood that might be left in him circulating again. Pull off them wet britches. James, get me some blankets but warm 'em up on the cookstove first. Good and hot, but, for Pete's sake, don't burn 'em lest Ole dock your pay. You, boy, take this here rag and wash your uncle down. Clean up all that blood. Smiley, I got some horse liniment in the barn that will draw out any poisons in those buckshot holes. You'll find it in a coffee can under my bunk. Make haste."

Tor dipped the rag in the bucket. "What about the pellets?"

"I ain't no prestidigitator, boy, just a plain old barn boss during winter and a farmer come spring. I would do far more harm tryin' to fish that buckshot out than if I just leave the pellets be. Should your uncle pull through, you can get him to Doctor Cox down in Hayward. He might be willin' to dig 'em out. 'Sides, your uncle would not be the first lumberjack 'round here with buckshot ridin' under his hide, though I 'spect most carry it in their backside."

As Tor washed away the sticky, clotted blood, he counted three holes in his uncle's chest and six more in his left shoulder. None of the pellets had passed through. Blood seeped from four of the openings. Clive Schmidt rubbed his homemade horse liniment into the wounds, applied folded, floursack rags, and bandaged Ingman with strips torn from old bedsheets.

"We should get him to Hayward—to Doctor Cox," said Tor.

"Too risky, boy. Your uncle might not survive the trip down the East Road to town. Best thing right now is to make him comfortable, keep him warm. There is a chance he will pull through if he is tough enough and the good Lord is on his side."

"And Wenebojo," said Tor.

"Hmm?"

"Wenebojo and Gitchee Manitou are looking after him. I know it. I can feel it. They are here. Right here." He rinsed the dishrag and wiped Ingman's brow.

"What the blazes you talkin' about, boy?"

"My uncle will pull through, I know it. The spirits are with him." Tor placed his hand on Ingman's damp brow. "C'mon, Uncle Ingman, show these fellas what we Lokens are made of."

"Son, we should leave him rest," said Clive. "What he needs most right now is to keep warm and rest up. Should your uncle make it through till daylight, well, he might just see the loons return in May. Course, that's supposin' he stays clear of your shotgun."

"What?"

"Your shotgun. Were you two huntin' deer?"

"When?"

"When you shot him."

"Shot him? Me? No sir. I never shot him."

"Oh, another hunter, then?"

"No, no hunter. A killer—a murderous, cowardly assassin by the name of Frank Derkson."

"What kind of bull you shovelin', boy? Ain't no shame in one hunter shootin' another by accident. Such things happen. Nobody will hold it against you. But, there is shame in lyin' about it."

"Look, I'm telling you, Clive, I did not shoot my uncle. We were followin' the fella who murdered Chief Namakagon up in the Marengo mining country last week. His trail took us down the river where he ambushed us. Peppered my uncle, but missed me clear."

"Paper said nothin' about no murder," said Smiley. "Said the old boy had too much fire water, laid down to rest, and plum froze solid."

"In a blizzard, yes," replied Tor. "I know full well what the Ashland Press reported. The writer of that article was dead wrong. Let me ask you. Would you get drunk and lay down to rest in a blizzard?"

"Well ..."

"That's what the newspaper reported. Seems everybody who read that paper takes it as Gospel. Think about it. Old Ice Feathers lived here forty years. He would not get drunk and lay down to rest on a trail near his camp in a blizzard. Nor did I ever know him to drink much and certainly not in the midday. Not Chief Namakagon."

"But, we ..."

"Did you see his body, Clive?"

"His body? No. But, ..."

"I did. I also saw the blow to his head. I saw the blood. I heard Frank Derkson confess to his murder, and I was with my uncle when Derkson shot him. What more do you want?"

"Son, you cannot expect me to ..."

Tor turned to the others. "You have to believe me. Just look at our canoe."

"Boy's right, Clive. There's a score of holes near the front thwart, 'bout knee-high. In one side, clean out the other. Looks like buckshot, all right."

Clive Schmidt put the lid on his liniment can. "Maybe that's the work of the boy, too."

"What?" snapped Tor, "Now, you listen here. I neither shot my dear uncle nor our canoe. We were ambushed, like I said. Whether it was the assassin's poor aim or my good fortune, God's will, or Wenebojo's, I somehow got missed clean. Now, somewhere out there is Frank Derkson with a double-barrel shotgun and a pocketful of spent brass shells. He murdered the old chief, tried to slay my

Uncle Ingman, and do the same to me."

Robert swiped Tor's hat from his head. "Clive, look here," he said, inspecting the brim. "Two holes—same size as them in the boat and in the boy's uncle."

Tor grabbed his hat, looked at the holes, and waved it in front of the camp doctor's face. "Clive, I need a horse and saddle. I'm headin' for town. Bill Burns needs to know about this post haste. He will know what to do."

"All right. I will ask Ole about loanin' you a horse when he returns tomor…"

"No, Clive. I need it now. And I want you to send someone over to the Namakagon Timber Company camp. Tell my pa what happened. He needs to be here … be with his brother in case … well, in case he does not pull through."

"Now, hang on there, boy. I don't know if …"

"Well, I do," said the cook. "Clive, I believe the boy's every word. We are gonna do what he says. Ole will approve. I know it. Your job is to keep Ingman breathin'. I'm sendin' Whitey Whitmann over to the Loken Camp." He turned to Tor. "C'mon, boy. This ain't no time for us to stand around jawin'. Let me get you that horse."

"Who put you in charge, Chauncey? I am the camp doctor and, dang it, I am runnin' things here."

Chauncey grabbed Clive by the collar and raised a clenched fist. "You ain't runnin' nothing nowhere, Clive. You have no say in this. One more word and you will be pickin' what few teeth you got left from out between the cracks in the floorboards."

"Ah, do what you want. 'Tain't worth neither of us gettin' busted up over it."

Chauncey turned to the others. "Now, I am fixin' the boy up with a horse. If Ole was here, he would do the same gol-dang thing. Anyone here wish to squabble 'bout that?"

The room fell silent.

"All right, then. C'mon, boy. You need to get to town."

<>O<>O<>O<>

Chapter 32
Behind Johnny Pion's Hotel

November 21, 1886

By the time the Omaha pulled up to the depot, darkness obscured Hayward. Tor jumped from the slow-rolling passenger car, running across the rail yard and down Iowa Avenue to the office of Doctor Arnold Cox. He pounded on the locked door with his fist, drawing attention from all those on the busy street. The shopkeeper next door poked his head out.

"Lord in Heaven, young man. What is all the dang ruckus about?"

"I need the doc. Fast. Where is he?"

"What for? You don't look sick to me."

"Where is the doc?"

"He ain't here."

"I see that. Where is he?"

"You ain't told me …"

Tor grabbed the clerk by the collar, jerking him out of his shop and onto the sidewalk. "Gol-dang it, my uncle has been shot. Where in blazes is the doctor?"

"You look in the hotel bar?"

Tor dodged lumberjacks and shoppers, racing down the wood plank sidewalk before bursting through the lobby doors. The doctor sat at the bar, an empty shot glass and half-empty beer mug before him.

"Doc! My uncle's been shot. He's in an awful fix. Lost a lotta blood. White as a ghost. You must come."

"Who?"

"My uncle. Ingman Loken."

"Can he pay?"

"What?"

"Can your uncle afford my services?"

"Of course."

"Then get him over to my office. I will be there soon as I finish my supper, sonny."

"You don't understand, Doc. He has been shot bad. Buckshot in the chest. Can't be moved."

"Where is he?"

"Ole Swenson's camp. East of Cable."

"East of Cable? I have no intention of traveling to …Look. You'll just have to bring him here."

"We are afraid to move him. Doc, he is in an awful way. You must come."

"In this weather? In the dark? On that god-awful, miserable East Road?"

"Doc, please! He'll die. I know it."

"What did you say his name was?"

"Not was, Doc, is. Ingman Loken."

"Ingman Loken. Olaf Loken's brother?"

"Olaf is my pa."

"You don't say! Seems I sewed up your uncle's chin once or twice. Tended to your pa, too. All right, off to the camp we go. Bartender, another pint of Old Crow. Looks like I have work to do."

The bartender handed him a bottle. "Thirty cents, Doc. Want it on your bill?"

"Here," said Tor, slapping a silver dollar and a hand-written note on the bar. "Get this note to the sheriff right away. Take out for the whiskey and keep the rest. C'mon, Doc, we have to catch the last northbound."

Doctor Cox slipped the pint into his coat pocket. "I need my medical kit, son. It's in my other office."

"Then, I'll meet you on the platform, Doc, tickets in hand."

As the day's last train rumbled north, two men quietly spoke in the shadows behind the hotel. One was Deputy Frank Derkson.

"Listen, mister," said Derkson, "this was s'posed to be simple. That's what you said, remember? Simple. Now they are after me. By morning, every lawman north of Chippeway will be keepin' an eye peeled for Frank Derkson. I need your help and, by God, you will give it to me. You hear? I swear, if I go to jail, you go with me."

"Calm down. I will see to it you do not face prosecution, my friend. We cannot have an upstanding officer of the law in the calaboose, ay, Deputy?"

"Look, you don't understand. They almost had me at the island, then again on the river. All because of that dead Indian. Now I'm in a real fix. I had to shoot Ingman Loken just to get away. Most likely killed him! On the way down here that damn nephew of his was in the next passenger car. I cannot show my face in public no more—cannot even go back to my shack to get my bankroll. I am flat broke.

x

I need money and I need to get out of town so I can hide out for a bit."

"That, Frank, is not my problem."

"Look, dammit. You got me into this. Now you are gonna help me get out of it. And, to start, I need more money."

"Here, take this." A thick roll of bills passed from one man to the other. "You lay low for a bit, then you finish the job, hear? Finish it. Then you get far, far away from here."

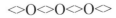

"All right. But I lost me my livelihood, my shack, my bankroll, too. Not to mention that silver mine, thanks to you. When they are dead, when it's over and done, I expect another payment to cover my losses."

"Done. I will see to it you are well-compensated."

"All right, then. I will finish it—the boy, his uncle, and his pa will join the Indian, as agreed."

"As agreed."

<>O<>

Constable Bill Burns arrived at Ole Swenson's Lumber Camp shortly after dark. He opened the cook shanty door. Stretched out on a table lay Ingman Loken wrapped in wool blankets, his breathing shallow and labored. Olaf Loken sat at the end of the oilcloth-covered table, his head resting on his folded arms. Olaf looked up.

"Bill! Thank God you are here. Is Tor with you? I tell ya, I been so worried about …"

"Your boy is fine, Olaf. I sent him to Hayward to fetch Doctor Cox. How is your brother doin'?"

"I can't tell, Bill. All he does is lay there, white as a ghost, barely breathin'. Sometimes he gasps for air. I wish I knew what to do to help him."

"He is a tough old bird, Olaf. If anyone can beat this, Ingman Loken can."

"That's the problem."

"Hmm?"

"Maybe nobody can."

"Don't give up on him, Olaf. Do not give up."

<>O<>O<>O<>

Chapter 33
Dead Sure

November 22, 1886

Negotiating the tote road to Ole Swenson's lumber camp was no easy task in the dark, though the kerosene lantern provided by the Cable stationmaster helped. The wet heavy snow slowed travel even more. Snow-laden overhead branches bent low over the trail. When brushed by the horse pulling the train station's cutter, it fell onto the mare and the men. Cold and wet, Tor and Doctor Cox finally entered the warm cook shanty at Ole Swenson's camp after midnight. Tor rushed to his father and uncle.

"Tor, thank God. I was so worried. Worried that ..."

"I know, Pa, I know. But I'm fine. How is Ingman doing?"

"He is still with us, though he has not stirred since I got here."

"Then we are not too late. I brought Doctor Cox."

Olaf turned. "Doc! Thank you for coming all this way. Ingman here is in awful, awful shape."

"Doctor Cox," said Tor, "my uncle will live, right?"

"Son, give the doctor a chance to look him over."

Doctor Cox placed his palm on the injured man's forehead. Lifting an eyelid, he looked into Ingman's eye. Next, he pulled back the wool blankets, placing his ear to Ingman's heart. Taking a scissors from his medical kit, he cut through the blood-soaked bandages, revealing the wounds, now swollen, red and oozing.

"Will he be alright, Doc?" said Tor.

The doctor reached in his bag, retrieving a brown bottle. He pulled the cork, saturating a rag before dabbing it on Ingman's wounds. Finished, he tipped the bottle up, swallowing two, three, then four times.

"Fair chance he might pull through. You were right in that he lost a lot of blood. But the bleeding has stopped. Had it not, he would be gone by now."

"What do you mean when you say, 'fair chance,' Doc?" asked Olaf.

"Infection might set in. Blood poisoning, fever. If he can stave these off, why, he just might recover. On the other hand, should his arm putrefy, we will have to take it."

"Take it?" said Tor.

"Amputate." He took another swallow and pressed the cork into the bottle.

Olaf shuddered from the word. "Do all you can, Doc."

"Of course, Olaf, of course."

Doctor Cox placed new dressings on Ingman's wounds and covered him again. "A night's rest for us now. We will be off to Hayward in the morning if Ingman is up to it."

Tor looked at his uncle, pale and still. "He will live though to morning, then?"

The doctor replied, "Day in and day out, every creature alive is in the Lord's hands, Tor. The best we can do is wait and see, pray, and have faith." He turned to Olaf. "Your boy says they were ambushed along the river."

"Appears to be so. Tor, you were not hurt?"

"Not a scratch, Pa. First load of buckshot hit Uncle Ingman square. Every shot after missed. We did not linger long enough to offer the coward another easy target. Hightailed out of there fast as I could paddle. Derkson either ran out of shells or figured he would never catch us by running through the woods. Either way, we never caught sight of the spineless murderer again."

"Derkson? You are certain? Frank Derkson?"

"Oh, it was Derkson all right."

"Tor, that's a serious claim you make. You absolutely sure?"

"Sure? I am dead sure, Pa. We watched him from afar as he ransacked the chief's lodge near Marengo. We managed to lay a snare for the fool and captured him at Chief Namakagon's island camp. Pa, Ingman squeezed a confession right out of him. He admitted killing the chief, though he showed no repentance for the deed."

"Derkson admitted killing Mikwam-migwan? He said this?"

"Yes. Derkson confessed, all right. Admitted to striking Chief, leaving him to freeze in the blizzard. Here. Look at this." Tor pulled the diamond-shaped silver medallion from his pocket. "Derkson gave me this. Said he took it off Namakagon's body after he bashed in his skull. Look at it. It belonged to Chief all right. I saw it many times, same as you, Pa."

Olaf inspected the medal, turning it over. "What is this 'J T' on the back?"

"J T?" said Tor. "Where?"

Olaf held it out.

"Hmm. J T, clear as day. Maybe Derkson did that. No matter, Pa. Derkson confessed to the murder of Chief Namakagon. Ingman and I heard him plain and clear. I'll swear it before any judge."

"So, how is it that Derkson found his way downriver?"

"He buffaloed Uncle Ingman and managed to escape by canoe. We took after him. He must've got wind we were close behind and laid for us. Pa, I am dead sure Frank Derkson is the scoundrel who shot Uncle Ingman. Shot Ingman, all right, and tried his best to slay me to boot!"

The cook shanty door swung open. Bill Burns and two Swenson camp men stepped in, stomping snow from their boots. Bill hung his lantern on a nail and peeled off his wet coat, shaking the snow from it. "Olaf, Tor, I fear Derkson gave us the slip. We tracked him only as far as the river. By the looks of it, he hightailed it downstream."

"You're sure he's not out there now?"

"I'd say when he spotted Tor's canoe and all the man-tracks at the landing he kept on a-goin. At dawn I plan to light out for Cable. I intend to get word out to every railroad constable and sheriff in the pinery to keep an eye peeled. We will catch him, Olaf. Frank Derkson will suffer for his dirty work, as God is my witness."

"Bill," said Tor, "I got word to the sheriff in Hayward. We should speak to every camp boss between here and there, too."

"We?" said Olaf.

"Me and Bill, Pa."

"This is a matter for the law, Tor."

"I can help. He is my uncle. I was right there when it happened, even got shot at. I have to help."

"You can help more by staying by his side. You can help me keep him comfortable on the trip to Hayward."

"But, Pa, I ..."

"Son, use your head. You know nothing about detective work. Bill does."

"Your Pa is right," said Bill. "Your uncle needs your help right now more than I do. But never you fret, Tor. We will find this polecat sooner or later. I will not let this go—not after what he did to your Uncle and to Earl Morrison."

Tor held out the diamond-shaped silver medallion. "And what he did to Chief Namakagon."

<>O<>O<>O<>

Chapter 34
By Dark of Night

December 13, 1886

Constable Bill Burns sat with his feet to the fire in the Namakagon Timber Company lodge. "Olaf, Tor," he said, "Frank Derkson seems to have vanished into thin air. I have had every stationmaster and railroad constable in the pinery and beyond watching for him for weeks. Nobody has seen hide nor hair ever since the shooting. I am convinced he fled this country for good."

"Bill," said Tor, "he did tell my uncle and me he was pulling up stakes on that dark day he ambushed us. Sounded to me like he was fed up and headin' out for good."

Olaf tamped the tobacco in his pipe and struck a match. "I s'pose that means he could be 'most anywhere by now. Bill, I appreciate the work you have put in on this. I imagine he is either gone for good, or he will show up in the hands of another lawman somewhere. Until we hear different, maybe life should be business as usual."

"I will keep on this murderous ne'er-do-well's trail as best I can Olaf. I'll do it for your brother. Seems it's the least I can do.

"Tor and I are off to Hayward tomorrow to visit Ingman. Come along if you want, Bill."

"No, you two go ahead. The little lady has been askin' me to tend to chores around home, especially with Christmas right around the corner. You tell Ingman I said to hurry up and get his lazy backside out of bed so I can teach him a few more lessons at the poker table."

"I will do that, Bill. I imagine he's champin' at the bit for it."

By dusk the next day, Olaf and Tor strolled down Iowa Avenue, turning into the office of Arnold Cox, M.D.

"Afternoon, Doc. My brother awake? Hope he is not givin' you too much guff."

"You brother? Oh, dear me, Olaf. Have you not heard?"

"Heard? Heard what, Doc? What is it?"

Tor interrupted. "Didn't take a turn for the worse, did he, Doc?"

"No, no, nothing like that. On the contrary, he is doing quite well. In fact, he's recuperating up at Adeline Ringstadt's Boarding House. I figured he no longer needed my care. What little infection he had is gone. So is the fever. Lucky man, your uncle. Seems as though anybody else would be in the graveyard after what he went through.

I told him I would haul him up to Adeline's in a wheelchair where he can enjoy some company and her good cooking. He would not hear of it. I swear, the stubborn old ox wanted to walk."

"Cannot say as I blame him," said Olaf.

"Isn't that just like Uncle Ingman for you, Pa? So, Doc, he walked all the way, I mean, up the hill?"

"He also insisted on stopping at Pete Foster's for a game of cribbage and a beer. I had a helluva time getting him out of there!"

"Yessir, that's Uncle Ingman."

"Olaf, I can keep an eye on him for a few more days. I 'spect he can head back to your camp by the end of the week."

"Wonderful, Doc. You do not know how much we appreciate ..."

"I know you do, Olaf. I am pleased I was able to help your brother pull through. Most men would not have made it, you know. He has quite the constitution."

"Doc, I will stop by on the way out of town and pay the bill."

"Fine. Fine. I will have it ready for you. If I'm not here, I will be around the corner."

"Around the corner?" said Tor.

"My other office."

"You have another office?"

"The hotel bar, Tor."

Oil lamps in the businesses along Iowa Avenue cast a soft glow onto the snow-covered scene. Garland, wreaths, and red bows in the windows invited shoppers. Lively piano music from the taverns drifted through the downtown. As Tor and his father passed by the windows of the Clark House, a man stumbled out of the bar.

"Why, if it ain't Tor Loken the bark eater," he said with a slur.

"Muldoon? I thought you left for a climate more comfortable for snakes and lizards."

"Hate to disappoint but, in spite of this infernal sawdust smoke and perspiration stench, I am still here. Don't ask why. Say, you heard about Billy and his little brother being lost in that shipwreck?"

"Of course."

"Raw deal. I lost a fortune."

"You?"

"I covered half the sale for Billy. Oh, well. Spilt milk, right? 'Sides, I have an insurance. Say, I heard about your uncle, too. Tough luck. First Billy and his brother, then the old Indian, then your uncle. Dangerous place this pinery. So, is he dead, then?"

"My Uncle? Takes more than a load of buckshot to hinder a Loken. Pa and I are headin' up to see him now."

"Pa? Oh, you must be Olaf Loken. You knew my grandfather."

"Not well," said Olaf. "Nobody did."

"You knew him enough to throw him to his death at the dam."

"That was your grandfather's doin'. I tried to stop him, to save him. So did my son."

Muldoon laughed. "Well, water over the dam, you might say. Grandfather is dead. Just more spilt milk."

"Son, time to be goin'. I dare say I would much rather visit with my brother than this souse." They continued up the street.

"Say, Tor," called Muldoon, "you tell Rosie 'Merry Christmas' from her old flame, Reggie Muldoon."

Snow falling now, Olaf and Tor climbed the boarding house steps. Christmas carols greeted them as Tor knocked on the door.

"My stars!" said Adeline. "Olaf! Tor! Come in! Come in! Oh, my, what a wonderful surprise!" She turned toward the others. "Ingman, Rose, everyone, look who came for supper!"

A grand meal of roast chicken with all the trimmings, carrots, squash, wax beans and baked potatoes, graced the dining room table. Soon pumpkin pie and whipped cream was followed by songs played by Rosie on her mother's piano and banjo tunes played by Walter Houghton, a missionary who had come to serve at the reservation.

The party carried well into the night. Ingman, still pale and weak, insisted on a nightcap before they retired. He raised his glass.

"To Christmas," he said, "and to life. I know, now yust how wonderful both are. Yoy be to you all, and good health, to boot!"

<>O<>

The streets of Hayward were quiet by two o'clock in the morning. Lights shone from only three of the thirteen taverns on Iowa Avenue. A woman's laughter came from one of the sporting houses, echoing down the side streets. A man in a dark overcoat crossed the railroad yard, moving in and out between flatcars loaded with pine slabs. He followed side streets and alleys up the hill past the courthouse. Slipping between Adeline Ringstadt's barn and chicken coop, he climbed the steps to the rear stoop. The kitchen door was unlocked. He pulled a small revolver from his coat pocket.

Seconds later, at the top of the rear stairs, he turned the first doorknob. Stepping in, he stood in the dark waiting for his eyes to adjust to the dim moonlight drifting through thin curtains. Realizing his error, he entered the next room. Again he left, entering the third. As his eyes adjusted, he slid the pistol into a pocket and drew his knife. Waiting until he was certain he had his victim, he silently approached the bed and the man who slept so soundly before him.

Seconds later, he was again in the hall, trembling, his knife now dripping with blood. Silently entering the next room, the assassin again stood in the dark, breathing rapidly, waiting to confirm his next victim's identity.

Stirred by the heavy breathing, Olaf looked up as the man came fast, knife held high. Olaf rolled off the bed and sprang to his feet. The blade sliced through the air past his face. Olaf grabbed the man's wrist, twisting with all his might. The knife flew to the floor. Adrenalin driven, Olaf spun the man around by the wrist and pushed him into the dry sink, smashing the porcelain bowl, pitcher, and mirror with a crash. The killer dashed for the door, fumbling for the revolver in his pocket.

Hearing the commotion, Tor opened his door as the man flew by. Fearing capture, the man turned, aiming at Tor just as he reached the top of the stairway. In the pitch-black darkness, a howl of a wolf sliced through the night. Startled, the assailant missed the first step, fired the pistol, tripped and fell, flipping, and crashing headfirst into the front door below. The thick glass shattered. One shard sliced his face. Another implanted in his neck. Reaching up, he found the latch, opened the door and stumbled down the steps into the street.

From her room, Adeline screamed, "Lord in Heaven! What is it? What is it? Daisy! Rosie! Violet!"

Olaf struck a match and stepped into the hall.

Rosie, a candle in hand, joined him.

"Tor? You all right?" asked Rosie.

"I'm fine. What happened? Who ...?"

"Someone tried to stab me, Son. I ran him off,"

"Tried to what?" said Rosie.

"Took a shot my way, too," said Tor from his room. "From the sound of it, that wolf's howl scared him and he fell down the stairs, busted the glass, and high-tailed it out—down the street."

"What wolf howl?" asked Rosie.

Tor pulled on his britches and boots and stepped into the hallway. "Didn't you hear it? I mean …the wolf?"

Adeline lit an oil lamp and carried it past Olaf toward the stairway. He pulled her back.

"Adeline, he might still be down there. You stay back a ways. That lamp of yours would make a fine target." Then, "Tor, what wolf? Outside, you mean? Did you …"

"No, Pa, Sounded close. Right here in the hall. Definitely a timber wolf. Just like those we hear 'most every night at the camp."

Ingman and others stepped into the hall.

"Folks," said Olaf, "until we know for sure if this assassin has fled, it might be wise to stay in your rooms." He turned toward the stairway. "Son, can you see anything from there?"

Tor peered around the corner and looked over the railing into the dark stairwell. "Nothing. I believe he fled."

"You sure?"

Tor looked over the railing. "Ya, the door is open. He left all right." Tor moved toward the top of the steps. As he tried to sneak down the stairs, each step seemed to bellow out a squeak. Reaching the bottom step, he stole a look through the broken window. In the dim light he made out a trail of blood.

"I doubt he is comin' back, Pa. He's bleedin'—bleedin' bad. Must've been cut when the window broke."

"You keep your distance, Son. Thus far it seems no one but him got hurt. No point in pressin' our luck."

Adeline peered around her doorway. "Where is Walter Houghton? Walter?"

There was no answer.

"Has anyone seen Walter?" she asked.

Ingman opened Walter's door. From the hallway, Adeline's flickering lantern revealed blood-soaked blankets covering his motionless body. Olaf entered the dark room.

"Adeline," he said, "I fear Walter has been stabbed. He's gone."

"Stabbed?" she cried. "Walter? Dead?"

"Addie," said Olaf, "as soon as we are certain it is safe, I want you and the girls to get over to Preacher Spooner's home for a time. Tor and I will get the sheriff up here. You tend to the girls. They need not be exposed to this dreadfulness. We will tend to things here and let you know when to return."

"Tor, Olaf," said Rosie, "why would anyone want to harm poor old Walter? He was so kind, so warm?"

"And why you, Olaf?" asked Adeline. "Why on earth would anyone want to cause you harm?"

"Pa, I see him!" whispered Tor from the bottom of the stairwell. "He's layin' out there, across the street, face down. Still as can be."

"You certain?"

"I am certain, Pa."

Tor slowly opened the door, and stepped onto the street. Oil lamps from within the boarding house now cast enough light onto the snowy street to show a large pool of blood soaking into the snow surrounding the fallen man. A pistol lay in the blood. Tor stepped closer, recalling his mentor's advice about approaching a fallen deer. He kicked the pistol away, then nudged the man with his boot.

"Oh, he is gone all right, Pa. No man nor beast I know could lose this much blood and survive."

Half-dressed, Olaf stepped onto the street to join his son. Tor rolled the corpse over.

"Recognize him, Tor?"

"You will not believe it, Pa. This is the man who shot Uncle Ingman and murdered Chief Namakagon. This here is Deputy Frank Derkson."

"Derkson? Why would he come after Walter Houghton and me? Makes no sense at all."

Ingman joined them. "I think the fool murdered the wrong man," he said. "I believe Derkson was after us, Tor. Planned to silence the only witnesses to his confession."

"Ingman," said Olaf, "you figure Derkson mistook both me and Walter for you?"

"That's my hunch. Had he succeeded in his plan, Tor, you might have been next. Me and you might both be gone if not for your pa flushin' him out like he did."

"Pa, thank God and Gitchee Manitou you were able to scare him off. No tellin' where he would have stopped or how many of us would now be layin' up there with Walter Houghton."

"Well, the Devil has Derkson by now," said Olaf. "We have nothing more to fear from this scoundrel. Thank God this is all over with—over and done. Now, tell me again about that wolf you heard."

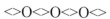

Chapter 35
Paths Cross

December 19, 1886

Louise Renshaw spread Chief Namakagon's bearskin robe on the floor near the Namakagon Timber Company lodge fireplace. With a snap of her fingers, Waabishki and Makade took their places on the robe, sitting at attention. She turned to Tor, handing him the chief's hunting knife and the diamond-shaped silver medallion.

"Mikwam-migwan wanted you to have his knife, Tor. Wanted you to wear the silver ornament, too. He said you would know why."

"Yes, Diindiisi, I think I do. It is the same symbol worn by the great makwaa—the bear that once rescued us. I would be proud to wear it. Miigwetch."

"And there is a walking stick. He was making it for you. He would be proud to know you carry it. I wish he could have handed it to you. It is in his home. You must find it. As you travel, so will he."

"On the island?"

"No. In his lodge near Marengo."

My uncle and I saw no sign of it when we were there."

"It is hidden. Look above the rafters. You must go there. Find it. I cannot. I will not return there. Too much pain."

"I will look for it, Diindiisi. Rosie is visiting the camp on Sunday. I plan to meet her at the Pratt station. We will take the trail to his lodge on the way back here."

The door swung wide. Ingman and Olaf entered. Sourdough's cookees, Zeke and Zach Rigsby, followed, carrying supper to the table. Olaf, Ingman, Tor, and their guest dined on roast beaver, wild rice, fried potatoes, baked beans, fresh bread, and warm peach pie.

As Ingman took a third piece of pie, Tor raised his glass and proclaimed, "Here is to Uncle Ingman, too stubborn to let a load of buckshot slow him down, especially when he's at the dinner table."

"And raise a glass to Tor, fastest paddler on the river. May no man or woman ever have to endure a paddle like that again!"

<>O<>

Early Sunday morning, Tor hitched the black mare to the small cutter and left camp. His first destination was the Omaha Railroad Station at Pratt. His second would be Ogimaa Mikwam-migwan's small cabin near Marengo.

As Tor made his way toward Pratt, miles away on another track, the Wisconsin Central southbound left Ashland, stopping at Marengo. A tall, thin man disembarked, walking west down the tote road toward Chief Namakagon's camp.

The Omaha pulled in to the Pratt station, bell ringing and steam rushing from below the undercarriage. Rosie waved from the passenger car window. As soon as Conductor Williams shouted the all clear, she stepped from the car.

"Rosie! So good you could come. I have quite a day planned. Ol' Sourdough is in the cook shanty right now fixin' up something special for a Christmas. My mare is keen on trotting this morning and the snow is just right. C'mon. No point in keepin' her waiting."

Beneath a bright blue morning sky, the cutter glided lightly down one trail, then another, over hills, across frozen lakes, and through the tall pines. They were headed for the Marengo silver fields and the cabin built by Chief Namakagon.

Miles later, they climbed from the cutter. Tor tied the reins to a stout birch limb overhanging the trail. "We have miles of snowy trails to trot before we reach the lake again, Lady. You rest up. We will be back soon."

Following a narrow path through dense balsams, the young couple walked the last quarter-mile, approaching Namakagon's camp from the west. Tor broke trail for Rosie, sometimes slogging through three-foot drifts until reaching a stand of white pines. Beneath the grand, pine canopy, their trek became easier, the snow only inches deep. Their footpath led to Chief Namakagon's lodge, now cold, dark, and still. They stomped snow from their boots and entered the lodge. Tor tossed some kindling and birch bark in the stove and struck a match. Rosie pulled open the flour sack curtains to let more sunlight brighten the room.

Not far to the east, the tall thin man followed Chief Namakagon's trail from the tote road to the cabin. His gate was rapid, his stride long, and he made good time along the forest trail in spite of the new-fallen blanket of snow. He noticed nothing as he passed the place where Mikwam-migwan was found dead along the trail, all sign forever erased by snow and wind.

In the cabin, Rosie righted a fallen chair. "Such a muddle!"

"Derkson did this," said Tor. "Ripped the place apart searching for clues to the silver mine. Least that's what Uncle Ingman and I figured. Seems a greater mess than how we left it. Could be that others have been here rummaging. With word out Chief is gone, many will want to find clues to the mine." He moved a stool to the middle of the room. "I s'pose folks will search for a long time to come." He stood on the stool. "Maybe decades." He reached up, feeling between rafters. "Look! It's here. Safe and sound, just like Diindiisi said—the walking stick Chief carved for me."

"Goodness, gracious, Tor. It is beautiful!"

The hand-carved, ironwood walking stick, whittled by the steady hand and sharp knife of the old Indian, showed images of birds and mammals winding around the shaft from top to tip. A whitetail buck fled from two wolves. A bear reached high for wild currants. A fisher chased a snowshoe hare. Ducks flushed from nearby cattails. An osprey carried a fish through the air as other animals looked on. Adorning the top was an eagle. Its tail feathers and head were inlaid with brightly polished metal. "Diindiisi said he had been working on it a good while. I see why it took time. It truly is beautiful!"

Rosie held it to the window light. "The eagle—is it silver?"

"Sure is. Must have come from the mine."

"Will you take me there?"

"To the mine? What makes you think I know the way?"

"You cannot fool me, Tor Loken. I know you have been there." She waved her hand before him, parading the ring he made for her two years earlier.

"Well, considering I'm the only one who knows its location now, I s'pose it would be good if someone else knew. And it's pretty close by. Yes, I can take you there, Rosie, but only if you promise ..."

"You can trust me, Tor. You know you can."

Tor in the lead, walking stick in hand, they headed east, crossing the chief's path to the Marengo Station tote road. Turning north, they followed a narrow creek bottom, leaving their tracks in the snow behind—tracks made especially distinctive by the mark left by Tor's walking staff. Steep ridges on either side of their trail cast jagged blue shadows onto the snow. Rocky outcroppings faced the trail from both sides. An eagle swooped down from its hidden perch, passing only an arm's length above Tor and Rosie, then sailed up the creek bed before them.

"He is here to guide us, Rosie. I have seen this before."

"He? You mean the eagle?"

"Wenebojo, Rosie. I wondered how long it would be till he joined us. He just gave us the answer."

"Surely, Tor, you do not really think this eagle is …"

"The eagle was only one of the creatures guarding Namakagon's mine. I am grateful to know this. It means the secret is still protected."

"Protected by animals?"

"Spirits, Rosie. This way. We'll take the back way in."

"Back way? You mean there is more than …"

"Two years ago, Chief found a new entrance. I am pretty sure his usual entrance is buried under snow and ice this time of year. It's down along the creek bed where the snow tends to drift in."

They climbed the steep bank and circled the rocky hillside. Tor leaned his walking stick on a sheer rock wall. A narrow opening angled across its face. "This is it, Rosie."

"What? This? This skinny … crevice?"

The eagle flew overhead again, landing on a nearby dead pine limb that bounced and bobbed under the its weight. Silently, the raptor stared down at the couple.

"It's the entrance, all right. He brushed snow from the opening."

"But, it doesn't look like it goes anywhere."

"Soon as you squeeze through, it gets wider. Opens right up. You do want to see the inside, right?"

"Well, of course. I did not come out here just to see a rock wall with a crack in it. Will we fit? I mean, we can't get stuck, can we?"

"We will make it."

She looked up at the eagle, now staring down at her. "Tor, you are certain … I mean … the eagle, the spirits?"

"Rosie, many times I heard Namakagon say that Wenebojo protected those with good intentions and punished those without. Like Mikwam-migwan, those with a pure heart will be smiled upon. I know you, Rosie. You have nothing to fear from Wenebojo. You still want to see the cave?"

She looked up at the eagle again. "Yes, but, this thin crevice …"

"Not to worry." Tor slid through the opening, right side first. "C'mon, Rosie. Nothing to it!" Rosie followed, wiggling, shifting, and squeezing through.

Tor struck a match, lighting a birch bark torch. The light exposed a low, narrow corridor twisting far into the darkness.

"Stay close. Keep your head down. Almost there."

Tor led Rosie around and through the narrow, twisting passage until it opened into a larger cavern. Its walls were wet and encrusted with silver tarnished black with age.

"Goodness gracious sakes alive, Tor. I never imagined …"

"Isn't it something? I get the same feelin' each time I come here. Rosie, take this torch while I light up another. Chief and I put up a bunch of them along with other supplies a while back. Just in case."

"In case of what?"

"Oh, um, Chief and I got sort of stuck in here once. After that, we decided it might be a good plan to keep some firewood along with extra birch bark for torches. Follow me, but watch your step."

"There are no animals in here?"

"Animals? Oh, I have seen some bats from time to time." Tor reached down to bend, twist and break a shard of silver from the wall. "Here, Rosie, take this for a keepsake. If you polish it up, it will shine like the stars on a clear January night."

"Are you sure I can take this?"

"Sure? Even though this is a sacred site, taking a small souvenir or two will not disappoint the spirits. On the other hand, Rosie, from what Namakagon told me, I would not risk taking it out by wheelbarrow."

On and on they explored the meandering passageways, Tor in the lead and Rosie astonished by the mysterious splendors of cavern after cavern. As each birch torch burned down, they lit another.

<>O<>

Approaching Namakagon's camp from the east trail, the tall, thin man crossed recent footprints in the snow. He stooped, inspecting the smaller tracks.

"Hmm. Namakagon's woman?" he whispered. "Yes. I'll wager it is so. Could it be she's heading for the chief's silver mine? Yes. That must be it. She is going for the silver. I'm sure of it. What great fortune! She's about to lead me to the old man's mine. It seems Lady Luck brought me here for good reason—and at the perfect time, too. What good luck!"

He turned his attention to the larger footprints. "Now, then… just who is this?" He studied the track and the mark of a hiker's staff. "Namakagon! Chief Namakagon!" he said with a groan. "By God, that dolt Derkson lied to me. The old Indian is still alive. I knew it! I should have handled this myself from start to finish. Dammit! All that time and money wasted on that bungling buffoon, Frank Derkson. Well, that does it! I swear I am going to finish this—finish this here and now."

He pulled a small revolver from his coat, checked to see it was loaded, and pocketed the pistol again. Following the fresh tracks, he soon found himself in a narrow creek bottom with steep rock walls on either side. An eagle swooped down, talons extended, brushing his hat from his head. He lost his balance, falling to the snow and rocks, bruising his chin. The eagle perched on a dead white pine limb above. It watched him as he stood brushing snow from his coat. He pulled his revolver, aiming it at the bird far above.

"No," he said. "Count your blessings, bird. I will not waste a bullet I may soon need each round for bigger game. But don't tempt me again. I am not inclined to allow you another pass at me."

Following the footprints, he plodded up the creek bottom, the eagle glaring down from above. The trail led him around a bend in the creek before suddenly turning uphill. He climbed the steep slope higher and higher until the tracks took him to a hand-carved walking stick leaning near a narrow crevice in a sheer stone wall.

"So, Chief Namakagon," he whispered, "this is where your treasure lies. 'Twas your fortune till this moment, old man. It shall be mine hereafter. Mine alone." His whispers were overheard by two others—the eagle, watching from above, and, behind, an old timber wolf bearing a white blaze on its black chest. The man slid sideways through the wall and into the cavern, then drew the revolver from his pocket.

<>O<>O<>O<>

Chapter 36
At the Heels of Their Prey

December 19, 1886

Far ahead, Rosie followed Tor through long passageways, some narrow, some wide, some so small the explorers were forced to crawl on hands and knees.

"Tor, you are certain we can find our way out, right?"

"As long as we stay in this corridor, we are fine. It would not be wise to venture off into one of the others. There are some awful deep chasms in here. Stay close now, only a stone's throw more."

The narrow tunnel opened into a series of large caverns, again encrusted with age-blackened silver. They followed a narrow ledge that dropped off into a deep pit. Tor lit another birch torch. He took the nearly spent torch, saying, "See this?" as he tossed it into the pit. They watched the flame fall and fall, then disappear into the blackness without a sound. "This is why you need to watch your step in here. No tellin' how far down this goes."

"I had no idea this cave was so dangerous. We should leave."

"I have come to know this cave over the past two years. As long as we have light, we will be fine."

From behind, the man now closing in, heard their voices. Near enough to be guided by Tor's firelight, he doused his torch in a pool and crept closer, whispering to himself, "Loken! Loken and Rosie. So, the old chief is dead, after all. Good. Fewer fish left to fry."

Tor, continuing on, used his torch to light another, sticking both into crevices in the wall. The torchlight revealed stone tools, piles of crushed silver ore, and other remains of ancient laborers. Abstract animal images danced across the cave walls in the flickering torch light. Rosie picked up a primitive stone hammer.

"Tor, I thought you said nobody knows about this place."

"No one but us. Over the centuries, Anishinabe elders came to fetch silver for ceremonies and decorations. They placed these drawings on the cave walls. Mikwam-migwan could not tell me their meaning. He thought it might be a warning of some kind."

"A warning? Warning of what?"

"No way to tell anymore. Their stories are long, long forgotten."

A voice came from the dark. "Perhaps, Loken, it's a warning that you and the girl will be discovered."

Reggie Muldoon stepped into the light, his pistol in hand. "Perhaps it's written notice that Reggie Muldoon will soon own the old Indian's secret silver treasury."

Tor stood. "How did ... Why are you here, Muldoon? And watch where you point that revolver. There is nothing to fear in these caverns. Put it away."

"I came to claim what is mine, Loken."

"Yours? Muldoon, this all belongs to the Ojibwe people. Nothing in here is yours. And, for Pete's sake, put your pistol away."

"Ojibwe people? Loken, by this time tomorrow, my mineral rights claim on this land will be on file in the county courthouse."

"Muldoon, we both know I will not let you file such a claim."

Reggie erupted with laughter. "That's the pleasure of all this—the satisfaction. You see, I am here to claim another right—the right of retribution, the settling of scores, Loken. You know, revenge!"

"Revenge?"

"Yes, revenge. Revenge for you and your family murdering my grandfather."

"What? Now, hold on, Muldoon. Your grandfather brought about his own demise. No one else."

"Liar!" screamed Muldoon, pointing the pistol at Tor. "Phineas Muldoon would still be alive and well—still be King Muldoon if not for you. You, Loken. You and the old Indian, and that uncle and father of yours."

"You are wrong, Muldoon."

"Don't deny it! You Lokens killed him all right. And though I don't give a tinker's dam about the old skinflint, the fact remains he was my grandfather. No one outdoes a Muldoon, Tor Loken, especially not a family of ignorant, immigrant woodsmen."

Rosie stepped between them. "Reggie Muldoon, do not be foolish. You cannot blame Tor for mistakes your grandfather made. It's wrong and you know it. Please put away your pistol and we will talk this whole matter out."

"The time for talk is over. Although I feel no remorse in causing your beau's demise, I truly regret such a tender, young miss, so ripe for the plucking, must perish with him. How different this would be had you not rejected my affections. I must say though, how very romantic it will seem—the two of you departing as one—lost forever in the snowy, snowy pinery. It's such a pity there's not a Harper's Weekly reporter here to record the tragedy. It would sell a million."

A faint howl came from far back in the cavern.

"Who is there?" Muldoon shouted into the dark.

"Looks like we are not alone," said Tor. "Hand me the revolver and I will guide you out of here."

"What do you mean, Loken? Is there …"

"Another way out? Yes. And I can take us there. Hand me the pistol and I will show you the way."

"No!" shouted Muldoon. "No, this is a ploy. I am not going to let some backwoods shanty boy hoodwink me. I shan't be duped by the likes of an immigrant shanty boy."

The howl came again, louder.

Muldoon cocked the pistol. "Tell me what that is. Tell me now! Tell me or I will shoot your girl!"

"No! Wait! Could be a wildcat. Or a bear. Perhaps you woke up the great Makwaa. That puny pocket revolver will not stop a she-bear trying to protect her cubs. Hand me the pistol and I will have the three of us out of here in minutes." Tor stepped closer, hand extended.

"Get back! I am not about to fall for your ruse."

"There is no ruse, Muldoon. If not a bear, perhaps a wolf. It could even be Ogimaa Mikwam-migwan seeking his revenge."

"Who?"

"Chief Namakagon."

Muldoon laughed. "My man Derkson saw to him."

"Your man? You hired Derkson? *You* were behind Chief Namakagon's murder?"

"What of it? My money bought me the failed murder attempt on your father in the lumberyard, as well. And your uncle at the bridge. And the train. And the fire. Yes. Had Derkson not been such a bumbling idiot, the fool would have finished you, your uncle, and your father at the boarding house, too. Now the idiot is dead. It is me who must finish this."

"You'll rot in prison, Muldoon."

"Never! My greatest regret, Loken, is that your father and uncle will remain alive. Although I must admit I relish the thought of them always wondering, always haunted by your mysterious disappearance. Yes, it does offer some consolation. I suspect, steeped in guilt, they will devote the rest of their lives to the fruitless search for you two. Your father and uncle will go to their graves never finding resolution—never knowing the truth—never!"

"Reggie," pleaded Rosie, "you are in a position to be a great contributor to society—another Andrew Carnegie. Think of all the good you can do. Instead, if you proceed with this, you will live your life haunted by murder. A worthless thug. Is that what you want? To burn in Hell and be known as a spineless, murderous fiend? Reggie, it is not too late. We can help you. There is still time for you to make a good name for yourself and your family."

"You are so naive. The handful of families who run this country know the name Muldoon. Nothing else matters. My place has been assured by my grandfather, now dead, thanks to the Loken family. He is dead. I am rich, and you? Well, you will be forgotten soon, like so many others who die in the pinery. A few will recall your names, but not for long. Nobody cares about the likes of you—about you commoners Meanwhile, my family name will live on and on."

Tor stepped forward. "Muldoon, you've gone plum daft. Now give me that pistol so we can get you some help."

"Silence, Loken! No more talk. Rosie, fetch me those torches."

"No!" snapped Tor. "Don't do a gol-dang thing he says."

"Do as I say, Rosie, or I will shoot him here and now and you will watch your beau die before your eyes. I mean it!"

"No, Rosie. Don't listen to him."

Muldoon leveled the pistol at Tor. "The torches, Rosie. Now!"

Rosie pulled the birch torches from the wall.

"Muldoon," said Tor, "you cannot get away with this. People know we are here. You'll be the first suspect on the Sheriff's list. He'll add things up and you'll spend the rest of your days in prison. Is that what you want, Muldoon? To die after rotting in prison?"

"That, shanty boy, is where you are wrong. I left Hayward yesterday with all my baggage, headed for New York. I disembarked, taking a hotel room under another name in Ashland. By now my baggage is in storage a thousand miles east, waiting for me. I shall arrive on a later train, retrieve it, with none the wiser. No one in Wisconsin knows I am here—no one other than you two."

Rosie burst into hysterics, dropping one torch, waving the other erratically, and screaming, "The Lord is my shepherd; I shall not want. He maketh me to lie down in green ..."

Muldoon laughed at Rosie's hysterical spectacle and arm waving as her volume and pace amplified.

"He restoreth my soul!", she shouted in near panic. Her arms flailing and the hand bearing the torch coming far back, she screamed, "Yea, though I walk through the valley of the shadow of Death, I—shall—fear—no—evil, Muldoon!" And Rosie hurled the blazing birch torch with all her might, striking him in the face.

Screaming, he fell into the wall, his pistol firing over their heads.

The blast echoed through the caverns as Muldoon, one hand to his burning eyes, fired a second wild, deafening shot into the air.

Tor lunged for the revolver. It fired again. The bullet ricocheted off the wall, through Tor's left arm, and into his chest, throwing him back onto the cave floor near the abyss. Muldoon kicked him, shoving him closer to the edge of the pit. Ignoring his pain, Tor reached up and grabbed Muldoon's leg. Tor twisted with all his might. Muldoon spun like a leaf in the wind and fell. Rosie picked up her torch and thrust it into his face again. Swatting the torch aside with his pistol, Muldoon fired a fourth wild, deafening shot. Tor struggled to his feet. He lunged at Muldoon who rolled out of the way, striking Tor's bleeding chest with his fist.

Tor screamed from the pain, falling again.

Laughing and rubbing his eyes, Muldoon leveled the revolver at Rosie. "Two rounds left, Loken. All I need to finish this task."

Both torches now lay on the cavern floor, their flames dying. As Muldoon picked one up, a deep, guttural growl came from the passageway behind. He turned, raising the flickering torch to cast light into the void.

Tor struggled to his feet. "Looks like two rounds will not be enough after all, Muldoon. Last chance. Hand me the gun. I can get us out of here."

Another growl came from beyond the darkness.

"Look," said Tor, "if any of us hope to leave here alive, we will need another torch. I have more in the next chamber. Without light, all three of us are bound to die in here. We must go. Now!"

"I've had enough of your damn tricks, Loken," Muldoon raised his torch, shifting his aim. "Farewell, shanty boy."

A horde of dark shadows suddenly splashed across the cavern walls. From deep within the cave came distant wails of a thousand hungry wolves at the heels of their prey. Their throaty bellows resonated throughout the passageways and silver-clad chambers.

Muldoon looked up. A great, black wolf flew through the air, torchlight reflecting from its eyes and a white, diamond blaze on its chest. The wolf's jaws clamped onto Muldoon's gun hand and wrist, its teeth smashing through bone like a steel trap. The howling of the wolf-spirits grew louder. Muldoon wobbled back, dropping gun and torch. Shrieks from his fear and pain melded with the wrathful wailing of the wolf-spirits—sounds now resonating into the jet-black depths of the cavern.

Chapter 37
The Wrath of the Wolf-Spirits

December 19, 1886

An eerie breath of icy air rushed through the cave as the howling echoed from every hidden recess. Muldoon reeled away from the snarling, snapping, fire-eyed wolves before him, tripping on rocks and rubble. He stumbled back and back, unable to regain his footing, then stepped back into nothing but the black of the pit. He screamed as he fell.

Now mute, the spirit wolves stood at the precipice, staring into the abyss until all became deathly still.

"C'mon, Rosie," whispered Tor.

The wolves turned.

Hearts racing, Rosie and Tor fled through the next narrow passageway. Tor looked back to see the wolves and the host of indistinct shadows disappear into the black of the caverns.

"Follow me," he said. "If our torch holds out, we can find the lower cave entrance."

"But, the wolves ..."

"They will not hurt us."

Clutching the torch in his right hand, Tor led the way, his left arm swinging erratically from damage done by Muldoon's bullet. He tripped, sprawling onto the cave floor, and they watched their only torch hit the cave wall. Flaring as it landed on the rocks, its flame died.

Now, spotting a single, glowing ember between rocks, Rosie crawled through the sheer black of the cavern. She fumbled for the ember, finally feeling the torch. She brought it near her lips. Hoping to give new life to the flame, she blew on the ember. It glowed at first, then darkened again.

"Try again," said Tor.

Rosie blew once more. As she did, she could hear Tor, behind, quietly chanting indistinct Anishinabe phrases. Rosie blew softer now. The faint ember glowed once more, then sparked and the birch torch burst into bright flames. She held the torch high.

Together, Tor and Rosie again made their way through the narrow corridors, stumbling over rocks, squeezing through tight passageways and clumsily tripping over silver ore rubble left ages before. Rounding a tight passageway, they entered a large, dead-end cavern.

"This is it. This is where the chief and I hid out from that rapscallion, Percy Wilkins."

Rosie stepped over the long-cold coals of an old fire. "Wilkins? You mean ... that outlaw who ...?"

"Someday I will tell you the whole tale," said Tor. "Maybe you can even write about it. Make a story of it."

On hands and knees, he fumbled for the opening. "Here! This is it—the exit. Let's pray it's not froze up."

Grimacing from pain in his chest and arm, Tor wriggled into the low, narrow breach near the bottom of the cave wall. Digging with his right hand, he scraped and plowed, snow and ice flying behind. Squirming his way through the tight, icy tunnel, Tor broke through to daylight.

"We made it, Rosie! Grab my ankles. I will pull you through!"

Rosie laid the torch on the cave floor and reached for Tor.

"Ready?" he said. "All right, hang on tight!"

Tor cleared more snow from the narrow opening, reached forward with his good arm, and pulled himself out. Rosie held tight to his ankles and both were soon safe, standing outside at the downhill entrance to the network of caves.

"Help me hide it," Tor said, kicking snow back into the entrance.

Together they shoved snow back into the breach. They stood in silence, staring toward the now-hidden cave entrance, hearing only the wind in the pines above.

"Follow me," said Tor.

They climbed the hill, Rosie in the lead. As they passed by the entrance they had used an hour earlier, Tor reached for his walking stick. They heard faint sounds from within the cave. Echoing through the many dark, narrow caverns and corridors came an eerie mix of mournful howls—the howling of wolves—wolves sounding as though they had been hungry for centuries.

Rosie leaned toward the crevice in the stone wall and listened. The wailing continued, intensified, then suddenly went silent.

"Tor, we must go back in and look for him. We have to do something to ..."

"It's out of our hands now. The spirits of the wolves are determined to protect the sacred holdings of their brothers and sisters, the Anishinabe. Muldoon is dead. 'Twas his doing, not ours."

Tor clutched his arm. "Rosie … Rosie, I am bleeding. I have to get to Sourdough."

Leaning on her for support, Tor followed the trail out, drops of red marking the snow behind them. Soon, with Rosie at Lady's reins, the mare drew their cutter through the pines.

In a faltering voice, Tor said, "Rosie, you know we cannot tell anyone, right?"

"Not even my …"

"No. No one. Any word of this will bring the whole outside world to Mikwam-migwan's secret silver mine. We must not mention this, not to even one, single soul. It has to remain our secret—our secret for all time—for eternity."

"But … what about Muldoon?"

"Muldoon? He is in other hands now. I believe his insults to the spirits, his violations, have determined his fate. The Devil will see to Muldoon, just as he sees to Frank Derkson."

"His family will search for him."

"But, like he said, as far as anyone knows, he is somewhere betwixt here and New York."

The horse and cutter splashed through the Marengo River, climbed the bank and caught the east tote road leading to the camp.

Rosie looked at Tor. "What happened back there? How did …?"

"I believe Wenebojo was with us … watching over us."

"Wenebojo? Surely you cannot believe …"

"Mikwam-migwan once told a tale of a dozen French voyageurs, fur traders. One night they camped along the Flambeau River. Five men dug a latrine back in the woods. The other seven laughed at them and used the riverbank. Rain fell hard when they broke camp the next morning. The rain washed everything from the riverbank into the stream. The rains fell harder. Wenebojo was angry at these men for soiling the river. So was the Flambeau, for the canoe soon capsized. Only the five voyageurs who used the latrine back in the woods survived. Those who used the riverbank perished. Now, some may say this was merely chance. But there are many, many such stories. It appears unlikely they could all be chance."

"You think the river was Wenebojo?"

"Rosie, do you believe God can be found only in a church?"

"Of course not. God is everywhere."

"And Gitchee Manitou? You think Gitchee Manitou is everywhere?"

"Well … Yes. Yes, I suppose it stands to reason that …"

"Then would Wenebojo not be everywhere? In everything—rocks, snow, trees, the air we breathe, and in every animal?"

"Well …"

"Everywhere, Rosie. In everything."

"The wolf in the cave, Tor … the wolf with the diamond blaze … was that … I mean … could that have been …"

"Old Ice Feathers? Is this what you want to ask? Rosie, I have seen many mysterious things take place in this land of the Anishinabe. Mysteries beyond explanation, beyond understanding, yet, somehow, not beyond belief. You know, if you listen closely to the wind in the pines, you will hear the chanting of elders from the past. They have the answers, Rosie. They have knowledge we can only dream of sharing. Two years ago, a great Makwaa saved my life. Was he Wenebojo? I still wonder. Is the wolf we saw today Wenebojo? Were either of them Chief Namakagon? I do not know. But, who is to say they are not?

"Rosie, Chief always said the spirits speak only to those willing to listen. Most of us do not listen. Most spend too much time talking to have time for listening. The Muldoons did not listen. They heard only jingle of silver and gold in their pockets. Until the songs of the wind through the pines become more important than the coins in our pockets, nothing will change. Let us hope it doesn't come too late."

"I hear it, Tor. I hear their songs—songs of concern, songs of courage. I hear it in the pines. I hear it in the rain falling on the rivers and lakes. I have heard it for quite some time. In fact, I have heard it ever since I met you."

As the cutter glided along the narrow trail between the pines, Tor took the reins in his good hand. He pulled back, and with a "Whoa, Lady, whoa," the mare slowed, then stopped. Tor turned.

"Rosie, there is something… well … something I have been wondering about. Something I have to ask you."

"Yes?"

"Rosie, do you suppose … um…"

"What, Tor?"

"Well, what do you think … What do you say you and me …"

"Yes?"

"Rosie, I … well … Rosie, would you marry me?"

Chapter 38
The Black Wolf

December 19, 1886

Olaf poured three fingers of brandy into a tin cup. He corked the bottle and handed the cup to Ingman who sat before the fireplace.

"Here. This might help the cough some."

Ingman took a sip, coughed again, and set it aside.

"Olaf, I cannot fathom this change in me. I used to be the gol-dang bull of the woods. I could lick any man in camp. Now, look at me. Why, I dassn't venture across the yard to the cook shanty for fear a slight breeze might set me down in a snow bank. I yust don't have no gumption left in me."

"Oh, for cryin' out loud. Quit your gol-dang bellyachin'! 'Twas only a month ago we were all wonderin' if you would live or die after that fella loaded you up with buck shot. Tor says some of those men at Ole Swenson's camp nearly had you boxed up and buried. Probably would have if not for their horse doctor steppin' in. You will get your strength back. Be patient. And, stop your gol-dang bellyachin,' for Pete's sake! I am tired of hearin' it, day in and day out."

A horse-drawn cutter on the east tote road caught Ingman's attention. "Well, what do ya know? Tor and Rosie are finally back. Must be they took the long way 'round."

"Leave it to the young ones, ay?"

"Can you blame 'em? Nothin' here but us crippled up, bellyachin', old fogies."

"Ingman Loken, there you go again. I swear! When are you gonna start to appreciate life? I would think of all people ..."

"Ya, ya, ya. Of all people I should be thankful that I wasn't killed by that scoundrel. Well, for you folks on the outside lookin' in, that may be the way it seems. For me it's different, see? I am not the man I used to be. Not half. Somehow, I know I will not ever be right again."

"Hog slop!"

"I been thinkin', Olaf. In a few years, 'most every white pine in Wisconsin, Minnesota, and Michigan will be cut, milled, and gone for good. Time for me to make a change. Olaf, I'm pullin' out. Takin' my share and headin' west to Washington. A. J. Hayward is goin' west, ya know. Freddy Weyerhaeuser just bought up a bunch of timberland out there, too. Out west—the new pinery—the place to be if you want to make a name for yourself in the timber trade. Pine and fir as far as the eye can see. Up one side of a mountain and down the other, on and on. No end to 'em, they say. Yep, I'm cuttin' out—headin' west."

"By God, Ingman, I do believe you have finally gone daft. Must be from your injuries. Lord knows when you will come to your senses. Maybe I should call in Doctor Cox."

"I've already come to my senses, Olaf. I will be leavin' next week on the Omaha."

"Next week? You intend to leave now? It's only Christmas. It's the start of the gol-dang season? Who is gonna be my woods boss, for Pete's sake?"

"Olaf, since you got your legs back you have done both your yob and most of mine. You have not let me run things 'round here for the last two years and you dang well know it. Seems this is your camp, not our camp. It is high time I strike out on my own."

"You didn't answer my question. Who'll take your place?"

Ingman pointed to the cutter now entering the yard. "Your son."

They watched the cutter pass the file shed, barn, and blacksmith shop. "Tor is just a boy. It will be years before ..."

"Yust a boy? Olaf, your son is all of nineteen years now. He is a true woodsman with a darn good head on his shoulders. Old Ice Feathers taught him well, as did you."

"And, you, Ingman. But that doesn't mean ..."

"The men respect Tor. They listen when he speaks. He's a born leader. 'Sides, takin' over this camp is his family right. You and Tor—father and son—like it should be. As for me, well, I've never been one to lollygag. I'm headin' west."

As the mare approached the cook shanty, Rosie jumped from the cutter and ran inside.

"She must be awful dang hungry," said Olaf.

Sourdough and two cookees shot out of the cook shanty and ran to the cutter. Rosie followed, heading for the lodge. The door swung open.

"Mr. Loken, Tor has been hurt. Sourdough's about to tend to it. You better come."

Before Olaf could reply, she was on her way back to the cook shanty. Sourdough helped Tor to the door, the cookees close behind.

Tor sprawled across an oilcloth-covered table while Sourdough pulled off his coat and shirt. With a butcher knife, he slit Tor's union suit from left wrist to neck, pealing the blood-drenched wool from his skin. Zach scooped hot water from the reservoir on the wood range, pouring it into an enamel pan. Olaf rushed in, followed by Ingman.

"Son, what in blazes happened?"

"Zeke," said Sourdough, "hand me a dishrag and two towels." He pushed back the bloody wool underwear. "So, Tor, you gonna tell your pa and us what happened?"

"Ricochet," he muttered.

"Ricochet? Some deer hunter, Son?"

"Can't say."

"You all right?"

"I'll be fine, Pa."

"Zeke," said Sourdough, "fetch me my boning knife, will ya?"

Olaf looked at Rosie. "You see him, Rosie?"

"Hmm?"

"The deer hunter. Did you see him?"

"Deer hunter?"

"The hunter who shot my boy."

"No, sir. I saw no hunter."

"You get a look at him, Tor?"

"Pa, all I can say right now is that I heard a shot, and something hit my arm."

Zeke handed Sourdough the knife who carefully wiped it clean using his apron.

"Hold on, Tor, this might pinch a bit."

Sourdough inserted the blade, probing the wound.

"For mercy sake, Sourdough! Is that what you call pinching a bit?"

"Aw, quit yer dang whinin'. Here is the culprit," he said, popping a deformed bullet from the chest wound. "Not very deep, thank heavens. The rib it busted stopped it short. Good that it went no deeper."

"Let me see that," said Olaf. He pulled a bandanna from a hip pocket and wiped the bullet. "This did not come from a hunter's

rifle. Too small. This was fired by a pistol."

Sourdough tore a corner from a flour sack dishtowel, folded it and placed it over the chest wound, then wrapped both Tor's arm and chest.

"All right," he said. "Best I can do for now. Let's get a hot cup of tea into you. Then it is off to Hayward to see Doctor Cox."

"Son," said Olaf, "I have to know who shot you."

"I am awful tired, Pa. Can we talk about this later?"

"Mister Loken," said Rosie, "if we hope to catch the southbound, we mustn't dally."

"Yes. You're right. I will see to it we make the train, Rosie."

He turned to the nearest cookee. "Zach, run over to the barn. Tell John Kavanaugh to hitch two horses to the company sleigh."

"Yessir, Mister Loken."

The sleigh ready, Rosie helped Tor into the back seat, then followed him in before covering up with heavy, wool blankets. Olaf climbed into the sleigh, taking the reins. Ingman handed his brother a double-barrel shotgun and stepped up and onto the seat next to him.

"This gun loaded?" asked Olaf.

"Double-ought buckshot. One in each chamber. Six in my pocket."

"Are they for the trail, the train, or for in town?"

"All three, considerin' the events we have seen lately."

Olaf flicked the reins and gave a whistle. The cutter soon sailed along the north trail to Pratt where they would meet the southbound train. Rosie by his side, Tor fell fast asleep. Above the treetops to the west, shafts of sunlight beamed through a bank of dark clouds.

"Rosie," said Olaf, "was a hunter to blame for the bullet in Tor?"

Rosie considered Olaf's question and her answer before replying, "Mister Loken, I am afraid I cannot say. If I did, it would be a betrayal of Tor's trust. I hope you understand, sir."

Olaf was silent. Then, "Yes, I do understand, Rosie. But, all these things that have happened … these terrible things … my God. Chief Namakagon murdered, Ingman shot and nearly killed. And, that horrible, nightmare we saw at your mother's home—your home! And now, Rosie, my boy comes home with a bullet in his chest. Surely you see why I must know what happened today. I must!"

"Mister Loken, I understand how you feel, trying so to protect your son. Oh, how I wish I could explain."

"Rosie," said Ingman, "if you are aware of any threats to us—to Tor, in particular—please, please tell us now."

"I will not betray Tor and I cannot tell you precisely what happened. That task must be left to him. However, I can tell you this, you may rest assured there will be no more murderous assaults on your family. Tor will explain all when he's up to it. Until then, please trust me when I say we are out of danger. We are safe. You shan't be in need of your shotgun for more than the occasional partridge along the trail."

The horse team whisked the sleigh through the pines, then down the long grade to the Pratt station. Rosie, lulled by the sway of the sleigh and the soft squeal of steel runners on snow, drifted off to sleep.

Cresting a hill not far from Namakagon's Marengo cabin, Olaf made out something dark, far ahead. He continued on, soon realizing what he saw was a wolf, a black wolf, and not about to leave the trail. Uneasy, the horses slowed their pace.

Ingman, apprehensive, reached down for his double barrel. The sleigh drew closer and closer until, when almost in shotgun range, Ingman noticed a white diamond blaze on the wolf's chest. Olaf drew back on the reins. The sleigh came to a stop. Ingman raised his shotgun. From the back seat came a weak voice.

"No, Uncle. No. Don't shoot. The wolf is our friend."

Ingman lowered the shotgun and turned to Tor.

"Friend?"

"See that diamond blaze on his chest?"

"Ya. So?"

"Remind you of anyone?"

"Anyone?" replied Ingman, "you mean … any person?"

"Only fella I know with a diamond on his chest like that was old Ice Feathers," said Olaf.

"What?" said Ingman. "Chief Namakagon? Nephew, are you tellin' me that wolf is …"

"Like I said, Uncle, don't shoot. That wolf is our friend."

The wolf turned, trotting down the sleigh trail as if escorting the Loken sleigh to the station. Rounding the bend, a murder of crows flushed from a nearby stand of black spruce, shrieking displeasure at being rousted from their evening roost. Far to the north, a train whistle echoed down the snowy valley, interrupting the crows' distant complaining.

With the engine's polished brass bell announcing the Omaha's arrival, the southbound rumbled up to the depot platform. Large snowflakes fell as Olaf, Ingman, Rosie, and Tor boarded the train.

Far above the rail yard, the wolf watched them board, then slipped into the evening shadows.

Towing two passenger cars and twenty-nine carloads of virgin white pine, the Omaha locomotive rolled south, its clear, resonant whistle echoing from the hills.

The black wolf replied with a long, mournful howl, a reply heard only by the tall pines bordering the Marengo Trail and the young lumberjack, Tor Loken.

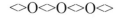

Epilogue

May 19, 1966
6 a.m.

The lonely wail of a loon came streaming into the old lumber camp lodge with the first light of morning. Aching from a night in Grandpa Tor's old chair, I stood, stretched, and bent to pick up my crumpled map. I looked at it one last time, laughed at my foolishness, and tossed it onto the embers. I watched as it wriggled and twisted, then burst into flames. I no longer cared about either map. The dreams I had experienced, if dreams are what they were, had me wondering about other things. I knew I would have to look deeper to find answers. Answers about those days, my ancestors, and their friends. I pledged then to learn more. But not today. Today would be a full day of work cleaning up the old lodge.

I soon had Grandpa Tor's aluminum percolator bubbling away. As it drummed out its "blip - blip - blip," the fresh smell of coffee filled the lodge. By the time the sun broke over the treetops, bacon sizzled. I cracked two eggs into the pan, then dropped two slices of raisin bread into Grandma Rosie's toaster.

It was well after breakfast that I noticed it—the silence. The old lodge was too quiet. Even though I had wound the mainspring in Grandpa's clock only a day before, it had stopped. I inserted the key but found it still wound. I picked up the clock. Something rattled inside. Flipping open the latch, a diamond-shaped, tarnished medallion fell to the floor. The clock immediately ticked again. I returned it to its home on the mantle.

The medallion was heavy, about three by four inches, and as black as coal. I felt sure it was silver. To prove this was the real McCoy, I turned it over, opened my pocketknife, and scraped some tarnish away. As I did, the letters J and T appeared.

"J T," I muttered to myself. "Just like in my dream. But ... was it a dream?"

A car pulled into the yard. The ladies from town had returned to sort Grandpa and Grandma's things for the church bazaar. I slipped the silver medallion into my pocket.

"Grandpa Tor," I said into the empty room, "these tales of you and the old chief have been buried for too many decades. I know there is more to tell—much more. I'm not going to stop searching till

I have the whole story. I'll need help from you and Grandma Rosie, the lumberjacks and Old Ice Feathers, too. I know I can count on you."

I stepped outside to greet the ladies from the church. There, staring at me from the porch railing, perched a blue-black raven. As it followed me with its dark eyes, I turned. "Oh, yes, Wenebojo, I will need your help too. We'll see to it the world hears these tales—the tales of Chief Namakagon."

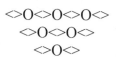

Raven   John James Audubon   1831

Appendix

Glossary to accompany the Chief Namakagon trilogy

Aft: Toward the stern or rear of the vessel.

Anchor: 1. A large, heavy weight designed to hold a sailing vessel in place when lowered to the bottom. 2. To lower a weight to the bottom, thus stopping the vessel.

Animosh: Ojibwe word for dog.

Anishinabe: *a-nish-i-NAH-bee.* Original Native Americans who lived north and south of the western Great Lakes region. Primarily Ojibwe but also Algonquin, Pottawatomie and others.

Barber chair: Slang for what is created when a tree is improperly notched prior to cutting, resulting in a tall splinter rising up from one side of the stump that makes it resemble a chair.

Bark eater: Slang term for a lumberjack. More insulting than its cousin, *shanty boy.*

Barn boss: Oversaw care and feeding of the animals and other barn chores.

Blackbird: A slang term for a log driver who was skilled at walking on the floating logs.

Blackjack: Gingerbread. A cake made with ginger and blackstrap molasses.

Boom: A large raft of logs held together by a ring of logs connected by chains. Boom companies were formed on parts of some rivers to sort logs and direct them toward the right mills.

Boozhoo*: Boo-ZHOO.* Hello. Possibly from the French term *bon jour* meaning good day. Probably from a contraction of Wenebojo and a greeting that acknowledges the omnipresence of Anishinabe culture and the strength of Native American camaraderie.

Boreal forest: Primarily coniferous. Found where long winters and high precipitation prevail.

Brakeman: Railroad worker whose job is to set and release safety brakes, among other jobs.

Breakup: The spring ice melt when logs could again be driven to the mills.

Bow: The front of a sailing vessel.

Bull Cook: A worker who did many camp chores including the feeding of some animals, bringing in firewood, keeping the stoves filled, fetching water for the kitchen, clearing paths through the snow, plus many kitchen chores. Not well-paid.

Calaboose: Jailhouse, prison, the brig.

Calked boots: Leather boots with spiked soles that helped men walk on the floating logs.

Camp dentist: The worker who sharpened the saws and axes.

Cant hook: A tool for rolling logs. Consists of a stout, wooden handle and a C-shaped hook. Similar to a peavey.

Caught in a bear trap: Lumberjack slang for getting into trouble.

Chain-haul team: The men who used horses or oxen and chains to load the logs onto the sleighs.

Chautauqua: *sha-TAHK-wa.* Traveling entertainment troupes that would set up large tents and then offer lectures, music, comedy, burlesque and theater before moving on to the next rural communities.

Chequamegon: *she-WAHM-a-gun. A large bay on th*e south shore of Lake Superior. Also a national forest in Wisconsin.

Chippewa: Originally pronounced *CHIP-ah-way.* Now usually pronounced *CHIP-ah-wah.* French slang for Ojibwe. Also a county, a lake, a flowage, and a river in Wisconsin.

Choppers: Heavy leather mittens.

Clydesdales: The largest of the big workhorses.

Cookees: Assistants to the head cook.

Corks: Calked (spiked) boots. Also called calks. Sometimes spelled caulks.

Creel: A basket on an over-the-shoulder strap that's carried by a trout fisherman.

Cross-haul: Loading the logs onto the sleigh by using a horse or ox to pull a chain that would roll the log up a ramp mounted on the side of the sleigh.

Cross-hauler: The man who loaded logs onto a sleigh using horses or oxen and chains that crossed over the load. Chain-hauler.

Crosstree: A cross-member on a mast from which a sail is hung. Runs perpendicular to the mast.

Cruising: Inspecting and estimating the value of standing timber. Timber cruisers were also called land-lookers.

Deacon's bench: A pine board attached to the ends of the bunks. It ran the full length of the bunkhouse and was usually the only seating, other than benches near the cook shanty tables.

Deadhead: To make a trip to deliver cargo with no prospect of coming back with a return load.

Dentist: Ax and saw sharpener. Third-highest paid worker behind the woods boss and head push.

Diindiisi: Blue Jay

Donkey engine: A steam engine used to haul full logging sleds up steep hills.

Double Eagle: Twenty-dollar gold coin.

Double sawbucks: Twenty dollar bills.

Double-bit ax: An ax with two cutting surfaces so it will last twice as long between sharpenings.

Dray: Hauling service.

Dressed:, Gutted. Entrails removed. Cleaned.

Engineer: The driver of the train.

Fireman: Railroad worker whose job is to move firewood or coal from the tender car to the boiler, keeping the steam pressure up.

Flaggins: Dinner carried into the woods for those men who were working too far from camp to eat in the cook shanty.

Foremast: The mast nearest the bow of a ship or boat when more than one mast is present.

Foresails: Sails supported by the foremast. Near the bow of the ship or boat.

Four bits: Fifty cents.

Galley: The ship's kitchen and eating area.

Gabreel: A long tin horn used to call the men in for meals.

Gandy dancers: Slang for railroad construction crews who, when tamping crushed rock under railroad ties with their Gandy brand shovels, appeared to be dancing a jig.

Gang saws: Powerful, multi-bladed saws that, in one pass, could cut many boards from one log.

Gee: A signal used to train horses to turn to the right. *Haw* turned them left.

Gitchee Gumi: *GIT-chee GOO-mee.* Lake Superior

Gitchee Manitou: *GIT-chee MAN-i-too.* The Great Spirit.

Graybacks: Body lice. A common problem in the lumber camps.

Grippe: Any of several flu-like illnesses.

Hay burners: Work horses.

Haversack: A canvas or leather bag with a shoulder strap and a flap to secure contents. Rucksack.

Head push: The camp boss.

Hoar frost: White, often thick crystals of frost that cover objects when the air is moist and warm and those objects are below freezing.

Hornswaggle: To swindle, cheat, deceive, or otherwise trick.

Iron Belt: The iron-mining region of far northern Wisconsin and Upper Michigan.

Jam crew: A team of log drivers that specialized in breaking up logjams.

Keep an ear to the rail: Stay aware, alert. Rails transmit sounds of an oncoming train. By putting one's ear on a rail, news of a train approaching comes faster than conventional listening.

Kerf: The groove cut by the saw.

Lac Courte O'reilles: *la-COO-da-RAY.* Ojibwe tribe in northwest Wisconsin, a village and lake.

Latrine: A pit or ditch used for human waste.

Liniment: A salve or ointment usually rubbed on a wound or sore area to relieve pain &/or heal.

Locomotive: Train engine. A steam engine, in the 1880s.

Log drive: Logs were floated down rivers in the spring. Men would drive the logs to the mills downstream much as cowboys drove cattle to market.

Log Scale: A measuring stick used to estimate the board feet of lumber in a log.

Lumber baron: A wealthy, powerful businessman who prospered from the timber industry.

Mainmast: The primary, usually tallest mast on a ship.

Mainsails: Sails supported by the mainmast. Near the center of the vessel.

Makade: *ma-KAH-day.* Black

Makwaa: *MUK-wa.* Bear.

Menoomin: men-OO-min. literally, good grain. Wild rice was plentiful in many Wisconsin waters before the logging boom altered the lakes and rivers.

Mikwam-migwan: *MIK-wam-MIG-wan.* Feathers of ice.

Mizzenmast: The mast nearest the stern of a ship or boat when more than one mast is present.

Namakagon: *nam-eh-KAH-gun.* 1. Ojibwe term for sturgeon. 2. A large lake in northwest Wisconsin and headwaters for the Namekagon River.

Namekagon: *nam-eh-KAH-gun.* An outstanding northwest Wisconsin river. On early maps, some cartographers spelled the river Nam*e*kagon and other map makers spelled the lake Nam*a*kagon.

Ogimaa: *OH-ga-ma.* Chief. Leader.

Ojibwe: o-*JIB-way.* Sometimes spelled Ojibwa. Correctly pronounced with a long *a*. French fur traders called most Anishinabe in the western Great Lakes region either Ojibwe or Chippeway.

On the up-and-up: Honest. Truthful. Out of trouble with the law.

Pac-wa-wong: *pa-QUAY-wong.* 1. A rice-rich lake downstream from Cable. 2. An Ojibwe village abandoned when a lumber company dam raised the lake level, killing the rice.

Peavey: A log-moving tool with a stout wooden handle, a C-shaped steel hook and a steel point.

Pemmican: A mix of grains, dried fruit and dried meat. A high-energy food, easy to carry and resistant to spoilage, making it ideal on the trail.

Percherons: Purebred work horses, originally from France.

Picaroon: An ax handle with a sharp, steel pick rather than a blade. Used to stab, and pull logs.

Pinery: The great stand of virgin pine once stretching from central Wisconsin to Lake Superior, into Minnesota and Michigan. By far, the richest range of white pine on Earth until the 1890s.

Pinkertons: A Chicago detective agency distinguished for investigating train robberies in the late 1800s. In 1885 the Pinkertons had more men and more weapons than the U.S. Army.

Port: The left side of a marine vessel when facing ahead (toward the bow).

Rack bar device: A T-handled box containing a magneto capable of generating an electrical charge. Used to detonate explosives.

Rail: 1: Railroad worker. 2: The safety rail around a large boat or ship. 3: Lengths of heavy steel, designed specifically to support a train when used atop crossties to build a railroad track.

River Pig: Log driver.

Road monkey: A worker who maintained the ice roads, trails and tote roads.

Rut: The deer breeding season when does are in heat and bucks often lack normal caution.

Rucksack: A canvas or leather bag with a shoulder strap and a flap to secure contents. Haversack.

Sand man: The worker assigned to slow down a timber sleigh by throwing sand in the track. Straw was also used.

Sault Ste. Marie: *SOO-saint-marie*. A settlement & military post on the east end of Lake Superior.

Sawyer: A logger who felled trees using a crosscut saw. Also mill workers who ran saws.

Schooner: A fore-and-aft rigged sailing vessel having at least two masts, with a foremast that's usually smaller than the other masts.

Scrip: A "company note", often mass-produced and offered to workers in lieu of U S dollars.

Shaving the whiskers: Wisconsin's pine was often compared to being *as thick as whiskers*. Clear-cutting a forest was compared to shaving the pine *whiskers* from the landscape.

Shoe pac: Rubber boots with leather tops.

Shypoke: Slang for a Green Heron.

Sky pilot: Clergyman. Preacher.

Silver cat: A stiff sapling bent over by a fallen tree. When the tree is moved, the sapling can snap up, injuring or killing a logger. Differs from a widowmaker in that it comes from the ground up.

Slats: Lumberjack slang for ribs. Barrels were made of thin, curved wooden slats that were held together by metal hoops. The rib cage was compared to a wooden barrel by some.

Sleep camp: Another term for bunk house.

Sluice: *SLOOSE*. A channel built to control which way a log can travel.

Slush bucket: A large metal scoop pulled by an ox. Used to move soil, create roads, and excavate.

Slush out: To remove earthen materials using a slush bucket and, usually, oxen.

Snow snakes: Mythical creatures that hid under the snow, waiting to steal the lumberjack's tools. Often blamed for this.

Stamp hammer: A hammer used to mark the lumber camp's name on the end of each log.

Standing part: The free or unattached end of a rope or chain.

Starboard: The left side of a marine vessel when facing ahead (toward the bow).

Star load: A very large load of the biggest and best pine.

Stern: The back of a sailing vessel.

Stove lids: Lumberjack slang for pancakes or flapjacks. Term was inspired by the heavy, circular, iron lids found on old, wood burning cast iron cook stoves.

Swamper: The saw crew member who trimmed branches from downed trees and cut any brush in the way of the sawyers and teamsters.

Switchman: Railroad worker who, by throwing a manual switch, shifts the position of the track, thus changing the train's direction.

Tender: The train car immediately behind the engine that carries the fuel for the boiler.

Three-master: A boat or ship with three masts. They are the foremast, mainmast, and mizzenmast.

Thwart: The cross-bar in a canoe. Its ends are attached to both gunnels. To portage a small canoe, the porter lifts the canoe by the thwarts, flips the canoe hull-side-up, then carries the canoe overhead, one hand on each thwart.

Top loading: Guiding the logs onto the sleigh while standing on top of the pile. Sky-hooking.

Travois: *Trav-OY*. A device used to drag heavy items. Made by lashing saplings together.

Trestle: *TRESS-sil*. A large railway bridge.

Two-man crosscut: A 5 to 9-foot-long saw blade fitted with a handle on each end. Perfected in the 1870s, it replaced the ax as the primary tool for felling trees, greatly accelerating the harvest.

Union suit: One-piece underwear. Longjohns.

Waabishki: wa- *BEESH-key.* White.

Waffled: Refers to scars resulting from being kicked by calked boots during a brawl.

Walkin' boss: A woods boss who managed several camps at once by walking to each.

Wannigan: *WAHN-i-gun.* Company store. Also a portable kitchen that was used to prepare food for workers who were too far from camp to return for dinner at midday.

Wash: The turbulent water behind a vessel.

Wenebojo: *we-ne-BO-ZHOO.* A key spiritual character to many Native Americans, His father was a man. His mother was the west wind. His grandmother the Earth. Wenebojo is often depicted as a half-man, half-spirit, who delights in playing tricks on and confusing people, both to demonstrate his talents and wisdom and to protect all plants and animals. Able to perform miraculous feats, but also vulnerable and capable of making thoughtless errors. He may take the form of animals, rocks and plants. Sometimes called Wenebush. Wenebojo is, to many Native Americans, what Jesus is to many Christians—the worldly manifestation of the great spirit.

Whiffletree: The rear wooden component of a horse team's rigging that connected the team to the load. and evened out the force of the pull from two horses. Also called an evener.

Widowmaker: A dangerous tree or limb that may injure or kill a logger when it falls.

Woods Boss: Foreman of the crews that worked in the woods.

Yellowjack: Cornbread. Also called johnnycake.

About the Author ...

2013 ABNA Award-semi-finalist, James A. Brakken, was a boy when he first heard stories of Chief Namakagon and his secret silver mine. Born and raised in Cable, Wisconsin, less than a mile from the Namekagon River where this story takes place, he heard the tales of the old lumber camps, explored the legendary river, and walked the ice roads in search of Chief Namakagon's treasure.

Brakken has been published in Sports Afield, Outdoor Life, Field & Stream, School Arts, and Boy's Life Magazines and has received awards from the Wisconsin Writers Association and the Lake Superior Writers in

 addition to being honored as an ABNA semi-finalist.

An educator and award-winning conservationist, James Brakken has earned statewide recognition for his work to protect and preserve the lakes and streams of Northwest Wisconsin through his writing, teaching, and leadership. Brakken now illuminates Wisconsin's "lumberjack" history through fictional novels and short stories.

More at BadgerValley.com, home of James Brakken's Badger Valley Publishing

Did the old hermit of Lake Namakagon fall victim to foul play on November 18, 1886?

The Mystery Surrounding Chief Namakagon's Death

Two divergent opinions exist regarding the 1886 cause of death of Mikwam-migwan (spelling varies), AKA Old Ice Feathers and Chief Namakagon. What little information exists is subject to interpretation.

One of the only two available documents regarding Namakagon's death is a brief, November 1886 newspaper article. This obituary, along with interviews of descendents of those who knew Old Ice Feathers, and several years of related historical research, has caused James A. Brakken, the author of this mystery novel, to join ranks with those who conclude Chief Namakagon was a victim of foul play.

Questions arise, beginning with this November 27, 1886 Ashland Press article by reporter, George Francis Thomas. Is Thomas biased? You are invited to draw conclusions of your own.

"ME-KWA-MI-WI-GUAN
The Hermit of Nema-Kagon Is Dead."

"The old Indian found a few miles out of Ashland, frozen to death in the snow, and who was buried in this city on the 20th, has proven to be no other than the old hermit of Lake Nema-Kagon, around whose life there hovered a most quaint and romantic experience.

"In my second [publication] is related the story of the old man, whose name, as given above, signifies *Old Ice Feathers*. A strange co-incident, for in death he was found covered with feathery icicles. One of the old fellow's peculiar fancies was that one of the islands in Nema-Kagon Lake was the happy hunting grounds set aside by the Great Spirit for himself alone in the future life.

"Some time ago Old Ice Feathers moved from Nema-Kagon to the Marengo river, in order to dispose of his pine stumpage. Since then he has been a frequent visitor in Ashland, as is well known by all the natives. Not unlike most of his race, "fire water" consumed the larger part of his little fortune, and eventually led to his untimely death, for there is hardly a doubt but he was drunk and laid down to rest during that fearful storm last week. He was seen in town on Wednesday, and was known to have started towards his home on the Marengo."

Geo. Francis Thomas. Ashland Weekly Press November 27, 1886

The Thomas obituary raises questions regarding Namakagon's death, and demonstrates the attitude of the many, recent white inhabitants toward Native Americans in those days. Thomas' conclusions are of no surprise, considering they appeared in 1886, a time when the Indian Wars were still fresh in the minds of all.

However, the brief obituary fails to offer some key information. In particular, Chief Namakagon's body was found in the vicinity of the silver diggings southwest of Marengo, Wisconsin, near the Marengo Trail. Namakagon had a lodge in this area and was returning to it with his companion when a sudden snow storm changed their plans. It caused her to return to the Marengo Station while he pressed on. Thomas concludes that Ice Feathers, a woodsman who lived a hermit's life near Lake Namakagon for at least 40 years, died because "he was drunk and laid down to rest during that fearful storm." The reporter's words succeeded in convincing many that the chief's death was caused by his own weaknesses.

Thomas neither observed the body nor the place where Namakagon died, yet drew the above conclusions. Again, there is little doubt his words reflected the attitudes of many, perhaps most Upper Midwest immigrants toward Native Americans at that time. However, the fact that the chief was a seasoned woodsman—a man who had lived through an estimated 40 winters in northwest Wisconsin, makes it very unlikely he would get drunk and lie down to rest in a raging snowstorm as Thomas reported. And, although it is likely that many who read the Thomas article at the time accepted his conclusion, the author of this book does not.

It should be noted that, although the Thomas article states Namakagon was buried in Ashland on November 20, 1886, there is no death record in the Ashland County Courthouse. The Ashland County official who maintains historical death records was surprised to find no entry in the 1886 record book for Mikwam-migwan's death or his burial. Additionally, the city cemetery staff have no idea where the remains rest. The have no marker for this quite well-known Ojibwe elder. Nor can the cemetery produce any record of his burial, in spite of the 1886 press report. No medical or police reports have been found regarding Namakagon's demise, increasing the mystery surrounding his death. The above Ashland Daily Press item tells us his remains were not taken to his cherished Lake Namakagon retreat in keeping with the Anishinabe tradition. James Brakken has not been able to uncover any information explaining why Namakagon was laid to rest in the municipal cemetery, clearly *not* in keeping with tradition.

Brakken, author of the Chief Namakagon trilogy, believes he knows how and why Chief Namakagon's perished that November day. Information surfaced in 1885 of Chief Namakagon trading silver for medicine and supplies. Soon, many sought to discover the source of his silver.* Considering the value of silver then (and now), it is quite likely that, after those press reports appeared, Ice Feathers lived in jeopardy, facing unknown risk until his November 18, 1886 death.

(*Although a friend of old Ice Feathers came close to learning the mine's whereabouts, a black bear blocked the trail, convincing Namakagon to neither reveal the silver's location to him nor to anyone else. Old Ice Feathers was found dead near the Marengo Trail not long thereafter.)

The newspaperman's conclusions set forth in the brief obituary may have caused many of his readers to conclude Chief Namakagon died of natural causes. Others, though, felt it was more likely someone may have tried to force information from Old Ice Feathers—information leading to the source of his silver. The possibility that Chief Namakagon died at the hands of another was not investigated by local or state officials, perhaps another indication of late 19th century attitudes toward Native Americans.

Historical and field research, along with information from descendents of those who lived there during the great timber harvest days have convinced this book's author and others that Chief Namakagon did not die from natural causes. Some feel the press reports were influenced by local authorities. Poor or non-existent record-keeping, lost records, fading memories, the attitudes toward Indians at that time, the suspicious disposition of Ice Feather's remains, the value of the silver, and many other factors raise suspicion. However, the tarnish of more than a dozen decades suggests we may never learn the full story.

New information revealed

Research conducted for James A. Brakken's Chief Namakagon trilogy has turned up fascinating facts regarding other aspects of Old Ice Feather's life. Records previously thought lost have now surfaced, leading to more questions about this remarkable man. Some of those questions have not been asked for well over a century. The third book in this Chief Namakagon trilogy, *The Secret of Namakagon*, will soon reveal astonishing information surrounding the life and death of this legendary Wisconsin woodsman.

Follow the news and progress of the next book, *The Secret of Namakagon*, at BadgerValley.com or on Facebook® at Jim.Brakken as James Brakken's fast-paced, fact based tales of Chief Namakagon and his Loken family friends continue to unfold.

Find *YOUR* "Treasure" today!

Clip or copy the order form or download one at <u>BadgerValley.com</u> where you can also order online using PayPal and major credit cards.

See <u>BadgerValley.com</u> for special sales, package offers, contests, and news of upcoming publications.

Badger Valley will publish *YOUR* book, too.

From who-dun-it mysteries to poetry anthologies to family reunion collections, science fictions, earth-shattering exposés, young adult books, memoirs, and even lumberjack adventure epic novels, BVP can do them all. BVP is faster and far less expensive than mainstream publishers. And, unlike them, the author needs not order large quantities that must be properly stored for ages before being sold. We specialize in orders of 50 to 100 books at a time, making your publishing experience affordable and enjoyable.

Inquire for prices and policies at <u>BadgerValley.com</u> soon!

The Stories within the "Chief Namakagon" Trilogy

A quick count of Book I of Brakken's trilogy, *The Treasure of Namakagon*, will yield no fewer than twenty-five stories combined to create the novel. Book II contains the same number of tales, all based on fact. Book III is likely to have more.

Often, the facts behind one story may come from several true events. (Such is the battle scene at the dam in Book I. It is a combination of the John Dietz trial transcripts (See *The Battle of Cameron Dam)* and the defensive decision made by A. J. Hayward's employees to dynamite the Namakagon dam in 1883 in order to save Hayward's sawmill from closing.

Northwest Wisconsin was once far wilder than Hollywood's Wild West boastfully proclaims itself to be. With no government regulation, no law enforcement, plenty of money, thousands of adventurers from all corners of life, the stories here abound. <u>Book III, *The Secret of Namakagon,* will share the same format and style as the first two in the series, though it will rely even more heavily on historical record.</u>

For a list of true events from the Wisconsin's "lumberjack" days that inspired these books, visit <u>BadgerValley.com</u> and select the "about us" page. There, you will learn much of the truth behind the fiction in the Chief Namakagon trilogy. If you like what you see, please share with your friends, thereby helping to preserve the rich history of Wisconsin's 19th century timber harvest days.

CLIP or COPY this order form and share with others.

The Treasure of Namakagon 2nd place winner in the 2013
ABNA out of 10,000 novels entered worldwide! *Find out why!*

Treasure of Namakagon Discussion & Study Guide
Questions and projects to accompany THE TREASURE OF NAMAKAGON. 186 questions
and projects covering all 43 chapters. Ideal for classroom use and reading discussion groups.

(Full version of) *DARK* (Call for price of poetry-only book.)
42 original, eerie poems & 14 delightfully frightening short stories with illustrations from long-
dead artists. *This is the perfect companion for those dark & stormy nights or near the campfire.*

NEW! *Tor Loken and the Death of Chief Namakagon* NEW!
Help solve the mystery of Chief Namakagon's death in 1886. Fact based and fast-paced. Part two of the
"Chief Namakagon trilogy. Join Tor & Rosie & help solve the mystery. Includes maps, illustrations

Item	Price	Quantity	Extended Price
Treasure of Namakagon	$15.99 ($17.99 after 4/1/14)		_____.__
Study Guide Only Study Gd & Ansr Key*	$3.99 $10.99		_____.__
DARK* (Full version)	*Incl. Dark, Darker, Darkest $ 17.99		_____.__
Tor Loken & Death of Namakagon	$ 17.99		_____.__
The Secret of Namakagon (Available 9/2014)	$ 17.99		_____.__
S & H in USA: $4 first item, $1 each added item			_____.__
US dollars only. 5.5% sales tax if shipped to WI address			_We pay sales tax!_
Please provide your email address (for delivery confirmation only):			
_____		**Total**	_____.__

[SPECIAL: Mail orders only: Order two <u>books</u> and deduct $3. Order any three <u>books</u> and deduct $6.]
FREE study guide & key with order of 10 books.   *Mail entire form and*
Quantity discounts available at 715-798-3163.   *check or money order*
Prices subject to change without notice.   *payable to:*

E-book versions for all E-readers available   **James A. Brakken**
At http://BadgerValley.com   **45255 E. Cable Lake Rd**
For online payment visit   **Cable, WI 54821**
BadgerValley.com   Email: BayfieldCountyLakes@Yahoo.com

Brakken's BADGER VALLEY PUBLISHING
45255 East Cable Lake Road
Cable WI 54821

Name _____

Address _____

City/State/Zip _____

*THIS IS YOUR **SHIPPING LABEL**: PLEASE PRINT CLEARLY*

REVIEWS

"TREASURE" outshines 9,975 other novels!

Seattle, WA, June, 2013: Out of <u>*10,000* novels entered worldwide</u>, *The Treasure of Namakagon* tied for <u>second place</u> in the 2013 *Amazon Breakthrough Novel Award* competition. This semi-final contender in the General Fiction category is the first "lumberjack" theme novel to rise to such heights. *The Treasure of Namakagon* is certain to become a classic.

Read this excerpt from the <u>Publishers Weekly Magazine </u>review of *THE TREASURE OF NAMAKAGON* to learn how it ranked so well in this worldwide competition:

"This is a fascinating tale of the men who harvested the pines in Wisconsin's North Woods. Namakagon, an Ojibwa chief, is the heart of this story of the land and its preservation. There is a strong sense in this book of oneness with nature." "There's rip-roaring action, a beautiful girl, and great yarns rivalling Paul Bunyan." "The book is so well-written." "Difficult to put down; a great read."

More "TREASURE" reviews:

<u>**Amazon Books review:**</u> *"The writing style of this piece is its greatest strength." "The flow of the words is like an old fashioned song."*

Michael Perry, NYT bestselling author of Wisconsin stories: *"Weaving mystery into history,* Tor Loken and the Death of Namakagon *vivifies the tumultuous nature of 19th-century life in the legendary north woods."*

LaMoine MacLaughlin, President, Wisconsin Writers Assn: *"Open with caution. You won't want to put this one down."*

Waldo Asp, Northwest Waters President & AARP Chairman: *"A twisting, thrilling mix of mystery, adventure and legendary treasure, still waiting to be found. .... A great fund raising idea for our lake association and schools. Wisconsin history buffs will find this book a treasure in itself. An exciting adventure for all ages."*

"... A very talented writer. Consider me fan!" **Jeff Rivera, Media personality, bestselling author.**

"I liked it!" **Larry Meillor, Wisconsin Public Radio talk show host.**

More *"TREASURE"* reviews, continued from previous page:

"Like a live history lesson, Brakken takes his readers on a ride down Northern Wisconsin's untamed Namakagon River, back when giant virgin forests lured heroic lumberjacks to seek their fortune. In scene after scene, the reader is surrounded by the beauty of pristine woods and lakes, rooting for the good guys to beat out the greedy ones, even learning step by step how to place the giant saw so the magnificent tree falls in just the right place." **Wisconsin writer, A. Y. Stratton, author of Buried Heart**

"Brakken's new book animates the long history of conflicts over Wisconsin's water and mineral resources. The interplay between citizens, corporations and government will be familiar to people following today's debates over mining and groundwater protection in Wisconsin, or energy development in other regions." **Eric Olson, UWEX-Lakes Director**

Book Clubs—Libraries—Schools: Inquire today about person-to-person **SKYPE® discussion sessions with the author**. Via Skype, James Brakken can be in your living room, meeting room or classroom, one on one. Email BayfieldCountyLakes@Yahoo.org today.

Find out why, **out of 10,000 novels** entered in the 2013 Amazon Breakthrough Novel Award competition, *THE TREASURE OF NAMAKAGON* **tied for 2nd place** in the general fiction category. **Order your *TREASURE* today or call your local library and request that a copy be ordered for your community or school.**

About Book I of James A. Brakken's Chief Namakagon trilogy:

The Treasure of Namakagon

Of the 10,000 novels entered in the 2013 Amazon Breakthrough Novel Awards competition, *THE TREASURE OF NAMAKAGON* surpassed 9,975 others. It tied for second place in the general fiction category making it ABNA's top rated "lumberjack" adventure novel of all time.

This fictional, **MAJOR-AWARD-WINNING** action-adventure is founded on historical fact. Like the other "Namakagon" books, most of the characters in <u>The Treasure of Namakagon</u> are not real, but they could have been. References to the Namekagon River log drives, life in the logging camps, and fraudulent timber sales are based on true events, as is the gunplay that resulted from a ploy to charge for timber floated over a dam near Hayward. The rivers, the lakes, the towns are all real. So are most of the hotels, taverns, depots, and other buildings mentioned. These and other historical references help bring this tale to life.

Add in historical accounts of silver and gold found in the region and Chief Namakagon trading silver for supplies. Although many still search for Chief Namakagon's secret silver mine, it has yet to be rediscovered. Perhaps, though, the real treasure was the vast white pine forest that, until the 1880s, gave northern Wisconsin its character, its life.

This book will plunge you into Wisconsin's single, greatest economic event—the post-Civil War harvest of the largest stand of white pine in the world. Estimates said that timber would take a thousand years to cut. It was gone in just fifty. Tens upon tens of thousands of lumberjacks descended on the north to harvest the "green gold" and cash in on the wealth. Many northern Wisconsin towns sprang up in the middle of nowhere and boomed into bustling cities full of life, fast money, fortune seekers, loose women, and lumberjacks. Rowdy wilderness towns quickly gained notoriety—and popularity. In the woods, wasteful harvest practices, poor forest management, and outright greed prevailed.

Most of those boom towns failed soon after the pine was cut, shrinking to impoverished settlements and, in some cases, ghost towns. Our forests will never be the same. The great Wisconsin pinery, as it was called, will never return.

What does remain are the tales of the lumberjacks. This adventure is based on those great men and the hard but colorful lives they lived. This story is also based on the history of Mikwam-migwan, better known as Chief Namakagon, and his legendary lost treasure.

Open this book and step back in time. Share in the rich history of life in the great Wisconsin pinery during the lumberjack days of the 1880s. Share, too, in a great north woods adventure.

Available only at select Indy bookstores, outlets, Amazon, & <u>BadgerValley.com</u>.

Other **Badger Valley Publishing** Books

Available at finer bookstores and at BadgerValley.com

The Treasure of Namakagon by James A. Brakken

A young lumberjack, his Indian mentor, and a lost silver mine—a **fact-based** tale of timber, treasure, and treachery in the 19th century.

Following a daring rescue from a dangerous child-labor scheme in 1883 Chicago, an orphan is plunged into the peak of lumberjack life in far northwestern Wisconsin. There, Chief Namakagon teaches him respect for nature and shows him to his hidden treasure—an actual mine, lost in 1886, and yet to be rediscovered.

Meet young Tor Loken whose family owns a wilderness lumber company. Join the fight when a sinister timber tycoon takes control of the river, threatening the camp's future and the lumberjacks' dollar-a-day pay.

Be in the cook shanty before dawn for breakfast. Then, it's out into the cuttings where, knee deep in snow, you will help harvest giant pine logs. Hitch the Clydesdales to the tanker. Ice the trails for the timber sleighs. Take the train into town, but keep one eye peeled for charlatans seeking an easy swindle. Back in the bunkhouse, spin a yarn with colorful lumberjack friends. Next, it's a Saturday night of merriment. Dress warmly, though. It's a four hour sleigh ride back to camp at twenty below zero.

Put on your red wool mackinaw. Grab your pike pole. You're about to plunge into 19th century lumberjack life and *THE TREASURE OF NAMAKAGON*, a thrilling adventure, thick with twists and turns, researched and illustrated by an author who lives there. And, yes, the boy wins the girl. But, as for the treasure …?

DARK James A. Brakken

56 very short, blood-curdling tales and delightfully frightening poems.

Lurking beneath the cover of *DARK* you will encounter a rare collection of James Brakken's spine-tingling poems and very scary, short stories. Your host through this macabre library of horrors is **"The Thief of Dreams"** who will help you explore more than fifty bizarre, sometimes humorous, and often downright disturbing tales. *DARK* is perfect reading before the campfire or by flashlight under the covers. For visual relief from the skin-crawling poems and stories, the author offers **53 mysterious, evocative engravings by long-deceased, ancient master artists.** *DARK is the perfect mix of scary short stories and poems for late-night campfire or cabin reading.*

Coming in 2014 … *The Secret of Namakagon*

James Brakken has unearthed long-lost records of Old Ice Feathers. *The Secret of Namakagon* is sure to be the jewel atop the crown of the Chief Namakagon trilogy as we learn more about Ogimaa Mikwam-migwan (also known as Chief Namakagon) and his Loken family friends. Watch BadgerValley.com for updates and news of the proposed 2014 launch of this engaging, enlightening adventure novel. In Blackie Jackson's words, "Tie your pant legs, fellas. This is bound to be a bone-shaker of a sleigh ride!"

May 1880 Ashland Weekly Press Mining Claims Southwest near the Marengo Trail

SPECIAL NOTICES.

To Whom it May Concern.

The undersigned has located upon the sw¼ of the nw¼, Sec. 15, Township 45, Range 4 west, for mining purposes, this 1st day of May, A. D. 1880.
48-3. JOHN DEACON.

To Whom it May Concern.

The undersigned has located upon the ne¼ of the ne¼, Sec. 15, Township 45, Range 4 west, for mining purposes, this 1st day of May, A. D. 1880.
48-3. S. S. VAUGHN.

To Whom it May Concern.

Notice is hereby given that I have located on the ne¼ of the ne¼, Section 21, Town 45, Range 4, for mining purposes. CHARLES GEHN.
May 8, 1880. 49-3.

Notice,--To Whom it may Concern.

Notice is hereby given that the undersigned has located on the ne¼ of the se¼, Section 15, Town 45, Range 4, for mining purposes.
47-3. W. G. FRENCH.

To Whom it May Concern.

The undersigned hereby claims the nw¼ of the nw¼, Section 27, Town 45, Range 4 west, for mining purposes, with all the rights and privileges pertaining thereto.
May 14, 1880. 49-3. ALPHONSE LEBEL.

To Whom it May Concern.

The undersigned hereby claims the sw¼ of the sw¼, Section 27, Town 45, Range 4 west, as a mining claim, with all the rights and privileges pertaining thereto.
May 14, 1880. 49-3. LOYD BURGES.

To Whom it May Concern.

The undersigned hereby claims the sw¼ of the nw¼, Section 27, Town 45, Range 4 west, as a mining claim, with all the rights and privileges appertaining thereto. n46-3t. HARRY GUY.
Ashland May 8, 1880.

To Whom it May Concern.

The undersigned hereby claims the nw¼ of the ne¼, Section 15, Town 45, Range 4, as a mining claim, with all the rights and privileges pertaining thereto.
May 14, 1880. 49-3. C. L. JUDD.

To Whom it May Concern.

The undersigned hereby claims the n½ of the nw¼, Section 15, Town 45, Range 4, as a mining claim, with all the rights and privileges pertaining thereto.
May 14, 1880. 49-3 D. MORGAN

To Whom it May Concern.

The unersigned hereby claims the ne¼ of the se¼, Section 27, Town 45, Range 4 west, as a mining claim, with all the rights and privileges pertaining thereto.
May 12, 1880. 49-4. J. E. PAGE.

To Whom it May Concern.

The undersigned hereby claims the nw¼ of the ne¼, Section 27, Town 45, Range 4 west, as a mining claim, with all the rights and privileges pertaining thereto.
May 14, 1880. 49-3. JACOB BECK.

To Whom it May Concern.

The undersigned hereby claims as a mining claim with all the rights and privileges pertaining thereto, the ne¼ of the nw¼, Section 27, Town 4 Range 4 west, Ashland county.
May 14, 1880. 49-3. JACOB WILHELM.

To Whom it may Concern.

The undersigned hereby claims the se¼ of the ne¼, Sec. 27, Town 45, Range 4 west, as a mining claim, with all the rights and privileges pertaining thereto.
May 14, 1880. 49-3. M. E. MONSELL.

To Whom it May Concern.

The undersigned hereby claims as a mining claim the sw¼ of the ne¼, Section 27, Town Range 4 west, for mining purposes, with all the rights and privileges pertaining thereto
May 8, 1880. CHAS. COHEN
49-3. JOSEPH FINN.

To Whom it May Concern.

The undersigned hereby claims the follow described lands for mining purposes, with all the rights and privileges pertaining thereto, viz: Garnich, the nw¼ of the se¼; Joseph Felden, the se¼ of the nw¼; Phillip Kohl, the ne¼ of the sw J. F. Patrick, the nw¼ of the ne¼, all in Sect 27, Town 45, Range 4 West.
May 8, 1880. 49-3

To Whom it May Concern

Notice is hereby given that we, the undersign have located for mining purposes the following scribed lands to wit: Ferd. Schupp, se¼ se Sec. 15, Town 45 north, Range 4 west; W. Hassa nw¼ sw¼, Sec. 15, Town 45 north, Range 4 we M. McManus, sw¼ nw¼, Sec. 23, Town 45 nor Range 4 west; A. J. McDougald, sw¼ nw¼, Sec. Town 45 north, Range 4 west; J. W. Moffet, n nw¼, Sec. 23, Town 45 north, Range 4 west; Ju Dore, nw¼ ne¼, Sec. 23, Town 45 north, Ran west; John Fraser, sw¼ ne¼, Sec. 23, Town north, Range 4 west; W. R. Durfee, se¼ nw Sec. 23, Town 45 north, Range 4 west; A. McK non, nw¼ sw¼, Sec. 23, Town 45 north, Rang west, and ask the permission of the State to pay it or to deposit the money with the State and t scrip with which we can settle with the railr company whenever they shall come into posses of the land.

This page from a May 20, 1880 edition of the Ashland Press shows some of the many mineral claims filed along the Marengo Trail, a trail frequented by Chief Namakagon on his walks to Ashland for supplies. The following map shows many of these claims. In late November 1886, the body of Old Ice Feathers was found in this general area, 8 to 10 miles southwest of the Wisconsin Central Railroad's Marengo Station.

The small map shows the proximity of the Marengo Trail to Lake Namakagon and the silver fields southwest of the Marengo Station. Note that the Marengo Trail goes through the silver-"diggings." (Chief Namakagon frequently walked this trail for four decades before this area had any mines.) The large INSET shows many of the mining claims documented on the previous page. Parcels with numbers or stars were owned by miners.

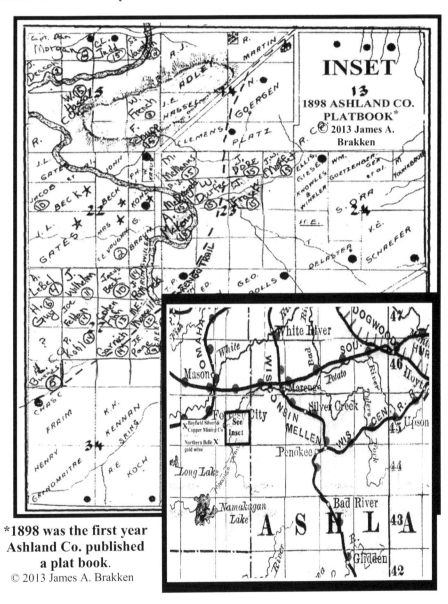

*1898 was the first year Ashland Co. published a plat book.

© 2013 James A. Brakken

- 255 -

Tor Loken and the Death of Namakagon

Like *The Treasure of Namakagon,* this novel is a <u>stand alone</u> action-adventure and founded on historical facts dramatized through fiction. Appropriate for ages twelve through adult.

Most of the characters in *Tor Loken and the Death of Namakagon* are not real, but they could have been. References to Chief Namakagon's death, like the peril faced by the schooner, *Lucerne,* are based closely on fact. The Namekagon River log drives, the lumberjacks' life in the logging camps, and charlatans' efforts to swindle the lumberjacks are based on true events, as are the chapters on river pirates who cheated the lumber camps out of many thousands of dollars. True, too, is the history of silver and gold mining in northwest Wisconsin. Many claims were filed and many mines yielded limitless wealth for a few, fortunate miners. The rivers, the lakes, the towns, in this story are all real. So are most of the hotels, taverns, depots, and other buildings mentioned. These and other historical references help bring this tale to life.

When we consider **actual newspaper stories** of Chief Namakagon trading shards of silver for supplies and the discovery of Mikwam-migwam's frozen corpse our story takes on more historical significance. Although many treasure hunters have searched for Chief Namakagon's secret silver mine, it has yet to be rediscovered. Perhaps, though, the real treasure was the vast white pine forests that, until the 1880s, gave northern Wisconsin its character, its life.

Like *The Treasure of Namakagon,* this book will plunge you into Wisconsin's single, greatest economic event—the post-Civil War harvest of the largest stand of white pine in the world. Estimates said the pinery's timber would take a thousand years to cut. Yet, it was gone in only fifty.

Thousands of lumberjacks descended on the north to harvest the "green gold." Many northern Wisconsin towns sprang up in the middle of nowhere and boomed into bustling cities full of life, fast money, fortune seekers, loose women, and lumberjacks. Rowdy wilderness towns quickly gained notoriety—and popularity. The term "Hayward, Hurley, and Hell" was coined for good reason—and rightly so, as the term remained accurate for decades. In the woods, outright greed, wasteful harvest practices, and nonexistent forest management prevailed, creating extremely dangerous fire conditions. The forest fire scene in this novel offers only a taste of the terror felt by all who settled in the north when dry weather resulted in forest fires that destroyed millions of acres.

Open this book and step back in time. Share in the rich history of life in the great Wisconsin pinery during the lumberjack days of the 1880s. Share, too, in a great north woods adventure.

Maps on preceding page.

56038993R00163

Made in the USA
San Bernardino, CA
10 November 2017